Knife of Truth

Road to Megara

Cynthia Willerth

A
SmatteringsBooks
Paperback

Contributing editor and cover design: Ruth Willerth

A special thanks to the Northside Writers for their many critiques and the folks in the mid-west who invest in prairie wildlife refuges.

Except for purpose of review, no part of this publication may be reproduced in whole or in part, or stored in a retrieval system, or transmitted in any form or by any means, electronic, mechanical, photocopying, recording, or otherwise, without written permission of the publisher. For information regarding permission, write to SmatteringsBooks, P.O. 556, Clarence, NY 14031.

13 digit ISBN 978-0-9800130-1-6
10 digit ISBN 0-9800130-1-1

Library of Congress Number: 2011905731

Printed in the U.S.A.
 First SmatteringsBooks printing April 2011

Chapter 1

Metrox, captain of the Delmarthian Guard awoke from a restless sleep. He opened his eyes, breathing heavily. A vivid memory of wild men, their bloodshot eyes blazing with hate, their long braids flying behind them, raced their warhorses down the mountain to Delmarath. They charged across the vacant market-place and salted black powder on the massive stone wall that protected the city. Rock evaporated into air. 'Black death' drifted into the city, coating everything it touched with a fine powder: It slipped into houses through cracks in windows and doors. It buried streets and gardens in a coat of black dust and piled around houses keeping the people prisoners. Some suffocated as they attempted to clean the powder out of their homes. Others starved unable to leave the city for the black death poisoned their skin while other victims breathed their last breath as the powder destroyed their lungs. His beloved city, desolate, devoid of life.

The horror that invaded his dream faded. "Just a nightmare," Metrox reassured himself. "It won't happen that way. The black death must have fire to work. It's not a poison; somehow it tears things apart."

The cot in the small room off the Hall of Justice was less comfortable than the bed in his private quarters, but he often slept there in the absence of Lord Betren, the rightful defender of Delmarath. The bedroom door to the hall remained open in a vain hope that the one source of heat, a huge stone fireplace in the larger room would provide some warmth.

Closing his eyes, Metrox pulled his coarse wool blankets over his head. *Barbarians! Wild, undisciplined scoundrels! Like to execute them all.* He rolled on his side hoping to find a more comfortable position. One particular barbarian intruded into his restlessness. *Curse Reig, that insolent prairie storyteller with his perfect rendition of our sacred historical ballad. How dare he recite Dana's rise from quarreling cities to a united country ruled by a high king. That story ruined Maris; caused my son to abandon his station just so he could fetch his lute. What magical charm did that barbarian use to compel Maris to forget that he was a guardsman on duty? Lousy barbarian forced me to execute my youngest boy.*

The captain sat up suddenly, his top blanket slipping to the stone floor. "Get off it, Metrox," he muttered in disgust. "I'm reasoning like a child caught in the marketplace stealing an apple. Can't blame Reig for Maris' behavior. Truth is Maris spent three years wrecking havoc in the guard. I was too blind to see it. Running after his lute was the spark that led to his demise. Our law demanded my son's death. I, Captain of the Delmarthian Guard had no choice but to carry out his punishment."

He rubbed his arm across his eyes as he reclined on his pillow. "Hate to admit the storyteller's right. Hurts to lose a son. It is as it is. Can't dwell on the past. Must concentrate on the present disaster."

He groaned. *Reig. Can't force that man from my thoughts: He did alert me to that inaccurate map depicting the route from Delmarath to Megara. Written on Danian parchment, but filled with pictorial symbols so stupid prairie-men can understand it. Prairie-men don't use parchment; completely ignorant; neither read nor write. Their hands are much too*

5

large to draw anything as small as the directions on that map. Some corrupt Danian lord behind this treason. The question is who? What motive could there be? Some insignificant lord's desire for revenge against the House of Bartran? Bromwell and Bart could have made a few enemies in Megara. Or is the real target Megara and the throne? One of the great lords would be involved if that's the case.

Metrox buried his head in his pillow. "Got to sleep," he yawned. He closed his eyes, but events of the last few days swarmed into his head, conquering his sensible intentions. *Lance and Sylvia — two more barbarians, conveying that hideous bag of black powder from Kans, our lovely neighbors on the other side of the mountains.*

"Barbarians armed with 'gunpowder.'" Metrox sat up and positioned the pillow hoping that it would smooth his troubled mind when he flopped back on it. "Gun? What's a gun? Doesn't matter. Enough to know that black powder can destroy our walls. It's a black death, that's what it is. Curse those men of Kans who intend an invasion in spring."

He rolled over on his side, rearranged the pillow and sighed. *Just to complicate my life, our respected Lord Betren decides that he and that walking disaster Lance, start out on a secret suicidal mission to Megara, not to mention Lance's dear little sister, Sylvia, and her homicidal refusal to go home. All these events create excruciating pain in my aging body.*

"Think of something agreeable," he murmured, "erase all this turmoil from my mind; need to relax." He yawned, deeper than before. "Greylen, that teller of tales whom Lord Bromwell sent me. That's encouraging." He added the blanket that had slipped on the floor to his coverings and turned on his side. *Greylen's good. Not as talented as Maris of course, but no one can play an instrument like my boy. Still, this teller of tales pleases me. He'll keep my men sane during the long winter ahead.* Metrox's eyelids grew heavy; he drifted into gratifying sleep which ended abruptly when a door to the Hall of Justice creaked open and then closed with a bang.

Metrox snapped to consciousness; every muscle readied for action. *What fool would risk his life sneaking into the Hall of Justice?*

6

Must pass five guardrooms on the way up; always post men on duty at night.

Hesitant footsteps stumbled up the last flight of dark stairs into the Hall of Justice.

Metrox snatched his knife from under his pillow. He reached for his belt, which hung next to his bed and fastened it around his waist over his woolen tunic that served as night clothes. He leaned back on his pillow and waited. Assailant? *Does some treacherous plot exist among my captains?*

Moonlight streaming through the window above his head revealed a giant advancing toward the little room.

Metrox tensed. *Easy, moonlight plays havoc with shadows.*

The footsteps quickened, then stopped; a large figure hesitated searching for his victim.

Metrox leaped to his feet, his weapon swinging into attack position. Two quick steps brought him out of the room, his weapon poised above his shoulder.

"Metrox, it's me."

Only one person in all of Delmarath, in all of Dana for that matter, spoke his language with a faint barbarian accent. "Sylvia, what in the name of all the gods are you doing in the Hall of Justice?" he roared. He flipped his knife across the room missing the girl's head by inches.

"Don't hurt me," she yelled. "I'm sorry. I had a bad dream."

Metrox noted the fear in her voice. "A dream? You dare disturb my sleep for a dream?"

"Sylvia, don't wake Metrox," Captain Evander, Metrox's nephew and second in command hissed loudly as he quietly closed the small unobtrusive door at the foot of the stairs.

"Something amiss, sir?" The guard in front of the main door to the hall inquired. "Sounded like a commotion up there."

"No, guardsman. Everything's under control." Evander's flickering candle lit his progress up the stairs, and framed his tan face surrounded by disheveled shoulder-length black hair.

"You're too late, Evander," Metrox snapped. "I thought you capable of keeping this young lady in your quarters. What's wrong?

7

Too slow on your feet to manage that task because you occupy the apartment directly below us? Maybe I should relocate your family to the first floor of this building. Six flights of stairs would allow you ample time to apprehend this girl and keep her out of trouble."

Evander withheld his answer until he reached Sylvia's side. His flickering candle illuminated the girl's distraught pale face.

"Well?" Metrox stood in the shadows outside the range of the candle.

"Sylvia screamed and woke me, and Lavine, and the baby, and the two older boys. Took me a moment to calm things down and that permitted Sylvia the opportunity to rush up here before I could detain her. I apologize, sir." Evander's voice, always controlled, always reasonable, no matter what the circumstance, had a smoothing effect on the participants of this unexpected late-night meeting.

"Expect more from my high-ranking officers. Perhaps you'd like to wake up as a sub-captain tomorrow." Metrox grunted. "As long as you're here, Evander, make good use of that candle; light a couple of torches and build up the fire. Excuse me while I change into more comfortable clothing."

"Yes, sir." Evander handed the candle to Sylvia. "Light the torches. It's dark; it's cold, and I await an explanation." He shuffled to the woodbox near the head of the stairs and chose two logs, which he set on the smoldering coals.

"Fire needs some small stuff," Sylvia ventured.

"Pile on your left," Evander answered. "Go ahead, build it up."

By the time Metrox rejoined them, fully dressed in his Delmarthian Guard uniform, the fire blazed, warming his snug fitting pants and black tunic decorated with an embroidered flying eagle. Sylvia huddled on the bench, hidden under a gray blanket. Evander propped against the stone fireplace, his rabbit fur-lined robe wrapped around his slender frame. At the sight of his uncle, he snapped to attention.

"So, you woke up Evander's entire family for a mere dream and now make us suffer your hysterics," Metrox said, retrieving his knife and then sitting opposite the girl. "Fortunately these walls are

8

thick otherwise Lavine's temper would have roused everyone in the building."

"I think she screamed louder than me," Sylvia said. "I'm sorry." She straightened on the bench letting the blanket slip to her shoulders revealing a tangle of blond hair concealing her face.

Metrox stiffened. *Surrounded by barbarians. And this barbarian girl is always prying into matters that don't concern her. Doesn't know her place in life. Danian women keep their dreams private. An outspoken busybody, that's what she is. She's not normal, not Danian. Never did approve of yellow hair. Black's the true color for a woman. She's much too tall. Requires me to look up to her when I speak. Why didn't she stay in the mountains?*

"Metrox?" Sylvia pushed her hair over her shoulder and regarded him with a pair of beseeching blue eyes. "Please, don't stay angry. This dream surpassed all of my dreams with eerie accuracies or least I thought them real."

Metrox glanced at his nephew. "Oh, sit down, Evander. We'll be here till morning." He focused on Sylvia recalling the first time he saw her, a little girl with golden curls bouncing around her face as she ran to him. She startled him by grasping his hand, babbling meaningless words in a foreign language and tugged him to the barn to see a new born foal. What amazed Metrox was his pleased reaction to the child's behavior. Danian children, even his two sons, maintained a respectful attitude toward adults.

She's the same child I cared about all these years. Just grew up a bit. It's been five years since her troubles began. Must be about fourteen now. Old enough to be married. Unfortunately she's on the wrong side of our wall. If she were sitting by the fire in her cabin, I'd see nothing unusual with her light skin or her knee length tunic over a pair of pants. It's not her fault she's a barbarian. His voice became sympathetic. "Now, Sylvia, tell us about this terrifying dream."

"It was more than a dream," Sylvia started, her voice unsteady.

"Why?" Metrox felt all desire for sleep drain from his body. He leaned forward his eyes focused on the barbarian girl.

"The vividness. It left me with a feeling of— terror. Something horrible happened. Lance screamed, his horse screamed." Sylvia stared into the fire.

"Has this happened?" Metrox prompted. "Or is it about to happen? Can it be prevented?"

"I don't know. But Bet— Bet—"

"What about Lord Betren?"

"He wasn't there. Not at first. Then Bet's voice came to me. It was so clear. He told me to wake up, warn you that he and Lance need us now; we must ride to Megara." Sylvia looked from Metrox to Evander. "Please," she pleaded. "We must save them."

"Fine, just fine," Metrox said. "Relax, Sylvia. I need a moment." *Lord Betren commanded me to act on this foolish girl's notions. Said she would know if something happened to Lance or Betren. Evander's aware of this— was on duty when I received those orders. Question is, did Sylvia actually have a vision or is she inventing it in an effort to join her brother? She has a mild case of the sight, sometimes gets a warning, but she's also an expert at manipulating us more innocent people.*

Evander glanced at Metrox. "Permission to question our visitor?"

Metrox nodded.

Evander smiled at the girl. "Lady, did you see Lance and Betren, or is this only a fear of disaster because you love both your brother and our Lord Betren?"

"Both, I think. A dire feeling of doom overwhelmed me like when my brothers died on the wall." Sylvia shook her head. "I never had a vision before. I actually saw Lance tumbling down a bank. I heard Betren's voice as if he stood next to me." She rubbed her forehead. "That's the strange part. I've had feelings about people, that they were in difficulty, or would be in danger soon, but I never saw any details, never heard any voices."

"Surely, Lance's cloak would have caught on something and slowed his fall," Evander suggested.

Sylvia shook her head. "Lance wore one of Val's jackets. He left his cloak home."

10

Evander frowned. "It's a dream, Sylvia. Lance wore a Danian cloak when he left Delmarath."

Metrox lurched to his feet. He snatched an iron poker and rearranged one of the logs. "'Lance ditched that cloak on the trail beyond the first lean-to on the other side of our outpost thereby lessening the chances of a successful mission.' That's a direct quote."

Evander almost smiled.

"My long-winded son, Captain Menes, wrote a two-page dispatch, stating that he tracked our fugitives a little beyond the Delmarthian border after he settled his men into the outpost barracks."

"Another direct quote, sir?" Evander's face seemed to grow youthful and compelling, as he asked.

"Your levity is unappreciated, Nephew. Although my dear son might have condensed his whole report into a single sentence, the fact remains." Metrox nodded at the girl. "She had no knowledge of what her brother wore."

"So Lance destroyed the mission and doomed them both," Evander stated quietly.

"Surely we can save them," Sylvia cried.

"Sylvia, your idiot brother insists on acting like a ten-year-old," Metrox barked. His voice softened at the sight of tears in Sylvia's eyes. "Easy, girl. Thanks to your father's books, Prince Conder's illegal abuse of our law, and your brother's exasperating attitude, you're caught up into a complicated mess."

Chapter 2

Metrox straightened his black tunic as he stared beyond Sylvia into the frigid gloom of the hall. An icy blast penetrated the mortar teasing the dark tapestries hung on the ancient walls. A clammy hand clutched his insides. *I pledged my life to Betren. His decision to take Lance to Megara is my doom. I'm destined to face the Knife of Truth. I knew that when I vowed to stand by my lord regardless of his decision. It is as it is.* He eyed Evander.

"That's it then." Evander said. "Her story rings true. Am I to replace you while you're gone?"

"It's either you or Lang." Metrox shrugged. "I trust you. Not always sure about Lang. I suspect his loyalties are not completely with the House of Bartran. No question in my mind that you can handle it."

"Lang is loyal to the King, loyal to Prince Conder as well as to the House of Bartran. Nothing illegal about that. The House of Langfield provides us with many good officers."

"Not questioning their ability," Metrox snapped. "Lang's a climber. Keep an eye on him."

"What about Storm?" Sylvia's blanket slid off her shoulders revealing her worn rumpled tunic.

Metrox scowled at her. "Your dog will not accompany us to Megara."

"But Storm's my dog," Sylvia cried. "Where I go, he goes."

"The palace is no place for dogs!" Metrox exclaimed. "Storm would end up in the kennels in the 6ᵗʰ ring. You will be confined to the palace." *Maybe confined to a cell.*

"Actually, the animal's taken a liking to Maris," Evander said. "I made Storm's care a part of the boy's duties before the law decreed his death."

"Where is Storm?" Sylvia demanded. "When I searched for him yesterday, Lavine claimed your men took him hunting. That they wouldn't be back until dark. He wasn't sleeping by my bed when I awoke."

"Most likely at your cabin," Evander said. "I ordered two guardsmen to take him for a run in the mountains near the path that leads to your home. Report has it, you are surviving since smoke pours out of your chimney. Tracks state that you have guests for the winter."

Sylvia stared at Metrox. "Did you allow some stranger to move into my house? How dare you give someone permission to live there."

"Reig's not a stranger," Metrox growled. "Storytellers often hole up somewhere in order to take part in our festival of the Gathering of the Greens."

"Yes, they've sheltered at our house this time of year," Sylvia admitted. "But why take Storm back home? Does Reig like dogs?" Her eyes narrowed. "Or is Maris with Reig?"

"Maris is dead." Metrox spoke without emotion. "His name has been stricken from the Delmarthian list of citizens. He never existed."

Sylvia stared, wide eyed at Metrox and sank onto the bench.

Evander took this moment to add another log to the fire. When he faced Metrox, his features were chiseled into the correct expressionless indifference of a seasoned guardsman. He stood at attention.

"Neither of you will speak his name again," Metrox stated.

"Understood, sir," Evander said.

Metrox glowered at him. "Mention that name again and you will feel the taste of my whip in the marketplace."

"Yes, sir."

Metrox shook his head in exasperation and sighed. "Take your seat, nephew. You look ridiculous standing at attention in your bed-clothes. Sylvia, you're not Danian. Since you have very little knowledge of our law, I'll explain. The law permits a choice in the punishment for guardsmen who disobey orders: It's certain death for the culprit. Branding comes first, then fastening the condemned to irons attached to the city wall, left there until the birds peck his flesh from his bones. The alternative is banishment: The criminal stripped of all clothing, weakened by a beating, driven from the city, is left to face death from starvation, inclement weather, and be devoured by wild animals."

The girl swallowed. "You— you banished Storm— without even letting me say goodbye."

Metrox groaned. "If you wish to support your brother, there is a price to pay. We all will make sacrifices before this deadly problem your family dumped into our laps is solved. In your case, you have to forgo your dog."

"It's not fair." Sylvia blinked back tears. "Storm's my faithful companion." She brushed her tears off her cheek. "But Lance is my long lost brother and Betren's my best friend. That's a terrible choice."

"You have no choice, not about Storm, not about a few other details. Your clothing for example." Metrox glanced at his nephew. "Evander, has Lavine finished fixing that dress so Sylvia can wear it?"

"Dress! I'll not be seen dead in a dress!"

"You're dead if anyone sees you in your tunic and pants," Metrox snarled. "Now, let's get something straight, Young Lady. I don't have to take you to Megara even though Lord Betren ordered

14

it. Much simpler if I send you home. If you put me or this city at risk because of your insolence, you will go home. The final decision is mine. As of the night when Lord Betren left, you are under my command and you will obey my orders without complaint. Your life depends on it. Do you understand?"

"But— yes, I understand." Sylvia dropped her head and studied her hands. "I'll do my best, Metrox."

"You'll do better than that. You will obey. Evander, did Lavine agree to the loan of her mare and sidesaddle?"

"Reluctantly." Evander grimaced. "Whatever you do, come home with both in mint condition."

"Understood. Unfortunately that horse is the only one in Delmarath trained for a woman."

"I've never ridden sidesaddle," Sylvia said her face puckered into a frown.

"You'll do just fine," Metrox said.

Sylvia leaped to her feet. "Please, let's leave now. It's dark; no one will see my clothes. And I won't have to ride sidesaddle."

"Sit down, Sylvia," Metrox ordered. "We won't be leaving immediately."

"Why— Oh!" Sylvia sank back on the bench. "I— I'm sorry; Lance needs me. Betren commanded it. Please Metrox, we must hurry."

Metrox gave Sylvia one of his best penetrating stares. "Sylvia, what was the exact message in your vision? Think, now. This is important."

"Bet said, he and Lance were in trouble, that we should go to Megara. Oh, I forgot to mention this. We must get the gunpowder to the King."

"Anything else?"

"No." Sylvia gulped. "I assumed that we would save Bet and Lance by taking the powder to the King. Betren said nothing about helping them."

"Your vision doesn't place them at the palace. I would surmise this happens on that risky shortcut, a day or two away from Megara. Betren has hope, despite your brother if he can find the

15

trail under the snow." Metrox touched her arm. "I share your concern, Sylvia. I wish we could help, but there are certain procedures that I must follow to keep this city safe while I am absent. Lance and Betren are expendable."

"Expendable? You're going to let them die?"

"It's a five-day ride to Megara. Our chances of finding our friends in time to save them from the fate you saw in that vision is slim. The people of this city count far more than two individuals. Yes, our loved ones are expendable, and I'll not listen to one more word about saving them."

"When do you want me to summon the citizens?" Evander asked.

"Ring the bells after people break their fast," Metrox said. "We'll inform them that I have been summoned to Megara and I leave Delmarath in your hands."

"It's my first time as acting defender."

"Don't worry, nephew. We'll do everything according to custom. We hold a public assembly this morning, and then delay a week or so until we summon the guard. That gives people an opportunity to accept the idea, a possibility for us to evaluate any protest to your promotion." Metrox sighed. "And I need a little time to instruct you in the details of my position."

"But, that'll take forever," Sylvia wailed, "Lance and Bet — " She glanced at Metrox and covered her face with her hands.

Chapter 3

"Danian roads are meandering dirt packed surfaces, mud rutted in spring and fall, dust choked in summer and snow clogged in winter," Betren grumbled as he tightened the ties to the hood of his scarlet cloak under his clean-shaven chin. The white powdered road to Megara wound its way through snow coated hills where leafless trees bent their branches in homage to the wind. "Careful. Could be ice lurking under that snow."

His companion Lance, the Citherian, laughed. "You should try riding any distance on the prairie this time of year. This is excellent compared to what passes for roads on the other side of the mountains. Relax, Bet. Stop acting like you're on Sunburst watching a review of your guard."

"I ride the way I was taught." Betren sat in his saddle— back straight, both hands on the reins, heels down, toes balanced in the stirrups. "The conformation of my mount makes no difference in my seat; good posture in the saddle is a must in Delmarath. Doesn't matter what caliber of mount I'm on."

"Why bother? You must be as bored as me." Lance grinned. "Now if I were riding Warrior, he'd keep me on my toes every minute, but these old nags are a disgrace to be under a saddle."

Betren raised his eyebrow. "It's unwise to look a gift horse in the mouth."

Lance laughed. "Would you believe this antiquated horse and I have come to an agreement? If I let her chose her own pace, she promises to stay on the road."

"Really." Betren guided his mount, a swayback gray around a large puddle. This maneuver forced him to drop behind Lance who allowed his horse to splash through the icy water, giving Betren an opportunity to evaluate the Citherian's outlandish costume. *Should have died his blond hair black. We did manage to tame the wild barbarian hairstyle, but he can't seem to keep that fur-lined hood on his head. Nothing we could do about his height. None of our clothes fit him, he's much too heavy, and so he's riding through Dana wearing that smelly sheepskin jacket and his loose britches. Backpack — standard equipment for personal items attached correctly. Wait one moment; that backpack should be covered by his cloak.*

Lance slipped his feet out of the stirrups, leaned back in the saddle, and yawned. He dropped his reins and stretched. His bay horse slowed and snatched a mouthful of dried grass.

Betren urged his gray to regain her position alongside Lance.

"It's just like the old days. You and me, riding together."

"Not quite. Then we were young and carefree. Now, we have this little problem." Betren touched a leather bag containing the small box of powder on his belt. "I'd be more comfortable if you kept your hands on the reins."

Lance groaned. "Always the sensible one." He straightened in the saddle, slipped his feet into the stirrups, and laid his hand on the rein. "Better?"

"Much." Betren sighed. "Do I have to remind you that a horse has a mind of its own? Just because these nags aren't Warrior and Sunburst, doesn't mean they're trustworthy. Be grateful that Captain Menes managed to obtain these horses without being noticed. The alternative would be walking to Megara."

18

"Nothing ever changes. Big brother takes care of me just like when we were boys." Lance scowled. "I'm not a boy anymore. I don't need you; don't need anyone."

"Hopefully, you're mature enough to realize that you are a stranger in this land. Your survival demands your obedience to my orders."

"I know, I know. We carry gunpowder that can turn city walls to rubble." Lance paused. "What's wrong, noble Danian," he drawled, "don't like the way I look?"

"It does seem to be lacking something," Betren said, his voice soft.

Lance stared at the space between his mount's ears. "Something bothering you, Bet?"

"Yes, something's bothering me." Betren ignored Lance's innocent tone and glared at his companion's averted face. "Just when did you get rid of that cloak Metrox gave you?"

Lance shrugged. "Not a problem. I'm plenty warm without it."

"I'm not concerned about your comfort."

"You'd think that cloak was worth a bag of gold. Bet, you're overreacting."

Betren's voice softened. "Without that cloak, you shout to anyone within a mile that you are barbarian. You didn't bother to listen to Metrox, did you? I know he emphasized the importance of your disguise."

"Well…" Lance petted his horse's neck. "Let's see… my cloak. Yeah, I had it this morning. Probably fell off when we had a little trot while these old nags were fresh. Come off it, Bet. I hate cloaks."

"So you dropped it somewhere between here and Delmarath, just because you dislike wearing a cloak." Betren allowed his anger to color the tone of his voice.

Lance flushed. "Who's going to see us? We've been on the road three days, not counting the two we spent on foot getting to your outpost. Come off it, Bet. Losing my cloak is not the end of the world."

"It could cost us our lives."

"I didn't drop it, at least not deliberately. I had it on until I started to sweat. Then I let it slide behind me. Honest, Bet, I thought it would stay on my horse, stuck between me and the back of the saddle. Besides, who's going to notice two vagabonds on two ancient horses?"

"Lords, en route to Megara to celebrate the Winter Festival." Betren urged his horse in front of Lance, emphasizing his anger— his back erect, his head high— his thoughts about Lance's incompetence filling his mind.

They rode in a signal file, plodding hooves spelling out their doom. Finally, Lance urged his horse forward.

Betren noted the bay horse's increase in speed. He turned his mount to face the Citherian. "Well?" Betren's cold voice stood between them.

"I really goofed, didn't I?" Lance looked Betren in the face.

"Yes, you 'goofed'. Losing that cloak is disastrous."

"Great. So, now what? Have I ruined all our chances of making Megara? What if I went on alone? I could take the powder to the King. You could go home."

"Lance, cut the nonsense. You act as if this was a pleasant jaunt into the mountains when you were a boy. It isn't. We'll lose another day if we retrace our steps to retrieve your cloak. Our food supply is limited. Thank you very much for diminishing our chances of success to practically nothing."

Lance sighed. "It would help if I looked more like a Danian." He studied Betren's foot. "We don't even wear the same kind of boots. Yours aren't cowhide, what are they made of?"

"Beaver skin. Suppose to be waterproof."

"That's the most sensible part of your outfit. Your long red cloak just gets in the way and your black uniform shouts that you are from Delmarath. What a great disguise for someone who doesn't want to be noticed."

"Unfortunately, you're the one who will draw interest." Betren urged his horse into a trot.

Lance let out a whoop. "Eat my dust," he yelled as he disappeared around a bend in the road.

Betren's horse slowed of her own accord as if a trot was a gait a little hard to handle. "Well, old horse," he said as he patted her, "you're right. Save yourself until we really need speed." *Have to form a new plan, thanks to Lance's stupidity. I intend to live, but if we're apprehended, Metrox has some of this powder and Sylvia. Her knowledge along with Metrox's presentation to the court should be solid evidence to convince King Cadamire of the truth.*

Betren chuckled as his horse ambled around the bend in the road. *How long will it be before Sylvia charms Metrox into taking her to Megara? My little adopted sister can be very persuasive.*

"Can't see what you're so amused about," Lance said as Betren rode toward him. "Have you thought of a new way to reach Megara without anyone seeing me?"

"Your behavior is not amusing. I was thinking of Sylvia."

Lance snorted. "You remember her as a child. She's grown some since then."

"She seemed changed to you?"

Lance shook his head. "No, she's as impossible as ever. All we did was fight."

"Pay attention to the road. Follow me." Betren guided his horse along the edge of slimy water that had oozed across the road from a green algae-covered pool. "Have to be more careful from now on. This trail skirts a marsh miles long. I think it's a branch of the Great Swamp. These nags will stumble into anything."

"Where will we spend the night?"

"There's a lean-to on higher ground. At this pace, we'll reach it about dark."

"Hope nobody's using that shelter like at the last lean-to."

"You have a wonderful imagination."

Lance scowled. "You sound just like Mother."

Betren shrugged. "I didn't see anyone. I was concentrating on the road. It was too soon to stop for the night. We had two or three more hours of daylight." *Sorry Lance, I'm sure you speak the truth, but so do I.*

The next morning they rode along the cattail edged swamp, Betren in the lead, Lance close behind him. Tall stiff sword-like

21

leaves rose over their heads, the ground often deteriorated into treacherous mud puddles. About noon, they left the swamp behind and soon arrived at a place where a road intersected their route.

Lance drew rein and stared at the crossroads. "Glad I'm riding with you, Bet. Never saw anything like this before. Which way do we go?"

"These roads lead to different cities." Betren pointed south. "That's the route to Chaleen."

"I don't think we want to go south."

Betren grinned. "Conder would be delighted to see us. North leads to the northern border cities. We'd have a rather difficult time explaining your presence there."

"So we veer off this way?"

Betren nodded. "We have a saying, 'all roads lead to Megara.' And they do, but not necessarily in a straight line. Don't you have roads on the prairie?"

"Our traders use some paths that lead directly to the next town. Trac used the position of the sun to check direction and studied the stars at night. Real prairie-men don't need marked trails."

"Danians use roads," Betren stated. "You don't see much sky in this wilderness. Come on. Megara waits for us." He studied Lance as they rode.

Lance turned in the saddle and met Betren's intent gaze. "What did I do now?"

Betren smiled. "It's what you're not doing that bothers me, my friend. It's time to pull your sixth sense out of wherever you have buried it. We need to know when someone is behind us."

"You think I've lost the sight?" Lance stared at him. "Is that why you refused to listen to me when I sensed a presence at the first shelter?"

"Let's say your talent's a bit rusty. You've been floundering like a drowning man. Came close to getting killed in Delmarath. Most men do very well with five senses, but you seem lost when you are out of tune with your sixth one."

"You may be right." Lance stroked his horse's neck, and then glanced at Betren. "I forget how well you know me." He silently

22

gazed off at the countryside for a while, and then nodded. "Yes, I will be able to sense what is behind us."

"Good." Betren brushed snowflakes off his arm. "From now on we must be alert. Remember, every hand is raised against us because you're not Danian. Even people I've known all my life will not hesitate to kill us. It's the law."

Lance spat. "Your law —"

"Rather not discuss it." Betren cut him off. *The very act saving my city condemns me; hard to believe the son of Bromwell is an outlaw. Let's face it; I'll spend the rest of my life in a cell. It's not just me. It's Bart. I've ruined him socially, destroyed his career. And Father? This will injure him too. Might even cause his death.* Betren became aware of Lance watching him. Concern filled the Citherian's face.

"Care to share those thoughts?"

"No." Betren glared at him. "And you stay out of my head."

"I'm not in your head. It's just that you radiate a feeling of despair. Give it up, Bet. You can't carry Delmarath — walls, houses, and the Hall of Justice on your shoulders."

"I'm defender. The welfare of my city is my responsibility."

Lance dropped his reins on the horse's neck and raised his arms to the sky. "May your gods spare me from your burdensome life!" He placed his hands on the reins. "Where do we sleep tonight?"

"Camp in the open and we just arrived." Betren followed a well-traveled path through a heavy thicket into a grove of pines. "We spend the night here. Shelter." He pointed at the thick branches above his head, then at a stream. "Running water, what more could two fugitives want?"

"Walls, a roof and a soft bed," Lance answered as he dismounted. "You care for the horses. I'll rustle up some wood."

"Those matches are wonderful," Betren said as he watched Lance ignite some tiny pine twigs. "Where did you get them?"

"Trac and I found them on a dead trader."

Betren filled a pan with water. "We need to go over our plans when and if we reach Megara."

"Again?" Lance groaned. He pulled apart a metal tripod then set it over the fire.

23

"How much do you remember?"

"Your father will recognize the black powder and understand the danger," Lance quoted mimicking Betren's voice. "The King will listen to his trusted advisor."

Betren's lips tightened. Water splattered into the fire as he dropped the dried meat into the pan. "Stay focused. Our lives depend on your actions."

Lance yawned. "What's the problem? I'll know what to do when we get there. You'll give me instructions each step the way."

Betren almost snarled. "Can't you treat this seriously?"

"I do." Lance said soberly. "I pledged my life to help save your city, to speak on the Knife of Truth, to prove that the powder is real. This will most likely kill me and destroy the House of Bartran, but you can't expect me to dwell on it every minute I'm awake. I mean to enjoy each day I have left before we reach your capital city."

Betren sighed. "We're not cut from the same tree; that's certain. I consider a problem, work out detailed solutions and search for flaws. When a plan seems promising, I formulate a new set of conditions to test my conclusions."

Lance stared into the fire. "I never wanted any of this. My idea of a good life is to make a decent woman my wife. I'd breed horses, train them, and sell them in the marketplace. He shrugged. "I guess that will never happen."

"I can't predict the future." Betren stabbed his knife into the meat. "I'm not sure about you."

Lance shook his head. "Mother could, but her visions were not always correct. The closest I ever came to visualizing future events was back in Delmarath. Then it seemed that Mother stood at my side opening my eyes for a few minutes." He paused. "It was horrible."

Betren nodded. "I watched you. I surmise you saw Delmarath destroyed. I said nothing then. I had no intention of permitting you to describe that scene in front of my men." He lifted the pot from the fire and set it between them. "Let's eat, and then call it a night. Tomorrow we ride through the Sistra Gap."

"Wonderful place for an ambush," Lance said the next morning as they entered the Sistra Gap. He gazed up at limestone cliffs towering above their heads. "It looks like some great monster slashed through solid rocks, just so the road could pass easily into the valley."

Betren nodded. "Perhaps the men who lived like gods built it." He took the lead, noting that this steadily rising incline was difficult for his mount.

"Bet!" Lance's hoarse voice warned Betren of trouble. He circled back halting his horse beside Lance's bay.

Lance slumped in the saddle, his breathing labored. "I can't go on," he gasped. "Something horrible happened. It crushes me. Terrible suffering. Lives snuffed out."

"Easy. There was a battle here. Long ago, against the prairie-men. We won."

Lance nodded. "Our storytellers tell different versions of that war." He groaned. "And now we ride over the bones of dead champions. Thousands died here."

Betren rode his horse next to Lance. He reached over and rested his hand on Lance's arm. "It was long, long ago, my friend, back in the time before we Danians built walls around our cities. These fallen men no longer feel pain, nor can they hurt us."

"They hurt me," Lance wailed.

"You no longer feel the ancient horror of soldiers in the midst of conflict." Betren allowed his compassion, his acceptance of Lance's emotions, engulf Lance's consciousness. Hopefully, he created a buffer for Lance like the wizard in Megara had instructed him in preparation for a moment similar to this. "You know how to block them."

Lance trembled. "I can't."

Betren tightened his hand on Lance's arm. "I imagine you as an expert at blocking others' thoughts — no other way you could survive on the prairies. This is no different. Block these atrocities from your mind. Do it now."

Lance slowly erected his back, turned in his knees so they rested against the horse's side, slipped his toes into the stirrups, his heels down— at last a proper Danian riding seat. He rested his reins on his saddle and touched Betren's hand. "I'm okay. We can go on."

"You are not alone, my friend. I ride by your side, my sword in your defense through this cursed valley."

"Thanks." Lance looked over his horse's ears. "I feel so— stupid."

"You are not stupid, Lance. It's just that you never received the schooling to learn how to control your special talents. Megara's wizard taught me much about people like you. We need to get out of here. Let's ride."

They descended into the great valley of Sistra; clouds played with the sun which seemed to be running ahead of the riders.

"Duck, Bet!" Lance yanked his mount to a halt, dropped his reins and covered his face with his arms. "We're riding straight into battle. Danians charging out of those caves on the hillside; it's an ambush."

"Lance!" Betren roared. He grabbed the reins of Lance's horse and kicked his own mount into a canter. The Danian was pleased to note the sudden movement of Lance's horse and the fact that Lance almost slipped out of the saddle, jolted the Citherian back to the present.

Betren brought both horses to a standstill. "Listen carefully," Betren ordered as he gave back the Citherian control of his horse. "One more bit of advice from our wizard. Repeat after me; we are going to Megara. We are going to Megara. Repeat this phase over and over."

Lance gulped. "I'll try it. I'm going to Megara."

"That's it. Keep that thought on the top side of your brain. Concentrate on the words. Say it over and over again."

It took them the remainder of the day to ride through that historic land. Exhausted, they set up camp near a stream and were asleep before darkness covered the earth.

The next day Betren kept the pace to a slow walk.

"What's wrong, Bet? Think we pushed these nags too fast yesterday?"

26

Betren raised his hand motioning to Lance. "I'll enjoy your silence for now. I'm searching for a trail that we can use instead of the main road."

"Wait a minute." Lance stopped his horse. "Riders behind us."

Betren glanced over his shoulder. Light snowflakes landed on the vegetation. His horse grunted a harmless happy snorting sound.

"Let's go. We don't have too much time." Lance urged his horse forward.

"Have to find that path. It's not far from here." *Snow makes this difficult. Surely it lies around here someplace. Ah, a large boulder shaped like a giant's chair marks the beginning, a stand of pines a few feet beyond* "I see it."

"Oh, no, how did I miss that?"

Betren tensed. "Missed what?"

"Wait, I need to be sure." Lance stared down the road. "Yeah, there's a large party of riders ahead. If we increase our speed, we'll ride right into them."

"We use the shortcut." Betren kicked his horse into a canter. "Follow me." He led the way onto a narrow path and halted behind some pines. Lance stopped beside him.

"This trail runs parallel to the road for a couple of miles," Betren said in a low voice. "No need to advertise our presence."

Shortly, jingling bells and drumming hoof beats told him that Lance had been correct. They heard laughter, lilting voices of women, deeper voices of men. Betren slid off his horse and held her head. He didn't want her to greet the oncoming riders. He motioned Lance to follow his example.

Lance remained in the saddle and grinned at him.

Betren stiffened. *Is Lance capable of keeping both horses quiet with his mind? Hope, he knows what he's doing.*

The leader of the oncoming party, dressed in his finest navy blue hose and jacket, led the way on a cream-colored stallion. A broad rimmed felt hat shadowed his wrinkled face. Two young women, their long blue-green cloaks flowing over their black mares' backs and sides, rode sidesaddle. Five armed attendants followed,

27

their swords loose in their scabbards. Two men carried crossbows, powerful weapons at close range.

Betren caught his breath. *I know these riders, Lord Famen of the house of Falen from the city of Pit. Pit's a two-day ride southwest of Megara, Chaleen ten miles farther from Pit. Now, what is the noble Famen doing so far from home when he's in charge of the Winter Festival in his city?*

"A short cut?" Lance questioned, after the riders disappeared around a bend of the road. "Do you think that's a good idea? You know the old saying, 'short cuts, the quickest way to disaster.' They tend to turn into long cuts."

"We have no choice." Betren mounted his horse. "Without your cloak, we're an easy bull's-eye for any archer who notices us. Most Danians are proficient bowmen. Follow me."

Chapter 4

It was easy at first. The narrow trail forced them to ride single file though a dusting of snow. Lance led; his horse disliked being second. Twenty feet below them, at the bottom of a slopping shale bank, little waterfalls splashed over rocks. The stream was full of deep pools, wonderful for swimming on a hot day. The creaking of saddles, the plodding hoofs of the horses on the snow covered dirt-packed route lulled Betren into a sense of relief. No one would use this trail this time of year. "Lance!" he shouted. "When we reach the place where our trail crosses the stream, we'll stop to rest the horses and have lunch. Then I'll take the lead. Trail becomes confusing a few miles ahead."

"Fine, just fine," Lance answered as he glanced over his shoulder.

Betren tried to stop laughing. Lance mimicked Metrox, captain of the Delmarthian Guard perfectly.

Chickadees called from tall stately hemlocks above him. One of Betren's fondest memories of Lance's mother, Anya, was watching her feed the cocky little black capped birds near the cabin during the winter.

Lance twisted in the saddle to get Betren's attention. He pointed to the trees above him and grinned.

"I see them," Betren called.

The flock darted to the opposite side of the stream. Several birds fluttered in front of Lance's horse.

The mare snorted, shied toward the edge of the cliff. She squealed as she crashed through undergrowth shielding the steep side of the precipice.

Lance kicked his feet out of the stirrups and tumbled free of his horse.

"Lance! Catch hold of something!" Betren shouted.

"Get your rope," Lance yelled as he grasped a protruding moss-covered rock halting his descent.

The mare tripped over a treacherous root, sliding head first toward the stream.

Small rocks showered Lance, ricocheting off his body. He raised his hand in a desperate effort to shield his head. Unable to support his weight with his other hand, he slipped off the rock, falling into the path of the screaming horse.

"That horse weighs over a thousand pounds, if she slides on top of Lance, he doesn't have a prayer." Betren unfastened the clasp on his cloak and dropped it on the ground. He swung out of his saddle and secured his mount to a convenient ironwood.

Snatching a leather bag containing medical supplies off his saddle, he strapped it securely across his chest and sprinted a short distance until he came to a place where sturdy oaks descended the bank to the stream. He half slid, half scrambled down the steep incline using tree-trunks and eroded roots to control his speed.

A shower of dead leaves, twigs, and pebbles accompanied Betren's feet as he skidded to an ancient beech, caught hold of it, utilizing it as an anchor. Below him, frigid water rushed over stones.

The mare wailed as she plunged into the stream, her legs churning the air.

Somehow Lance followed her, desperately clawing at numerous roots. He shrieked as the force of his fall propelled him into the shallow water licking the stony ground opposite the cliff. The brook trickled over his motionless limbs and teased his blond hair, inviting it to float downstream.

"At least the horse missed him." Betren muttered as he caught his breath. *Like to silence those blasted chickadees. How dare they continue that cheerful chirping? That horse is badly hurt; otherwise she'd be on her feet. Easy, now. I'll be no help if I'm injured.*

He worked his way downward using roots and protruding rocks to keep his balance until he reached the edge of the rushing stream. *Water's deep. Current's fast.* He lowered himself into the icy water and waded toward Lance and the horse. *Curse these rocks. Balance — must keep my balance. Water's almost up to my knees. Easy, that rock is covered with green slime. Slippery, but it's the best way out of this current.*

The mare attempted to regain her feet as Betren approached. Her head flopped uselessly; her legs thrashed the water disrupting the stream bed, turning clear water into mud. Her eyes were glazed with pain.

Betren drew his sword and slashed her throat. Blood spurted from the animal and colored the water red. As he stood up to put the weapon away, he noted that the horse's body rested on top of the saddle bags attached to the saddle. Lance's backpack had burst open during his fall. Most of its contents spilled into the water and floated around a curve downstream. He sighed as he splashed to Lance's side.

"Lance, you big oaf, now look at what you've done. As usual, I have to pick up the pieces." Betren grabbed the Citherian under his arms and tugged unsuccessfully. Drawing a deep breath, he braced his feet against a rock and clutched Lance under his armpits. Utilizing every ounce of strength he possessed, the Danian lord dragged his barbarian friend to dry land.

Panting for breath, Betren rested a few minutes and then struggled to his feet. *I'm all right. Still dry except for my hands. Remarkable, those beaver skin boots that Metrox insisted I wear, actually do work. Means I'll be able to cope in this weather. Lance's forehead is cut. Only the gods know what other injuries he sustained.*

Lance groaned. "Bet?"

Betren knelt beside him. "I'm here, Lance. Are you all--"

"No," Lance cut him off. "I'm not all right. I can't move my arm."

"Easy." Betren removed a clean cloth from his medical kit. He wiped the blood off Lance's wounded forehead. "It's only a scrape. Nothing serious."

"Bet? The powder? Do you still have the powder?"

"I have the powder. It's safe." Betren pressed the cloth against the wound to stop the bleeding.

"My horse?" Lance brushed Betren's hand off his face.

"Dead. I had to kill her. Keep your hand out of my way."

"The supplies?" Lance clutched a rock with his good hand. "Oh, you're hurting me."

"Sorry, had to clean the dirt out of that cut. I'm finished now."

"The supplies?"

"Rapidly floating downstream. Saddlebags— under your horse. No way we can budge her." Betren sat on a rock and considered Lance. "That wound will heal better without a bandage."

"The matches— I had the matches." Lance shut his eyes; he remained silent for a long moment.

"Lance?" Betren leaned over him and slapped him on the face. "Stay with me, Lance."

Lance opened his eyes. He caught his breath. "I'm okay. Bet, just tell me one thing. Tell me you brought your tinder box."

Betren slowly looked up at the tree lined sky. "Wasn't necessary. We had matches." Realization of their predicament settled somewhere in his stomach. They had no way to make a fire, no way to dry Lance's clothes, no way to cook food, no one to turn to for help.

Lance sighed. "I wish Bart were here. He would have brought a tinder box."

"I know." Betren kept his voice matter of fact and forced a smile. "Remember how crazy my little brother made us when we planned to spend time in the woods? He always lugged twice the equipment as anyone else."

"And we always used whatever he brought," Lance whispered. "You know, little things like tinder boxes." He closed his eyes.

Betren laid his hand on Lance's arm. "That's enough. Can you stand? We can't stay here."

Lance struggled into a sitting position. "My arm," he moaned. "I think I broke it. And — and — I'm soaked."

"Let's see." Betren cut the straps of the useless backpack and threw it aside. "Help me, Lance. We must remove your sheepskin coat. That's it, I got it off your good arm, now try to relax." Betren studied the problem. "I don't want to pull that heavy material over your arm. Sit very still, I'm going to snip this sheepskin until it's above your elbow."

Lance gritted his teeth and nodded.

"Easy, easy, hold still. Your jacket's tougher to slice apart than the backpack." Betren cut the sleeve exposing Lance's wool garment. "Finished. Now the tunic."

"Shirt, Betren. I don't wear tunics."

Using his knife, Betren half tore, half slit the material away from the skin. Lance's forearm dangled limply below his elbow.

"All right." Betren nodded. "Stay where you are. I'll make a splint, put your arm in a sling and fasten it close to your chest."

"Bet, I won't be able to use it."

"That's the general idea. The healers will look after it when we arrive at Megara."

"How am I going to climb out of this gully?"

"One detail at a time. Remain still until I prepare your arm for traveling." Betren quickly hacked the correct size branches for splints. Treating injuries on the trail was part of the training every member of the Delmarthian Guard received. Betren had protested that a lord of a city needn't know about caring for the wounded, but Metrox insisted. More to the point, Bromwell backed his captain. Metrox and his father were dangerous adversaries when they agreed.

"It's a clean break." Betren wrapped a dry towel and Lance's jacket's sleeve around the splinted arm which he fastened to Lance's chest. "Should heal just fine. Let's get your good arm back in your jacket. Keep you warmer when it dries out. Stay put until I fetch your pack. Maybe something's still in there that we can use." He retrieved the leather bag and shook it. Two soggy trail bars, consisting of nuts and dry berries held together by honey fell to the ground. Betren handed one to Lance. "Eat."

Lance pushed the food away. "Not hungry."

"We both must eat." Betren shoved the food into Lance's hand. "Our bodies must have nourishment to combat this damp miserable weather." He bit into the soggy bar.

Lance shook his head. "I'll never make it."

"You must try. Eat while I'll replace the water in my canteen." Betren concentrated on keeping his hands dry as the icy water flowed into the metal container. He faced Lance. "Finished?"

Lance nodded. "What about you?"

"Finished." Betren held out his hand, planted his leg firmly on the ground and pulled Lance up onto his feet. "How do you feel?"

"Cold.. A little dizzy. No, my head's clearing now. I guess the food helped." Lance took a couple of steps. "I can walk, but I don't see myself climbing that bank."

"Neither do I. We're near the bend where we ford this creek. I don't recall any really rough places from here to the crossing. The rocks are mostly smooth shale. Besides, flat land lies on this side of the water. How do you feel about walking downstream while I retrieve the horse? We'll meet at the crossing."

Lance studied the stream. "It's better than trying to climb that bank. What if I can't make it?"

"Don't worry. I'll secure the horse and amble upstream until I find you. Ready?"

"I think so." Lance stumbled, caught a low hanging branch, steadied himself and slowly maneuvered along the edge of the water. He glanced back at Betren. "I can manage."

"All right." Betren took a quick breath. He raised his voice. "But if you run into trouble, wait for me to find you. Don't do anything else foolish."

"Okay, okay. I hear and obey."

Betren gathered his medical supplies and struggled back up the bank to his horse. "Stupid," he muttered. "Stupid, stupid. Just because these horses don't measure up to what we usually ride, we became careless. We both know anything can spook a horse. Lots of them fear birds." He whipped his cloak over his shoulders, mounted his mare and kicked her into a trot.

Lance was nowhere to be seen when Betren reached the crossing. He tied his mount to the nearest tree and hurried upstream until he saw Lance sitting on a ledge at the top of a small waterfall about three feet high. "Hello up there," he called.

Lance gazed at Betren sheepishly. "I looked down and felt dizzy. I thought I'd better wait."

"Glad you did. Don't want to further damage that arm. Come on now, step down on this rock. I'll steady you. We don't have far to walk."

The gray mare was a welcomed sight when they struggled across the stream to her side. Lance sank onto a large boulder.

"Drink." Betren handed him his canteen, a frosty metal flask that he had purchased in the marketplace.

Lance swallowed a little and handed it back to Betren.

"No, take a good long drink. I'll have some too. You relax while I refill this and water the horse."

Lance stared at the mare. "Bet, I think that animal's grown. I don't suppose she's been taught to kneel?"

Betren chuckled as he led the mare to the edge of the stream. "A guardsman's nag from Chaleen? The noble Prince Conder wastes neither time nor money on good horses for his guard. He left us quite a few worthless mounts five years ago when Father forced him to walk home."

"Conder? Walking to Chaleen? From Delmarath?"

Lance's astonished tone warned Betren to be careful. "Never mind." *Lance will learn about this when he speaks on the Knife.* "Tell

35

you later when we reach Megara. We have more important things to consider." After the horse had satisfied her thirst, he led her to dry ground and pointed to a fallen tree that lay by the side of the trail. "Can you scoot up on that?"

"Of course I can." Lance stepped up to the log, placed his good hand on it and stopped. "I not going to be able to balance; wish I had two hands."

"Try over here." Betren pointed to a place where a branch jutted out from the log.

Using the branch to steady himself, Lance managed to crawl up on the log and rested on his knees.

Betren held his breath. *He has to stand if he's going to mount the horse.* He backed the mare along the log until the saddle was within Lance's reach.

Lance grasped the saddle and pulled himself upright. He eyed the stirrup. "Hold her steady."

Betren tightened his hand on the horse's rein close to her head. "Easy, girl— stand."

Lance lifted his right leg and shoved his foot into the stirrup. He gripped the front of the saddle with his good hand while he raised his left leg over the horse's back and plopped into the seat.

"I feel ridiculous. Never have any trouble getting on a horse. Oh— not as good as I figured. Dizzy again." Lance braced himself. "I..." He stopped and listened. "I thought I heard a howl."

"Let's hope it's your imagination. Take the reins, can you hold her steady?"

Lance managed a smile. "Still capable of handling this horse, Big Brother. She neck-reins. I can control her with one hand."

Betren took out his blanket from the pack fastened to his saddle and jumped up on the log to obtain some leverage. "Here, wrap this around you." He helped Lance pull the blanket over his shoulders. "Better?"

"A little." Lance scrutinized him as the blanket slipped off his shoulder. "It's up to me, isn't it?"

36

"What?" Betren hopped off the log, slipped his medical bag over his head, fastened it to the saddle, dug out his rope and cut off about four feet.

"If we get to Megara. It will depend how long I can hold out in this freezing weather."

"Most likely. Hold your position." Betren leaped onto the log. "Let's fix that blanket. Hold her steady." He repositioned the blanket over Lance and tied his rope around Lance's waist.

"This is my fault," Lance said slowly. "I had a chance to think while I waited for you. I realized I've been acting as if our lives hadn't changed... as if the last five years had never happened. Why did it take until now to realize we can never go back?"

"It's all right, Lance." Betren slipped the reins over the horse's head and started to lead them toward Megara.

"No. Will you look at me? Listen." Lance's body stiffened. "If I'm too badly injured, you abandon me; keep the powder and go on."

"It's not going to come to that. We're going to reach Megara." Betren urged the horse forward.

"But if it does, promise me one thing. Get the powder to the king. And Bet, let my death have meaning; don't leave me to be tortured by your law-abiding Danian citizens. Be sure I'm dead before you leave."

"Lance..." Betren halted and stared up at the Citherian.

"But if it does, you must do as I say. Swear it on the horse."

Betren sighed. *Strange, that each of us holds sacred that day on the mountain when James gave us each a little wooden horse, on which we pledged ourselves to one another — two Danian boys, three Citherians and one small girl.* He raised his eyebrow. "Do you realize what you're asking?"

"Betren, please." Lance's hand tightened on the front of the saddle.

Betren studied him. "Contemplating on quitting on me?"

"No! But if I can't think straight and things get really bad and you know the only way you can get to Megara is without me..."

37

Betren nodded. "I'll consent to your demand, only when you understand that you are putting your life completely in my hands. I, not you, make that final decision."

"Understood." Lance breathed deeply, his shoulders slumped, his hand slipped off the saddle but the blanket stayed on him.

"Then I swear it." Betren laid his hand on Lance's knee. "I swear that I will take your life if necessity demands it. I swear it on the horse, even though we left both halves of that horse in Delmarath."

Chapter 5

The cold hard leather reins stung Betren's hand as he led the old mare along the trail. He kept a watchful eye on Lance who clung to the saddle as if he had never seen a horse before. *More than his arm must be hurting. Wish I could do more to make him comfortable, but our only hope is to reach Megara. Must keep moving.*

Eventually, the motion of the horse revived Lance. "You don't have to walk. Why not ride behind me?"

"Not yet. You've had a nasty fall, my friend. If it were possible, I'd have you flat on your back next to a warm fire. Since that's not an option, we take it easy for awhile. You relax. I walk." Betren sighed. "Must have had a wind storm in this part of the country. There's a downed tree blocking the trail here and I see several more ahead of us. We'll go around. Watch for low branches."

Time inched by while they maneuvered for ground open enough to lead a horse around fallen timber. They had just returned to the trail, when they heard a barely discernable low-pitched howl.

"That's no wolf," Betren said.

"Horrhound. Last time we ran into those things, they almost ripped us apart."

Betren met Lance's eyes. "Are they coming this way?"

Lance shook his head. "Can't tell. Too much distance between them and us."

They stood at the edge of a clearing choked with shoulder high bushes, dogwood, arrow wood and willow. Their hard packed trail deteriorated into a soggy uneven path which seemed to be losing a battle with the encroaching vegetation. Puddles of icy water lurked under clumps of grass.

Lance drew the blanket closer to him. "I'm cold, so cold."

Betren sighed. "I know. Not much we can do about it. Stay on the horse until we get through this mess. Then maybe you should try walking. It might help to warm you a little. But now I think I'll ride with you."

Betren slipped the reins over the horse's head and handed them to Lance, then vaulted up on the horse behind the saddle. "Come on, scrunch forward. This saddle is big enough for both of us." Betren hugged Lance's waist, pressing his body against his friend's back.

"Bet? What are you doing?"

"Figured my body might give you a little warmth."

"You idiot. You'll only get yourself wet."

"Shut up, Lance. Let's go."

Lance obeyed the first part of that order, but he held the horse still.

"Well?" Betren's voice softened.

"Horrhounds on our trail!"

"Go!"

Lance touched his heels to the mare's side keeping her at a walk.

Come on, Lance. A little speed here. A branch snagged Betren's cloak. He yanked it loose. *Those hounds are strangely quiet. Have those demons found some other prey or is this a new breed that hunts silently?* "Lance, move it."

The horse stumbled; the riders lurched forward in the saddle.

Lance cursed as the mare recovered her footing. "Ground's too rough. Don't want our horse to break a leg."

A bramble snared Betren's boot. He jerked it free. *I should have taken the reins; I could do better than this.* "Lance, a little more speed would be good."

"We're almost there, hang on."

A hideous howl sent shivers down their spines. The savage animals were closing the distance between them.

The mare bolted out of the brush staying on the trail.

Lance urged her on. "Hang on!" he shouted. "Log in our path. We're going to jump."

Betren tightened his hold on his friend.

The gray gathered herself together and leaped over the hurdle. Lance cried out as the landing jarred him.

The horse slowed to a bone-shaking trot, but broke into a gallop as the hounds resumed their howling. Two or three trees barricading the trail forced them off the path. Underbrush whipped the riders' legs. Low hanging branches threatened to sweep them into a net of thorny brambles.

A whoosh of frigid air rushed at them as Lance guided the horse back to the trail. Both men sighed in relief.

The animal cantered a short distance, slowed to a trot, and then a walk. Behind them the yelping dogs gained on them.

Lance drew rein. "We've had it. This horse can't go much further." He stroked the mare's neck, quieting her. "It's all right, girl," he whispered.

"Get off." Betren shoved himself over the back of the saddle and landed on his feet. "Hurry up!"

Lance managed to pull his leg over the back of the horse and dropped to the ground. His legs buckled. He caught onto the mare's creamy mane and leaned against her. "Steady girl, steady."

"Let go of her!"

Lance stroked the horse's neck and soothed her.

Betren rammed Lance, barely aware that the Citherian tripped over a log and crashed to the ground.

Snatching the reins, Betren wrapped them around the nearest sapling pulling the mare's head against the trunk. Drawing his knife, he slit the girth causing the saddle to fall off the struggling horse and yanked the bridle over her head.

The mare rolled her eyes in terror and pawed the ground with her two front hooves.

Betren slapped her hindquarters with the bridle and sent her bucking away from them.

The men froze.

Horrhounds, large black and tan beasts the size of the prairiemen's ponies crashed through the undergrowth. Long red tongues lolled out of muscular jaws revealing needle sharp pointed white fangs. Their gleaming eyes focused on the galloping horse. With a triumphant cry the dogs tore after the doomed animal.

Betren dropped the bridle and seized Lance's arm. He jerked him to his feet. "Lance, if you ever block me with your mind again, I'll kill you." His tone masked his anger, but he knew Lance was not fooled.

"Ow. Let go. Please." Lance looked dazed and shook his head as if to clear it. "How did you know?"

Betren smiled, that smile sent chills through any man in the Hall of Justice. "No horse stands quietly when horrhounds are on top of it. You almost got us killed."

Lance gazed at him. "I'm sorry, Bet. She was a good horse. She shouldn't have to die."

"Your death doesn't seem right either, nor does mine. But that's what will happen if we don't reach Megara soon." Betren released his grip on Lance's arm. "How do you feel?"

Lance looked at him, confusion in his face. "Does the word idiot mean anything to you? I don't believe I did that. You had to sacrifice the horse. What's wrong with me?"

"Let's say your judgment has been impaired by your accident." Betren paused. "Now, you must keep your part of our pledge. You placed your life in my hands. Now, you do exactly what I say when I say it."

Lance drew a sharp breath and nodded.

Betren snatched the medical kit and the food sack from the saddle. Snarls and growls came from the direction of the fallen mare. *Speed's our only chance.* He hesitated, watching Lance trip on the blanket as he slung the packs over his head."Stop before you hurt yourself. You'll find that soaked blanket worse than a cloak." Betren untied the rope securing the blanket around Lance's waist. "Let's get out of here. I'll lead. Keep close to me. Yell, if you fall behind."

They plodded through the woods all night guided by the light of a full moon reflected on white snow. Instead of speaking, they concentrated on picking the right foot up, putting it down, then doing the same with the left, progressing forward, always forward.

Behind him, Lance mumbled. Betren caught the names Val and James, the older sons of Robert, heard Lance call Warrior and realized the Citherian believed he was riding through the mountains to the high pastures.

Dampness penetrated Betren's bones, his feet and hands tingled with the cold. His legs protested every step. His shoulders ached. *Must have pulled a muscle when I pried Lance out of the stream. At least the hounds are no longer on our trail. Only five. Where's the main pack?*

"Bet, hold up." Lance trudged through the snow toward Betren.

Concentrate on Lance. So preoccupied, I failed to realize he was so far behind.

Lance stumbled, but managed to maintain his balance. He was shivering and breathing heavily. "Slow down, Bet," he panted. "I can't keep up any more."

"All right Lance."

"I'm not quitting. It's just that you walk too fast."

"Understood. Actually, you're doing just fine. I don't mind walking a little slower. Trails wider here. Let's walk together." *His strength is failing. Thank the gods we're almost to the main road.*

The trail crossed a small stream. The bank on the side nearest them was steep. Lance tugged Betren's hand, recognition of their situation flooded his face. He pointed down the bank. "I can do this." He sat and slid.

43

"Wait for me," Betren yelled. *Don't want him crossing that water without me. Good, for once he's listening.*

Lance slipped on a algae covered rock halfway across the stream and turned his ankle, but Betren caught his arm and steadied him. The land ahead of them was easier, just a long incline starting at the water's edge. A loaded wagon pulled by a tired old mare could roll along this section of the trail effortlessly. Normally, Betren and Lance would have raced to the top, but in their condition, each step was agony.

"If I only had use of two hands," Lance groaned as he supported himself by leaning on a tree.

"Here, grab mine."

Lance took a breath. "No, I'll hurt my colt. I need both hands to hold him. No," he wailed as Betren grasped his arm. "We'll hurt the colt."

"Not likely, my friend." Betren ignored Lance straying from reality. "Hang on, I have myself well supported. Besides, it's not that bad. Push yourself up with your legs."

Lance managed to climb next to Betren. "How would you get a horse up here?"

"Oh, we have a couple of detours for places like this, but this is the quickest way."

Lance let out a heavy sigh. "Is Warrior all right?"

"He's fine. Metrox will take good care of him. Come on, it's not much further to the top. Then we can rest."

When they reached the open flat land, long since cleared for firewood, they collapsed on the ground panting for breath. Betren's legs felt useless, his heart pounded in his chest. He handed Lance his water flask, and then realized that Lance's trembling fists made it difficult for him to drink without aid. Betren snatched the canteen back before Lance could spill the precious liquid.

"Let's try this again." Betren lifted the canteen to Lance's lips. "Now drink, easy does it. Not too fast."

"Thanks." Lance panted. "Here, you finish it."

Betren divided the last of his trail bars between them. *Thank the gods he can still eat. It's not much. I still feel ravished.*

44

Clouds circled the moon, and then covered it. The wind picked up and it began to snow. Betren scrambled to an upright position. "Come on, Lance, onto Megara." He watched Lance struggle to his feet, estimating the distance they still had to travel to the remaining strength of his friend. He breathed a prayer to all the gods that the Citherian maintained the stamina to get to the King's city.

The sky lightened as they reached road. The snow stopped, but heavy clouds hid the rising sun. *Only one more mile to go, but the distance seems impossible.* He glimpsed the city perched on its rocky hill. The road to the city wound through open fields like a white ribbon. Dried stalks of corn lined the right side of the road. A stone fence kept stock out of the plowed fields on the left side. There were no tracks. It had snowed since the last party of nobles had passed this point.

Wet heavy flakes floated to the earth, slowly at first, then faster until they could barely see a foot in front of them. Betren felt as if he and Lance were the only living creatures in the world creeping along a perpetual road to nowhere. The snow had been ankle-high when they started. Now it was deepening, forcing their exhausted muscles to lift their legs through the heavy slush. Betren's foot scraped something hard. *The stone wall on the side of the road; we must stay in the middle. There's a covered bridge around here someplace. If we miss that...*

"How much further?"

"Not far. We'll be there soon. How are you doing?"

"I can still walk." Lance staggered forward.

Betren caught his shoulder. "Lean on me. We're going to make it."

"Riders behind us," Lance gasped his voice hoarse. "Might as well wait for them. We can rest here."

"No!" Betren forced him to take a step. "Obey me, Lance. Walk with me. We still have some time before they catch us. Look, the bridge is in front of us. We're almost at the city. Easy now, it's slippery."

Lance's feet flew out from under him on the icy boards hidden under the windblown snow.

45

Betren had just enough strength left to drag Lance to his feet. *The glazed look in Lance's eyes scares me. He's fighting to breathe. And he's not shivering like he was.* "Come on, Lance, one step. Now another."

They floundered on, slower than before. The small hill seemed like a mountain. It took forever to reach the top.

"Men riding from city."

"You're imagining things." Betren pushed forward.

"We're trapped. It's over."

"Not yet. Keep moving. It's our only chance." *Please, every god in heaven and on earth; let Lance be right. Let it be the King.*

Betren could hear the riders behind him now; heard the horses' shod hooves, the silver bells on the harness, voices complaining about the weather. Betren didn't glance behind him. He really didn't want to know who the riders were.

"Can I believe my eyes? A barbarian," someone shouted. The riders halted.

Lance cried out as an arrow penetrated his shoulder.

"Bet," he cried as he fell. "Kill me. Go."

"If there's one thing I'm proficient at, it's killing." Betren drew his sword. "Your death will take a matter of minutes. The results will last forever." He gazed into Lance's pleading eyes. "Trust me, my friend. I still have time to keep my pledge."

Chapter 6

Plodding hooves and voices engaged in excited conversation advanced toward the fugitives. Betren stood poised to ram his sword up through Lance's vital organs, yet delayed, hoping against odds for some miraculous reason to postpone Lance's death.

"A horn," Lance whispered. "I thought I heard a horn — beautiful music."

Lance was right. A horn pealing over the snow-covered fields answered Betren's prayers. It was beautiful music. Only it wasn't being blown for anyone's enjoyment, it gave definite orders. The King's horn was directed at the party behind them commanding them to stand down. This matter was the King's business and there would be no interference.

Betren glanced behind him. The riders halted, respecting Cadamire's authority.

"Lance," Betren said. "Can you hear me?"

"What?" Lance moaned.

"King Cadamire's coming." Betren sheathed his sword and knelt beside Lance. "Remember the words you need to request permission to speak on the Knife?"

"Yes..."

"Now is the time to petition the king. Ask to speak on the Knife. I cannot do this for you. Our lives depend on you speaking to the king. Understand?"

"Yes."

Betren could see the king's horsemen quite clearly now. Bart, his green hood thrown back, mounted on his black mare, led the riders down the hill. The horsemen from the city formed a single line, each horse's head even with the saddle of the green cloaked umber uniformed rider ahead of it. They urged their horses into a slow collected canter. Down the hill they came, a solid line of guardsmen who swung wide of Lance and Betren and cut them off from the party behind them.

Good maneuver, Nicely executed. Betren recognized some of the riders and realized that this was the King's Personal Guard. *Rumor control must have exaggerated their uselessness in the field.*

He rose to his feet and watched four horsemen break out of the formation and canter toward him. He had led this particular tactic a thousand times, training men in Delmarath how to apprehend a thief. "Steady," he muttered to himself. "I can't reach for my weapon. It's my turn to surrender." The word surrender choked in his throat.

The four horsemen circled them forming a tight moving ring. Betren struggled to keep his footing unable to avoid the snow and mud kicked up by well-trained horses demonstrating an excellent piaffe. *Like to swap secrets with their trainer. They cover less ground trotting in place than our horses in Delmarath. No way could anyone penetrate this formation.*

Several notes on the bugle ordered the horsemen circling Lance and Betren to withdraw to a position directly behind them.

Three riders advanced toward them.

48

Betren recognized them even though they were all cloaked in green. *King Cadamire, haven't seen you in five years. You're our only hope. And Bart, your black mare clued me in, even as you left the city. Oh, yes, brother, Bart. This meeting will bring neither of us pleasure. And what's this? Talman rides with the King? The wizard never rides. Hope, he doesn't fall out of his saddle.*

The King raised his hand signaling his companions to halt.

Bart dismounted and approached them. "What in the name of heaven?" He stared first at Lance, then at Betren. "Brother," he managed. "Give me your sword."

Betren realized he had never faced this moment when he stood before the king, in the eyes of the guard, a felon. His reputation, his achievements as Defender of Delmarath meant nothing here. Slowly he unbuckled his weapon and handed it to Bart. Betren felt that he lost his right hand.

Bart fastened the sword to his saddle, then turned back to Betren. The Captain of the King's Personal Guard chewed his lip. Finally, he shook his head. "I can't believe this, Betren. What a fine mess you've made."

Betren smiled wearily and raised his eyebrow. "As always, Brother, no matter what I do, I do it well."

"How dare you destroy my life," Bart snapped, clenching his fist and slamming his brother into the snow.

Betren waited for the kick he was sure Bart intended to administrate to his ribs. He lacked the strength to roll out of range of his brother's foot.

"I have always heard of the high regard the sons of Bromwell hold for each other. It is interesting to see it firsthand." The King's sarcastic comment caused Bart to freeze. He stepped back from Betren, his eyes smoldering.

"Indeed it is," Talman was the only one in the party who seemed pleased with the proceedings. "Look, Great King, a lord of the land and a stranger."

"It is as you said, Wizard," King Cadamire said. "And I don't want to hear another word about it."

Betren struggled to his knee. "Great King, take us under your sword." He fought to keep his voice steady. "I ask your protection for myself and this barbarian."

"The Knife of Truth," Lance gasped. "Let me speak on the Knife."

King Cadamire dismounted, drew his sword, let it hover over Betren's head and then touched Lance's forehead with it. "These men are under my sword," he declared. "We'll escort them to the palace. Death to any man who harms them."

Betren lurched to his feet. *Well, Bart, it's up to you now. How strange, my life rests in your hands.*

"Captain," the King said to Bart. "Did you hear me? Or have the gods deprived you of your senses? Accompany these men to my palace immediately."

Bart saluted. "Understood, my King." He knelt beside Lance and laid his hand on the Citherian's neck. "Sedrac, we need a litter."

The Captain of the King's Guard unfastened his cloak and rolled Lance up in it. "More cloaks, gentlemen. We've got to warm him."

Sedrac's fleshy hand snatched a hatchet attached to his saddle and called to some of the men to help. He handed the ax to the first man to answer his call, supervised the men as they found two saplings and cut them down. Guardsmen removed their cloaks and wove them around the branches. When their handiwork was strong enough to carry a man, they approached Lance.

"My word, Captain," Sedrac said to Bart, "he's branded." The guardsmen's expressions reflected the revulsion on Sedrac's double chinned face. The men glanced at each other; several turned toward the king.

"Get him in the litter," Bart ordered. "Now."

Gingerly the men rolled Lance on the litter and proceeded to fasten it between two horses.

"Captain," King Cadamire said, his dark eyes wide. "I'm curious. When did my guard learn how to move a wounded man?"

50

"Sometime after they learned to saddle and bridle a horse," Bart said. "What good is a King's Guard that isn't prepared to protect their king no matter the circumstances?"

"Interesting concept. I'm sure these over privileged sons of my illustrious nobles found it so." The King pulled his hood over his frosted black hair and tightened the ties under his square chin.

Sedrac strode over to them and saluted. "The prisoner is ready to travel, my King."

"Good," Cadamire said. "Captain, I'll ride with the litter. Half of my guard will accompany me to ensure the barbarian's safety."

"Yes, my King. "

"See that your brother gets to the palace alive and undamaged."

Bart saluted and then mounted his horse. "And now, brother..."

Chapter 7

Exhausted, Betren gaged the leering expressions of the green and brown uniformed men astride restless mounts. *Abandoned by my king — and they crave blood.*

Bart and his rich enough to be stout, second in command perched on their horses engaged in earnest conversation. *Social climber.*

A rider near Betren fiddled with his rope. *My brother's going to kill me.* The King's Personal Guard would bind his hands in front of him and force him to run behind their horses all the way to Megara. They'd claim that their charge fell, their horse's hooves accidently trampled him. *Ironic, Lance makes it and I don't. Just look at those vultures.*

"Betren, can I give you a ride? You seemed to have misplaced your horse." Bart's words, although never spoken so coldly, were familiar.

It took Betren a moment to recognize his brother's hand. He clasped it and Bart hauled him up on top of the black mare. Betren swung his leg over the horse and balanced behind Bart. "Thank you," he said softly as he grasped his brother's waist. "You will pay dearly for this kindness."

"Do you really suppose anything I do now, will matter?" Bart allowed bitterness to color his voice. "I obey the King's order."

Betren gazed over his brother's shoulder at the city on the top of the hill. *Will I ever see Delmarath again?* He focused on the wizard bouncing in his saddle. "Why is Talman riding with you?"

"King's command," Bart said sharply.

All too soon, they clattered through the city gates where most of the guard turned their horses in the direction of the stables. Only three riders continued to the palace slowly up the slippery stone streets.

People stared at the two sons of Bromwell riding double on Bart's black horse. Voices commenting on the fact of two men on one horse changed to shouts of, "hail Buris, hail Sedrac!"

Buris' paint gelding would be recognized anywhere, but he didn't need the horse to be noticed. Lanky Buris was one of the few guards with a receding hairline.

Sedrac's hefty body and double chin shouted that he was the richest man in the King's Personal Guard. The farmers of the first ring claimed his horse was part draft. If an animal could carry Sedrac, it would do well pulling a plow.

"What's wrong, Brother? No cheers for the King's Captain of his Personal Guard?" Betren couldn't resist the taunt.

They're high-ranking lords," Bart muttered. "Border Lords don't rate cheers. Except for Father." The horses clattered across the drawbridge.

Dismounting in the courtyard, Betren felt Bart's hand on his arm and he permitted his brother to lead him into the King's Great Hall. He lacked the will to protest. His legs would collapse under him any moment.

As they proceeded across the hall, Betren recognized his father assisting the king with his outer clothing. Bromwell froze momentarily, his dark eyes widened in recognition at the sight of his eldest son.

Cadamire turned and beckoned the sons of Bromwell to him.

Betren sank to one knee. It took all the concentration he had left to remain in this position. He could not, would not disgrace his family by collapsing in front of the king or his father.

"Elder Son of Bromwell," King Cadamire said, "I will keep this short. We will investigate the cause of your highly irregular behavior when the barbarian is able to speak on the Knife. Until that time, I place you in the custody of your father. I grant you the protection of my sword and the freedom of the palace as long as you stay within its walls. For the time being, you may keep your knife. Do you understand?"

"I understand and will obey, my King," Betren murmured. "Thank you, my King."

"Good. Bromwell, stop fussing," Cadamire ordered. "I'm capable of handling things here without your assistance. Escort your son to your quarters so he may rest. Bart, see to your normal duties."

Bart saluted and started to leave.

"Captain."

Bart halted and pivoted facing Cadamire.

"I expect you to attend me at dinner tonight."

"Yes, my King." Bart saluted one more time and exited the throne room.

Betren leaned on his father's strong arm as they climbed the stairs. He could barely believe the King's leniency. Instead of a cold damp cell, he had the comfort of his father's quarters, and the freedom to place inquiries that may bear fruit in saving his city throughout the palace.

Bromwell led him inside his fire-warmed chamber. "Give me your cloak, Son."

With numb hands, Betren managed to unfasten the clasp.

His father lifted it from his son's shoulders. "You've had a rough journey."

Betren fumbled with ties attaching the small leather bag and handed it to his father. "Gunpowder— what we call the black death."

Bromwell peered into the bag and removed the little box. He lifted the cover off and gazed inside. "Robert described this to me once. I never thought to hold some in my hand."

"The prairie-men have it. They attack Delmarath in the spring." Betren sank into the nearest chair.

"I'll keep this safe. I imagine Robert's books are at the bottom of this."

"Probably." Betren leaned back in the chair and closed his eyes. "When will you inform the King?"

"This will keep until Lance is able to speak on the Knife. Know that the law decrees a king must have no knowledge of the circumstances that brought you two to Megara until then. First we must heal you and Lance."

Bromwell had barely time to hide the powder before there was a knock on the door. He opened it to see a boy dressed in a healer's white smock, a medicine bag slung over his shoulder, ready to knock one more time.

"My Lord, King Cadamire, may he live forever, requests your help with the barbarian," the boy said, "and I'm ordered to tend Lord Betren." He handed Bromwell a silver ring with a crowned eagle etched into the metal. "The Great King Cadamire sends his token to prove that my words are true."

Bromwell looked amused. "And you are?"

The boy drew himself up as tall as his twelve years permitted. "I am Josu, apprentice to the healers. I know enough to care for a man who has been out in the cold too long."

"Of course, I recognize you now. You're one of the first that participated in Cadamire's new program to match ability with position." Bromwell walked over to Josu and studied his thin face. "What happened? Did someone strike you?"

"The Senior Healer, my Lord." The boy's words fell out of his mouth, one on top of the other. "I was trying to stop the barbarian's wounds from bleeding. The Senior Healer told me to leave him alone; he's going to examine the barbarian when he is good and ready. Then he told one of the other healers that he just might set the barbarian's arm so he can never use it again." The boy paused, his eyes on Lord's Bromwell's broad face. "I'm sorry, my Lord. I always talk too fast when I'm scared."

"And what scares you? Surely not me?" Bromwell smiled at him.

The boy took a breath. "The healers, my Lord. They'll murder me when they get an opportunity. I told my King what they were doing. That wasn't too smart, but I didn't know what else to do. I took the oath to heal the sick and they prevented me from doing anything to aid that stranger. I understand he's a barbarian, but he's a man. He's hurt and needs us." The boy fidgeted. "And my King — well, he looked angry. At me I suppose. He sent me to fetch you."

Lord Bromwell's lips tightened, his eyes became cold dots of obsidian. "Lance needs me more than you do, Bet. You'll manage just fine with this boy's help. I'll send my attendant, Sagu. He has the authority to obtain any provisions you might require."

Chapter 8

Already reports of the downfall of the House of Bartran flew through the court. Two young ladies, last night so delighted to dance with Bart, brushed past him without a word, then shook out their skirts as if they had touched something filthy.

Bart fled into his office near the throne room. He slammed the door, sank into his chair behind his table and buried his head in his hands. Thanks to Betren's disastrous appearance at court, Bart's workload for the day had tripled.

He reached for a roll of parchment kept on a shelf next to his table. An overwhelming desire to fling the scroll out the window into the moat soared through every nerve in his body, but a lifetime invested in self-control saved his career, the window and the records of the King's Personal Guard. He opened it and wrote a concise report of the morning's activities starting when the wizard, Talman, had persuaded King Cadamire to ride out of the city.

When finished with his written report, he tapped his quill on the desk. Duties forced him out of the comparative safety of his office. "Curse the results of Betren's repulsive behavior." Checking on the welfare of the prisoners, in this case his brother and Lance, was priority number one. No secret passage existed between the main floor and the dungeons making desired avoidance of the Megaran court population impossible.

The corridor to the holding room in the lower levels of the palace forced Bart to pass one of the sitting-rooms the woman used in their leisure. He gritted his teeth as feminine voices floated through the hall.

"They're alike and not alike," a woman's voice rasped as he approached the open door. "Both are blessed with that oval face that seems to run in the House of Bartran. Bart's taller of course, but his face is fuller. Result of all the good food he eats at the King's table. What a shame. I was beginning to admire the younger son of Bromwell."

Bart quickened his pace.

"Not that handsome features matter of course. There's only one end for those committing treason," squealed an older woman. "They'll be hung on the wall— all three of them."

That's actually possible. Bart grimaced. A few more steps and they would see him.

"Fortunate for this to happen before any of you girls married into that disgraceful family," a deeper voice added.

"It's all because of that obnoxious brother. What a disaster, bringing disgrace and death to the House of Bartran because of a filthy barbarian."

"And to imagine, I bestowed a dance on him," another woman whispered, "Oh, there he is." In a louder voice she added, "Do you fancy we will have more snow today?"

Bart recognized that voice. *Alisha will never dance with me again.* He held his pace as he strutted down the hall, their barbed remarks ringing in his ears.

Before entering the holding center, he ducked into an overlook, a small room protruding over the area where a man could observe proceedings undetected.

Lance lay shaking on a grimy bed dragged out from one of the side-cells far from the fire, still wrapped in the cloaks that his King's Guard had provided.

His father, Lord Bromwell strode into the room followed by Regis, the king's scribe.

Bromwell glanced at Lance, then hurried to the door leading down the hall to the sickrooms and bellowed, "healers! To me! Immediately!"

"My Lord, we're organizing our supplies," a slender man wearing a medical tunic rushed into the room.

"Indeed."

Bromwell's calm cold voice warned Bart of his father's anger. *Glad I'm not the one responsible for Lance's neglect.*

"They'll, they'll be right in," the healer stammered. He drew his knife. "I must cut his clothes off so we can work."

"Hold it." Bromwell stepped in front of the man.

"My Lord, stand aside. We cannot treat our patient while wearing those foul rags."

"Keep your knife away from this man." Bromwell lifted the green cloaks off Lance and handed them to the healer.

"My Lord, state your business?" The head physician hurried into the room wringing his hands. "What is Regis doing here?"

"King's orders," Bromwell said as he carefully unfastened the material cradling Lance's arm. "He wants a full report of how this man is treated and I'm ensuring that the king's order is fulfilled. Word for word, action for action. Have you got that, Regis?"

"Yes, my Lord. Word for word, action for action, to the letter. I can read everything that has been said, and everything that has been done for the barbarian back to you, if you desire."

The head healer cringed.

Bromwell returned to Lance's side as the rest of the medical staff rushed into the holding center with blankets and medical supplies.

Bart grinned. *Nothing I can do here. Lance is in no condition to talk. Besides, I wouldn't consider interfering with Father. Wonder who's caring for Bet?* Bart climbed the stairs toward his father's quarters. He winced as Luciana entered the hall from her room and strolled toward him.

Alisha's little sister, held her pert little nose high, her ebony eyes straight ahead as she passed him. Her lilac and cream-colored satin dress rustled as she moved to accent the snub.

Not Luciana. Bart's heart sank. *I hoped she'd be different.* He struggled to act like he didn't care and opened the door to his father's quarters. He halted in the doorway, surprised to see his way blocked by twelve-year-old Josu.

"Captain," Josu stood motionless in front of Bart. "Your brother is resting and cannot be disturbed."

"Move aside, boy. I have official business with my brother. This is ridiculous. Since when does a child issue me orders?"

Josu refused to retreat. "It can wait, Captain. I am in charge of this sickroom. You will not interfere." He seemed to grow in stature as he opened his right hand revealing a silver ring with a crowned eagle etched in the metal. "King's orders."

Bart retreated into the hallway and closed the door quietly. *Bet's enjoying this if he's awake. His condition is nowhere as serious as Lance's. Oh, to have the pleasure of visiting my brother in the lowest dungeon in a dark, damp cell with water oozing from the slime-covered walls.* He sighed. "Two jobs completed. Onto the stables. Heaven help the man who fails to cool off his horse before turning it into its stall. I'm just angry enough to make it a five-lash offense."

Inspecting the condition of horses used by his guard was not a normal duty of previous captains of the King's Personal Guard, but Bart, scandalized with the lack of knowledge of the King's Guard in military procedures, initiated a training program. Unexpected problems arose when Rauf, the lowly stable master, held Bart responsible for the health of the horses used by the guard. That underling insisted that Bart check the animals daily after being cared for by the sons of Dana's high ranking nobles. Bart had filed a complaint that this reduced his position of captain to the job of mere stable hand but the King backed the stable master's mandate. Indignities like this could only happen to a border lord.

Bart paused at the head of the stairs to the great room. Below him people gathered in small groups all engaged in serious conversation sounding like a swarm of bees. *I'm sure they're chewing the House of Bartran to shreds. Unfortunately, it's the fastest way out of the palace. Here goes absolutely nothing.*

Luciana's father, Lord Andros stood on the landing briefing his retainers as Bart descended the stairs. The wealthiest man in the kingdom usually so cordial, ignored Bart's greeting.

"The Great Hall..." Bart muttered to himself stopping at the foot of the stairs. "It's the same as running a gauntlet, but the blows are much more devastating."

He took a deep breath as he gathered his courage. "I am a son of Bromwell of the House of Bartran," he reminded himself. "My brother has done enough. I refuse to further disgrace my family." Head held high, Bart started across the hall.

Lord Famen who just a few weeks ago had been hinting to Bromwell via carrier pigeon that a marriage between Bart and his older daughter, Falina would be advantageous to both houses, scowled. Falina and her younger sister drew their matching crimson capes tightly over their white dresses. Famen deliberately stepped in front of his daughters, and shielded them from Bart's eyes with his large rimmed hat.

Bart kept his pace brisk in the manner of a man attending important business. *Still have two-thirds of the room to cover.*

Lord Robo lifted his tri-colored beret and bowed mockingly. He dramatically tapped his knee-high deerskin boots with the blue jay feather sown on his cap. "A few embarrassing family problems, Captain?" Conder's ambassador laughed loudly. He turned to his companions, guardsmen wearing the purple and gold Chaleen uniform.

"I suppose that Prince Conder will disinherit his favorite foster son," snorted one of the guardsmen.

"The upstart House of Bartran falls," Robo sneered. "Maybe Buris will finally be appointed Captain of the King's Guard."

"Well, he deserves the position. He's served long enough."

Bart didn't recognize the last speaker. *Underling! I'll take care of him if he ever joins my guard.* Realizing that his fingers curled around the hilt of his sword, he quickly let his hand fall to his side.

A stocky heavy youth dressed in a vibrant orange tunic looked darkly in Bart's direction, then joined a group of young nobles.

Bart held his head higher. *There's that nosy Gilmore, collecting information for Talman.*

"Will the father die with the sons?" One of Sedrac's personal attendants whispered.

Bart strode by them. *I'm certainly not going to acknowledge these idiots.*

"Why isn't the noble captain in a cell?" Buris' personal servant's voice raised his voice loud enough for all to hear.

"Perhaps a test," Gilmore hissed. "The King allows the son his freedom. Ability over birth, you know."

Bart forced himself to maintain his normal facial expression. *Career, acceptance, and chances of a good marriage gone in one fell swoop. How could Betren do this to me? At least the gods have granted me an inch of mercy. No more people between me and the door.*

On entering the courtyard, Bart discovered Nightwind missing. *She'd better be safely in her stall.* He seethed as he crossed the drawbridge. *One of my lovely lady's less endearing traits is her knack of untying knots. Last time my horse freed herself, she managed to trample everyone's front yard in the first ring. That's all I need.* He jogged down the hill to the horse barns.

Only horses happily munching hay accompanied him in the stable. Bart's black mare, Nightwind, nickered a greeting as he stepped into her stall. He ran his hand over her back and under her neck. *She's cool. Hay is fresh. Clean water in her bucket.* He picked up her foot. *Hooves cleaned.* His mare's neck felt warm and comforting as he buried his face in her mane. *At least I have one friend in Megara.*

Hearing footsteps, Bart stepped out of Nightwind's stall, picked up Rauf's checklist and started to examine the horses that had been ridden that morning. A chestnut gelding had a loose shoe.

Holard appeared with Rauf, the stable master still dressed in his green cloak covering his brown leather uniform. Holard saluted Bart. "Captain," he said. "My horse has a loose shoe. I reported it to the stable master as you require."

Bart returned the salute.

"I'll take over from here, Captain." Rauf stepped into the gelding's stall.

"Well done, Guardsman," Bart said to Holard. "Go care for your saddle. I'll be there shortly." He continued with the inspection of twenty horses, checking them off his list as he worked. *Well, this is a first,* he thought as he completed his inspection of the last stall and attached the papers to the wall near the cloak room. *Rauf is going to fall over in a faint when he sees this. Not one mistake made by my guard.*

Bart strode past the cloak room into the tack room where the men were cleaning mud off their saddles. The complete silence that greeted him told him that he had been the topic of conversation.

Finally, Sedrac said, "Captain, that barbarian... we touched him. Isn't it against the law to aid such a man? Will we be punished?"

"You acted under orders," Bart said. "Which puts the blame on the one in charge, me. However, we all acted under the King's command. We did nothing wrong, none of us."

"But your brother; he's under the King's sword; that means you—"

"Quiet," Buris growled, his long lips curling with disgust. "He's captain until the King says he's not captain. Don't forget it."

"That's exactly right." Bart paced through the room checking the work. Everyone was being extremely careful. Saddle blankets hung on the rails. The bridles suspended on their hooks, bits polished, the reins carefully draped over the headpiece. The saddles had never received so much effort, the leather gleamed. Bart had no excuse to vent his anger on them. He surveyed the scene. "Attention!"

Every hand ceased movement. Heads turned toward him, their faces betrayed no emotion. They awaited his orders. Anyone

63

stepping into the room would never suspect that these men represented the wealth of Dana.

"When you finish here, you're free until dinner. Report to the Main Hall prepared for the evening routine." Bart left without another word. *I've absolutely nothing to occupy my time until dinner. Should have ordered some drills instead of indulging my men in the liberties of R&R. The palace! Oh, the desire to hack off the head of the first person I meet.*

"Fine," he muttered, "just fine. I'd be hung on the wall for murder. Got to get control of myself. Maybe a brisk run on the city walls will rein in my temper."

Usually Bart enjoyed the view from the walls, the wide-open farmlands that supported the city, or the houses and shops crowded behind the walls full of life and enterprise. Unlike Betren, he enjoyed the city, liked living in the capital of Dana. Today, none of this mattered.

The younger son of Bromwell paced along the wall, seeing nothing except the stone masonry under his feet, unaware of anyone on the battlements.

"Watch it, Captain. Who gave you orders to knock me off the wall?"

Chapter 9

"My King?" Bart gasped. "I'm sorry; I should watch where I'm going. My mind was elsewhere. I would never —" He tried to kneel but King Cadamire caught his arm.

"Well met, Younger Son of Bromwell," the King said, silencing Bart's profuse apologies. "Enough of this foolery. If I wanted court behavior, I'd stay in the palace, out of this wind and command you into my presence. Since we both seem to have a need for exercise, let's accompany each other. You are just the man I want to see." The King gave his Captain of the Guard a shrewd look. "How are things with you?"

Bart held his tongue. Unintelligent words, unconnected scenes collided in his mind.

"Nothing like frigid air to clear one's head. I might as well come to the point. What does the elder son of Bromwell — Betren hope to gain in presenting that barbarian at the palace?"

"Unknown, Great King," Bart could see his breath as he spoke. "I'm sure my brother considers his reasoning sound."

"You didn't speak to either of them?"

Bart blew on his hands and rubbed them together. "Tried to see Betren, but was apprehended at the door by a determined twelve-year-old boy, who let me know that his Lordship, the Defender of Delmarath, was sleeping and gave the impression that not even you, the King, was going to wake him."

Cadamire laughed. "Oh, good, I see that Josu is obeying orders. I had to remove him from the medical wing and I didn't want him to surmise he was being punished. Not after alerting me on the outrageous behavior of my healers."

"I'd like to remind my King that I live there too."

"I thank you, Son of Bromwell, for not pressing the matter."

Bart shrugged. "I had business at the stables, my King. The boy's right. My brother verged on the rim of collapse when he was brought into the palace. He needs undisturbed sleep."

"If Bromwell thought the problem needed an immediate solution, I would have been advised. I suspect the life of the barbarian is the first consideration here."

"I took a moment to look into the holding room. Father is on the rampage. The healers are moving faster than I've believed possible. Father stands beside Lance overseeing every procedure." Bart couldn't help smiling. "I don't envy them."

The King nodded as he gazed over the wall. "I've seen your father in action when he's angry. He is calm, composed and deadly. The perfect Danian way of handling trouble. Don't feel sorry for the healers; they deserve everything they are receiving and will receive." The King glanced at Bart. "And what about yourself? I imagine Betren's actions are responsible for your recent lack of popularity."

"Yes, my King." Bart sighed. *Now don't say anything stupid. It's pointless complaining about the snubs and snide remarks I've endured.*

"This will pass, Captain." The King said quietly. "In a few weeks there will be a new crisis for the court to chew on and you and the barbarian will be forgotten."

"Unless my brother is found guilty of something." Bart could have bit his tongue. *May the gods help me; this self pity is unbecoming behavior for the Captain of the King's Personal Guard.* "Forgive me, my King. I'm still reacting to the fact that Betren would even contemplate escorting Lance to the palace."

"I understand your feelings." Cadamire laid his gloved hand on Bart's shoulder. "But you had better stay on top of them if you wish to survive."

"Yes, my King. That's what I'm doing out here. Trying to gain control of my emotions."

"It might help to discuss it."

Never! Bart stared at the massive stone under his feet. *I know too much about Lance and Betren.*

Cadamire applied force to Bart's shoulder, an unspoken suggestion that his captain face him. "Well, I need to converse, and you are the only one available. Would you deny your King?"

Bart glanced out at the snow-covered fields. "No, Great King. Of course not."

"Excellent." The wind blew Cadamire's cloak around his legs as the king increased his pressure on Bart's shoulder.

Bart squirmed inwardly, unwilling to meet his king's brown eyes and continued walking.

"What can you tell me about the prize your brother brought me today? You called our barbarian visitor by a first name. You know of him?"

Bart caught his breath. "He resided in the mountains of Citheria, my King. His family raised horses. My mare is from there." *A discussion on bloodlines might save me.*

"I wondered at her breeding. She's a cut above most of the horses in Megara, only my brother owns something similar."

The King halted and grasped Bart's arm, forcing his captain to face him. "Now, I have a question which must be answered with some thought. The way I handle this case depends on it."

"My King."

Cadamire looked at him searchingly. "Your brother's barbarian. I have never seen one before. I have no expertise in this and I feel at a disadvantage. Is such a one capable of truthfulness? How long

67

will he last holding the Knife? No barbarian has ever asked for that questionable privilege. Does he know what he is in for?"

"As much as any man, Great King. Betren would not trick any man to speak on the Knife, no matter what the consequences to himself, the House of Bartran or Delmarath, or even to the kingdom. You can be sure that Lance is here because he chose to be. He knows as much about the Knife as any Danian brought in from any city in the land."

"So your brother isn't doing this just to dishonor you?"

"Of course not! Oh." Bart groaned. "I've been giving that impression, haven't I?"

Cadamire refrained from answering. He released Bart's arm and proceeded along the wall.

Bart paced beside him, head down, deliberating. *Any man under my command would gladly seek a way to dishonor me. It's common practice in Megara. My current dilemma delights most of them. But Betren? If Betren has a problem with someone, there's a face to face confrontation. If the problem's unresolved, his victim learns exactly what is wrong before he dies.*

"No," Bart said slowly. "Betren would neither stab me nor any man. That's not his style. The danger to our land is real enough. The key lies with Lance. How bad is he?"

"He could be better, if our so called compassionate healers had been obeying orders. However, at this point with your father in charge, I'm sure our barbarian is receiving the same excellent care I'd be given if I were in his position." The King smiled.

"You inquire of Lance's ability to speak the truth, my King?" Bart paused, trying to organize his thoughts. He stood still, his eyes on the horizon.

The King waited patiently.

"It's not that Lance is just as capable of lying or telling the truth as any Danian, he can sense when a man is lying. He has the sight, my King. Sometimes he can control the actions of an animal with his mind."

"And the mind of a man?"

Bart shook his head. "Unknown, my King."

68

Cadamire frowned. "But at the very least he can perceive what men's feelings are for him, whether they hate him, tolerate him, or like him without them saying so?"

"Yes." Bart grimaced. "He certainly can do that." The wind caught his green cloak.

"It's too cold to stand in one place. Let's continue our stroll." The King tugged his cloak tightly around him. "Tell me, does this — what did you call him?"

"Lance, my King. His name is Lance."

"Does this Lance have any concept that men must live under law, must obey it or die?"

"Do you mean could he live under our law? No, he couldn't. His people had a code of behavior, that I know. You have to be born Danian in order to embrace our rules and regulations. The law controls practically every facet of our lives."

"Then how can such a one speak on the Knife?"

Bart stared out over the snow-covered fields. *What a tricky question. If I admit how well I'm acquainted with Lance and his people, The King will suspect my House is involved in treason. If I say too little, I can avert Lance from speaking on the Knife. Tempting... No one need learn about the friendship of the House of Bartran with a family of barbarians, but then if I end this here and now, what disaster is Betren risking all to prevent?*

He turned to the King and saw that Cadamire watched him, expecting an answer. "Lance, his family, they were decent people, my King. They knew right from wrong, truth from lie. Loyalty to friends and family — the same qualities which go into a decent Danian, make a decent Citherian. Lance is no monster, my King. He looks different from us, that's all."

"And doesn't think like us."

"In many ways, no, but in many other ways, yes. There is no doubt in my mind that if Lance can focus on the Knife, if he doesn't try to protect any of us of the House of Bartran or himself, he might succeed." *And may all the Gods that exist help us when he does.*

"Thank you, Son of Bromwell." Cadamire studied him for a moment. "You know this man as a friend, strange as that may seem.

You speak truth at great cost to yourself. I appreciate your candor." The King frowned. "However, I have more questions, but not such heavy ones. When I checked on the barbarian, he kept repeating the word, Sylvia — a name I think, but I ponder whether it is a place or a person or a horse."

"A person. Lance's younger sister, my King. I surmise she is in Delmarath, or if not there, I know where to find her."

"You presume your current acting Defender holds her in custody?"

"I would assume so, my King. It's the only legal way for a barbarian to be in Delmarath." *Unless Sylvia winds Metrox around her little finger as she often did in Citheria.*

"Of course," Cadamire agreed. "Lance rambled on about Metrox. Partly in our language, but also in one I can't understand. Obviously, he must speak something besides Danian." The King leaned against the cold snowcapped wall overlooking Megara. "Metrox, that's Betren's second in command." He looked at Bart questionably.

"Lance must be delirious."

"I sense you are protecting this Metrox. No matter." Cadamire raised his hand to halt Bart's protest. "I desire those two here. Sylvia, because Lance's recovery will be faster if his sister is near. Metrox? No real reason, just a premonition he's involved in this matter. The Knife will prove it, one way or another. Are you ready for your orders?"

Bart concentrated on keeping his face expressionless as he saluted.

"Take a patrol. Use some of my guardsmen; I appreciate what you are doing with them. Let them experience some simple guard duty. Escort Metrox and Sylvia to Megara. Will you have trouble carrying out my orders?"

"How so, my King?"

"Will Sylvia and Metrox accompany you willingly?" The King strolled along the outer wall.

"My King, I have no idea what impression Lance gave you of Metrox." Bart hurried after him. "The man is completely loyal to

Betren and the House of Bartran, to Delmarath and to you. Not necessarily in that order. He will do as you command. Sylvia will wish to be with her brother. I don't foresee any problems." *Well, that isn't quite true. Metrox just being Metrox is a problem and Sylvia can match him any day.*

"In that case, set out tomorrow at dawn." Cadamire turned and faced Bart. "Dine at my side tonight. It won't stop tongues from wagging, but it will show everyone where I stand on this matter."

"My thanks, Great King."

"And Captain, are there men in Delmarath who would not consider this Lance some kind of animal?"

"The main purpose of the Delmarthian Guard is to keep peace in the marketplace. They know barbarians, even have a grudging respect for some of them."

The King nodded. "Bring me back some Delmarthians to guard this Lance. Our visitor needn't feel that he is some kind of freak while healing."

"Great King, you mean to give a barbarian a chance." Bart eyed the King in amazement.

"He's under my sword. I don't abuse men who find shelter there. And Captain, your brother also is under the protection of my sword. No one who risks his life to request that favor is considered guilty of anything until he has a chance to speak at the proper time."

Bart saluted the King and then wished he hadn't. *I'm acting like a fourteen-year-old recruit. Metrox's youngest son acts like this.*

The King grinned. "Captain, who can handle Delmarthians better then one who was raised in Delmarath? Now, assemble your guard and get yourselves to Delmarath come morning. Considering the inexperience of your men—"

"I'll start preparations immediately, my King." Bart finished the sentence.

The King and Bart exchanged salutes.

Bart turned and headed for the guardsmen's quarters.

Chapter 10

Trac's arms and legs ached. Unused muscles protested his every motion. For the first time in his life his bearskin cloak left him feeling clumsy. The prairie-man leaned on his ski poles and caught his breath. *At least I'm a better skier than I was seven days ago. I almost keep up with these Merkans.* He glared at Marcia's retreating back as she skied effortlessly out of sight.

He pushed forward and concentrated on gliding over the snow. "Doing fine," he muttered. "It's a matter of rhythm. Actually, this motion would make a great dance step. Slide, slide; add one or two hops — I'll introduce it at the next ceremony when I get home. If I get home."

The rays of the sun with the help of a mischievous breeze snatched snow off a branch and dumped its cold wet substance on Trac's head. It slid onto his face, frosting his checks, slipping into his eyes, and sticking to his beard. Blinded, he skidded to a halt as more snow followed obliterating the trail in front of him.

"Stupid trees." He wiped the frigid white moisture off his face and brushed it off his beard. Noticing that his bearskin cloak had not escaped the sudden downfall, he dusted the snow off his clothing, a maneuver that resulted in a sapling snatching his ski pole with its slender branches. He yanked the pole free and managed to maintain his balance as he pressed on through the soft snow.

"Trac! Hurry up, slowpoke; we're almost home." Marcia skied toward him, the brilliant sunlight streaming through the trees brought out the red in her long brown hair. The close-fitting woolen pants and jackets she and the other Merkans wore seemed appropriate for this new mode of transportation.

Too many trees; they confine my vision. Trac watched the Merkan girl skim over the snow. *Give me the prairies where I can see for miles following a clear trail of bent grass and golden-rod. I swear that every bush in this entire forest conspires with those huge moss-covered trees to frustrate me.* "Had a little problem with a tree," he complained as Marcia snowplowed to a stop in front of him.

The rosy-cheeked girl smiled. "You're in my country, Prairieman. How does it feel to be in a place where everything is strange?"

"I can survive better in this miserable forest than you and Peter did when you attempted to live in my country."

"Hello-o-o." Allen's deep voice floated through the air.

"We're coming," Marcia yelled, skiing in the direction of his voice.

Trac followed at a slower pace. *Never intended to enter Merkan. Strangers rarely receive a warm welcome in a new land and Merkans don't sound especially friendly. 'The only people who survived the great disaster.' Indeed. Sounds completely unpromising.*

"Do try to keep up," Allen said. "We must stay together." The Merkan retied his fur hood covering his short brown hair as he eyed the plainsman, a worried look on his lean face, red from the cold. 'We're almost to Trail's End. I want you close to me when we greet some of my people."

Peter loosened the knit scarf that partially covered his boyish face. "Do you expect trouble?"

Definitely. Trac noticed fear lurking in the boy's brown eyes. *For once, Peter and I agree on something.*

73

"No." Allen smiled reassuringly. "Just good to stick together until we get to Trail's End. A lone stranger could be picked off without thought. A group will cause our people to talk first, shoot later. In this case there's safety in numbers."

Liar. Trac felt like screaming. *If I introduced you, a stranger who doesn't speak our language, dressed in those tight fitting clothes and that ridiculous short hair cut and trimmed beard to Cole, headman of Kans for the first time, I'd be worried; someone might panic and—*

"Come on, we're wasting time." Allen continued down the trail. "Trail's End waits for us."

"Trail's End— even the name has an ominous sound," Trac muttered. As he waited for Marcia and Peter to resume their positions behind Allen, his keen ears caught the sound of strange voices. "Allen, wait! We're about to meet some people."

Before Allen could answer five armed men dressed in woolen plaid coats and coonskin hats skied toward them. They carried long knives on their belts and bows slung over their shoulders.

Trac reached for his knife, but his ski poles slowed his hand. His skis imprisoned his feet. *They're armed and I'm trapped. Steady.* He straightened up to face the strangers.

"What in thunderation is that?" The leader gawked at Trac. His men pushed their ski poles into the snow, freeing their hands to grab their bows and draw arrows from their quivers.

"Hold it, Chad," Allen said, positioning himself between the newcomers and Trac. "Tell your men to relax. This is a friend. Don't harm him."

"A friend? A friend who looks like that?" Chad's chunky face registered amazement.

Allen glared at Chad. "Believe me; my Aunt Sybil won't be happy if you try anything. You could lose your job over this."

"Well, if you say so." Chad rolled his eyes in disbelief, then glanced at his men. "Put your weapons away, boys," he ordered. "We don't want to make Councilor Aunt Sybil unhappy."

Trac admired the expertise of Chad's men as they slipped their arrows back into their quivers, shouldered their bows and retrieved their ski poles.

"The team those two borrowed last fall—" Chad pointed at Peter and Marcia, "wandered home two days ago, followed by a strange pony. When the kids didn't show up, we figured that they might of found trouble." He shook his head. "See they found plenty. Didn't expect to find you here hanging out with a mutant."

"Councilor Sybil commissioned me to check out the absence of the Saunder family," Allen said as he pivoted on his skis and slid backwards to Trac's side, so Trac now had full view of the new-comers. "Let me introduce you. Chad, this is Trac. He lives in the forbidden lands beyond the forest."

"Do I wave or something?" Chad asked. "Does he understand what that means?"

Allen grinned. "Why don't you just try saying hello? He'll understand you."

"If you say so." Chad looked skeptically at Trac. "Hello."

That 'hello' sounds unfriendly but it's better than an arrow in my chest. Trac placed both ski poles in his left hand and raised his right arm with his fingers spread apart in the formal greeting of a prairie-man.

"That's a prairie-man's way of saying hello," Peter explained.

Everyone started talking at once.

"No more questions until we get to Trail's End," Allen insisted. "We've been traveling seven days; let's not stand in the cold jabbering."

"That's right!" Chad yelled. "One side, boys."

Chad's men sidestepped off the trail giving Chad room to turn on his skis. He led them to a clearing where several low log buildings surrounded a two-story log house.

"Welcome to Trail's End," Peter said. "We made it, Trac. See, I told you it wouldn't take that long to get here." He stopped in front of the tallest building.

"Took a few days longer than you said." Trac unfastened leather straps on his skis. Since everyone leaned their skis against the log wall, he followed their example. One ski remained motion-less in the upright position, but the other slid along the wall knocking neighboring pairs into the snow as it toppled.

This mishap delighted the Merkans who broke into a roar of laughter. "Look at the stupid mutant," someone yelled. "A four-year-old can handle skis better than that."

Trac felt his face go hot as he bent to pick up the wayward ski. *Traitorous skis, I never want to be involved with another pair.* He felt Peter's hand on his arm and noted anger in the boy's brown eyes.

"Trac, don't mind those idiots," Peter said. "You just need more practice. Go on inside and get warm. I'll fix this."

"Yes, do come on in," Allen said, holding the door so Trac could enter. "We hang our coats on pegs. Hope you manage coats better than you do skis."

A few of Chad's men snickered.

Before Trac had a chance to locate which wall held the pegs, Chad unbuttoned his coat and took off his hat. His sandy hair touched a solid red scarf tied around his neck.

"Alan, your mutant is slower than a snail. Bet they don't have hooks wherever he comes from." Chad hung his outer clothing on a peg.

Trac took in his new surroundings as he shook the snow off his bearskin cloak. *This must be the main room like Lance's cabin in the Citherian Mountains. Furniture looks similar, but there's more of it because it's a bigger room serving many people. Wonder if they all sleep here. Lots of doors; could lead to bedrooms. I don't think that fireplace is used for cooking. No pots surrounding it. Lance's mother, Anya would have liked that. Funny looking lights. Wonder what they use for fuel? Hope those hooks are strong enough.*

"Come and warm yourself, everyone. I'll bring you a rib-filling meal fresh from the kitchen," Chad said.

"Chad, we've got trouble." Allen handed Marcia his jacket.

She gave him a nasty look. "What's wrong, can't you hang up your own jacket?"

Since Allen ignored her, she hung it up next to Peter's and slipped into an adjacent room.

"Well yeah, I see trouble standing right in front of me." Chad said. "Where did you find the mutant?"

"He's a plainsman and he's only a small part of the problem. I've got to summon the Council. Does the magic ball still work?"

"Council?" Trac repeated the word under his breath. *Is that what they call their king or headman? It can't be the same as in Kans when everyone in town is involved. Just a few buildings here. Not enough people to make a legal decision on anything.*

Chad lifted a ball about the size of a man's head off a shelf and laid it on the table. "Takes me a minute to set it up," he said as he carefully removed the cloth wrapping.

Trac rubbed his hands together and blew on them. *Feel cold. Wonder if anyone will mind if I warm myself by the fire.* He ambled over to the fireplace and held his hands near the heat, then turned to warm his back. *All the men wear their hair short just like Robert and his sons.* He tossed his long braids over his shoulders. *And they trim their beards. I've found Lance's people. Hope, we both live long enough to meet again.*

Everyone in the room seemed fascinated by the thing that interested Chad and Allen. Trac shrugged. *What's so important about that ball?* He casually joined the group by the table.

"Let me help." Allen extended his hand toward the ball.

"Don't touch it," Chad warned. "It's not to be trusted. My daughter Dotty was cleaning, thought she'd dust off the ball. Rubbed it the wrong way and disappeared with a flash."

A ball that makes people vanish? Magic? Trac stepped next to the table for a better look.

"Disappeared? Where did she go?" Allen stepped away from the table and clutched his hands together behind his back.

"Never saw her again. She went wherever she was day-dreaming about when she touched the confounded technological antique." Chad glanced at Trac. "How much does he understand?"

"Every word," Allen answered. "He speaks Merkan real good."

"What?" Chad exclaimed. "How's that possible?"

"Long story," Allen answered. "I don't even know it all and I refuse to say another word until I get in touch with the Council."

"Oh, wait one moment," Chad said as the ball emitted a blue glow. "Picking up some strange signal. Comes and goes. It must be

77

a disturbance in the weather." He slid the ball to a slightly different position on the table. The blue light disappeared. "There, now we're ready."

Trac caught his breath as the image of a room appeared inside the ball. It was similar to Chad's cabin, but a brown and black blanket covered the floor, and the chairs had red pillows. He didn't have time to take in any more details because a man's head replaced the vision of the room. *Feel like I could touch that short gray hair, wonder if those hazel eyes can see us?*

"Karl Sorrison here. What may I do for you?"

Magic. The man not only sees, he speaks too.

"Councilor Karl Sorrison, Trail's End calling," Chad said. "You better hop on the train and hustle on over here. Bring the others. Allen Stacy's here with a— a—" He looked at Trac blankly.

"A prairie-man." Trac struggled to keep his voice steady. He glanced away from the ball and noticed that the men Chad called 'his boys' had stepped back, fear in their faces.

"Prairie-man?" Chad repeated, "I thought Allen said plains-man."

"Prairie is my home. Plains further west and much flatter. I am a prairie-man." Chad's ignorance of what was beyond the forest gave Trac a little confidence.

"Chad, what's going on there?" Karl asked. "With whom are you conversing?"

"A Prairie-man— some sort of mutant. Oh, sorry sir; I was distracted. Allen Stacy says there's trouble."

"Put on Allen."

Chad stepped back. He motioned Allen to stand in front of the ball.

Allen cleared his throat. "Karl, I found a human who is not from Merkan. Found him on the prairie— ah, what we call the forbidden plains on the other side of the forest. Better summon the councilors. Our prairie-man is only the icing on the problem."

"You brought him with you? Oh... Only John and Sybil here; the others returned to their districts as soon as our Director's meeting concluded. We'll be there as soon as the engine can be stoked.

Fortunately, we had some unfinished business delaying us another day. Thanks for calling."

Chad waved his hand across the front of the ball and the man and the room disappeared.

The minute Chad put the ball away, everyone relaxed. The men swarmed around Allen and Trac.

"Where did you find this bit of cow dung," one of them shouted pointing at Trac.

"I know," another bellowed. "Allen Stacy captured the wild man who lives in the middle of the forest."

Every hair on Trac's skin stood up. He was in the wrong place, alone in a room full of five short hair strangers who were noisy, boisterous and much too curious. He forced himself to remain calm as they plied Allen with questions about Trac as if he was some brute animal that understood nothing. He was about to explode when he became aware of Marcia's voice rising in protest from the next room. She screamed.

Trac bolted through the door to see Marcia struggling with one of Chad's men.

The Merkan clutched her close to him as he tried to plant a kiss on her mouth. He was too busy trying to molest the girl to notice Trac until he felt the prairie-man's knife against his throat. He loosened his grip and Marcia sprang away.

"Trac," Allen shouted. "Let him go. Don't kill him, he's not worth it."

Trac slammed the man on the floor and sheathed his knife.

Allen yanked the Merkan to his feet. "Out!" he ordered shoving him into Chad who was first of the Merkans trying to crowd into the room. Allen drew his knife from his boot. "Get out of here," he repeated. "All of you. We'll wait for the councilors in here."

"Allen, come on," Chad pleaded. "Bert didn't mean any harm. Figured she was available. Oh, she's the Plains— ah, the Prairie-man's woman. Forgive and forget, you know it's lonely out here for unmarried men."

"Out," Allen said stepping toward Chad, holding his knife low ready to attack. "I mean it. Take your boys and leave my cousin alone."

"Cousin?" Chad sputtered. "You're related to her?"

"Yes, I'm related," Allen growled. "She's the daughter of my father's half-brother." He approached Chad threatening him with his knife. "Out. I won't say it again. Your behavior disgusts me."

Chad and the others backed into the safety of the other side of the door.

Allen slammed it. "I'm sorry, Trac. You just met some of the worst sort of Merkans. I can imagine what you're thinking. Are you all right, Marcia?"

"Yes." She nodded.

Trac put his arm around her and drew her close to him. The girl hid her face in his shoulder. She was shaking.

Good thing Allen has some kind of authority here. Trac stroked her hair. *These people certainly have no feeling for a stranger in their midst. They barely respect each other.* "Easy, lass," he said. "You're going to be fine. Come on now, sit here." He led her to one of the chairs. She looked up at him through her tears and tried to smile.

Trac touched his knife as the door opened, then relaxed as he recognized Peter, somewhat thinner in his brown wool shirt than the padded woolen jacket he wore while traveling.

"What happened?" Peter asked. "Things seem a little ugly out there." He glanced at Marcia, her face in her hands and Trac comforting her. "I'd say they were a little ugly in here too."

"I'm all right," Marcia whispered. "Honest."

Trac nodded and straightened up to meet Allen's questioning eyes. The prairie-man turned toward Peter. "Where have you been?" He asked more sharply than he intended.

"Out in the barn, checking the horses. They made it back in good health, even your pony." Peter ran his hand through his curly brown hair as he leaned against the door and looked at Allen. "You summoned the Council?"

Allen nodded. "They'll arrive shortly."

Peter blew on his fingers. "I'm in for it, I guess." He rubbed his hands together as he walked over to a metal drum and warmed them. "Marcia too. They won't like what we have to say."

"I know my aunt," Allen said. "We've been neighbors for a long time. Trust me on this one. It's better to tell Sybil the truth immediately rather than have her find it out from someone else."

"So this is where the heat comes from," Trac said, walking over to the metal drum. "Where's the fire?"

"Oh, that's right, your people don't use stoves." Peter opened the door and added a log.

Trac bent down and peered inside as the glowing coals embraced the fuel with tongues of flame. He stepped back and noticed that the drum was fastened to long pipes that reached the ceiling and then traveled through the wall. "Wonder if Lon, our blacksmith could build such a contraption. The lack of smoke in the room is amazing. Now what in the name of the Great God above all others is that groaning shriek outside?" As the noise increased, the sound changed to a dull repetitive rumble.

Trac glanced around the room. *What's wrong with these people? That monstrosity threatens the cabin and none of them pay any attention.* He spun toward the window, his hand on his knife as a monstrous smoke-bellowing dragon charged into sight emitting a series of piercing war cries.

Chapter 11

"Trac." Marcia laid her hand on his arm. "You've never seen a train before." The girl smiled at him. "It's a machine. Very common in ancient times."

Trac caught his breath. He stared at the steam train as he gained control of his emotions. "It's a wonder. Yes, I see now. It's metal. Your people must have great knowledge to create such a marvel. On the prairies our blacksmiths shoe horses and work on small items like kettles and hooks, swords and knives."

"We only have one," Peter said. "Sometimes, they let me help repair it. And it often takes a year or two to fix." He joined them at the window. "We use horses to pull the cars when the engine doesn't work."

"Cars?" Trac blinked hard.

"Those buggies, carriages." Peter sighed. "You don't know those words either."

"A type of wagon with a roof?" *Feel like a child not knowing simple words.*

"Yeah," Peter said, "sort of. They have more comfortable seats than wagons. Intended for important people, not produce."

A man climbed out of the monster's head, hurried to the first car and opened the door, bowing as three occupants hurried outside and strolled toward the house.

Trac stared. *Those men wearing dark loose-fitting trousers remind me of the man Lance and I found dead on the prairie near home. His jacket was leather, lined with wool — different material than his pants. These men wear matching jackets and pants. Those tall black hats perched on their heads look ridiculous. A strong wind will carry them over the mountains. And the woman? She's wearing the same type of clothes Sylvia and Anya wore in Citheria. Anya had a cape like that one. She wore it at the market. And there's the guardsmen, dressed in brown. Hats must determine whom they serve. They don't ride in the same vehicle as the great ones. Huh, they're armed with long wooden staffs. No swords? However, those crossbows slung on their hips look efficient.*

Allen laughed. "Chad's going to be upset. Our wonderful leaders each brought a full honor guard. Three rangers for one councilor — fifteen more mouths to feed, plus the train's crew."

"This council," Trac asked, "what is it exactly?"

"It takes the place of the King of Dana, or whoever is in charge of things on the prairie," Marcia explained.

Peter groaned. "We had a chance to gain sympathy from Councilor Sybil if she were alone, but those other two with her — John — that's the fat one, has the reputation of being the greatest executioner in the land. And Karl, he's the one with the silver hair; he's nice, but not too effective."

"Peter, you've been listening to common gossip," Allen hissed as he cracked open the door of the small room where he and the children had waited with Trac.

"Well, it's true." Peter scowled as he clenched his fist.

"Behave." Allen caught Peter's arm. "You don't want to make a bad impression. "

Trac struggled to peer around Allen's head into the main room.

"Welcome, Sirs; welcome, Madam. Welcome to Trail's End. You honor our outpost." Chad's voice had changed from its normal

83

forcefulness to a polite whine. "Come in, come in. Let me take your coats. Your rangers are welcome to make themselves at home in the guest lodge. You may post two outside the door if you please. We can have a meal ready for you shortly. "

"Didn't come to eat. Drop that sirs, and madam stuff." Sybil slipped out of her black cape revealing a cream tunic and black pants. She removed her tall black hat and handed the garments to Chad. "We're merely elected public servants. Rangers, we need two men outside this door. The rest of you may proceed to the guesthouse. Where's— Oh, there you are, Allen," she exclaimed as the vendor stepped into the main room.

Trac felt his jaw drop and struggled to close it. The women's long gray braids tightly circled her head. Wrinkles crossed her forehead. Lines formed around her mouth. *Rarely see a woman as old as she must be. Prairie-woman seldom reach the age to acquire that color hair. Most die young from overwork or childbirth.*

"Your mother is sick with worry, Allen. You have no business being away when the snow comes," Sybil said.

"Sorry, Aunt Sybil," Allen said. "Winter came early this year."

"It was fortunate that your arrival coincided with the Director's Meeting at Thunder Hills. Otherwise, John and Karl would need a few days to travel to Trail's End from their districts and we'd have to recall everyone. Three is the proper number for a committee of inquiry. Any news of Paul Saunder?"

"Dead," Allen answered quietly. "Died near a place called Kans. Come on in, I want you to meet someone."

Trac and the children retreated from the doorway.

Sybil stepped inside and gasped, placing her hand over her heart. "Oh, my Lord! Who is this?"

The prairie-man returned her fixed gaze as Sybil beheld his long brown braids, his sheep skin vest, brown woolen pants and knee high boots. *No woman stares at a man unless they're united in marriage.*

"This creature must be half woman, half man," Sybil murmured. "It has a beard, but wears its hair in long braids just like a girl. I can't believe my eyes."

84

"Aunt Sybil, a show of manners would be appropriate," Allen said. "This is a man, not a monster. This is Trac who lives on the other side of the forest. It seems he rescued Peter and Marcia who lost their way on the forbidden plain and brought them safely home. And yes, men on the prairie braid their hair."

"Well, well," John waddled into the room. "A mutant. I never saw one. Now we can prove they exist. Sybil, we must transport him to New Hope and dissect him. Then put his bones on display in the museum."

Allen drew his knife while he stepped to Trac's side.

"What's going on here?" The oldest member of the council closed the door behind him. "Allen, put that knife away. John, we're not going to dissect anyone." Karl faced Trac. "Forgive my colleagues. It's just that we've never met anyone like you." He cringed. "Oh my! Allen does he understand anything I'm saying?"

"I understand your surprise," Trac said using the language he had learned from Lance. "I don't expect much from people who believe they are the only ones who live on this earth."

Sybil gasped. John and Karl stared at each other with furrowed brows.

Allen grinned. "Oh, didn't I mention that Trac speaks our language? He may not have caught every word, but I think by his response, he understands you just fine. I'm sure he's positive he has stumbled into some barbaric land where the inhabitants are all ignorant mutants."

"Mutant!" John repeated. "Allen, are you saying this un-cultured monster dares to judge us civilized people?" He stormed toward Trac, his broad jaw twitching.

Trac fingered the hilt of his knife.

Allen touched Trac's shoulder. "Let a Merkan handle Merkans."

Trac nodded, and folded his arms.

Allen raised his knife. "Back off, Councilor John. You're no match for me, a champion who has won many prizes in competition at the games."

"John!" Karl maneuvered between the two antagonists. "Take a seat. Now! Allen, sheath that knife."

"Allen," Sybil said. "It's inconceivable that you would call this man a friend."

"Aunt Sybil, I can't imagine anyone I'd rather have with me when traveling though the forest."

"Trac's our friend too," Marcia said. "He saved our lives, shared his food with us and taught us many things about the prairie."

"You better not hurt him." Peter positioned himself in front of Trac.

"No one is going to hurt anyone," Karl said. "Calm down, though I must say that I approve of a young man who sticks up for a friend. John, Sybil, your silence would be most welcomed. Allen, would you introduce us properly?"

"Trac, you have the questionable pleasure of meeting three of our notable officials in Merkan. Each one governs a certain part of our country. May I present Councilwoman Sybil, of Thunder Hills, Councilman John from Hio, and Councilman Karl of the state of New Hope and director of the 12 districts that make up Merkan? New Hope probably holds the same position as Megara where the Danian high king resides. You can't call Karl a king but he's a —"

"Headman?" Trac questioned.

"Ah— close enough."

Trac raised his right hand in greeting. "I'm Trac, a prairie-man from the village of Kans."

"Does he shake hands?" Karl asked.

"No," said Peter. "Hold up your right hand in answer."

"Welcome," Karl raised his ink-stained hand.

"This goes against centuries of belief!" John gasped.

"I know," Allen said soberly. "That's what I thought until I stumbled on the market near Chaleen. And then I wasn't sure the men were human until I met Trac. He claims that his people are numerous and live on the great prairies north of here."

Sybil's eyes narrowed. "Why did you decide to keep an entire race a secret?"

"Who'd believe me? Everyone knows that we are the chosen, the only true humans to survive the great disaster. And as long as Trac's people stayed on the forbidden plains and we stayed on our side of the forest, what difference did it make? Thanks to Marcia and Peter, we have a problem. Aunt Sybil, why don't you sit down? You look a little pale." Allen pulled a chair from under the table and offered it to her.

Chad hustled into the room balancing a stack of ceramic plates, followed by three of his boys bearing pewter goblets filled with wine on a tray, a plate of freshly sliced bread, and piles of cheese. "Councilor Sybil, I understand you didn't come here to eat, but that was before you met our problem. Somehow, I foresee you visiting a day or two."

One of his men placed the food on the round table near the stove and arranged the plates and goblets. Two other men positioned four more chairs from the main room in front of each setting.

"This should suffice until supper." Chad bowed and backed out with his men, before anyone could protest. "Oh," He peered back in at the councilors. "I asked the women to prepare your rooms. Just in case." He closed the door quickly covering his retreat.

"What are you? Where and what is Kans? And why have you invaded our land?" Karl demanded, pointing his finger at Trac.

"You better answer," Marcia said. "No one's acting rationally. Normally, we sit down and discuss things around a table."

Trac nodded. "I came because I wanted to see what kind of people would sell my people the black magic that turns city walls into rubble." *So far I'm not impressed.*

"You speak our language!" John exclaimed, jumping out of his chair. "Unbelievable!" He paced around the room. "How did you ever learn it? From whom?"

"Take a seat, John," Karl ordered. "We would enjoy your patience. Eventually, we'll discover the answers to your questions, but let's take one step at a time, please. What black magic are we inquiring about?"

87

"Aunt Sybil," Allen broke in. "Don't you think you should ask the rest of us to sit at the table? I know from experience that our prairie-man considers you all very— ah— unfriendly."

"I second that motion." Karl laid his slender hand on John's bulky shoulder. "Let's both sit down, John. Allen's right. We are behaving badly." He waited until John complied. Karl sank into a chair and drew a deep breath. "Now, that we have obtained some order, we need to define the problem before eating. I'll ask the question: What is this black magic?"

"Gunpowder." Allen leaned over the back of an empty chair. "It seems that a group of our young people took it upon themselves to make it, and then sell it to mutants."

"What?" John burst out. "That's against the law. You must be mistaken."

"John! Silence!" Karl roared. "Give this prairie-man a chance to explain. Go ahead, Trac."

"At the time of last full moon, these two," Trac indicated Marcia and Peter, "and others drove a wagon to our village with two kegs of powder. They claim this powder can take down the walls of Delmarath, a border city of Dana."

"Delmarath? Dana? Walled cities?" John snatched a goblet from the table and gulped some wine. "How can this be? We're the only ones to survive the great disaster."

Karl pushed back his chair, rose to his feet, a look of horror crossed his face. "All right, Peter, would you explain what in heaven's name possessed you to make gunpowder and sell it to mutants?" He reached for Peter's arm.

"I didn't do it," Peter wailed, dodging behind Trac. "Mike did it and Tom."

Trac shifted his weight so that he blocked Karl from grabbing Peter. The Merkan and the prairie-man sized each other up.

"Karl, stop it!" Sybil snapped. "Sit down. This is my district. These are my people. It is my right to do the questioning. And we can wait until we all have something to eat."

Trac eyed the food. *Seems to be enough for everyone, but no one has the courtesy to invite us. Are they going to let us stand here and watch?*

Marcia touched his hand. "You'll have to excuse them," she whispered. "They'll feed us. You'll see. They brought dishes and chairs for all of us."

"Councilor." Karl nodded abruptly and sank into his chair. "Be my guest."

"Thank you." Just two words, but the sound of Sybil's voice would have turned water to ice. "We're giving this prairie-man a terrible welcome. We need proper introductions before we dine."

Trac stroked his beard as he raised his eyebrows. Since the councilors arrived, everyone spoke too fast for him to understand every word. It had all started with that train...

"Slow down, Aunt Sybil," Allen said. "Trac has an amazing grasp on our language, but he doesn't speak it like a native."

"Prairie-man, it is our custom to learn the names of the people who eat with us," Sybil explained slowly, "your companions are unknown to my friends." She smiled at the youngsters. "Let me refresh my memory. Marcia, I recall, and Peter— last names, please."

"Peter Thomson and Marcia Saunder," they answered.

"Ah— was Paul your father? You mentioned Mike and Tom. You're related to Mike, aren't you— his sister?" Sybil indicated Marcia.

"A distant cousin. He lived with us after his folks died in a fire," Marcia explained.

"And Tom's your brother, isn't he, Peter?"

"Yes, Councilor."

"And both of your families homestead land near Trail's End?" Peter and Marcia nodded.

Sybil rose from her seat and approached Trac, her hand extended. "I'm sorry, Trac. I suddenly realized you are our first ambassador from a different part of the world. I'm afraid our manners have been disgraceful. We treated you improperly. You raise your right hand in greeting. In Merkan, we shake hands so I offer you my hand in welcome."

Trac gazed at her extended hand. *Ambassador? There's one more word I don't understand.* He slowly grasped Sybil's hand.

89

"Thank you," Sybil said. "Come; join us at the table— all of you. We'll feel better after we eat." She glanced at the other councilors. "We will not speak of any of this, until we finish the meal."

"Wait, one minute," John said. "Explain the meaning of the word 'ambassador'. Some foolishness you invented, Sybil?"

Glad I don't have to ask that question, Trac thought.

"Oh, I know the word." Karl smiled at John. "It's found in that ancient book I'm working on. It means someone who is not one of us, someone from a distant country who represents his government. Such a man's life is sacred in the land he visits. Do I need to translate the word 'sacred', John? It means our Lord and Savior protects the life of an ambassador, so the consequences are death if you try to harm Trac."

'Ambassador.' Sound's important. Sent to visit another land? Well, yes, I suppose.... The Order of Storytellers sent me. Trac touched his medallion. *Thank you, Reig, for this little metal.*

"Ah, but is he an ambassador? Let's find out." John leaned back on his chair which groaned under his weight. He smiled a toothy grin at Trac. "So, Prairie-man, did some high official commission you to find us?"

Trac stroked his beard and squinted. "Commission?"

"Let me rephrase my question," John snapped. "Did someone important order you to seek us out?"

Trac lifted the "S" shaped medallion that he wore around his neck. "This represents the Order of the Storytellers, some of the most powerful people on the prairies. I was sent by their leader, Reig, a most respected member of their organization."

"That should suffice, John," Karl said. "Trac is an ambassador sent to us from the forbidden plains. As head of this council, I demand your silence on this matter."

"Karl, as Director of our 12 Districts, would you ask the blessing before we eat?" Sybil smiled as she made this request.

"Gladly." Karl bowed his head and the others followed suit. "Our Father in heaven, bless this food and all of us seated around this table, amen."

Trac raised his eyebrows. *Don't they know that the Great God above all others created people in his own image? The great one doesn't require a bow. We raise our hands to the heavens in supplication when we address him.*

"Now," Karl said. "Let's eat. Please pass the bread."

Trac watched the Merkans lift two slices of bread off the main dish, and set them side by side on their individual plates. The cheese and meat had also been cut in thin pieces which were then stuffed between the two slices of bread. *Glad they use no utensils for this meal; when spending the winter with Robert and Anya, they expected me to balance food on something called a fork.*

They ate in the customary silence found everywhere on the civilized prairies, which gave Trac opportunity to collect his thoughts: *Karl reminds me of Lance when he was a boy, can't quite put a finger on the similarity, but I have a feeling I'm right.*

John's full of bluster and dangerous. Met many like him, men who gain position by conniving and betraying friends and allies, grabbing power wherever they can.

Sybil's age fascinates me. It's more than that. Although her hands are smooth, indicating that she belongs to a privileged class, this woman is strong. Her very walk; in fact her every move speaks of power and confidence that a man would have to work very hard to match.

He chewed his bread. *The only Merkan women I know are Sylvia and Anya. No, Anya was different, or was she? She could hold her own when it mattered. And Sylvia never backed down to her three brothers or to the sons of Bromwell. She might as well have been a boy. Marcia isn't afraid to say what she thinks about anything either. Women enjoy a different position here than in my world.*

The meal soon ended.

"We should have stayed in Kans," Peter muttered. "Now, we're in for it. They'll settle down to business and decide the best way to execute us."

Chapter 12

Sybil rose to her feet to resume the Merkan's relentless series of questions as soon as the table had been cleared of the remains of their lunch. "Trac is an ambassador from the prairies bringing us disturbing information and many inquiries. His person is protected by sacred law." She smiled at the Prairie-man.

Trac relaxed a little. *So, being named an ambassador is a good thing. That position should allow me to live until they figure things out. Hope it takes them a long time.*

"I shouldn't have to mention how serious this is," Sybil continued. "Not only are we faced with the fact that an unforgivable sin, possibly murder or treason has been committed, but we are overwhelmed by the fact that other races survived the great disaster besides ourselves. It is embedded in us since childhood that we are chosen by the Lord, the only ones left on earth." She paused taking a breath. "It seems that our perceptions are false. We must also determine the guilt or innocence of these young people. This investigation will shed light on this momentous situation."

Peter gulped. "We didn't—"

"Silence, Peter." Sybil sounded annoyed at the interruption. "You will have your turn to explain at the appropriate time." She looked directly at Karl. "Now, repeat your original question, Karl. I think we're ready for it."

John lumbered to his feet. "Wait! I have a question. We should start—"

Karl rose from his chair. "John! As Director of the 12 Districts, I order you to be quiet. Take a seat."

"What question, John?" Sybil asked. "Does it concern the gunpowder?"

Karl glared at John and Sybil as he resumed his seat.

"Hear me out, Karl," John leaned on the back of his chair, his brown eyes focused on Trac. "I'm unsure how much this pertains to the stolen gunpowder, but we certainly need to consider what I say. This man, Trac speaks our tongue amazingly well. That means someone from Merkan spent many years among these—these mutants who, it seems are not beasts but men."

Karl sighed. "Get to the point, John, if you have one. I'm not following you."

"I am." Sybil folded her hands on the table. "John suspects someone left our country and succeeded in living among foreigners, perhaps even selling our secrets."

"Foreigners?" Karl looked thoughtful. "No one has used that word since before the great destruction. It means other people living in some remote place. Since we know, or knew that there are no other people in the world, the word is one of those forgotten ones unless read about in a book. The strange thing about this is that I just finished copying a book about how the ancient world was organized."

"Yes." Sybil nodded. "That's where I found the word. Remember, I'm editing your work, but all that happened centuries ago."

"Forget that blasted book," John snapped. He pulled his chair out and lowered his bulk on it. "Let's get back to here and now. Did any of our people escape justice by fleeing to other lands via the

93

forest? We are talking treason; that's a mortal sin." John pounded the table as he emphasized his words. "This prairie-man knows, I'm certain of that. We—"

"Trac," Sybil cut John's speech short. "Where, and how, and more important, who taught you our language. Do you understand the question?"

Trac stroked his beard. "Hmm... No one leaves their own country unless their life is threatened, usually because of some crime. It is true on the prairie; it is true in Dana; I see it is true here. I learned your language from Lance, son of Robert, who lived in the mountains of Citheria. Lance had no knowledge of Merkan; he considered himself a Citherian. He lived with me for five years."

"Son of Robert—of where? Citheria? That word means nothing, but Robert?" Sybil tapped her fingers on the table. "The name, Robert, has a familiar ring."

"Wait a minute." Karl settled back in his chair. "Robert, thief and traitor. He disappeared fifteen or twenty years ago with our books."

"See! A mortal sin!" John's flabby face nodded like nags in a Delmarthian stall at the market.

Trac frowned. "Robert of Citheria, a thief! That's hard to believe. The Robert I knew was an honest horse trader, never tried to disguise the age or condition of an animal he sold. Couldn't be the same man."

"Maybe," Karl said. "Are you willing to elaborate about this man you call Robert?"

"Elaborate?" Trac frowned. "Tell?" He looked directly at Sybil. "Does he want me to tell what I know about Robert?"

Sybil nodded. "Yes, unless there is some reason you feel you need to protect him."

"There's no reason to protect the dead. Robert stood in judgment before the great god over all gods, years ago."

"He believes in God," John burst out.

"John, I'll enjoy your silence unless you have something to add to the subject on hand, mainly this mysterious Robert." Karl glowered at the heavy set man. "Do you understand?"

94

"You are Director of the 12 Districts, Karl. I understand perfectly. You're pulling rank." John tightened his lips and leaned back in his chair, and folded his thick spongy hands on his stomach.

"How well did you know this Robert?" Karl asked.

"Karl!" Sybil exclaimed. "I'm doing the questioning."

"Oh, sorry, Sybil." Karl grimaced. "I didn't mean to step on your toes. I usually run this type of proceeding."

"In New Hope, Karl, not in Thunderhills." Sybil's lips twisted into a slight smile. "Apology accepted. Answer the question, Trac."

Trac took a deep breath. "As a trader— no, you use the word 'vendor' to describe what I do. I first met Robert in the Delmarthian Marketplace. If I remember it right, he had brightly woven cloth and two or three horses to trade. Two of his sons accompanied him. Hope, you understand. This was a business relationship which lasted a long time. We were never friends— didn't even come close until he gave me shelter the year of the great snow and shared what little his family had with me."

"So you knew him for many years," Sybil said.

"As a vendor," Trac said, "Robert seemed an honorable man. Several times I traded at his place in the mountains to fill an order for a good horse. Robert raised some beauties."

"That's one thing these two Roberts have in common," Sybil said. "Robert and his wife Anya were neighbors of mine. When our Robert left, he took his herd with him."

"The horses were his to take," Karl said, "and the Robert Trac knows raised excellent horses. What kind of lodging did Robert live in?"

At least I haven't been dealing all these years with a horse thief, Trac thought. *I'd have a hard time explaining that to anyone on the prairie.* "I'm sorry, what was the question?"

"I'll slow down a little," Karl said. "What kind of house did Robert have?"

"Very much like this."

"Cabin made of logs?"

Trac nodded. "Our Roberts might be the same. What crime did yours commit?"

95

"A hideous sin mandating the death penalty. Fifteen years ago or so, Robert Robsen who lived in the Thunderhills district, broke into the cave at New Hope where we housed our books." Karl raised his eyebrows. "Oh. Do your people use books?"

Trac shook his head.

"Then how do I make you understand?" Karl pushed his chair back and walked to the window.

Silence reigned in the room as everyone waited for Karl to speak. He turned and faced Trac. "You know about the great disaster?"

"My people have stories of horrors of long ago."

Karl cleared his throat. "All right, I'll start at the beginning. Years before the actual destruction, there were many signs that this terror would come upon us. My people, who rested in the arms of our Lord, understood the signs and made ready for the coming of the end. They prepared the caverns so we could live, stored provisions to last years. And one of their greatest fears was that all the knowledge of their world would be destroyed.

"Some of our wisest men prepared a room underground fixing it so the books would last forever, and another room where we could read them. After the disaster, our books became our most precious treasure. We sought their knowledge to solve troublesome problems.

"Over the centuries, the books stayed the same, but our lives changed. We no longer had access to the things the ancient ones took for granted. As time passed, thousands of words lost their meaning. The very letters became unknown marks on the page, especially in the technical books Robert cherished. We consider those books our last link with the old times. It is our source of pride, that we were chosen by our Lord to preserve the knowledge of the past. The books are considered to be the saviors that kept us alive."

Karl's intense greenish-blue eyes seemed to look straight through Trac. "Did your Robert own books? Do you have any idea what I am talking about?"

Trac nodded. "The treasures of the House of Robert. They told of unbelievable wonders. Robert and his sons read them to us. Yes, they called them books." *Reig has the same problem with his tales of when the men lived like gods. Some he no longer tells, because no one understands them.*

"The treasures of the House of Robert," Sybil repeated as her wrinkled lines in her face softened. "It's a wonderful way of saying it. I remember Robert now, a strange man. His head and heart were always in our sacred books. He soaked up knowledge as other men soak up food and wine. Anya often complained that he neglected his family because he spent so much time in the cave at New Hope."

Karl walked back to his seat and sighed heavily. "A group of us reached the conclusion that the books now were useless. People came to read, claiming that eventually the Lord would open their eyes and we could live life as our ancestors did. They wasted hours peering at pages, praying over them, waiting for a sacred revelation while their gardens turned to weeds, their cattle strayed or sickened, their families lived in want. Others spent their time trying to build something they saw in a picture unable to fathom how it worked.

"It was the year before I was elected to the council. Our leaders had voted to destroy books with technical material. Only the technical books. No others. At the time, I approved. The books had flowered into something evil.

"Robert gathered men that opposed the destruction of any knowledge, no matter how useless. These men rode into the council cave and wrecked our meeting place as a protest while Robert broke into the room where the books were kept. In the process he broke the sacred wall that protected our knowledge of the ancients.

"We caught some of the agitators and punished them, but Robert escaped with his family and our books."

Trac stroked his beard. "If Robert saved you the trouble of removing books you planned to destroy, why should his act bother you? Seems like he did you a favor."

"The equipment Robert destroyed couldn't be repaired," John said sadly. "All the words are fading. The pages have become so brittle they turn to dust in our hands. We loose knowledge even as we sit here. Most of those books are unreadable now. I would have enjoyed Robert's execution."

"I thought students at the School at the Great Cave were copying those books by hand," Marcia said.

"They are," John said. "But there were so many books. Only a few will be preserved." He shook his head. "Is this how precious knowledge is lost? Destroyed by a criminal gone mad?"

Trac didn't understand everything that was being said, but his thoughts focused on the winter he spent at the cabin in Citheria. *The older sons of Robert didn't particularly think ancient things were wonderful. Only Val spent time reading them. I grew sick of listening to the eldest son of Robert read about ancient weapons that could throw balls of death from the skies. Senseless nonsense.*

Robert, on the other hand, spent every moment of his free time buried in his library. When he read from books that were not about weapons, it was like listening to the old tales Reig told; the ancient ones had a good imagination.

"Those books should have been destroyed before our ancestors ventured out of the caves," Karl muttered. "Tell me, Plainsman, I mean Prairie-man. You said Robert was dead. What about his family?"

Trac shook his head. "All the males except Lance died on the wall."

"Danians?" Allen asked. Marcia and Peter gazed at him.

Trac nodded.

"Died on the wall?" Karl repeated. "You crucified them?"

Trac looked at him blankly.

"I'll answer that." Allen rose to his feet, surveyed his audience, his brown eyes serious. "Prairie-men obviously don't crucify anyone. Danians, however, do something similar. They string up a criminal to irons attached to their city walls to hang until death rescues him from agonizing pain." He paused and shook his head. "You folks don't understand what a vast world we inhabit."

98

Sybil and Karl glanced at each other, consternation in their faces.

John stared at the table. "Unbelievable."

"Let's see if we can get one little fact straight." Allen raised his voice. "There is no way to compare Danians with prairie-men. It would come close to looking for similarities' between night and day."

"You folks are straying from the current subject." John said with a slight sneer. "What of the books?"

Trac stroked his beard. "I have no idea. They looked like they were falling apart when I saw them."

"They wouldn't last too long," Sybil said.

Trac gazed at the council in wonder. *The death sentence for stealing an object as fragile and useless as a book? It surely isn't the same thing as stealing a horse. A man's life depends on his horse.* He continued stroking his beard. *Of course, if a storyteller should meet a violent death in a prairie village, the people who lived there would be severely punished. It takes years of training to be able to tell the old tales without changing one word.* He stifled a yawn. *I'm sick of hearing about books; will these people ever get around to talking about the black magic?*

Chapter 13

"John, are you satisfied with the answers to your questions?" Sybil asked. "If so, let's concentrate on the gunpowder."

"It was Tom's fault," Peter interjected. "Tom had a passion for learning about the old days. He stole books from the school in the Great Cave so he could read them."

"Slow down, Peter," Karl said. "Stick to the gunpowder."

Peter nodded and swallowed. "Tom found one book on gunpowder, a much more detailed book than the one Robert stole. Tom could write fast and clearly, so when he finished the required assignment, he copied the information out of the forbidden book."

"I can understand doing that. I did some of that myself when I was young. But selling our secrets to mut—" John glanced at Trac and changed the word to prairie-men. "That's treason, boy."

"I didn't do it," Peter protested. "Honest, I had nothing to do with selling anything. It was Tom's idea to try to make gunpowder from the information he'd stolen from the cave. He forced me to help. Tom insisted that we explore them for the right ingredients.

Marcia had no idea what we were doing. Tom told her absolutely nothing."

"And you manufactured gunpowder," Karl said with a deep sigh and a slight shake of his head.

Peter nodded. "Tom made me do it. He threatened me; said he would lock me in the spring house and leave me there to die if I refused."

"How fortunate for you that Tom is no longer around to defend himself," John muttered. "I suppose he forced you to go with him though the deadly Greenwood into the forbidden lands beyond."

"We wanted to go," Marcia said. "Children who live around here aren't afraid of Greenwood. We played hide and seek near the edge of the forest. My father hunted there for meat and furs. When he didn't return from his last excursion, we decided to find him. His trail led to the prairie where it disappeared into grass and flowers that towered over our heads."

"Tom said we should do a little exploring and somehow we ended up in the Chaleen Market," Peter said. "The first time we were there, a ranger gave me a yellow slip of paper."

"Ranger? Do you mean guardsman?" Trac interrupted.

"They were in some sort of uniform, armed, doing same job as our rangers." Peter scowled. "What difference does the word make?"

"When talking about Danians, the correct word is guardsman," Trac stated. "Use it."

"Anyway, the guardsman insisted that I try reading it. I was about to shove it back to him when I realized it was written in Merkan. I read it, understood it was a sentence or two from one of our books, but it didn't make any sense. Something about a glass slipper and a prince or a king."

"Glass slipper?" The council around the table looked mystified.

Trac slid his chair back, allowing his legs room to stretch. *Glass slipper. Where have I heard that before?*

"I don't know what book it came from, but I read the words easily. I didn't think the ranger— I mean, guardsman understood, but obviously, he was impressed. Anyhow, they escorted us into a

101

small room on the edge of the market and a rich Danian greeted us. He knew about gunpowder. The real shocker came when he produced a copy of the Book of Weapons. He demanded Tom read some of it to him, but none of us knew enough Danian speech to enable him to understand the material."

"The Book of Weapons!" Karl exclaimed. "How could any ah—foreigner get his hands on one of our books?"

"From the House of Robert," Trac said.

"Are you naming Robert Robson a traitor?" Karl demanded.

Trac shrugged. "I only know that Robert shared the knowledge of those books with us when we were stranded at his cabin during the long winter."

"We're getting off the subject," Sybil said. "Peter, what happened next?"

"Somehow, this rich Danian using sign language along with a limited knowledge of our language, made some kind of a deal with Tom. It took forever. All I wanted to do was get away from there. Tom agreed to make that rich man enough powder to blow up a troublesome stone wall. We had no idea he meant the wall of a city.

"So we went home, made the powder in our spare time and experimented with the finished product. We didn't want to sell something that didn't work. That would be immoral."

"Experimented with the finished product?" Sybil leaned forward, her blue eyes focused on Peter. "Is that where my cousin, Charles got those burns. He never really recovered; he's dead now. And Kevin lost his hand from experimenting with the powder?"

Peter's face paled, his body stiffened as he nodded gravely. "Yes, Councilor. We were more careful after that. First, we ignited small amounts and then figured out how to use a lot at one time safely."

"You said Tom used threats to make you break the law. Did he also threaten Charles and Kevin?" Sybil questioned.

Peter gulped. "I don't know. They were Tom's friends, not mine."

"You didn't say anything about the powder being responsible for Charles's death," Marcia snapped. "You told me Kevin had an accident with an ax."

"Tom told me to keep my mouth shut," Peter muttered as he studied the table.

"Go on, Peter. Tell us the rest of it," Sybil said.

"Tom and I took a trip to Chaleen with a sample of our work to impress the Danians. They introduced us to a small man who guided us to Kans where we proved gunpowder could destroy a large rock. The prairie-men were impressed. We spent the next year making enough powder to demolish a wall.

"Tom agreed we would winter with the prairie-men and teach them how to use gunpowder. If the prairie-men liked the idea, we would even help them take down the walls of someplace called Delmarath."

"Delmarath?" Sybil asked as everyone looked at Trac.

"A Danian border city," Trac said. "The Delmarthian Market-place is known as a good place to trade."

"City?" Sybil folded her hands and shook her head venomously. "Cities are a thing of the past."

Trac grunted. "I wouldn't say that to a Danian if I were you. They live in cities."

"Easy Sybil," Karl said. "I find this just as perplexing as you do, but let's take one thing at a time. Stay with the powder."

Sybil nodded and drew a deep breath. "You're right Karl." She stared across the table at Trac. "And what was the price of this powder?"

Trac unfastened a bag from his belt. "This bag of bloodstones." He handed her the bag.

"Garnets?" Sybil held a stone up to the light. "Garnets, the price of a war? These stones are not all that valuable. What did you call them, Prairie-man? Bloodstones? Well, it's a good name for them."

"Tom thought they were rubies," Marcia said. "He read about them in a book."

Sybil seemed to look far off into the distance, somewhere through the cabin wall. "If anyone has a ruby, it is something that survived the great horror."

"Exactly why those books should have been destroyed centuries ago," Karl growled. He glanced at Peter. "Did I hear you say you planned to live with these people?"

"It was after the harvest that we went to Kans," Peter explained. "The Prairie-men didn't want to use our merchandise until the next spring."

"But you didn't spend the winter in Kans," John stated flatly.

"No," Marcia said. "Those people live in mud huts. Besides, we didn't know the language. Can you imagine spending all that time without being able to talk to anyone?"

"How did Mike and Tom die?" John asked.

"Danians! We were supposed to meet them and get paid," Peter said. "Well, they brought the bloodstones, and then they killed Tom and Mike and wounded me."

"I don't understand," John said. "You delivered the powder for these Danians and they turned on you. Why?"

"I don't know." Marcia shrugged. "It didn't make any sense."

"You broke a contract," Trac explained quietly. "It's death to break a contract with a Danian."

"What?" Marcia stared at Trac.

"Didn't you promise the men of Chaleen you would stay the winter?"

"Well, Tom promised somebody, but—"

"They considered that a contract, a promise you did not keep. It's a saying on the prairie, 'Never make a Danian a promise you're not going to keep; the end result? You'll be buried deep.'"

"We had no idea, Marcia," Peter said. "None of us wanted to stay in that wretched little village."

Trac crossed his arms and rolled his eyes toward the cabin rafters. "That wretched little village happens to be my home. And as far as I can see, a sod house is warmer than anything you've built."

104

"I'm sorry," Peter said. "I have a knack for saying stupid things."

"That powder — you must show us where you are making it." John did not hide his eagerness. "We can put it in the common stockpile — we're almost out."

"Now, I wonder." Sybil eyes narrowed. "Would that powder ever find its way to New Hope? Or would something happen to it and then it would show up in Hio?"

"Sybil, my dear, how could such evil utterances fall from your tongue?" John's lips curled into a fake smile. "All ancient things like gunpowder are kept in the Caves of New Hope. I often conduct Sunday morning services in honor of the Lord. Do you think I, of all people would break the law?"

"Only if you could get away with it," Sybil answered.

John laughed, his chunky face reddening with the effort. When he caught his breath, he said, "Marcia and Peter must show us that cave. If all the ingredients are there, we'll have an unlimited source of gunpowder. Think about it. No one would ever dare to attack us. We could even do a little conquering on our own."

Trac clenched his fist. He glared at John, then glanced at Karl who rose to his feet, a shocked look on his face.

"Just kidding, Karl," John added quickly.

Sybil frowned. "Easy, Trac. John's talking foolishness." She sighed. "Enough of your humor, John. This is serious. Peter, did this rich Danian have a name?"

"Yeah, it was strange sounding. Let me think. Conray. No, that's not right. Cooner — "

"Conder," Marcia said. "I'll never forget that name."

"Yeah, A rich Danian," Peter said. "You're right, Marcia. His name was Conder."

Trac drew a sharp breath. *May the Great God above all other gods be merciful, don't let this be true.* He grasped Peter's arm. "Are you certain?"

Peter winced. "What's wrong, Trac? Did I say something wrong?"

"No." Trac released the boy's arm. "You don't understand the enormity of that name. Are you sure, beyond a shadow of a doubt? Would you stake you life that the man you just named is Conder?"

"Who is this Conder?" Karl demanded, as he returned to his seat.

Trac raised his finger to his lips using the prairie-men's sign to remain silent. "Wait. Let me ask Peter and Marcia a few questions." He surveyed the council's amazed faces. "I beg you to be patient with me. What this boy knows may affect you as well as the Danians and us prairie-men."

"Karl," Allen said. "Give Trac the floor. This man has much knowledge of lands and people we know nothing about and his questions may have bearing on the subject at hand."

"Who gave this mere vendor permission to interrupt Council proceedings?" John sputtered.

"I did," Sybil answered. "Allen holds the title of Deputy in Charge of the Forest Border. Any objections?"

"Well, you could have made his position known to us." John glared at Sybil.

"I just recently received the appointment." Allen smiled. "There hasn't been time for the proper announcements."

"My other objection is that we don't know if this prairie-man is capable of conducting part of our investigation," John sputtered.

"Silence, John," Karl snapped. "This man is an ambassador from beyond the forest. According to the scared text, any man who holds the rank of an ambassador is capable of conducting an investigation. If you and Sybil agree, we can continue."

"Certainly, I agree," Sybil said.

John nodded. "Obviously, I'm out-voted."

"Go ahead, Trac," Karl said, "we will listen."

Trac circled the table until he was in a position where he could look directly at the young people. "Peter, Marcia, I want you to describe this man to me. I want you to tell me everything you remember about the time you saw him."

106

"He was shorter than us," Marcia said, "and had black hair, but then everyone one who is Danian seems to have black hair. And his skin was tan."

"He wore rich clothes," Peter said. "A long embroidered shirt that almost reached his knees. He wore really tight pants, and soft leather boots."

"So far, you've described any Danian Lord you might meet in one of the markets. Now, tell me something that made him different from other men."

"That's hard." Peter screwed up his face in thought. "Danians are small boned; they all looked alike to me."

"He was fatter than most of the men we saw there. Not as fat as Councilor John, of course, but —" Marcia rested her chin on her folded hands. "I guess you'd call him plump. And he was important. Everyone addressed him as 'Lord.'"

"Lord? How dare you use the name of our God when speaking of a mutant!" Karl exclaimed.

Marcia gasped. "I'm not speaking blasphemy, Karl. 'Lord' was the word these men used to address the rich Danian. Oh, and they all knelt when they spoke to him."

"Huh," Trac said. "Lord is a title used for ruling Danians. They would never use the word, 'Lord' to mean one of their gods. Danians do a lot of kneeling. Typical behavior. What else?"

"I don't know, let's see." Marcia looked thoughtful. "Oh, he knew a little of our language, and he had one of our books — the one on weapons. Although Tom read before, he wanted Peter to read it."

"Did you, Peter?" Trac eyed him.

"I tried. The room was full of rangers — I know, you don't call them that. They were armed. I had no choice, but my lack of the Danian language made my attempt impossible."

"Guardsmen, Peter. Anything else?"

Peter shook his head. "That was a couple of years ago."

"I remember something," Marcia said. "The rich man wore several rings. One was especially beautiful. It was a silver stag surrounded by red stones worn on his index finger. The ring on his

third finger was made of silver and had a raised eagle's head on it."
Marcia closed her eyes. "There was something else... Oh, I remember. A crown floated over the head of the eagle."

Trac felt his insides churn. He wanted to yell his protest to the top of the ceiling. Instead he returned to his seat and sat. Marcia's description of the second ring proved his greatest fear. *The Prince of Chaleen's signet ring. I admired it that snowy day Conder showed it to Sylvia and demonstrated how it made a mark on a piece of parchment.* "I've seen that ring. It is the signet ring of Prince Conder, next in line to the Danian Throne.

"Conder," Trac repeated after a silence, not wanting to believe this piece of information. "Prince of Chaleen and Brother to the High King Cadamire of Dana." He felt his eyebrows rise as a sudden rush of adrenaline caused him to bolt to his feet. "Conder is a very powerful man." He stepped away from the table, turned his back on the council and stared out the window.

"Are you finished with questioning these two?" Karl asked. "I'm unsure of its relevance."

"I've learned more than I ever wanted to know," Trac answered. He touched the metal S shaped medallion hanging around his neck. *I've failed. Conder has the power to gather an army at the gap of Sistra. It's a trap, just as it was when we tried to revenge the death of Megu thousands of years ago. Conder will sacrifice Delmarath and lure Cole and whoever follows him into the valley of Sistra. Garth, Lon, all my friends will be slaughtered. Even if I return, I'll never see any of them again. I'm stranded in this miserable place with strangers I don't trust. I can't warn Reig, a snow bound prairie lies between me and home. If I survive this predicament, I'll be alone in the world.*

He turned and scanned the people still engaged in heated discussion. He noticed Marcia, her head in her arms; her sobs racked her body. Trac returned to the table and put his arm around her. "Easy, Lass. What's wrong?"

"I killed Tom and Mike," she sobbed. "We should have spent the winter in Kans."

Chapter 14

Sick of complaints and grumbling from his mud splattered men and amazed that these fifteen over-privileged sons of high-ranking nobles could be so incompetent, Bart welcomed the sight of the open climax forest. The huge maples marked the Delmarthian border, an hour's ride would see them to the outer fortifications that guarded the city.

He smiled. *Almost home. Tomorrow night will find us safe behind walls. It'll be good to see Menes and Evander. Enjoy spending time here. Maybe I can celebrate the beginning of the Winter Festival with friends. The Megara dances never matched the Delmarthian celebration of the Gathering of the Greens.*

He turned Nightwind so he faced his men. "We're at the Delmarthian Border, gentlemen," he called. "Tonight we sleep under a roof." *The outpost's vacant this time of year. An excellent location for cleaning muck off our horses and gear. Unsure which is worst, snow or mud? We've only had to deal with the latter, thanks to the slight rise in temperature.*

Two horsemen approached from the direction of Delmarath. The man dressed in a red cloak and black military uniform, his grizzly thatch of hair escaping from under his leather helmet, rode a terribly familiar white stallion.

Bart groaned as he raised his hand signaling the men behind him to halt. *Metrox on Warrior. Always means trouble. Hello, who's riding with him?*

He squinted at the Delmarthian captain's companion. *That's Lavine's bay mare, but that definitely isn't Evander's woman. Too tall. Uncomfortable in that side saddle.* Bart frowned. *What are you doing, my Lady? Do we look so dangerous that you must hide behind those trees?*

Metrox advanced on Warrior holding the stallion to a high-stepping trot.

"Show-off," Bart muttered. "He has that beast behaving as if he were performing in the King's Annual Horse Show."

Metrox halted within speaking distance and greeted Bart with a Danian salute.

Bart scowled as he returned the salute. "By all the gods, why are you riding Lance's horse?"

"Just exercising him, my Lord. You know how miserable Warrior is if he doesn't get a chance to run." Metrox favored Bart with his innocent look.

Before Bart could answer, the Delmarthian Guard materialized from behind nearby trees at a canter. They fanned out to encircle Bart's men and Metrox.

The white stallion screamed and reared, striking out with his front hooves.

Bart's mare squealed as she leaped to one side.

"Delmarthians! Back off!" the Delmarthian captain yelled.

"Menes!" Bart recognized his old friend's voice as the Delmarthians turned their horses away from the plunging stallion. *What are you doing here?*

Metrox brought his crop down hard on Warrior's head.

The white horse screamed again and whirled toward the King's Guard who scattered in several directions.

"Easy." Metrox yelled. He forced Warrior into a tight circle and halted facing Bart.

The stallion tossed his head, his ears back, his eyes blazing.

Bart backed Nightwind to a safer position.

The Delmarthians regrouped on the road leading to Delmarath, blocking the way to their city.

A quick glance informed Bart that the King's Guard had gathered in a loose formation behind him, but a safe distance from the commotion, awaiting orders.

The woman maneuvered her horse through the trees to a position beyond the King's Guard.

Menes rode his gray gelding toward Bart. "My Lord, why do we have the pleasure of your company?" Menes' voice sounded as cold as the wind whistling out of the north.

"This isn't quite the welcome, I expected." Bart held Nightwind steady. *Pleasure of our company indeed! Menes desires us elsewhere. He knows I wouldn't forget that when a Delmarthian captain inquires the pleasure of anyone, there is only trouble ahead for that person.*

"Plan to ride into the city?" Menes' voice went from cold to hostile as he halted his grey beside Nightwind. "Sorry, my friend," he murmured in Citherian.

Haven't heard Lance's language, since I joined the King's Guard. I taught Menes Citherian. We adopted it as our secret language. Something's wrong.

Menes raised his voice so everyone could hear, and announced in Danian, "I'm under orders to allow no one into the city. We lack food to last the winter."

"Not even for the space of a night?" Bart asked in the same tone. *Oh great. Can't return to Megara without Sylvia. If she's not in Delmarath, we'll have to ride through the city and the marketplace in order to use the trail to her cabin.*

"I have my orders," Menes repeated. "No visitors during the cold months. You have too large an escort, my Lord. Even the King limits five armed men as the maximum attendants for a Lord when entering Megara and I count fifteen. Surely, the same law applies to Delmarath."

111

"Easily arranged, Captain. I'll post ten men at the outpost and order five to accompany me into Delmarath."

Menes switched to Citherian and said softly, "Bart, you must realize one Lord would be one too many."

Bart bit his tongue and breathed deeply. *Betren's in Megara, so is father. Even Metrox is not of the nobility and he and Warrior stand over there ready to travel.* He swallowed. *Only a third or forth ranking captain can be in charge. Any one of my men could evoke 'Right of Rank' and claim the city. Wouldn't put it past either Lord Sedrac or Lord Buris.* Bart hoped his face betrayed nothing. *The last time a Lord entered Delmarath while our entire house was away, Conder managed to order the House of Robert's execution. My brother never got over it.*

"Understood," Bart nodded as he replied in Citherian. "However, we follow the king's orders to provide an escort for Metrox and Sylvia to safely reach Megara. Perhaps you forget, Sylvia is a barbarian. Anyone who sees her is legally required to kill her. Figured the sight of fifteen lords protecting her would stifle anyone's desire for heroics. I can't leave without her." Bart turned to Metrox using the Danian tongue. "Captain, I take it that you head to Megara?"

Metrox laughed. "Exactly right, my Lord." He turned Warrior away from Bart. "And I'm leaving immediately. Let's ride, my Lady." The woman smirked before urging her mare to follow Metrox.

Sylvia! I'd recognize that expression anywhere. "Hold up! The King orders me to escort you to Megara!" Bart yelled. "Would you disobey your King?"

"What? I can't hear you, my Lord," Metrox called back. "See you in Megara."

Well, that solves one problem. We no longer need to ride to Sylvia's cabin door, just move out and apprehend her. "So much for a rest at the outpost," Bart said.

Menes grinned. "My father's difficult at all times; on Warrior he's impossible."

Bart shrugged. "Captain, I need a favor."

"A favor, my Lord?"

112

"The King requires six Delmarthians to guard Lance. Can you spare them?"

"Guard Lance?" Menes smiled and spoke in Citherian, "Bart, you bring wonderful news. I'm delighted to hear that Lord Betren and our barbarian are safe. I was so sure that they'd arrive to Megara that I wagered Evander a new barbarian western saddle from the Chaleen Market, the kind with the genuine silver fasteners for the rear rigging ring, the rope strap ring and stirrup irons. No one expected our resourceful heroes to fail, even without our assistance. With the noble Lord Betren in command of the action, how could it be otherwise?"

Bart nodded and glanced at the sky. *Five years distanced me from your confounded long-winded boring speeches!* He glared at Menes. "I need those men today, Captain," he said in Citherian. "We still have a few hours of daylight left. I just as soon start back now."

Menes grinned and switched to Danian. "Did you say six men, my Lord? I expect we can handle that." He returned to his men and spoke to them. A lengthy heated conversation followed. Eventually, six riders pulled away from the Delmarthian Guard and formed a line near the King's Guardsmen.

Menes turned to Bart indicating that they retreat a short distance from both bands of mounted men.

Bart nodded and followed him out of range of the hearing of the guardsmen.

"I too have a request, my Lord." Menes spoke in a low voice. "May I borrow six of your men? Even exchange so to speak."

"Hostages, Captain?" Bart matched Menes quiet voice aware of his guard's annoyance of being excluded from this conversation.

"No, my Lord. My orders are to gather information for Lord Betren. I require men who can blend in with the Lords in Chaleen and other cities close to the border." Menes smiled slightly. "You seem to forget, we're Delmarthians, my Lord. We can filter into the stables and towns easily enough, but we are not exactly respected socially in the upper circles of the inner cities."

Bart's lips tightened, his eyes narrowed. *No one knows that better than me.*

"There is only one slight incongruity that may raise eyebrows." Menes continued speaking in Danian keeping his voice low. "I'd require these men to answer to me, personally. They'd have to swear an oath of loyalty to make their positions official."

Bart stroked his mare's mane. "My guard? Sons of the Great Houses lower themselves to serve a mere captain of Delmarath? You ask a great deal, Captain."

"You have not spoken to Lord Betren?"

"I haven't had time," Bart explained. "The King ordered me to Delmarath before either Lance or Bet was in any condition to talk. If you want my men, I need to know the problem."

Menes sighed heavily. "I assumed that we are honored by your company because you were advised of our current situation. I have no desire to be the first to inform you of this."

Bart stared at his friend, aware his first reaction to Menes' actions had been correct. "What current situation? What compels Metrox and Sylvia to risk the trip to Megara? Get on with it, Menes. You have to tell me sometime."

Menes nodded. "It's horrible, Bart. I mean my Lord. I wish we were in Delmarath sitting around the table in Lavine's immaculate kitchen savoring the aroma of her special rabbit stew while chatting about this over a cup of mulled sweet port."

"Captain Menes," Bart snapped. "Enough. Tell me now, and that's an order."

Menes stroked his gelding's neck and took a deep breath. "The prairie-men wield a new weapon called the black death, a foul-smelling powder, something like a soured mix of pepper and salt, which left a stingy sensation in my nose. It possesses the potential to demolish the walls of Delmarath— reduce our beautiful secure walls into rubble."

Bart felt his insides do a somersault. He struggled to control every muscle on his face. "So Delmarath prepares for war," he muttered in Citherian. *Be nice to report to father how our people are dealing with this catastrophe.*

Menes eyed him. "From here on let's stick to our language. My Citherian is rather rusty."

114

Bart nodded. *Rusty indeed. How convenient, especially when current conditions in Delmarath are the subject. I'd interrogate him, even put him on the rack but he'd die before incriminating his family.*

"As unbelievable as Sylvia's story of 'Cinderella'," Menes continued. "Lance of Citheria snuck into the Hall of Justice with a sample of this black death in order to warn us."

"Lance? That makes no sense at all! He should want to kill us, not save us." *I should have known that Bet had good reason to bring Lance to Megara. No one would believe him about this dangerous powder unless he had proof.*

"Long story, my friend. Too long to tell here. Of course, if you want Father to ride into Megara unescorted, accompany me to the outpost and I will fill you in all fascinating gory details. Even scrape up some wine for your men." Menes grinned. "I'd enjoy the expression on King Cadamire's normally regal face when you and your guard drag into Megara a day or two after Father and Sylvia."

"Captain Menes." Bart scowled. "For once in your life, make this short."

Menes stiffened into military correctness. "My Lord, should I speak to your men, or do you want to do it? I promise I'll keep my words as simple as if I were drilling first year guardsmen."

"Permission granted, Captain, You know more about this than I do." Bart motioned the King's Guardsmen to join them.

Menes raised his voice. "My Lords, the barbarians have discovered a terrible weapon which can destroy city walls. They plan to attack Delmarath as soon as the snow melts off the Citherian Pass."

The King's guardsmen looked at each other, but did not interrupt.

"It gets worse, my Lords," Menes continued, "much worse. We have reason to believe a Danian Lord might be in back of this."

"That's treason," Buris muttered. The others nodded and grumbled.

"Exactly," Menes agreed. "Consider this. If Delmarath fell to the prairie-men and they continued on to Megara, they could be apprehended and destroyed in the Valley of Sistra like in the tales

115

of old. The Lord in charge of that feat would rise to the position of Savior of Megara. He might even entertain thoughts of over-throwing our noble King Cadamire — may he live forever. I need help, my Lords. Would you serve your King by submitting to my command?"

The King's guardsmen, sons of rulers of the cities of Dana sat motionless on their horses.

Bart shifted in his saddle. Nightwind shook her head. *As I thought, no one will swear an oath to a Delmarthian Captain. Maybe I should pledge myself. And be the only fool to kneel before the man who's under my brother's command? No, I'll wait a bit. How long can this silence last?*

The man next to Bart dismounted.

What? Sedrac, nephew of Andros, one of the richest, most powerful men in the kingdom willing to humble himself?

"This sounds interesting," Sedrac said. "Something to while away long winter nights. I'll do it." He checked the ground under his leather embossed boots and chose a dry spot to kneel before Menes. He regally lifted up his cloak as he sank to his knee. "I swear to serve King Cadamire, may he live forever, by serving you, Captain Menes of Delmarath, for as long as this emergency lasts."

"I wouldn't call treason fun or even interesting." Buris turned his long chiseled face toward Bart. "Captain, why would this Menes be in charge instead of you? Give me a reason why I, a lord of the land, should answer to a second or third ranking captain of a mere border city, who lacks any title whatsoever, even the lowly position of Captain of the Delmarthian Guard?"

"Because —" Bart glanced at Menes who sat rigid in his saddle, his face expressionless. "This particular third ranking Delmarthian captain is a genius at gathering details, stringing them together and deriving the right answers. I vouch for this man. We grew up together."

Buris nodded. "And you, Captain. Will you swear your allegiance to Captain Menes of Delmarath? Obviously, he serves the House of Bartran, so he is under your command."

116

Sedrac's riderless horse picked this moment to nip Bart's mare. Nightwind reared, preventing Bart from answering the question immediately.

When he had her under control, Bart glared at Buris. "Of course I pledge myself to Menes!" *Oh, to knock that noble piece of misery off his horse.*

The corners of Menes' lips twitched.

Bart ignored his old friend. "I simply prefer to refrain from being counted in the six men the good captain requests," he said in a more reasonable voice. "Yes, I pledge myself to Captain Menes. It's my city that's threatened. I planned to add my efforts as the seventh man."

"Thank you, Captain. If I needed anything to convince me that this is a serious situation, your words are sufficient proof." Buris dismounted from his sleek spotted gelding and dropped to one knee beside Sedrac. "I too will serve my King by serving you, Captain Menes. This I do swear."

"I also will take the oath," Wilfred said as he dismounted and knelt in front of Menes. "Buris and I have leave to spend the Winter Festival in Chaleen. We can see what we can learn while we visit our fair city."

Bart nodded. *Wilfred and Buris are a team. Or I should say Buris and Wilfred, for Buris is the leader.*

Three other men dismounted, knelt and agreed to the pledge. *Logmore, Calif and Ebin. All members of lesser nobility. Never had to impress them, so never paid them much heed. Hope, they'll do.*

"I can serve you best in the palace," Sedrac said as he rose to his feet. "I have connections." He smiled smugly and brushed the dirt off his knee before he mounted.

"Captain Menes." Rieman of Casein dismounted and knelt. "This guard is loyal to the King. A pledge signifies that we make this our only concern until the problem is solved. Not everyone can do that." He gazed up at the riders, his round boyish face grim. "I feel I speak for everyone here, that if we come across information pertaining to this, we will report it immediately to Captain Bart, our commander, or contact you, Captain Menes."

117

A general assent erupted from the men on horseback.

"Thank you, my Lords." Menes placed his hand on his heart and bowed his head. "I wish I had some tidbit to give you narrowing the search. All I can say is, keep your eyes and ears open. Anything— anything at all that seems out of line from normal behavior of our Danian citizens, report to Captain Bart or me. Every little insignificant detail will lead us to the traitor. I surmise that the best course of action is for you all to return to Megara as planned. Behave normally. We wish to avoid rousing anyone's suspicions that we suspect treasonable behavior among the Lords of our land without solid proof."

"You have no suspects?" Buris questioned.

Menes smiled. "No, no one specific. Oh, I have a few ideas, mere hunches, so no reason to name anyone. I need an honest search, gentlemen, not a preconceived witch-hunt."

The men nodded in agreement.

Menes gazed down the road toward Megara, glanced at Bart and grinned. "It's an awful empty road, my Lord. It was my understanding that your orders concerned my father's safety as he traveled to meet with the King."

Bart reined his horse close to Menes and struck him on the shoulder. "Oh, wipe that smirk off your face, Menes. You needn't be so delighted that I'm going to eat your father's dust all the way to Megara."

"My apologies, my Lord." Menes' features changed into the correct expressionless face that was expected of a captain addressing a lord. "Is this better, my Lord?"

Bart started to laugh and then remembered he was in charge. "Gentlemen of the Guard, make ready to ride back to Megara. Delmarthians, when we catch up with Metrox, flank that horse. Give him plenty of space."

As one the Delmarthians wheeled their horses around and raced after Metrox.

Bart swore. Under his breath he used every Danian, prairie-men's and Citherian invective that he knew while the King's Guard obeyed his order with the usual arguments of who had the highest rank and who should be riding directly behind Buris and Sedrac.

Sedrac approached him and saluted. "We're ready to ride, Captain."

"Move out," Bart ordered. He raised his hand in farewell to Menes. *At least Menes has the courtesy to keep his mouth shut on my men's lack of discipline.* Bart turned his horse toward Megara.

Chapter 15

Long shadows crossed the road. Bart glanced at the sky. *About two more hours of daylight; should find a campsite now, but we must apprehend Delmarath's Captain of the Guard and the lovely Sylvia. Thanks to Metrox, we'll spend one more night in the open. And just to keep life interesting, that Delmarthian Guard showed so little respect for me, they didn't bother to wait to be dismissed.*

"Captain!" Sedrac shouted as he rode his heavy chestnut mare alongside Nightwind. He eyed Bart, anger simmering in his dark eyes. "It was my impression that we'd enjoy some leisure time in Delmarath. The men need the R&R. You should've pulled rank on Captain Menes. May I remind you, you are a son of Bromwell, a Lord of Delmarath. What on earth were you mumbling about?"

Bart urged his mare gently. "Just ride with me and listen." Nightwind lengthened her stride.

Sedrac's fleshy face hardened as he kicked his horse into a jerky trot in order to match the black mare's smooth gait.

120

"You're right, it's a pity, we aren't going to refresh ourselves in Delmarath," Bart raised his voice so he could be heard over the drumming hooves. "Our mission is to escort Captain Metrox and his lady safely to the king."

"Another detail," Sedrac responded. "Are we to ride behind common Delmarthians all the way to Megara? What's wrong, Captain? Afraid to assert yourself and put those men in their place? Or do common Delmarthian guardsmen ride off before being dismissed by their commander? I'd submit that they have very little respect for the Younger Son of Bromwell. Furthermore, why not surround Metrox and the lady and do it the proper way?"

Bart pulled his horse to a stop. "The proper way would get men killed." He spit out each word with the fury usually reserved for his brother, Betren. "No, you don't want to circle that stallion. No, we aren't going to put an arrow in Warrior's neck. Which one of you remembered to bring a bow? For that matter, who in this guard knows how to use one? I wouldn't want to guess how many that horse would take down if the arrow veered one hair from the intended target. Yes, we are going to hold this formation all the way to Megara. Yes, we will be the laughing stock of the palace when Metrox leads us through the city. And you want to know something? My brother's got me in so much trouble that I don't care about appearances anymore. We will do what is necessary. But you will remember I am still your commanding officer and you will keep that in mind. Any more questions?"

"No, sir."

"Then drop back and order the King's Guard to hold their line. No switching positions."

"Understood." Sedrac scowled. "They're Lords, Captain. It's difficult for them to follow."

"They're guardsmen, and it's high time they start acting like guardsmen. You're second in command, see to it," Bart snapped. "Continue to ride toward Megara. Keep an easy pace, no faster than a trot. I'll wait for you wherever I bring that Delmarthian Guard to heel." Bart and Sedrac exchanged salutes.

121

Bart touched his heel to Nightwind's side. *I'd like to wring Metrox's neck,* he thought as Nightwind broke into a gallop. *Once I've the Delmarthians and the King's Guard together, it's only a matter of riding until we come to whatever spot Metrox chooses to spend the night. Of course that means setting up camp in the dark.*

The King's guard caught up with Bart and the Delmarthians as the sun slipped behind the horizon. They found Metrox as dusk grayed into night.

Bart knew this area, had stayed there many times with his father when they had occasion to visit Megara. Metrox had chosen his location well. A ridge protected the area from the wind out of the North. Towering pines grew near the road, concealing possible campsites in the open clearings behind them. However, the small size of the sites prevented convenient places for large groups of men. The spot closest to the road would accommodate the King's Guard. The Delmarthians would use one of the smaller areas.

"Sedrac, set up camp," Bart ordered as he dismounted. "Delmarthians, follow that path. It will lead you to a satisfactory location to spend the night. Buris, take my horse. She's worked enough for today. I'll join you shortly."

Bart found a narrow footpath leading to the smaller sites. Anger gave him speed as he noted the distance separating campfires. He stepped into the firelight of the closest tent where Metrox was adding wood to a fire. The Captain of the Delmarthian Guard straightened into a salute.

"It's nice of you to pick our campsite," Bart said. "Not exactly the spot I would have chosen."

Metrox grinned. "We like our privacy, my Lord. It's better for Sylvia and much better for Warrior."

Bart nodded glumly. "Have enough food?"

"Of course." Metrox eyed Bart. "I have a very interesting map to show you."

"Evidence?" Bart felt his eyes narrow. "Anything we need to take care of now?"

Metrox shook his head. "Nothing conclusive, just a piece of the puzzle."

"Keep it safe until we reach Megara."

"Yes, my Lord." Metrox frowned. "Why are we honored with this escort?"

"Lance and Bet are alive, but Lance had a fall, is in bad shape. He's calls for Sylvia and raves about you. I suspect he's delirious."

"Fine, just fine." Metrox stood erect, straight-faced. "So tell me, my Lord; is this an escort, or am I your prisoner?"

'Prisoner?'

As Bart considered that solution to his problems, the stallion raised his head from snatching bites of grass and snorted. He laid back his ears and gave Bart a long level stare.

Oh, I understand, Warrior, old boy, Bart thought as the horse drew back his lips revealing large yellow teeth. *Curb Metrox with you around? Forget it.* "By all that's holy, Captain, the King ordered an escort."

Sylvia poked her head out of the tent. "Bart, how good it is to see you."

Bart turned to her and smiled. "Sylvia, Little Sister, it's been a long time." He whistled as she stepped toward him. "By all the gods, Sylvia, how you have grown. You're almost taller than me."

"I am taller than Bet," she said as she twirled a long strand of blond hair between her fingers, "but then I'm not Danian. Which brings me to a question: You're higher in command than Metrox, right?"

"Yes."

"My lord, watch out," Metrox hooted.

"Then will you please tell the good captain that I don't need to wear this stupid dress or ride on that hideous sidesaddle?"

"No," Bart said, "absolutely not. No Danian woman rides astride. They all wear dresses. Your tunic and pants will not do."

"Oh please, Bart, I feel so uncomfortable."

"No!" Bart and Metrox chorused.

"Oh, all right." Sylvia wrinkled up her pert nose. "It was worth a try." Her blue eyes twinkled. "I must have lost my touch. I seem to remember talking you into doing most everything I wanted."

123

Bart scowled. "Your memories are faulty, Little Sister. And please, call me Captain when others are around."

"I won't talk to you at all." She tossed her head. "That way I won't embarrass the noble captain. How about that?"

Bart laughed. "As you like, Sylvia. I must leave you now. Duty calls." He bowed to her and continued on.

The Delmarthians built their fires on the hillside above Metrox's camp close to the ridge. Neat windproof shelters positioned to make the best use of the heat from the fire were being erected. Bows and arrows lay within easy reach in case of trouble. A nice fat rabbit roasted on a spit. *Now, when did they have time to catch that?*

One of the men noticed him and yelled, "Lord Bart in camp." The men ceased their activities and lined up in front of him.

Bart returned their salute as he inspected the guardsmen. Three of them were recent recruits. He knew the others. One of them wore the badge of a sub-captain. "Fredren," he said, "I see you have risen in rank. Congratulations."

Fredren kept his square jawed round face expressionless.

"However, that makes you responsible for these men. Therefore, if you ever dash off without waiting for me to dismiss you again, I'll whip you so hard that the skin falls off your back. Understood?"

"Yes, my Lord." The sub-captain's small nut-brown eyes stared back at Bart.

"Good. Tomorrow, you and your men will maintain a loose flanking position. I know you have a good idea of how much breathing space Warrior requires. Metrox will set the pace. Don't go ahead of him. If we meet small parties of Lords en route to celebrate the Winter Festival, your main duty will be to shield them away from Warrior and Sylvia. I don't expect trouble."

"Understood, my Lord." Fredren saluted smartly.

"Good. Carry on."

Bart evaluated the competence of his guard as he joined his own men. *They require at least another month of practice before they construct a weatherproof shelter. No one has the courtesy to care for my horse.* He unsaddled Nightwind and tied her to the picket line, then helped himself to the last of the stew made from dried mutton and sat to eat. *They even managed to burn the meat. Should have commandeered a piece of that rabbit.*

"Captain?" It was almost a chorus.

Bart took a bite of bread and analyzed the faces of his guard. *Most of these men consider me temporary. Everything that's happened right down to my friendly behavior to Menes will be reported to the court as soon as we return. The King will get fifteen different versions.*

"Captain," Buris said, "your behavior was astonishing."

"How so?" Bart took another bite and chewed it slowly.

Buris glanced around at the men's intent faces and said, "back there you treated Captain Menes as an equal. Anyone can see he's not of a great family. Why?"

"Although I spent my early years in Chaleen, I did my training in Delmarath. Learned most of what I know from Metrox, Menes' father. Menes is my equal in everything except birth." Bart glared at his men. "Unlike the guards in the inner cities who spend most of their time parading during holidays, our guard preforms actual military duties keeping order in the marketplace. A man's ability is more important than his lineage in a border city. That's one of the differences between Delmarath and the rest of Dana, gentlemen. May I remind you that our King was so impressed by this strange notion that he adopted it as his own?"

"Captain, one more question please." This time it was Sedrac. "Who is this lady who rides with Captain Metrox? I saw her eyes. They're blue. Captain, she is no Danian."

"She's Lance's sister."

Sedrac looked at him blankly.

Bart sighed. "The sister of that barbarian my brother hauled to the palace."

The men glanced at each other.

Bart put his bread down and stood up. "Now listen; for the first time in your lives you are performing actual guard duty. As captain I don't need to explain my decisions, but I will. Surely, I don't have to remind you that it is death for a barbarian to be in our land? That anyone who sees the girl riding with Metrox, has the moral obligation to kill her? Since her brother now rests under the King's sword, the lady's life is also under the King's protection. We're here to ensure that she arrives at Megara alive."

The men looked to Buris who nodded.

"My responsibility is to get everyone in this little group safely home. Rank, birth and all those great things we value so much in the palace has nothing to do with it. Survival does. So you will obey my orders without question. Understand?"

The men eyed him. "Yes sir."

Bart recognized their expression. *They'll obey because they must, but they loathe it.* "That white horse can and has killed," he continued. "Metrox and that barbarian we took into the palace a few days ago are the only ones who can handle the brute."

"If the horse is so dangerous, why is Metrox riding it to Megara?" Sedrac asked.

"Protection for him and the girl. The last thing Metrox expected was an escort." *The last thing Metrox expected was to see the King's Personal Guard blundering around in the wilderness.*

Bart returned to his seat and picked up what remained of his supper and ate it, ignoring the probing eyes of the men around him. When he finished his meal, he rose to his feet. "Good night gentlemen. I suggest you turn in. We leave at dawn." He picked up his saddle bag with his blanket and retreated into the best built lean-to.

Chapter 16

When Bart crawled out of his blankets, the stars were fading into the pre-light of dawn. Unable to sleep any longer, he took some of the remaining wood and fed it to the glowing coals of last night's fire. The men still slept; some spent the night in the open.

He stretched. *A moment's peace before the day starts.*

A long low wailing howl ended his sense of well-being. Shivers crept up and down his back. *Horrhounds?* He drew a sharp breath. *Miles away. Anyone notice that howl? No, no reaction from my men, but then only those who have experienced these monsters would recognize that sorrowful moan.*

He stood still, sifting through the night sounds. Close by men snored, the fire snapped. Wind whispered through trees.

Again the fearful cry penetrated the wilderness.

Rieman of Cassiae quietly joined Bart by the fire, his olive face taunt, fear lurked in his dark eyes. "Horrhounds, Captain. Did you hear them?"

"Yes." Bart scanned the darkness surrounding the camp. "Prefer wolves, much easier to deal with, but we can't be that fortunate. That's definitely the demon voice of horrhounds hunting prey."

A moment later Metrox appeared, his weathered face grim in the firelight. "The quicker we depart the better."

"I'll have to explain to the men—"

"Time enough to do that when we camp tonight."

Bart stiffened. *When will Metrox realize I'm in command?*

"Heard one— no two howls. Expect two hounds hunting together," Metrox continued. "Means that the pack is widely scattered. Fortunately the devils are miles away." He glanced at Rieman. "Anyone one else awake, Guardsman?"

Rieman saluted. "Questionable, sir, and even if they heard that howl, I doubt our men have any idea of what it means."

Metrox returned his salute. "My Lord, we must use what time we have to ride as many miles as we can before these monsters catch sight of us. Explaining to your men will just delay our departure." Metrox saluted, pivoted on his heel and disappeared up the trail to where he and Sylvia had spent the night.

"Rieman, get your horn," Bart ordered. "Sound the wake-up call. It's time to move out." *What am I doing? Blindly following Metrox's orders? Trouble is— he's right.*

Men slowly struggled to their feet at the insistence of the horn.

"The captain said, 'wake-up call was at dawn,'" Wilfred muttered. "It's still dark."

"They must consider this dawn in Delmarath," Buris answered. "What would you expect of Delmarthians?"

Sedrac groaned. "I'm sure he said we were to leave at dawn so I suppose we're on schedule."

"Oh, shut up, and roll up that blanket." Rieman sounded disgusted.

"What? No breakfast?" The voice came from the shelter next to the fire.

"No food, didn't you hear?" The answer floated from the same place.

"So that's why we didn't continue on to Delmarath? They lack enough food to survive the winter?"

128

"What would you expect? Stupid Delmarthians. Ability over birth! Ha!"

Bart didn't recognize the voices. "Look sharp." His command cut across the low mummer. "Gather your gear, saddle your horses. We're moving out."

"All here and ready to ride, my Lord." Fredren saluted. The Delmarthian sub-captain surveyed the scene in front of him focusing on two men struggling to roll up their blankets. He shook his head. "My Lord, what's wrong with your men? Any patrol of Delmarthian fourteen-year-olds do better than this."

"Secure your mounts," Bart ordered, "then give a hand with getting these—" He paused. Several choice words came to mind but it was better not to air them, not to Delmarthian guardsmen. "Ready these men and horses. We ride immediately."

Fredren relayed his orders to the Delmarthians and they made their way through the camp.

"Hey, watch where you're going!"bellowed one of the nobles. "You almost stepped on me."

"So, what are you doing still in your blankets?" Fredren snapped. He stepped over the prone man to check the first horse that had a saddle on its back. "Son," he said to the man pulling the stirrup in place, "unless you want to ride upside down under your horse's belly, you better check that girth. It's loose."

"You're putting the saddle on backwards," one of Fredren's men yelled.

"I can't see what I'm doing. It's too dark." The voice sounded close to panic.

"Well, turn it around," the Delmarthian shouted.

"Move aside." Fredren snatched the saddle out of the King's Guardsman's hands and positioned it on the horse's back. "Next time let your hands tell you front from rear. There's a slight difference, you know."

"Listen, Dean," he addressed the Delmarthian Guardsman who had backed out of his way. "We're under orders. Our Lord means to high tail it to Megara. That horse over there thrashing around, hold it steady while his rider saddles it and don't take any backtalk from these elegant inner-city guardsmen."

"Yes, sir."

"Captain!" Buris faced Bart. "What right do these underlings have to order us about?"

"I authorized them to do just that," Bart snapped. "We're moving out as soon as you're ready. Since no one seems capable of obeying my command, I ordered the Delmarthians to take charge. Buris, you don't even have your horse saddled. Move!"

"Yes, sir."

"My Lord." A young Delmarthian, about fourteen years in age, approached leading Nightwind. "Your horse, my Lord, saddled and ready to ride."

"Your first assignment, lad?" Bart put his foot in the stirrup.

"Yes, my Lord."

"Good. Now help collect the gear and load it on the horses."

"I tried, my Lord. Your men refuse to allow me to touch their gear."

"You're following my orders, lad. Just tell them 'Captain's orders' and do it. Any objections and they answer to me."

"Yes, my Lord."

Sylvia and Metrox joined Bart. "We're prepared to ride, Lord," Metrox said saluting. "What's holding things up?" He listened a moment to a noble's surly reply to Fredren's instructions. "Fine, just fine. I'd say you're in charge of idiots."

"The only idiot thing here is this sidesaddle," Sylvia complained before Bart could answer. "I hope we go over high land today. I plan to throw it down the first cliff I find."

"You'll do no such thing, my Lady," Metrox growled. "That sidesaddle belongs to Lavine."

"It's a good thing. I'd cut it up into little pieces if it were mine. I might do that anyhow. It's ridiculous to perch like a bird on a horse."

By this time, night had given way to the drab light that precedes the sun. Bart felt a certain satisfaction of seeing Metrox's agitated expression each time Sylvia spoke.

130

The sun left sunrise behind and was moving toward midday by the time everyone was ready to ride. Bart glanced at Metrox. "Let's hope those hounds find better prey."

Metrox smiled a nasty smile. "Don't count on it. We're the biggest meal between Delmarath and Megara. I'm sure they're anticipating full stomachs."

They rode the rest of the day without incident. Bart heard no more howls. Late afternoon, they camped near the place where the road skirted the swamp. Bart chose a field near open woodlands.

"No shelters," he ordered. "We need firewood. We encircle our camp with fire tonight."

"Horrhounds, my Lord?" Fredren questioned. The sub-captain managed to keep his face expressionless, but his clenched hands betrayed his apprehension.

"Heard them howling before dawn." Bart surveyed the raised eyebrows, frowns, and tilted heads of his guard. "You will form six groups. Collect enough firewood to keep a blaze going all night around the camp's perimeter. A Delmarthian will be in charge of each group."

"What?" Sedrac gasped. "You must be out of your mind! We, the King's Guard, are answerable to common guardsmen?"

"You dare question my orders?" Bart's sword was out and pressed against Sedrac's flabby chest.

"No sir!" Sedrac glowered at him.

"If you have complaints, submit them to the King," Bart snapped. "Until then, do what you're told."

The Delmarthians proved themselves equal to the challenge of having lords under their command. In fact they relished the opportunity. The King's Guard had never been worked so hard. Soon a campsite was marked out by wood piles.

"How are we supposed to sleep?" We'll be crowded inside these fires like a herd of horses in a pen," Buris complained.

"Would the noble Lord rather be slowly digested?" Metrox said as he added an armful of wood to a pile. "Just be glad there's no wind tonight. Smoke shouldn't be too bad."

131

"Listen to him, Lord Buris," Rieman said. "It's better to live and be uncomfortable than be eaten alive by those ferocious dogs."

Buris glanced from one man to the other. His lip curled as if it had become part snake. "You're serious about this. The danger is real?"

"Deadly serious," Metrox said. "Horrhounds, large as prairiemen's ponies, traveling in packs of sometimes twenty or thirty animals, destroy everything in their path. In this case, their main meal is horse. They'll enjoy us for dessert." He considered Buris. "You, however — they'll probably spit you back out."

Bart struggled to suppress a smile.

"Exactly what is a whore's hound?" Sedrac asked before Buris could respond to Metrox's last words. "Never heard of that breed of dog."

Rieman raised his horn and blew three low notes summoning the men to muster around him.

Activity ceased as the men obeyed the horn's command.

"Now, what?" one of the nobles muttered.

'Haven't we had enough for one day," another answered.

Rieman waited until everyone joined the circle. "Gather round all ye Lords and guardsmen. Listen to my tale.

"Captain's orders?" Sedrac inquired.

"Oh…" The sixteen-year-old guardsman glanced nervously at Bart. "Permission to continue, Captain?"

Bart checked the perimeters of the camp. "No sign of immediate danger. Proceed."

Rieman located a large rock and scrambled on top of it. He surveyed the group of nobles as he raised his hands commanding silence.

"Back in the days when life for men who lived like gods was ending — back before the great disaster, a man named Horace Pelderson wearied of his neighbors and retired to a mountain in the northlands. There he built a house and barns and lived in comfort.

"As the disaster grew nearer, men fled to the mountain seeking a safe retreat, but discovered great fences built around the base of

Horace's mountain. Packs of fierce dogs lived off his land and fortified his holdings.

"Inevitably, the catastrophe struck the earth. Horace died, some say slaughtered by the very dogs he bred. The fence rotted with time. The hounds multiplied and freely terrorized every community in the north.

'Horace's horrible hounds,' the people wailed as they shivered in their houses listening to the death cry of their livestock. Men who fought the animals were eaten alive. And eventually, the name of this terror was shortened to Horrhounds. Every so often the northlands fail to support those brutes so they roam south ravaging our lands."

"Rieman," Bart said. "Where did you learn this tale? It sounds like something a storyteller from the prairies would spin."

"A real compliment, Captain." Rieman stepped off the rock. "The storytellers are exceptional in our marketplace beyond our walls."

Buris and Sedrac exchanged glances. "Trust the son of a border lord to idolize a lowly teller of tales," Sedrac muttered.

"Typical," Buris sneered. "Typical, uncivilized border town behavior."

A howl floated across the camp.

"Gentlemen," Bart ordered, "light those fires!"

Chapter 17

Hours of darkness dragged slowly toward dawn. During the night the woods rustled as if an evil god found pleasure in tormenting men by breathing life into every branch. Hideous shadows slunk close to the camp, but nothing crossed the line of fire. The horses fretted on the picket lines. Men took turns keeping the fires burning; others reassured the horses.

Sometime before the sun rose, the hounds disappeared.

Bart stood on one side of the camp with the horses between him and the men. He turned as Metrox and Rieman approached him and saluted.

"Captain," Rieman said, "the horrhounds are gone for now. We found the tracks of five animals heading northwest."

"Figure they were scouting," Metrox said. "Let's hope the main pack is days behind us. The hounds won't touch us while we're protected by fire, but they'll be back. They'll harass us on the road."

Bart nodded. "Rieman, summon Sylvia, Sedrac, and Fredren. Metrox, one moment," he added as Rieman disappeared in the direction of the men. Darkness concealed Metrox's weathered face, but Bart knew it would be expressionless.

"Well?"

"Metrox, there is no one I respect more than you, except perhaps my father." Bart paused. *How do I tell the man who taught me everything I know about leadership that I'm in charge, not him?"*

"So? Bart, say what you're going to say. Get it over with."

Bart cleared his throat. "This is my command, such as it is. I'm captain. It is my place to make the decisions."

"In other words, keep my mouth shut; don't offer advice unless it is requested, even if I'm right. Bart, I understand. Listen, Son of Bromwell, you can handle this. You have dealt with these animals before."

"But never in a position of authority. I need this success. You don't know how I need it." Bart pushed back a panic-stricken small voice inside his head. "But not at the cost of lives. You have ten times more experience with these hounds than me. If I'm about to do something that's going to get everyone eaten, I want you to countermand it."

"Lord, the cost to you—"

"Is immaterial. We may not make Megara alive, but that failure won't be because of my inexperience. I trust you not to interfere unless I'm doing something that will end in death."

"Understood, Lord." Bart felt the Captain's hand on his shoulder. "Lad, you're more than reaching for your spurs. In my mind, you have already earned them."

"Everyone you requested is here." Rieman held a flaming torch which cast eerie shadows on the meeting.

"You've neglected to include me," Buris complained. "I rank next to Sedrac."

"We're breaking camp," Bart said. "The hounds have moved off and we need to put as much distance between them and us as possible. No horn. No reason to announce my decision." He waited for some comment. When no one spoke he went on. "Sylvia, do you have your own clothes with you?"

"Of course, I'm wearing them under this stupid dress."

135

"Good. Give your dress to Metrox to store in his pack. Place that sidesaddle as close to that outcropping of rocks as possible. You must retrieve it on your way back to Delmarath."

"That's the best command I've heard since we met."

"Hold on, Sylvia. I'm not finished yet." Bart drew a quick breath. "I want you to lead. You're the best rider we have, most competent to keep your horse under control under any circumstance. Can you handle it?"

Sylvia was silent for a moment. "You know how those horrhounds terrify me," she said in a low voice. "All I want to do is to ride out of here as fast as my horse can run."

"I know," Bart said. "I hesitate to ask this of you, but none of these men have any idea what we're up against. I know your courage, I admire your horsemanship."

"Captain," Sylvia said quietly. "You don't have to flatter me to gain my help. I understand what you need and why. I'll keep my horse at any pace you desire no matter how many hounds are on our heels."

"What? Captain, she's a girl." Buris laughed. "How do you envision a girl riding a horse without a saddle? Do you expect us to follow a woman?"

"Shut up, Buris," Sedrac snapped. "We are the King's Guard. We obey orders."

"Thank you, Sedrac," Bart said. "Keep that in mind, Buris. And Buris, one more objection from you, when we return to Megara you will be up on charges of insubordination."

Buris snapped to attention. "Yes sir."

"Sylvia, keep the pace at a trot. When your horse needs breathing, slow to a walk. Everyone's mount will need the rest."

"Captain, I thought you meant to put as much distance as possible between us and the hounds," Sedrac said. "Why the slow pace?"

"We need to save our mounts until it's absolutely necessary for speed. Those hounds travel miles like lightning streaking across the sky. We are days from Megara. Once the main pack overtakes us, it's the end. One more reason for caution: Loose a mount due to a

136

damaged leg because of these slippery mud covered roads equals losing two men to horehounds. Keep our welfare in mind."

"But Captain," Buris said, "surely we can handle a few hounds."

Bart glared at him. "Have any of you besides Rieman had any experience with these beasts?"

His men exchanged glances, a few shrugged, followed by the wind blowing through the leafless tree branches.

"No? All right then; listen. A few horrhounds won't attack if we stay together. They'll nip at our heels; try to separate a rider from the main group. The minute we attempt to flee, we lose our tight formation which gives the hounds a chance to invade our ranks and spook our horses. Fail to control of your horse and it bolts out of our ranks; you're dead."

"Captain, why don't we just set them up?" Buris asked. "Bait them with one man and horse, and then the rest of us rescue the rider by killing the hounds?"

"Are you riding a war-horse, Buris, experienced in battle?"

"Don't be ridiculous, Captain. The only horses trained in battle skills are those we school for show. We left those mounts in Megara. Oh." Buris' eyes narrowed, he looked grim. "You think our horses would become unmanageable if we tried to attack the hounds?"

"I don't think. I know! The only horse we have capable of that kind of action is Warrior."

"Captain, may I speak?" Rieman asked.

"Permission granted."

"Gentlemen, I too am the son of a border lord. We've had to deal with these monsters from time to time. What we will see today are scouts for at least twenty or thirty more animals. Sure, we can kill some of them. It's the one or two we miss that are the problem. They will return to the main pack. The next thing you know is that the whole pack is on our heels ready to attack. May the gods favor us and we be within sight of Megara before that happens."

"Captain," Buris said, "what do we do if the main pack hits us before we reach Megara?"

"Good question," Bart said. "We scatter. Rieman will give one blast on his horn and it's every man for himself. Do not stay together, do not look back, do not try to save anyone. Just ride out of here and hopefully some of us will survive. If you escape the horrhounds, head to the nearest city. If we reach sight of Megara when they attack, ride home as fast as your horse can carry you."

"You will tell the men this?" The sound of Sedrac's voice told Bart his second in command was horrified.

"As much as they need to know." Bart continued his orders. "Metrox, you and Rieman take the rear. You have the most experience with these hounds. If they act like they mean business, rejoin the guard immediately. Rieman, you can borrow my mare if you like. She's faster than your horse."

Rieman gulped. "No, Captain, my own horse has been through several such raids as this. He's steady. That might count more than speed in that position. And Captain, I brought my bow."

Bart nodded. "Good man!"

Rieman's boyish face positively glowed at this praise.

Bart almost grinned. *Did I look like this border guardsman the day I received my rank as captain?* "Fredren."

"My Lord."

"Take two Delmarthians and flank us on the left. Let no hound pass."

"Understood, my Lord. Keep close to our men and don't shoot unless those puppies try something foolish like breaking our ranks."

Fredren saluted, his small dark eyes full of pride at being singled out for a chance to prove his worth in a crisis.

"And Fredren, make every arrow count. When you've shot your last, we're out of ammo. I'll take the other Delmarthians and do the same on the right." He frowned. "I wished I had my long bow. This crossbow lacks range."

"Captain, use my bow," Metrox said. "Warrior's never been trained for an archer. Last night I fashioned a spear." He raised it above his head, a long stout pole on which he had lashed his knife. "Gives me more reach than a sword."

138

Bart saluted Metrox, turned to Sedrac and Buris and sighed. "Sedrac and Buris, you have one of the most difficult jobs. You must keep the men in line. If anyone panics, loses control of his horse and rides off, that man is expendable. Understand? If you abandon your position, those horrhounds will gain an advantage. It's your job to see that the remaining men close ranks and remain in line. Dismissed."

Bart hoped that the predawn light found his face expressionless. *Father's right; I should have relied on my lesser nobles years ago. Hate to admit I'm wrong. Especially to father.*

For once everyone worked together. Horses were saddled, girths checked, equipment packed.

"We're ready to ride," Sedrac said saluting Bart.

"We're finished in excellent time. We're improving," Bart said. "We're—"

"Will you look at that?" one of the men shouted. All movement ceased. As one the King's Guard turned and gaped.

Sylvia, dressed in her tunic and pants, put her foot in Metrox's clasped hands and mounted her chestnut mare. The hood of her blue cape fell back and her long lustrous blond hair flowed in the wind. The mare arched her neck and pranced.

"The girl's immoral," one man gasped.

"Indecent," another agreed.

"We should yank her off that horse and stone her...."

Fredren and his men exchanged glances and grinned.

"Will you look at that," Fredren spoke loudly to the Delmarthians around him. "These high and mighty nobles expect barbarian women to dress like our Danian ladies. Never shop at our market, my lords. You'll grow faint with righteous indignation."

"Mount up!" Bart shouted. "Fall into your positions behind Sylvia."

Several of the men turned toward Buris.

"Disgraceful," one of them muttered.

"Outrageous!" another agreed.

"You heard the order, gentlemen," Buris snapped. He drew his sword partially out of his scabbard. "Do it."

Shaking their heads, the men mounted their horses and fell into line.

The sun had barely risen when the hounds materialized. Not many. Only two brown and white dogs flanked the guard, one on each side. Three black ones followed behind Metrox and Rieman.

The horses wanted to bolt. They fought their riders, pulled on their bits, tried to break into a gallop. One of the horses veered, but its rider forced it back into line.

"Keep together, men. Keep your horses under control." Buris' voice was calm, encouraging. "If a mere girl can hold her horse to a walk, you certainly can do the same."

On the opposite side of the group, a horse grabbed his bit in his mouth and darted out of the formation. Sedrac was there with his crop to turn it back. "Hey, remember you're boss," he shouted. "Keep that pony's head up."

The hounds on the right held their distance, staying way beyond arrow range, but the Delmarthian cry of victory proclaimed that Fredren and his men had killed one of the beasts. Warrior screamed. Metrox's victory yell and the death cry of a hound told Bart that the stallion had attacked and won.

A sharp yip and the hounds vanished as quickly as they had appeared.

For the remainder of the morning, the company rode without a canine escort. It was a pleasure. The horses calmed down and followed along peaceably. The men relaxed in the saddle.

About noon the hounds reappeared, more of them this time. They seemed content to travel with the guard, staying within sight, but showing no desire to attack. Occasionally, one dashed toward the riders, turning away before the archers could respond.

"Easy boys," Fredren told his men. "Those puppies are teasing us. Don't shoot unless I give the order."

Sylvia sang as they rode. The Danians behind her recognized her song; a lullaby most had heard all their lives. The riders behind her first hummed, and then joined her until everyone except the

140

Delmarthians on flanking duty sang. As men sang, they relaxed in the saddle, their horses feeling their riders' confidence settled down.

"She's a wizard who controls her horse's mind," Buris grumbled that night as they built a barricade of brush around the camp near the Sistra Gap. "Whoever would think that a song could calm frightened horses?"

"She's the better rider, my Lord." Metrox threw a pile of branches on the ground.

"Take this wood and fill in this section," Bart instructed two young lords. He pointed to a low point on the perimeter.

Metrox faced Buris. "I know her people used song while they drove their herd home from the mountain pastures, especially in the spring when the mares were in foal. Why do you think the captain made her leader? The girl was practically born on a horse. She's playing the part of the bell mare."

Buris stared at him. "What?"

"Wild horses, my Lord. They're always led by a wise old mare, which knows the trail, sets the pace and leads the others down the safest routes. The stallion roams along the sides and back of the herd, keeping his band together, watching for trouble. Your captain is using that strategy to get us all to Megara. It's in a horse's mind to follow a leader."

"There's more to that little Delmarthian upstart than I gave him credit for," Buris muttered as he reached for more wood.

"The horrhounds are gathering, Captain," Rieman said. "Listen to those howls— some close to us, others further away."

A howl, much louder, much nearer, told Bart it was time to light the fires.

They spent another restless night as hounds circled their camp hoping for someone to leave the safety of the flaming circle.

"Remember to check your girths," Fredren yelled as the guard collected their equipment and prepared to mount the following morning.

"They're doing better, my Lord," Metrox said as he mounted Warrior.

141

"Those hounds provide good incentive," Bart agreed. "We'll be in the saddle before the sun rises."

"My Lord, I respectfully suggest we push the horses until we're through the Gap," Metrox said. "If those hounds manage to trap us in that narrow passage to the great valley, we're in big trouble. Once out of the valley we can camp early to rest the horses for the final race to safety."

Bart studied Metrox's grim face. "So, we have one more day before they attack?"

"Those sons of evil are gathering behind us, a few at a time. Rieman and I back-trailed a few miles with dawn's first light. Spied three or four of the pests traveling fast. When they reached the road, we noticed several other curs waiting for them. Another group could be seen in the distance. The drought favors our cause. Most of the game migrated to greener pastures late summer forcing our four-legged friends to cover miles in search for snacks to endure until they capture their main meal, meaning us. You know they won't stage an attack until they are one united pack. Yesterday, we killed two hounds proving that we have sharp teeth."

"Thank you, Captain," Bart said. "Next time, notify me before leaving camp. We're almost ready to ride."

"Yes, my Lord." Metrox saluted, and then scowled. "Amazing! I foresaw one of those two great nobles murdering the other in broad daylight." He indicated Buris and Sedrac directing the placement of riders according to each man's horsemanship and then reorganized it once more as the behavior of their mounts warranted. Inexperienced riders were placed between more competent guardsmen.

"Adversity, nothing like it," Bart agreed. "A temporary truce or a lasting friendship? Only time will tell."

"Orders, Captain." Sylvia's mare pawed the ground, anxious to start the day's journey.

"Sylvia, we're going to make tracks today. Let the horses warm up; then a little speed would be nice."

142

"How much speed?" Sylvia shot him a tight little smile. "Please be specific, Captain Bart. If I consult my horse, we will be traveling with the wind."

"Ground's fairly dry here. Try a collected canter. We must hold our formation. If Rieman gives a long blast on his horn, ride for your life, but try to stay on the road. It's our only route to Megara." Bart raised his hand and shouted to the guard, "move out!"

The riders proceeded though the gap, slowing as they climbed the narrow road, barely wide enough for three horses to trot abreast. Towering gray limestone cliffs jutting straight into the air, lined both sides of the formation. The rugged terrain seemed to capture a ribbon of blue sky as if the Danian land presented a banner to salute her guardsmen on the eve of battle.

The hounds were voiceless; the horses obeyed their riders with ease. As they reached the summit, the valley stretched before them, open land surrounded by steep ridges, filled with scattered boulders and random rock formations providing great cover for a lurking enemy.

It took a good part of the day to ride through the Great Valley of Sistra. Men glanced nervously toward the surrounding cliffs riddled with caves encircled by grotesque boulders. Ghosts of fierce barbarians still attempting to conquer Dana haunted this valley. No traveler would voluntarily spend the night here.

"Perhaps those devil dogs fear this creepy hell hole as much as us," one of the men muttered.

"Maybe we've seen the last of them," another answered. "It's been an easy ride, thus far without a peep from those miserable hounds."

Bart kept his own counsel on overhearing this conversation. No sense in alarming the riders unless it was necessary.

Memories of how the hounds had silently followed the men of Chaleen who were entrusted with escorting Bromwell's youngest son, a child of three, to their city, relaxed their guard thinking the enemy had gone. Suddenly, the huge dogs attacked. Bart never forgot the sight of men pulled off their horses by these beasts, or the men's screams as they were eaten alive. Years later, he learned that he survived that day because loyal Delmarthian guardsmen had attacked the hounds giving the leaders of the column the chance to reach Conder's city where he had been raised by his aunt. Not one Delmarthian survived.

Bart dropped back to the end of the column where Metrox rode Warrior. "So far, so good," he muttered.

"They're gathering, Lord," Metrox responded. "They're watching us, hoping we're become careless. When those hounds reach full strength, they'll strike."

Bart sighed with relief when they rode out of the valley. He led his men to a familiar clearing large enough to accommodate everyone. They pitched camp near a bubbling spring which provided them with a good source of water.

Leaving Sedrac in charge, Bart, Metrox and Rieman backtracked to a location looking over the edge of a cliff where they could view the road crossing the great valley.

"They're coming," Bart said.

"Some of them already here." Metrox shielded his eyes.

"Count about twenty," Rieman said. "They don't seem to be in a hurry. Must be waiting for a few more puppies to join up."

Metrox nodded.

Warrior pawed the ground.

"Let's get back to camp," Bart suggested. "Before those monsters realize that they have an opportunity to snack on us."

"At least it's the last time we set up camp on this journey," Rieman said. "Let's pray that we survive tomorrow."

Chapter 18

Sylvia met Bart's eyes. "Not one bird greeting the sun this morning. It's too quiet. How far to Megara?"

"Be there before dark at the pace we're traveling."

"Should I increase it?"

"No. Save the horses until necessary." He drew a quick breath. *It's a sad day in Dana when I opt to surrender the leadership of my men to this young girl.* "You can't assume that I'll be able to advise you at that point, but try to keep the pace under control until the end. Your experience with these hounds will enable you to handle this."

Fredren urged his horse in front of Bart and saluted. "We're ready my Lord. All bows strung, arrows equally divided among my men."

"Good, carry on." Bart turned to Sylvia. "As you say it's too quiet. We'll have plenty of warning before the horrhounds attack in force. I'll guess we'll see them soon."

"Yes, they'll strike from behind." Sylvia touched her mare with her heels.

"Move out!" Bart commanded.

Rieman's horn signaled the outriders to hold their positions and the King's Guard to keep close ranks. The men fell into formation and rode for an hour, hound free.

Their horses sensed the danger before the hounds became visible. Warrior snorted a warning. The guard's mounts pricked up their ears, caught the terrifying scent, and fought against the riders. Sylvia quickened the pace to a trot.

By mid-morning the horrhounds appeared. The huge black, tan, and white dogs loped along both sides of the column most of them staying out of arrow range.

"Good that Metrox insisted that Nightwind be trained to carry an archer," Bart muttered as he twisted his mare's reins around the saddle horn and lifted Metrox's bow off his back. A shadow crawled toward him through the brush. He pulled an arrow from his quiver and waited until the hound emerged from the undergrowth. He drew back on the string and released the arrow.

"Got him," he shouted as the snarling animal gave a sharp yip and collapsed.

For the remainder of the morning, aggressive hounds attempted to break past the bowmen but were forced to keep their distance because of the accuracy of the men's arrows.

It was well past noon when Fredren and his men merged with the King's Guard.

"Out of arrows," Fredren reported.

Bart and his men joined them minutes later. He raised his hands, bow in one hand, nothing in the other.

"The pack has increased in size," Metrox stated as he reined Warrior next to Bart. "I'd say we have at least thirty on our heels. That's not counting the ones we killed. Now, it's up to our horses. Orders, my Lord?"

"It's time to give Warrior his head. Let him help keep this group together."

Metrox nodded his face expressionless. "Ever see this horse in action under saddle? A quick prayer to the gods might give me the

146

ability to stay on him. I'll circle him around, give him the idea what I want, my Lord."

Bart raised his eyes to the sky and muttered, "may all the Gods in heaven protect us." He returned Metrox's salute and rode to the head of the line. "Sylvia, we are almost home. No more than an hour or two until Megara. Try a canter, put a little space between us and the hounds." He paused. "When you sense the need to increase our speed, do it. Don't wait for my orders. One more thing. Don't be surprised if Metrox takes the lead occasionally."

"Heaven help Captain Metrox," Sylvia said. "You're just ordered him into a deadly position. If he's thrown off Warrior, he's dog food."

"Enough. Sylvia, listen closely. We will approach a covered bridge soon. Delmarthian mounts aren't trained to cross wooden bridges. The thunder caused by hooves beating against the wood may spook our horses to the point that they'd rather be horrhound food than charge across that bridge. Our custom is to dismount and walk our steeds over it."

"While being chased by hungry horrhounds, we're supposed to dismount and — "

"Sylvia, I said 'listen.' When you see the bridge, bear left along the stream. You'll find a cattle crossing not far from the bridge. Use it." Bart glanced at his men surprised to see everyone mounted and ready to ride. "Look sharp," he shouted. "Move out."

Bart rode Nightwind beside the column paying close attention to the side of the road. *Hope none of those devils are on that trail that we used sometimes in the summer when visiting Megara. It intercepts us somewhere near here. Don't need an attack from the side. There it is. Good. All clear.* He glimpsed the city perched on the hill. *Only a mile to go.*

A spine chilling howl split the air. The hounds that had been harassing the guard drew back and answered. Sylvia urged her mare into a gallop.

As the guard neared the bridge, Metrox raced Warrior toward the front of the line along the right side of the guardsmen.

Sylvia's mount showed no desire to cross the bridge. Her mare skidded to a halt and reared in protest to all commands.

The guard's horses bunched up behind her as the girl fought to regained control of her horse.

Warrior's white head, ears flattened, teeth barred, loomed beside her. His long flat teeth racked Sylvia's mare's red-brown neck convincing the horse that galloping along the bank of the stream was the desirable direction to travel. Most of the formation followed.

Some of the King's Guard headed toward the bridge, but veered when they saw Warrior demonstrating an unthought-of use of a piaffe. The stallion bared the bridge trotting in one spot. Metrox sat on the prancing horse, his spear in his hand ready to use it on the first man who tried to pass him.

"Good job!" Bart, the last rider in the troop, yelled. "Come on!"

Howls of thirty wild dogs filled the air. They surged into sight.

Metrox urged Warrior to close the gap between him and Bart. As he reached Bart's side, the two horses splashed through the stream and caught up to the guard.

A few dogs attempted the bridge, falling on the slippery boards; the rest tore along the stream after the men. The dogs easily forded the river.

Rieman pressed his horn to his lips and the distress call pealed through the air. Horns on the city's wall answered, summoning archers to their positions.

Warrior wailed a sound no one had ever heard a horse utter before.

Sylvia allowed her horse to leap forward across the flatlands and up the hill toward the city gates. Several riders astride faster horses than Levine's mare galloped ahead of her.

Bart held Nightwind back. His mare could have easily been the first horse into the city, but his place was in the rear where danger threatened.

Rieman, leaned close to his gelding's neck whose eyes rolled in terror and raced by spattering a shower of mud.

148

"Ride you fool," Metrox yelled to Bart. "Out of my way!" The Delmarthian Captain of the Guard no longer attempted to control Warrior.

The stallion raged a running battle with the hounds. His teeth raked the neck of one black and tan cur who tried to bite his nose.

The hound yelped and fell back, then renewed the attack by leaping at Warrior's flank.

The horse screamed and lashed out with his hind legs.

The lead dog fell to the ground with an agonized yelp.

Warrior sprang away and stretched out into his fastest gallop. As he reached Nightwind's side he barred his teeth and nipped her neck.

The mare squealed, grabbed the bit and raced toward the city gate.

The hounds paused to sniff their fallen leader. An immense black hound bounded into the center of the milling dogs and growled. Every canine head swung in his direction. Dog after dog dropped their eyes before the black's challenge. The black hound howled once more and leaped after the horses. The pack tore after him.

Again the hounds gained on the horsemen. The leaders nipped at Warrior and Nightwind's heels, but now the last two riders were within range of the Megaran archers. A shower of arrows flew past them.

Hope those guys know how to shoot. Bart instinctually flattened himself on Nightwind's neck as an arrow whistled close to his ear. The shift of his weight broke his mount's gait; she stumbled, slipped on the wet ground and went down. She regained her feet in a second, but Bart was no longer on top of her.

Metrox roared the Delmarthian war cry, pulling Warrior around. The stallion wheeled back to challenge the oncoming hounds.

A tan hound leaped on top of Bart reeling him back on the ground preventing him from gaining his feet. Horrendous jaws armed with long white fangs sought his throat.

149

Warrior joined the fray, his front hooves crushing the dog's skull. Bart rolled out from under the rearing horse and caught Metrox's hand as the stallion landed on four feet.

Metrox yanked him up in front of him.

Warrior gave Bart no chance of gaining a seat. The stallion whirled toward the city. His long strides quickly overtook the riderless Nightwind.

Bart closed his eyes helpless while being held like a sack of grain, his head hanging on one side of the horse, his feet dangling on the other. Metrox tightly gripped his belt.

The archers' accuracy increased as the dogs neared the city wall. Hound after hound fell to the ground. Still the others advanced, crazed by the lost of a meal.

Warrior drove Nightwind through the open gates which were swung shut by guardsmen, but not before the black lead dog evaded the men and dodged into the city. Nightwind galloped into the square, but Warrior wheeled to face the dog.

Metrox jumped from the saddle, supporting Bart. The two men fell to the ground behind the stallion.

"Let me go, I'm fine." Bart gasped struggling to his feet. He backed away from Warrior. *Feel dizzy.*

The hound yelped his death cry as he fell under the stallion's pounding hooves.

Sedrac caught Bart's arm and steadied him. His dust covered, mud splattered second in command showed no evidence of being the nephew of one of the richest men in the land.

Bart managed a grin. "I'm all right, Sedrac. Just need to sit a while. Your orders are to get to the palace before Sylvia. Quarter our barbarian princess with Alisha and Luciana. Remind them she is under the king's sword."

"Yes, sir." Before Sedrac disappeared into the mass confusion, he ordered a convenient guardsman to Bart's side.

Warrior reared and pounded the hound one last time, then whirled as Metrox whistled.

The horse whinnied and permitted Metrox to catch hold of his bridle and lead him to the stables.

Chapter 19

Sylvia awoke to the monotonous clanging of city bells rung every morning to command the Megaran population to crawl out of bed and start a new day. As the bells ceased, masculine and feminine Danian chatter mixed with hurried footsteps echoed from the hallway outside her room.

"Where am I? Oh yes, the palace— safe from horrhounds, but surrounded by Danians. What are they going to with me?" The sound of her own language gave her courage. She hugged her pillow.

"How wonderful it is to lie in a real bed after sleeping on the cold sloppy ground for the last few nights." She yawned as she stretched. Crinkled scratchy bed linen irritated her limbs. The soft fur robe lay uselessly beneath her shoulders but somewhere rumpled near her side. *I'm not dressed.* She cringed as she felt a dungeon door creak open on the floor of her stomach. *Where are my clothes?* Tight fingers gripped her covers in an attempt to maintain decency. "No one's here," she reassured herself. "Creepy, waking up in a strange potentially hostile bedroom."

She sighed and opened her eyes. "Mother sewed quilts like this, one from scraps of material stitched together. Never seen such gorgeous crimson wall coverings." *Hello? Company!*

A slender Danian girl sat next to the window doing needlework with colored threads, taking advantage of the daylight. She pushed her straight black hair out of her eyes, frowned and stabbed the needle into the cloth.

"Bother!" she said and stood up, her soft yellow skirt flowed around her ankles. She placed her work on the table next to Sylvia. "Oh," she exclaimed, "I'm sorry, I hope I didn't wake you."

"No," Sylvia mumbled. "What happened to my clothes?"

The girl smiled shyly. "Welcome to the palace of the King. I'm Lady Luciana. I'm glad you're awake." She clapped her hands and a servant came to the door. "Is the dress finished?"

"Yes, my Lady." The maid curtsied and left the room. She returned with a dress of light blue wool and laid it on the chair next to the window.

Luciana dismissed her with a wave of her hand. "This color should match your eyes," she said to Sylvia. "The dress is one of Alisha's. You'll have to try it on. Hopefully, the alterations are correct. We worked late last night to restyle and resize it. I hope it fits."

"I'm not Danian," Sylvia protested as she struggled to a sitting position clasping the scratchy bed linen to her neck. "Why should I dress like one?"

Luciana giggled. "You can't wear those filthy pants and stained tunic here. Our people would shun you."

"Why should what I wear matter?"

Luciana shrugged. "I don't know. It just does. You have to be like my sister, Alisha, to get away with overlooking conventions. She knows exactly how far to go and when to stop. When you've had something to eat, we'll fix your hair."

152

"My hair! What's wrong with my hair?" Sylvia's hand flew up to touch it, the linen fell to her waist. "You're not going to dye it black, are you?"

Luciana smiled. "No, of course not. We'll just tame it a little. Come on; dress. Cousin Sedrac will arrive soon. He desires to speak with us." She clapped her hands and her maid reappeared. "Everything you require is right here. Mara will assist you."

"I can dress myself," Sylvia blurted, about to send Mara away. She looked at the pile of garments on the chair. "Good heavens, does one person wear all these clothes?"

Luciana rolled her eyes and shrugged, her face puckered into a frown. She gathered up her full skirts and hurried out of the apartment.

What a strange girl, Sylvia thought as she picked through the pile of clothing. "Does the white dress go over or under the blue one? How do those long stockings stay up? Ooh, I guess I could use some help."

***

Feeling horribly awkward in her unfamiliar heavy clothing and heeled shoes with pointy toes, Sylvia teetered into the next room. It was comfortably furnished with cushions on the benches, and even a couple of chairs. Luciana sat at the table near the fireplace. Two maids were placing food in front of her.

"Come and eat." The Danian girl motioned to a seat opposite her. "You must be famished."

"Bread takes the place of plates?" Sylvia stared aghast at the meat, and hard-boiled eggs arranged on a cake-sized slab of bread sitting directly on the sandy colored hardwood table. "Danians are more barbaric than the prairie-men told us. How on earth do I eat that without a fork? Surely you eat the chicken and eggs first and then the bread."

"Sit down, my lady. What's wrong?" Luciana gaped at her.

"No forks. How do you eat your food without a fork?" Sylvia plucked a spoon from near the middle of the table and slid it under the eggs. They wobbled, shivered, and then plopped back onto the slice of bread. "I thought everyone used forks. The sons of Bromwell did when they ate at our house. Maybe that's why Mother valued her forks so much. She counted them after every meal. Maybe owning forks is something special, rather than something commonplace."

"We manage very well without whatever you are talking about," Luciana said as she cut her bread in small squares, each one supporting part of the meal.

"Aha, they're supposed to be eaten like a sandwich without a top. At least the milk is served in a cup." Sylvia sipped her milk and cut the bread into four pieces. "Oh, don't mind me," she added noticing Luciana's puzzled expression. "I'm so glad to be here. I'll never use a stupid sidesaddle again. Horrhounds. What a nightmare." Sylvia took a big bite of her sandwich. "Thank the Lord for Buris. I never thought I'd be so relieved to see that paint gelding. What a well-trained horse. I understand Bart dislikes that man, but Buris sure knows how to ride through a crowd."

Luciana set her cup on the table with a thump, glared at Sylvia with wide eyes. She leaned across the table and snatched the spoon. Her dainty hands wiped it with a cloth napkin and sank it into a cup full of honey.

"Oh, so I wasn't supposed to use the spoon either. Oops... Well never mind. As I was saying, Rieman's sword insisted those ruffians keep their distance until Buris caught my mare's bridle." Sylvia chewed as her words rattled from her throat. "Then he and Buris rode alongside me, up and up. We climbed and climbed until we clattered across a bridge into the palace."

"My lady, it is impolite to cut such big pieces."

"I'm so hungry and my method is easier than using two fingers like you're doing." Sylvia swallowed, took another bite and continued. "Well anyway, inside this dark cold palace my legs felt like jelly. Those people! Unbelievable how unfriendly they are. I was so glad of Rieman's arm as we staggered into the biggest room I ever saw. Buris led the way. He must be important because the people we met stepped aside so we could pass. Oh, pardon me, I must be babbling. I don't usually run on like this."

Luciana forced a smile. "You've been though a lot, my lady; I can't imagine."

Sylvia sipped her milk. "I fell asleep as soon as my head hit the pillow." She swallowed the last of her bread. "Never enjoyed a breakfast like this before. I really liked it. What's going to happen to me now?"

"We're finished with breakfast. Come with me." Luciana led Sylvia into another bedroom. "Sit here," she said, indicating a cushioned bench. "My maids will fix your hair."

"I can comb my own hair," Sylvia protested. "No one has brushed my hair since I was ten and old enough to take care of it myself."

"You're in Megara now; our maids always style our hair in the morning."

"Oh. Sort-a like Bart, the first time he stayed at our cabin. You can't believe how he protested caring for his horse."

Luciana wrinkled up her nose. "Bart always tends his horse. So does Lord Bromwell. You're sprouting nonsense."

"I'm sorry. It's just that everything is so strange."

Fascinated by Sylvia's blond hair, the maids had a lengthy discussion of how to style it. They took turns running their fingers through it, yanking it one way or another.

When Mara took three strands and started to braid, Sylvia wanted to cry. "What are you doing to me? Mother braided her hair and wound it tightly around her head. Old people wear their hair that way, not someone who is fourteen."

"Hush. Let me finish," Maria said. She continued braiding. At last she stood back and surveyed Sylvia with a smile. "That's better. Look in the mirror."

Relief flowed over Sylvia as she gazed into the glass. "That can't be me. Never thought of fixing my hair like this. What a marvelous idea. Braiding my hair using only the front strands keeps it from falling into my face." She spun slightly so she could see a side view. "I love the way my hair flows over my shoulders." She twirled around. "Wish I could see my back."

Luciana's jaw dropped. "You've never seen a mirror before?"

"Oh yes, but I was very small when my big brothers crashed into it while wrestling."

Sylvia peered down and raised her skirts slightly. "How on earth will I ever walk in these pointed toed shoes?" She caught Luciana's reflection behind her and noted the smirk on the Danian girl's face. "You find me amusing, I suppose."

Sedrac strode into the apartment. He was off duty for he wore a short gold brocaded cape over his forest green tunic and stockings, causing him to appear slimmer than he had in his uniform. The top of his soft tan leather boots reached his knee. A silver headband held his black wavy hair in place which freely hung over his shoulders softening his double chins. He strutted by Sylvia as if she didn't exist. He greeted Luciana with a low bow, and then kissed her hand, pivoted back toward Sylvia and bowed slightly.

Sylvia's heart pounded wildly as he stuck out a chubby hand and puckered his lips. *Disgusting!* She quickly darted away from him and hid both hands behind her back.

His expression darkened. "You got her looking fit for the ballroom," he said to Luciana, "now you need to teach her some manners."

Chapter 20

"Manners indeed," Sylvia snapped.

Happy voices reverberated down the corridor outside the apartment walls as Sedrac, Luciana and Sylvia locked eyes.

Alisha's giggles floated through the hallway into the room. "It's gorgeous, Lord Robo. Thank you so much for the ring. I'll wear it tonight at the dance."

"You honor me, my Lady," Robo answered. "Your beauty will remain in my memory until I feast my eyes on you again." His heavy footsteps continued down the hall.

"My Lord Robo, one minute please." The squeaky masculine voice sounded like he was short of breath from running up the stairs.

"Gilmore, the wizard's apprentice and Robo, Ambassador from Chaleen," Sedrac muttered. "What are those two up to now?" He pivoted toward the door as Alisha burst into the room, her red skirts swirling around her ankles, her long black curls flying behind her. He glared at her as he bowed and kissed her hand. "And where have you been my sweet lady? I don't approve of your escort."

Alisha curtsied. Laughter filled her eyes as she teased, "wandering through the halls dreaming about the wonderful lord who someday will carry me away to his own palace. And then Cousin, the noble Lord Robo appeared out of nowhere to present me with this breathtaking ring." She wrinkled her pug nose. "I enjoy his favor, but he isn't the man I dream about." Alisha spun graciously toward Sylvia. "Ah, my Barbarian Princess, you're awake. Did you enjoy breakfast?"

"Enough of your foolishness, Alisha." Sedrac scowled at the girls. "Dismiss your maids. I need to enlist your assistance."

When they were alone, Alisha said, "you mentioned that yesterday. I wondered what the noble Sedrac, nephew of one of the most powerful lords in the land, could possibly want of me."

Sedrac bowed. "Your woman's charms, Alisha. There isn't a man in the palace who isn't enthralled by you."

Alisha frowned as she smoothed out a wrinkle in her dress. "Don't forget Father's lands."

"Yes, that helps, but that's not what's involved here." Sedrac became quiet for a moment, staring into the fire. "What I want you to do is dangerous, my cousin. I doubt if I should involve you in this. Maybe I should hash it over with Bart, Son of Bromwell first. After all he is captain."

"It's about the gunpowder," Sylvia said.

Sedrac whirled and faced her, his heavy features glazed with horror. "Is that what you call the weapon that destroys stone walls?"

Sylvia nodded.

"Then the less you speak about that the better, my Lady."

It wasn't the words so much as the tone Sedrac used that bothered Sylvia. "Now, what's wrong? I didn't insult you, or call you names."

"Cousin, perhaps you had better tell us what this is about," Luciana said.

158

Sedrac nodded as he reached out toward both sisters and drew them close to him. "Know you that I bound myself to serve Captain Menes of Delmarath," he said quietly.

"But Sedrac," Luciana said as she stepped away from him. "He can't be of a great house. This is the first time we have heard that name."

"He's not, but sometimes circumstances force the unspeakable." Sedrac stared at the cold stone floor.

Alisha draped her slender arm around his waist as if this was a matter that she should feel sorry about. "I'm sure you had a good reason," she said soothingly.

"Oh, for heavens sakes," Sylvia said. "You make the simple so complicated. Prairie-men have acquired what we call gunpowder, what the Lords of Delmarath call the black death and we need to stop them."

As he looked up in astonishment, a spasm of irritation crossed Sedrac's face. He rotated out of Alisha's arm towards Sylvia. "No woman interrupts me." He slapped her cheek.

Sylvia slipped her foot between his legs and threw him to the floor. It was a trick she had learned from wrestling with her brothers and the heeled pointed toe shoes weren't as troublesome as she had thought.

Alisha laughed.

Sedrac leaped to his feet, his face contorted with rage, his golden cape askew.

Luciana slipped in front of Sylvia. "Easy, Cousin," she said softly. "Calm down."

"Luciana, you enjoy living dangerously," Sedrac bellowed. "I almost struck you." He glowered at Sylvia. "I never conceived any woman perpetuating such anger. You act just like a man."

"How am I acting like a man?" Sylvia asked, bewildered.

Luciana turned to Sylvia. "My sweet Barbarian Princess, you should have permitted Lord Sedrac to finish what he was saying. Danian women never interrupt a man when he speaks."

"Why? He never gets to the point."

159

Alisha smiled. "Danian women don't throw a man flat on his back, even if they are slapped."

Sylvia placed her hands on her hips. "No man slaps me and gets away with it."

Sedrac bowed, struggling to regain his composure. "I'll keep that in mind," he said coldly. "Finish your story. You probably know more about this than I do."

Sylvia retreated to a padded bench on the opposite side of the room and took a couple of deep breaths to calm herself. "Reig, a storyteller from the prairies, gave Metrox, the captain of the Delmarthian guard a map he found on the prairie drawn on Danian parchment. It showed every landmark from Kans to Megara including the Citherian Mountains except for one thing— the Gap of Sistra. We all rode that trail. It's a wonderful place for an ambush."

"What could a woman know about ambushes?" Sedrac ground out the words between clamped teeth.

"I'm not stupid," Sylvia sputtered as she jumped to her feet. "It doesn't take any brains to ride though that gap and figure that one out."

Sedrac clenched his fist as he muttered peevishly under his breath.

Alisha laid her hand on Sedrac's arm. "I'm confused. Everyone uses parchment," she said calmly. "What's so unusual about parchment?"

"Not on the prairie," Sylvia retorted. "The prairie-men neither read nor write. Reig says that a Lord of Dana somehow got the powder and gave it to the prairie-men, so they can destroy Delmarath and be destroyed in turn at the gap of Sistra just like in the old story."

"Reig— Reig, he's our primary informant? How could any barbarian be so credible that the King's Personal Guard should tear apart the kingdom searching for a possible traitor? Prairie-men are animals." Sedrac shoved Alisha's hand away and turned toward the mirror and straightened his cape.

Sylvia stared at the back of his gold brocaded cape . *Reig dared to stand up to Metrox. He fought to save Maris from execution. He's so*

160

kind. "I should have hurt you, you obnoxious Danian instead of merely tripping you. A good kick in your ribs would be extremely satisfying." She bit her tongue. "I'd guess you have never met a prairie-man," she added stiffly.

"Sedrac, Sedrac," Alisha said shaking her finger at him. "This is getting us nowhere. Sylvia's not Danian. Why on earth would you expect her to act like one of us? Now what is the purpose of your visit?"

"I was about to tell you when I was so rudely interrupted," Sedrac stewed as he faced the girls.

"Sedrac," Alisha admonished. "Calm down. You're like a stallion in the palace kitchen. Sylvia, please refrain from saying anything else unless one of us asks you a direct question. You fluster Sedrac. Let's sit down over here by the fire and chat about this reasonably."

No one budged.

"I'm wasting my breath," Alisha muttered as she turned away. "Oh!"

Bart, dressed in his official brown and green captain's uniform leaned against the door watching them.

"Sylvia, Sylvia, sweet daughter of the forest," Bart spoke in Citherian as he sauntered over to Sylvia and laid his hands on her shoulders. "Little Sister, please sit down and try to be reasonable."

"Reasonable? I am reasonable," Sylvia declared in the same language. "It's those Danians who are unreasonable. Just look at them. That Sedrac acts like a puffed up rooster and those girls act like I'm something out of the Great Swamp. What's wrong with them? Why are they looking at us like that?"

"They have never heard me speak your language," Bart answered softly. "It never occurred to any of them that people exist in this world who do not speak Danian." He smiled at her and took her hand. "Come on, be a good girl. Sit over here." He led her to a chair by the fire.

"Lance, when can I see Lance?" Sylvia asked as she complied. "Now would be fine," she pleaded. "If I were with Lance, I wouldn't have to deal with these ridiculous Danians."

161

"Lance almost didn't make it," Bart said soberly. "He's going to be all right, but he's very weak and is sleeping now. You will have to wait for the King's permission."

"You're sure he's going to be all right," Sylvia clutched Bart's arm. "We left for Megara right after I felt something terrible had happened to my brother."

Bart nodded. "He's doing fine."

Alisha planted herself between them, her dark eyes blazing. "Captain," she protested, "how dare you wander into my quarters without announcing your presence? What kind of gibberish are you speaking? What are you doing here?"

Bart stepped back, glanced around the room and said in Danian, "I come in my official capacity as Captain of the King's Guard to inquire about the welfare of Megara's newest visitor."

"Well, that's no excuse for not knocking." Alisha's red lips curled into a pout as she pointed toward the door. "Go away. No one invited you."

"Alisha," Sedrac exclaimed as he caught her arm. "You can't order the King's Captain of the Personal Guard to leave. He has the authority to enter any room uninvited." Sedrac peered down at her. "This barbarian's manners must be affecting your wits."

"They are so stupid. The things they think important are ridiculous," Sylvia said in Citherian.

"And they think you are impossible." Bart smiled at her, again speaking in her language. "Little Sister, I know how you feel. I guess you were too young to realize what I went through when my father brought me to Delmarath from Chaleen."

"Captain," Alisha snapped, "how dare you talk in a language I don't understand. How rude! Is she telling you how terrible we treat her?"

Bart winced as he switched back into Danian. "Of course you don't understand our ways, Sylvia. Pleasantries before important conversation are expected in Megara." He turned to the others. "Sit down everyone, please."

Alisha flounced over to a bench, spread her red skirt over its surface as she sat. Luciana lifted her yellow skirts and daintily arranged the material so that it hung gracefully around her stool. Sedrac stepped outside the room and shouted some muffled orders to his attendants and then returned.

"I'm hoping we can put aside our differences so we can work together to save Delmarath," Bart said. "We are ensnared in something that outweighs our birthplaces. I assure you, more evidence than the mere word of a barbarian initiated the protective measures we're engaged in to serve our King. Somehow we must rescue Delmarath from the prairie-men and their new weapon. The consequences of the fall of my brother's city could eradicate Cadamire from the throne. We need to determine who is responsible and work out a way to terminate this madness."

"Captain," Sedrac frowned. "How long have you been in this room?"

Bart grinned. "Long enough to see you pick yourself off the floor. Believe me, it was a pleasure."

Sedrac stiffened.

"Sit down, Sedrac," Bart ordered. "Now that all these preliminaries have been taken care of, let's get down to business. Sedrac, you said you had some ideas of how to gather information utilizing the girls."

"Utilizing?" Alisha flushed as she leaped to her feet. "Captain, no one utilizes me."

"Guardsmen's term, Alisha." Bart looked at her seriously. "If you aid us, you will be stepping into a different world, almost as different for you as being in the palace is for Sylvia. Sedrac?"

"I mentioned a pledge I gave to Captain Menes of Delmarath," Sedrac said. "My mission and that of Captain Bart is to ferret out information about this powder. We suspect the involvement of a Danian Lord, but we have no idea if this is true or who it could be." He drummed his fingers on the arm of his chair. "While looking over possible candidates, Conder came to my mind. He has access to the border and could gain the throne."

Bart's dark eyes narrowed with contempt. "Not Conder. I would never question his loyalty."

163

"Nor would I," Sedrac agreed easily. "Allow me to finish, Captain."

Bart nodded and sat next to Sylvia.

Sedrac spoke resentfully as he eyed Sylvia. "I was counting on presenting this barbarian princess at the first ball of the Winter Festival three days hence, but I see now this is impossible."

Bart rubbed his pointed chin as he suddenly found something fascinating to look at on Alisha's ceiling. "Sylvia will have a hard time with this, harder than she did riding sidesaddle."

"Her presence on the dance floor will loosen people's tongues," Sedrac explained. "We have so little information. Anyone in the palace could be involved, but we can't go about asking people if they're committing treason. However, with everyone chatting about the barbarians in our palace, we might be able to pick up some leads and narrow the field."

"Good idea, but —" Bart looked at Sylvia.

Alisha smiled frostily and folded her hands on her lap. "Why is it impossible, my Lords? Do you really suppose we are incapable of teaching this young lady everything she needs to comprehend so she can survive the dance floor?" She glared at Sedrac. "Really, Cousin, you underestimate us."

Sylvia caught her breath. "No, no, no. I don't want to do this. Is it necessary?" She turned to Bart. "Lance will speak about the powder on the Knife of Truth. Isn't that enough?"

"Perhaps, if he knows enough. Could he identify the map before the King?" Sedrac asked.

Sylvia sank back into her seat and shook her head.

"That's why you must be at that dance." Sedrac glared at Sylvia. "You, with your strangely colored hair, and your rude manners are already the topic of private conversation. It'll provide Alisha an opportunity to gather information. And once open dialogue starts about current happenings," he bowed to Alisha, "my beautiful cousin is an expert at extracting details from the men that surround her." He looked at Sylvia blankly, shaking his head. "I don't know how to make it any clearer."

"I suppose I could try," Sylvia offered.

164

"I need you to succeed, Sylvia," Bart said. "Any lord who would stoop so low as to sacrifice an entire city to his ambitions must be stopped."

"Alisha, Luciana, teach this barbarian princess some manners," Sedrac ordered. He yelled some command to his men as he stormed out of the room. Bart bowed to the girls and followed him.

The three girls looked at each other. "Now what is wrong with my manners?" Sylvia asked.

Alisha laughed. "My dear child, five minutes at the ball, you'll have everyone so angry that I'll never be able to find out what Sedrac needs to learn. Comprehend this — you know nothing about this affair. No one will expect you to know anything about it. No woman in Dana would have such knowledge. Do you understand?"

"Yes, yes, I understand," Sylvia said. "No woman should be so ignorant, but I'll go along with it. In other words, you want me to make a fool of myself."

"No one is going to expect perfection," Alisha said as she glided toward Sylvia and smiled encouragingly. "We need to teach you enough that your mistakes will amuse people, not create a disaster. Are you game for this adventure?"

Sylvia stood looking gravely into Alisha's dark eyes. "If I can't talk about what's happening in Delmarath, what do I talk about?"

"The latest gossip, who's going to marry whom. You spend your time inventing compliments."

"Good heavens." Sylvia shook her head. "I don't know any of those things."

"You curtsy," Alisha said, "smile a lot, answer questions if they are not too personal. You can always pretend not to understand our language, if you feel people are being too inquisitive."

"We have no idea how you'll be received," Luciana said.

"How I'll be received?" Sylvia gasped. "What do you mean? Will your people throw stones at me if they don't want me at this silly dance?"

"Of course not. We're civilized people. I only meant that they may not dance with you." Luciana frowned. "Do people throw stones at each other from where you come from?"

"I lived in the mountains with my parents and three brothers," Sylvia moaned. "Until now, I have never been inside a Danian city. I've never had any reason to dance. I don't know how to talk to you people. Everything I say seems to make you angry." She sat trying to hide the tear that burned her cheek.

"Tonight, we will watch," Luciana said as she handed Sylvia a handkerchief. "I have a secret place where we can see and not be seen. You'll see, it's not so bad." She smiled. "Come on now, let's try a curtsy."

Chapter 21

The loathing of the healers who obeyed Bromwell's every command, quickly, efficiently, without compassion, jolted Lance in and out of consciousness, sometimes burning up with fever, sometimes shaking from cold. Lord Bromwell's powerful steady presence in the room offered security, a sanctuary where he could rest safely. Once he remembered waking to see Betren's dark eyes, felt Betren's concern as he relaxed his hand on Lance's shoulder.

Lance missed Sylvia, wanted to see her. He sent his thoughts out to her then realized she was neither at the cabin nor in Delmarath, but somewhere nearer.

Then one morning, he woke to see Metrox standing beside his bed. The healers' revulsion no longer saturated the room. Instead Delmarthian Guardsmen surrounded him. He welcomed their indifference. "Metrox, what are you doing here? Where are the healers?"

Metrox grinned. "Me? I'm here at the order of the King. The healers— well... I hear they have some unpleasant business to discuss with His Majesty. Nothing for you to worry about." He snapped his fingers and a guard approached with a mug of broth. Metrox propped Lance up with some pillows. "Now drink this. We're going to get you well."

"Is that an order of the King?"

"Well, he didn't say it in so many words, but you've caused me too many headaches to let you die. Drink."

Lance took the mug and drank. The hearty fire near his bed warmed the cushion beneath him. The plain wood chairs sat vacant under matching tables. Guardsmen dressed in black with red capes stood at attention on both sides of the heavy oak door. "I thought Lord Bromwell was at my bedside and I remember Bet."

"They're resting," Metrox said, "up in Lord Bromwell's quarters. They spent the last few weeks taking turns watching over you and keeping those excuses for healers in order."

"Sylvia?"

"She's in the palace. She accompanied me. Sooner or later, they'll allow her to visit. Oh yes, I rode Warrior here. He's in the King's stable."

"They'll take good care of him?"

"The best. I'll see to it myself."

Lance sighed in relief. "Thank you," he whispered, "thank you."

Metrox stripped off Lance's coverings, stepped back and surveyed the Citherian as if he were a newly purchased horse. "Betren must have been a little rough with you. Nasty bruise on your shoulder. Scrapes and cuts from your fall seem to be healing. How long have you been off your feet?"

"I— I've been in bed since I came." Lance closed his eyes, trying to remember. "I doubt I can stand. Besides, I heard the healers say that I should stay in bed until I felt better."

"Imbeciles," Metrox growled. "Don't they know a man's muscles weaken if they're unused? Or was that their point? We'll get you on your feet today."

"But my arm," Lance protested.

168

"We'll keep it in a sling, and I'll examine what's under that bandage. I've been told that you received an arrow in your back."

"The healers hate me. Hated to touch me. They wanted to let me die."

"I know." Metrox sympathized as he pulled the blankets back over Lance. "But what do you expect from Megarans? They never seen anyone like you except in their worst nightmares."

Lance twisted away. "I shouldn't have come," he whispered. "I'm nothing but trouble for everyone."

"You're wrong, Lance," Betren said, stepping to Metrox's side. "If you weren't with me, nothing would be done to stop the destruction of Delmarath. No one would believe a barbarian threat possible."

"My Lord, how long have you been here?" Metrox stepped back, snapped to attention and saluted.

"Only a few minutes, Captain." Betren returned the salute and smiled. "For some odd reason the guard at the door recognized me and let me pass. Didn't expect men in Delmarthian uniforms."

"Last time they'll permit anyone into this room without warning," Metrox growled.

"Oh, don't punish them," Betren said. "They expect me to wander where I please in the Delmarthian Hall of Justice without any fanfare. You haven't addressed my question: What are my Delmarthians doing here?"

"King's order. The Great King Cadamire decided Lance would gain a better chance of healing if he wasn't surrounded by men who find it impossible to cope with a barbarian."

"And somehow the King has come to the conclusion that you are involved in this business concerning Lance," Betren said soberly. "I hoped you would escape the Knife."

Lance winced. *I called for him? The King overheard me. It's my fault Metrox is in trouble.*

"Perhaps it's my destiny, my Lord. I pledged my life to you. I'd go mad if I remained in Delmarath after Sylvia swore you were in grave danger, and we needed to act. You orders — remember, my Lord? At least I can be some use here."

169

"So who did you leave in charge of my city?"

"Evander, my Lord. He has the most experience."

Of course. Evander. Remember hearing first-year guardsmen praising him in the marketplace. Everyone liked him.

"I ordered him to close the eastern gates and allow no one inside except you or Lord Bromwell, or of course the King."

"That could look like an act of aggression, my friend, explain."

"The good old Right to Rule Law. We don't have a loosely formed guard in Delmarath, we have a well-trained army. No lord with treason on his mind needs to acquire them. Evander can handle this or any other emergency that arises."

"Right to Rule Law," Lance muttered. "That's the law Conder used as an excuse to destroy me and my family."

"Understood," Betren ignored Lances outburst and answered Metrox. "He would be my choice. Menes?"

"The Eastern Outpost. With orders to spy out whatever is known in the neighboring cities about anything remotely connected with a certain black powder."

"With his love of detail, he should excel at that assignment. And Maris?"

"I have no son named Maris."

Lance's muscles tightened. *Something happened to him. Metrox's pain cuts right through me.*

Betren touched his captain's arm. "Whenever you are ready to talk about that one, I'll listen. Preferably in a more private place."

Metrox nodded briefly. "Thank you, my Lord."

"Rumor has it, you experienced difficulty with horrhounds," Betren remarked. "The people I've seen speak of nothing else."

"Horrhounds," Lance wailed. "Bart wasn't the only one who had trouble with those monsters."

Metrox, face expressionless, continued to converse with Betren as if both men had forgotten Lance was in the same room. "A little, my Lord, those hounds trailed us for three days. You can be proud of your brother. Bart handled the situation well."

"With you along, he should have won an easy victory."

Metrox shook his head, his eyes full of pride. "He handled it himself. I was there for him in case of an emergency which never developed. He's doing well, maturing into the kind of man I thought he was capable of becoming."

Lance's stomach did a somersault. *Oh, something's wrong between Bet and Bart. I suppose it is something I did. That's why they're ignoring me.*

Metrox studied Betren's stony face and drew a deep breath. "Fine, just fine," he said. "Keep up that attitude, Son of Bromwell and you're sliding off a slippery precipice. If you allow the Knife to divide the house of Bartran, none of us will survive."

Lance closed his eyes. *These men are from another world, one where I don't belong. Strange, it's taken me so long to realize that. Where do I fit in? Not on the prairies, stealing the powder closed that door. My beloved mountains? The brand on my forehead leaves that impossible. Not unless I want to live like a hunted animal.* "If I survive the knife, where will I go?" He muttered to himself as he tried to roll on his side. Unfortunately his broken arm prevented him from easy movement.

"Lance." Betren sat on the bed. "Talk to me, my friend."

Lance sighed. "Oh, I guess I'm just feeling sorry for myself."

"Worried about the Knife?"

"No, somehow I don't think I'll have a problem with that. It's just that..."

"Go on."

"It's just that when we are finished here, what do I do? Where will Sylvia and I live? I have no country that I know of. I have no place where I can call home. You can't possibly know what that feels like." He turned his head toward the wall and closed his eyes.

"No, I don't." Betren laid his hand on Lance's good arm. "You're right, and I have no answers. It's something that will require thought."

Lance stared up at his friend. "Bet? What is it? You look worried."

"I'm worried. You are falling into a common trap of the Knife. Even entertaining the idea of speaking on that weapon causes a man to look inwards, twists his mind to ordeals which have no

171

bearing on why he requested to speak on it in the first place. Often men are so confused by the time the Knife is placed in their hand, they can only babble. The Knife quickly ends their misery."

"You mean thinking about the future could kill me?"

Betren smiled. "Only if you allow thoughts of what happens when we are finished here, consume you so you are unable to concentrate on anything else."

"One detail at a time, lad," Metrox agreed. "Unless you regain your strength, you have no future. So let's concentrate on getting well. When you are strong again, we take on the Knife of Truth. It's a strange weapon. Men who survive, often find their lives going in directions they never considered."

Lance relaxed. *They're my friends, even if they are Danians.* He smiled weakly. "All right. One day at a time. One thing, though. I don't ever want to see those healers again."

Metrox snorted. "No worry on that score, lad. No man ignores the King's commands and gets away with it. The healers won't bother you again. You'll—"

"Be quiet," Lance whispered.

The Danians glanced at each other and waited.

"Someone is coming for you, Bet."

"Friend or foe?"

"Neither. A messenger. I can't tell anything more."

The guard at the door challenged someone, then stepped inside. "An attendant of the House of Andros would speak with you, my Lord."

Betren nodded. "Let him enter."

Metrox's hand automatically found the hilt of his sword.

"I'm unarmed, my Lord," the man said, spreading his hands apart. In his right hand he held a carved little horse of cedar."

Chapter 22

Gilmore burst through the door into the wizard's customer service area, the stocky youth winded from the long fast climb up the narrow winding stairs which led to Talman's quarters.

"Master," he panted, "the Captain of the King's Guard is coming. Be careful. He's involved in some devilment. I don't know what yet. He spent the last hour with Lady Alisha and Luciana. That barbarian girl is quartered with them. Lord Sedrac was there too. His personal attendants guard the area."

"Well..." Talman said. "The King hasn't removed Bart from his position. He's still Captain. His business could be official. Remember that girl is under the King's sword." He laid down his quill and put the parchment he was working on away. He frowned. "Sedrac's personal attendants?"

"That's it exactly." Gilmore shook his head emphatically. "The King's Captain needs no special guard to see this Sylvia. What a strange name. And there's more."

Talman smiled. "Later, over a glass of wine, some bread and cheese." The wizard sat in his chair, his mind full of questions.

"Haven't seen much of the Younger Son of Bromwell. He's too busy cultivating the rich and famous to remember an old friend."

Gilmore's breathing slowed as he handed Talman his blue robe. "He's a climber, but he seems to have fallen off the ladder."

"Britches and tunic occasion, Gilmore. No reason for me to be involved with Bart's current disgrace." Talman pushed the robe away. "I have my position at court to consider." He laughed shortly. "I have no intention of becoming ex-wizard to the King."

"He's almost here," Gilmore said as he laid the robe on a box and straightened his dark brown tunic. "Should I open the door?"

"No, wait for the knock. No reason to make him feel welcomed."

"Is this to be a private audience?"

The wizard shook his head. "No, I desire a witness. Who knows how many eyes spied our less than noble captain climbing up here?" Talman straightened some stray pieces of parchment and pretended to be busy.

At the sound of the knock, Gilmore opened the door and bowed. "Welcome, Captain. We don't see much of you up here."

Bart acknowledged the greeting and faced Talman.

Gilmore closed the door and took his place beside the wizard.

"Well?" Talman felt annoyed. "What did I do to achieve this honor? Does the noble captain fancy a love potion?"

"I hoped, maybe we could talk." Bart glanced pointedly at Gilmore. "Alone."

"Alone?" Talman shook his head and folded his arms. "My Captain, as the King would say, this is as private as it gets."

"Gilmore, leave us," Bart commanded.

Gilmore stepped around a box of love potions and headed toward the door.

"Gilmore, stay where you are!" Talman counter-ordered.

Gilmore slid the box across the room and returned to his place beside the wizard.

"Gilmore, go," Bart laid his hand on his sword.

Gilmore eyed the wizard and waited.

"Gilmore, stay." Talman shoved back his chair as he rose to his feet. "How dare you order my servant, Captain! How dare you order me about in my own quarters! May I remind you that I out-rank you? Only the King is above me. I suggest you remember that little fact."

"My mistake." Bart dropped to his knee. "I'm sorry, Wizard. I assumed that you, at least, would be willing to speak to me. Forgive me for bothering you." He rose to his feet, not waiting for Talman to respond, and spun toward the door.

"Captain, stay." Talman returned to his chair. "The sons of Bromwell usually exhibit better manners."

Bart pivoted on his heel and faced Talman. The Captain of the King's Guard looked both angry and embarrassed: His face was flushed, his eyes narrowed, his lips drew tight.

"Why should I be delighted to see you here? I sense that the winds have changed since your brother brought that barbarian into the palace." Talman smiled. "I must tell you I'm fresh out of popularity pills."

Bart toyed with the eagle on his signet ring. "Really, Wizard, we were friends once. Not that it matters. Nothing you could do could restore what I've lost." He sighed. "The tragedy is much bigger than one family's position at court."

Talman glanced up at his servant who shook his head slightly. *Interesting. Gilmore has no knowledge of Bart's purpose here. Whatever is bothering the captain is a deep secret.* The wizard glared at Bart. "Come, Captain, I'm a busy man. What do you want?"

"Your quarters." Bart sat on the first available box.

Talman rose from his seat and pointed his open hand, fingers spread apart. "A curse on you, Captain. A curse on all unwelcome guests."

Bart held his position.

"What?" Talman exclaimed as he examined his hand critically and repeated the motion. "You do not fear my curse?"

"Wizard, what's one more curse to a man whose future will end in death on the wall in a few days?"

Talman squinted, curled his upper lip and put his hands on his hips. "I have no intention of relinquishing my living quarters, not even my shop to you or anyone else in this palace. It's the only place in the whole castle that lacks listening posts. There's nothing but solid stone wall around this tower and I like it that way. Even if it's a little chilly sometimes."

"Chilly? It's down right cold." Bart tugged his cloak around him. "It's the absence of listening posts that intrigues me."

"Oh, really." Talman plopped on his chair in disgust. "What wonderful treason are you involved in? If I let you meet here, I'm implicated. Thank you, but no thanks."

"That's what we need to chat about." Bart leaned forward. "Talman, I seem to recall that a short time ago, I caught the King's ear for you."

"True." Talman relaxed and folded his hands behind his head. "Still an inadequate reason for me to be involved in treason. Even my stellar regard for the House of Bartran isn't enough. You're not exactly a polished piece of goods, Captain. Your services have diminished in the last few days."

"Undoubtedly, all you say is true." Bart smiled ruefully. "But my past assistance with the King should be sufficient price for you to at least listen to what I have to say."

"All right, all right." Talman threw up his hands. "You have my ear, but Gilmore stays."

Bart negotiated his way around several large jugs to the window. He stared out over the rooftops for a moment, then returned to his seat. "You trust him?" he asked indicating Gilmore.

"Implicitly. Listen, Captain, you either trust me, or you don't. Give me your reason for this visit or leave."

Bart surveyed the cluttered room, then focused on the wizard. "I have to trust someone, Talman." The Younger Son of Bromwell drew a deep breath. "I'm placing my life in your hands."

Talman waited.

Gilmore shuffled some items from a chair and sat.

"Well, Bart?" Talman spoke quietly. "Out with it."

"The prairie-men acquired a weapon which can demolish the walls of our cities," Bart said slowly.

Talman shook his head in disbelief. Gilmore glanced sideways at the wizard then stared at Bart.

"It's the truth. I'm not in the habit of spurting lies."

Talman gripped the table. "Unbelievable. What facts brought you to this unlikely conclusion?"

Bart rubbed his forehead as if he were gathering his thoughts. Finally he said, "you recall that I lived in Delmarath with Father and my brother for several years."

"Go on," Talman encouraged him. "Whatever you have to say, won't leave this room. I give you my word on that."

"My family befriended barbarians who lived in the Citherian Mountains."

Friendship between the Lords of Delmarath and barbarians? Intriguing.

"They weren't prairie-men. They originated from some unknown land." Bart sighed. "We spent time sharing their hospitality."

"Did I hear you right? You said befriended?" Talman couldn't hide his amazement. "You were friends?"

Bart grimaced. "Yes, I meant friends, we bought all our horses from them, but that's immaterial. What's really important, their house was filled with books."

"Books?"

"Think of small pieces of parchment bound together on one side, only these were made of something called paper. Similar to what we use, but thinner and more brittle. One of these books held information about weapons out of the ancient past, horrible contraptions like powder that could set walls on fire and leave them in rubble."

Books? Written tales? What an innovative idea.

"Lance, that's the barbarian Betren escorted to the palace, brought a sample of that black death to Delmarath. His reason for speaking on the Knife is his claim that Prince Conder stole that book of death. He accuses him as being responsible for the powder falling into the hands of the prairie-men."

Conder? Stealing a book? Could he be inciting the prairie-men to war? Now there's a dangerous thought. The Great Wizard's words are true: 'The barbarian who will save Dana.'

Doom settled inside Talman's gut. *The black clouds over Delmarath and Chaleen that I saw when I peered into the crystal ball, back before the first snow – it really is an omen of disaster.* "You lack enough evidence on the King's brother to warrant his death, or any other man for that matter." Talman shot Bart his well-rehearsed appraising glance. "You obtained proof that Conder stole the book. True. But that's not enough. You can't prove that he armed the barbarians with the powder. Careful, Captain. If you accuse any man of treason on such flimsy grounds, it will be you and any who aid you who will find death on the wall."

"I know," Bart said. "Conder wouldn't stoop to treason."

"I agree," Talman said. "He has too much to lose."

Bart sighed. "The problem is that I found reason to suspect some kind of Danian participation."

"The Order of the Glass Slipper," Gilmore interrupted.

"The what?" Talman and Bart chorused.

"Oh, I never imagined that was important or I would have told you." Gilmore met the intent gaze of the captain and then the wizard.

"Order of the Glass Slipper?" Talman leaned toward Gilmore. "What's this about? Do you have names?"

"All I know is a matter of hearsay. I shared a glass of wine with Lord Robo. He talked about a secret society of honorable men who meet in a small room near the King's dungeons. They recite strange words from an object fashioned from material similar to what you described."

"What does this have to do with the destruction of Delmarath?" Talman asked.

"Unknown. It just seems that the object the captain described as a book matches exactly what Lord Robo described."

"How very interesting," Bart said. "Can you find out more? There's a group of us who have sworn to do everything in our power to discover the truth of this matter. That's why we require a private place to communicate."

"With my master's permission, my Lord." Gilmore bowed slightly. Talman stood up and started to pace.

"It's even colder on the ramparts this time of year than it is here," Bart pleaded.

Talman slid a box out of his way with his foot, then stubbed his toe on a bigger box that was too heavy to budge. He felt like screaming, but he wasn't going to admit neither to Bart nor Gilmore that he had hurt himself. He sighed.

"We wouldn't meet here, often, Talman. Just when we all need to be present," Bart said.

"I don't know, Younger Son of Bromwell." The wizard walked back to his chair and sat. "Even if you're discrete, you're asking me to stick my neck out for you. I make it a practice never to involve myself in politics. And yet, if you speak true..." He studied the young man sitting on his box of good fortune charms. Bart's blank face stared back at him. *This is merely a plot to discredit the Prince. It's a well-known rumor that there's no love lost between Delmarath and Chaleen.* He chewed his lip. *However, Bart sounds factual. Who'd expect him to admit friendship with barbarians? Yet he freely acknowledges it.* Talman absently patted his magic ball covered with the scarlet cloth. *I hold the means of determining the truth. Do I have the courage?* Finally he said, "Gilmore, fetch that box, the long narrow one on the shelf."

Gilmore's eyes widened in surprise, but he obeyed. "This one?"

"Yes, that one. Bring it here." Talman opened the box. Inside was a knife giving off a blue glow.

Bart stiffened. "Surely you're not going to request me to repeat this story holding the Knife of Truth?"

Talman gave Bart a long look. "This idea distresses you, Captain? Maybe you told half the truth? If I'm fool enough to involve myself in a conspiracy against the King's brother, I must be convinced that what you say is not some way of disgracing an innocent

179

man. Son of Bromwell, place your hand on that knife and swear to me that what you have just told me is the complete truth."

Without hesitation Bart laid his hand on the Knife. "I do so swear."

The Knife emitted a white blazing light.

Talman nodded. "All right." He replaced the cover on the box. "You may meet in this room only. My sleeping quarters are personal and off-limits."

Gilmore stepped in front of the wizard's table and knelt before Bart and took his hand. "Captain, I make you a pledge. I will do everything in my power to uncover information about this matter. And Captain," Gilmore pressed Bart's hand against his forehead. "I will share what I unearth with only you and my master. I swear that your secrets are safe."

"I accept your pledge," Bart said quietly. "Thank you."

A knock on the door interrupted this little ceremony. Gilmore stood up and shuffled to Talman's side. He reached for his knife. Bart spun toward the door, his hand on his sword.

Talman eyed Bart. "Captain, were you expecting company?"

"Perhaps." Bart stepped to the center of the room.

"Captain, you invited someone up here without my permission? Do I need to tell you that you presume too much?" Talman glared. "Gilmore, open the door. Let's have a look at our next visitor."

Betren stepped inside. His red cloak set off his black Delmarthian uniform. It almost made the Delmarthian appear sinister.

Talman nodded as Betren bowed. "Ah, Betren, I see that the King doesn't find you particularly dangerous allowing you to wander around the palace, fully armed." *Obviously, the King never listens to rumor control. Betren springs like a great cat. The man's all muscle. Wouldn't want to meet him in a dark hallway and there's lots of dark hallways in this palace.*

The Defender of Delmarath's face was expressionless. He faced his brother. "I've been summoned by the horse," he said, his voice dangerously soft. "I return this to its rightful owner."

"Thank you." Bart slipped the pendent over his head.

180

"I expected Sylvia required my services." Betren rested his hand on his knife.

Bart shook his head. "We should talk."

"Really." Betren eyed Bart. "I'm unsure I have anything to say."

Bart twisted his signet ring on his finger. He glanced at Talman. *Our noble Captain is not comfortable in the company of his brother.* Talman rose to his feet. *Of course when Betren gets his dander up, only a fool would feel secure in his presence.* "Gilmore, I have a sudden desire for some of Cook's biscuits to eat with our lunch. She should be taking them out of the oven right about now. Fetch us some."

Gilmore's eyebrows raised as he silently mouthed, "why?"

"The House of Bartran has been good to me over the years. I mean to repay their kindness, by granting the sons of Bromwell some privacy. Neither of us need witness this family squabble," Talman whispered earnestly into Gilmore's ear, his hand on his apprentice's shoulder.

Gilmore glanced from Betren to Bart. "Understood, Master." He bowed and left the room, shutting the door behind him.

Talman yawned. "Gentlemen, my lunch must wait. Hate these confounded interruptions. You must excuse me. I'm long overdue for my noonday nap. Please close the door when you vacate my shop." He stood erect, squared his shoulders and yawned again. "No bloodshed. Don't break anything," he added, his head held high as he retired into the other room and slammed the door.

181

Chapter 23

A tense silence reigned in the wizard's tower as Gilmore's footsteps retreated down the winding stairs. The wind whistled around the window rattling the small glass panes. The conservative fire in the fireplace in the wizard's sleeping quarters had never attempted to warm the room next to it. As the two men regarded each other, their cold hard expressions lowered the temperature in the room from chilly to something far below freezing.

"Well?" Betren spoke softly. "You summoned me. Why?"

Bart dropped to one knee. The law protected any man who knelt and guaranteed his right to speak to the other party in a disagreement. A numb finger rubbed his signet ring tracing the raised image of a flying eagle. "Betren, thank you for trusting my messenger."

Betren raised his eyebrow. "Not one word of an apology for knocking me flat on my face before the King? Deny me one last shred of dignity?"

Bart kept a watchful eye on his brother's hand. *Why'd the King let him keep his knife?* "Bet," he spouted, "I doubt I'd drag Lance to Megara. It puts everyone at risk."

Betren smiled.

Bart had seen men led off to die on the wall after that smile. "I mean I'm uncertain I'd muster the courage to do what you did." He paused. *Why can't I say, sorry I knocked you down in front of the King? I disgraced you and myself before the King and my guard. Maybe I can't because I enjoyed seeing you lying in the snow.*

Betren stepped back, obviously appraising his brother, despite his expressionless face. "You'd love to kill me, wouldn't you, Little Brother? What's holding your tongue? Why don't you just blurt out that I disgraced our family, destroyed your career and robbed you of a good marriage? That Delmarath— the lives of my people mean nothing to you?"

Bart forced himself to meet Betren's eyes and realized that Betren considered him the same as a prisoner on trial in Delmarath.

"What? Nothing to say for yourself? Not even to admit I speak the truth?"

"I don't wish to see Delmarath destroyed."

"And the rest of it?"

Bart stared into his brother's dark smoldering eyes.

Betren nodded and his lip curled into a sneer. "Your silence is most elegant, almost as elegant as that uniform you wear. What would people say if they witnessed the Captain of the King's Personal Guard kneeling before me, the man who destroyed your reputation?"

Bart studied the wizard's bedroom door. *Is Talman listening?* He forced himself to look back at Betren who scrutinized him with an amused expression. *He's baiting me. He'd like me to punch him in the mouth. Yes, I'd love to wipe that smirk off my brother's face, but then he'd gain an excuse for killing me. I won't give him that.* He shrugged. "Why shouldn't I kneel to you? You are my brother after all."

"I wonder which of us is the angriest," Betren mused. "We both have cause." His eyes softened. "I'll accept your last words as an apology. I'll do that because if I'm honest, I wonder how I'd react

183

if I found you and Lance at the city gates, knowing that everything I'd worked for was history." He raised Bart to his feet.

Probably run me through with your sword right then and there. Bart shied away from his brother.

"Hopefully, I'd handle it as well as you did."

Bart felt on the defensive like he always did when he tried to reason with Betren. "Bet, it's been almost five years. I wonder if I know you anymore." *That was not what I meant to say. Betren always leaves me feeling foolish.*

Betren raised his eyebrow. "You're right, Bart. You don't know me. When we lived in Delmarath, you were too busy trying to be better than me to set aside time to discover who I am, my emotions, thoughts, my deep hidden secrets. Every time I wanted to sit and chat, you ran out on me."

An awkward silence followed. Bart despised that eyebrow. *Talking with Bet never works. I always think of the right words later.*

"I hear you handled the horrhounds well." Betren changed the subject, his voice casual. "Everyone in the palace proclaims your feats. Some are even sorry you're related to me."

"Every man and horse back alive." Bart felt a quick prick of pride.

Betren smiled. "Of course they missed your real achievement. You actually put a rein on Metrox. Good work, Little Brother. I was older than you when I managed that."

"He told you?"

"He's proud of you. Not one word of criticism when he bragged about your success."

Bart gave a short laugh. "I can focus on that accomplishment as we die on the wall."

"Death's a possibility. Depends on Lance."

"Oh, Lance will do just fine," Bart snapped as adrenalin circulated throughout his veins. "It's what happens in the aftermath of this caper that concerns me. You must admit we never were a conventional family."

"How could we be? Not only is Delmarath a border town, it's the home of the Delmarthian Marketplace. Men from all parts of the prairies, even some from the far unmapped territories to the west come to exchange goods with Danian merchants. You can't be part of that without it touching the way we view other races." He smiled. "By the way, do you still call Sylvia, Little Sister?"

Bart nodded. "Point made. I considered treating her like a barbarian, but I couldn't. We must be the only Danians in the world who acknowledge a sister with bright blue eyes, long blond hair and is a head taller than most Danians." He squatted on a box and invited Betren to join him on one opposite him.

Betren smiled. "I wonder what magic mastery we're sitting on. Will the charms still work when we leave?"

Bart grinned. "Talman had no problem with me sitting here. Hopefully, he'll have none with the box you picked." *We did have some fine times. Why do I always focus on the bad?*

"Hope, I sit on charms of good fortune. We could use some." Betren's mood changed. His expression sobered. "I grew up in Delmarath. It was normal for me to converse with prairie-men. I learned to respect them."

When Father dragged me to Delmarath, the marketplace was a shock. Never seen barbarians before. Never expected to treat them as equals.

"There's a reason we keep a tight guard in our city," Betren droned on. "Not only to control trouble in the marketplace, but because we acquaint ourselves with the caliber of the enemy. If they see a unified army behind our walls, they'll think twice about attacking."

"You love your life on the border. I'd never make a good Defender." *Father's decision to present me to the King, then being accepted into the King's Guard instead of you saved my life. For the moment...*

Betren stroked his chin. "All the prairie-men needed was reason to unite, with or without the black death. The drought this summer gave them cause. I added fuel by closing the market early. A definite oversight. I fancied grain was the only commodity they purchased. Lance informed me that I didn't know what I was talking about." He slapped the box under him with a bang. "All I succeeded in was adding wood to feed their anger."

Bart grinned. "I'm sure Lance felt— oh— just a little pleasure to be able to tell the mighty Betren that he made a mistake."

"And then someone, perhaps Conder, gave them confidence to actually attack when he sent powder to Kans."

"Conder!" Bart jumped to his feet kicking his seat into a box in front of the shelf opposite Talman's table. "Conder's no traitor!"

"Lance witnessed Conder steal the 'Book of Power'. You remember, that book about the ancient weapons?"

"And you believe him?"

"He's here. Has requested to speak on the Knife of Truth. Of course, I believe him." Betren studied his brother. "Don't you?"

"Yes, I'm sure Lance saw Conder walk away with one of the treasures of the House of Robert. But that means nothing."

"Why should Conder take anything from the House of Robert? Robert provided shelter from the storm that lasted the whole winter. If anything, our good prince should have showered the House of Robert with gifts."

Bart leaned against the table. "Conder blamed Robert and his sons for Crito's accident. You recall how the prince adored his boy. Maybe he felt Robert's family owed him one. Maybe he was just fascinated with the book. By all the gods, taking that blasted book does not prove the Prince of Chaleen guilty of treason." Bart returned to his seat and scrutinized his brother. "Do you realize what a complicated plot you're inventing? Those books were filled with words unknown to us. Just how do you suppose Conder or any other Danian could fabricate anything from those books?"

"If someone from Lance's country showed them?"

"Impossible! Lance doesn't even know where his country is."

"But it exists." Betren's voice softened. "Someone from Lance's homeland must have either manufactured the powder and sold it to Conder, or helped him make it."

"Or sold it directly to the prairie-men. There's no reason why any Danian lord should be involved." Bart leaned toward his brother.

"Except that Conder has the most to gain if my conjectures ring true. Especially if he follows up with an ambush at the Gap of Sistra

186

and defeats the prairie-men. Our good prince would even the score with us, by wiping out my Delmarath and then being crowned a victorious hero."

"Really, brother, you're in the wrong profession. Have you ever considered becoming a teller of tales?"

Betren's eyes glittered, his knife flashed into his hand. "No man calls me a liar, not even my brother."

"All I meant is that you possess an excellent imagination." Bart rose to his feet and backed into a box. "Calm down. We need to figure this out."

Betren nodded, but fingered his weapon. "Conder had no business taking over Delmarath while we visited the King. Lacked legal justification in ordering an execution on the House of Robert."

"But that's only one incident." Bart attempted to unglue his eyes from Betren's knife. "He overstepped himself, that's all." He forced a smile. "I'm enough of a Delmarthian to be glad we put him in his place, but you're wrong on this one. I mean to prove Conder's innocence."

Betren raised his eyebrow. "Good. You do that." He returned his knife to its sheath. "So far, all I have on him is my own wishful thinking and Lance's glimpse of Delmarath's future. One way or the other, we need to discover the whole truth." He wandered to the window. When he spoke, the tone of his voice sounded bleak. "Brother, I feel blocked, unable to visualize my next play. Unless we solve this riddle, Delmarath will fall."

"Betren." Bart could barely comprehend that his competent brother would admit defeat. He waded though Talman's clutter to his brother's side. "I refuse to believe Conder is involved. I'd dismiss these accusations as ludicrous, Delmarthian revenge a-gainst Conder, some stupid ruse to tarnish his reputation, except for one detail— you. You don't dally in Megara's favorite occu-pation, ruining a man's reputation. There must be more to this than deluded fantasies on your part." Bart searched his mind for the right words to make Betren understand. Finally, he said, "my first memories are of Chaleen. Conder's like a father to me, his son, Crito, my best friend." He groaned. "And I just spent half the

187

morning telling Talman the story of our life and I painted Conder as a possible villain. I feel like a traitor."

Betren laid his hand on his brother's arm. "You actually idolize the King's brother. Besides my destroying your career in one foul plunge, I point my finger of guilt at someone you trust and admire."

Bart snorted. "Do you really care?"

"Do I care about Conder?" Betren's features hardened. "No. At one time I accepted him as Father's friend, but that friendship died five years ago. Do I care what this does to you?" His face softened. "Of course. You are my brother."

Bart attempted to recall his brother acknowledging any special tenderness for him. Uncertain how to respond, he switched the conversation to their immediate problem. "I'm starting an impartial investigation. We haven't learned much, but I suspect that the prairie-men really do wield a weapon as dangerous as you maintain, otherwise Lance would be dead in Delmarath. And I can't help but speculate that there may be Danian involvement. Not Conder, but someone."

"You found evidence?"

Bart sighed. "A little."

"Well?"

"Later. I have people working with me. I want them to witness your reaction to this piece of the puzzle."

Betren unleashed his penetrating gaze. "My little brother has grown in wisdom. I never thought of you not being as good as me. You were just younger, that's all. I never expected you to match me until you were grown." His eyes narrowed. "I wager you could put on a good showing against me now."

Bart brightened. "Anytime you want, Brother. My sword against yours. Let's do it. After this is over."

"No."

"What? Afraid of losing?"

Betren folded his arms. "I'd never forgive myself, if in the heat of the match, I manage to forget myself and kill you. I couldn't live with that."

188

"Has that ever happened?" Bart felt stunned. "You killed someone when it was just in fun?"

"Before you came to Delmarath. He was a friend. We argued about something, I forget what — some stupid issue that boys fancy as important. He challenged me to prove myself and drew his sword. I lost my temper and murdered him. I already was close to being the best swordsman in the Delmarthian Guard. I could have disarmed him. The vivid memory as he gasped his last breath haunts me still. I swore that the only time I'd use my sword would be in defense of my city, my people, or my life. I'd never, ever engage in a match just to tout my ability."

"That explains a few things. That's why—"

"Enough," Betren cut him off. "Our skill with weapons is not in question."

Bart dropped his eyes before his brother's gaze. He never had been able to handle that look. *Definitely time to change the subject.* "Let me fill you in on what has been done so far. Metrox ordered Menes to investigate the matter, and being Menes, his inquiry will be thorough."

"Down to the very last minute detail."

"Perhaps in the next few weeks some proof will surface." Bart stared over Betren's shoulder at Talman's cluttered shelving unit. "Hope so. Menes is organizing a search that will reach into all the cities on the Western Border. Sedrac and I are starting the same operation here." He sighed. "Hopefully, the King will show you mercy even contemplating that Conder could be involved in this." He glanced at his brother. "Our first step is to introduce Sylvia into Danian society."

Betren laughed. "Poor Sylvia." He looked thoughtful. "However, it might work if she cooperates. Certainly will loosen tongues." He paused. "Feel slightly nauseous about our privacy becoming public."

Bart snorted. "You've always tended to understate the obvious."

Betren grinned. "I forgot to bring the gift I meant to present you on the day of the Great Feast. Left it in Delmarath. However, accept this one. I give you one impossible situation."

"What impossible situation? The black death? That's not much of a present. Why don't you keep your gifts in Delmarath like a good Defender?"

"Don't understand what I'm getting at, do you Bart? It is such a pleasure to see you struggle."

Bart grimaced. *Why can't my brother state a concept plainly and be done with it? He's so annoying.* "I've been wondering what decision I'd have chosen if I walked in your shoes. I might have put a knife through Lance as he stepped into the Hall of Justice."

Betren frowned and shook his head. "It was tempting," he said quietly, "but I couldn't do it. There was too much between us all those years. Lance was confused, full of hate for me, for our house. His mind had blocked out most of what happened when Conder hung his family on the wall."

"And somehow you took him from that point to the place where he agreed to come here and speak on the Knife." Bart whistled. "You have a way with people. I have often envied you for it."

"Don't. Your own strengths, although different from mine are just as valid." Betren tilted his head thoughtfully. "I'm out of my element. I'm here under the King's sword, suspect because I brought Lance to Megara; furthermore I'm only a defender of a border city. Even if I visited under normal circumstances, people would snub me." He studied his brother for a long moment, then dropped to his knee before Bart and took his hand.

Bart felt his mouth drop open.

"You must lead. I will assist wherever and however I can, but will refrain from interference. At this point, my life and my city are in your hands. I make you this pledge."

Bart thought he understood. "Because of my position? Yes, I outrank you here. I'm glad you've noticed."

Betren sighed. "Little Brother, you can be so dense. Any fool can be appointed Captain of the King's Personal Guard. I yield leadership to the only man I deem capable of dealing with this problem. You know the ins and outs of this palace. I do not. This is not a question of which of us is better. It is a question of working together to save Delmarath. You and I are different. By combining our strengths, we will win this one."

"Oh." Bart choked back his amazement. *Betren's not treating me as his little brother, he's treating me as a respected officer under the King's command.* Bart had no words to express his feelings. He bent over his brother and raised Betren's hands to his forehead. "Betren," he said quietly. "I pledge myself to solve the problem of the black death, to bring anyone guilty of this to justice, no matter who they are. I pledge my life to save Delmarath."

Chapter 24

"Are you ready?" Alisha whispered as she strutted over to the mirror which occupied a corner in her room near the fireplace and fluffed her skirts.

"Almost." Sylvia struggled to squeeze her foot into a dainty blue slipper that the girls insisted that she wear. "Proper shoes to wear to a dance, indeed. I'd like to throw them into the fire."

Luciana giggled and curtsied. "My dear sister, is your magenta dress really the right outfit for spying about the palace?" Luciana circled her older sister critically eyeing her full skirts falling over several starched petticoats. "This lavender dress I borrowed from Mara is so much more appropriate. Unfortunately, Sylvia will have to wear the dress she has on. Aside from that border town garment that Delmarthian captain delivered, it's the only set of clothes that fits her, so far. Fortunately, it's tailored from two of your discards. Father use to bring home plain simple gowns back then. If we're seen, people will mistake us as servants."

"I've studied the masters," Alisha answered smugly. "If one usually dresses flamboyantly, then one would certainly call attention to oneself if all of a sudden one was to dress inconspicuously. Isn't that how it is where you come from Sylvia?"

"I've never spied on anyone," Sylvia answered.

"Of course not." Luciana curtsied. "Good barbarian princesses would never stoop so low as to spy on anyone. Alisha, I don't really think that dress is going to work."

"Fine, then I'm not going with you two scoundrels." Alisha scrunched her nose as she tiptoed toward the door. "Watch me carefully tonight, Sylvia. I'll show you how it's done on the dance floor." She pressed her skirts against her side and struggled out the doorway.

Luciana waited to speak until her sister started down the stairs. "Good, Alisha's such a spoil sport when it comes to stuff like this."

"And I really don't think I'm a princess," Sylvia said.

"Of course you are a princess, my dear. We wouldn't entertain anyone of lesser rank than a princess. Especially, if the person in question is a barbarian. We are the daughters of the richest man in the kingdom, you know."

Alisha's footsteps could no longer be heard on the stairs.

Luciana's face glowed with excitement as she grabbed Sylvia's hand. "Come on. Let's go. Spying is fun."

The music grew louder as Luciana led the way down a series of empty shadowy winding stone passages. Their pointy-toed slippers clicked on the hard stone floor. Whenever Luciana spotted someone walking toward them, they dodged into the nearest doorway and hid until the halls were empty again. When they saw someone in the distance Luciana chose another hallway so they would not be seen.

Sylvia wondered if they'd ever reach their destination. At last Luciana stopped before an opened door. They heard masculine voices inside.

"King's Guardsmen," Luciana whispered. She pressed her finger to her lips and they snuck by.

"How much further?" Sylvia asked softly. "Wouldn't it be quieter if we took off the shoes?" *My feet hurt.*

"If anyone saw us, that would draw attention. Besides, we're almost there. It's just up these stairs. Don't fall. It's dark near the top." She pulled open a door and disappeared.

Sylvia scrambled up behind her into a small curtained balcony.

Luciana drew the curtain back gently. "Careful so no one sees you. Your blond hair will betray us."

Sylvia peered through the opening. *So many people in one place.* Women's swirling skirts gracefully whirled and pulsated around men outfitted in fantastic costumes— tights and brocade tunics. It seemed that she was gazing at a meadow of flowers dancing in the wind, red, blue, purple, and white. Every color imaginable flowed across that floor. Amazingly, everyone was in step to the music. Musicians played horns, fiddles and drums all at the same time. "Not sure I like the sound of all those instruments played together. It doesn't compare to the birds singing in the spring."

"There's Alisha," Luciana said. "Watch her. Sedrac is asking her for a dance. He nods his head slightly, because he is our cousin. She smiles and gives him her hand."

Alisha murmured something in Sedrac's ear and he glided her in front of the balcony.

"Oh, good, Buris is approaching," Luciana said. "Alisha is so popular that she changes partners often. See, Buris is tapping Sedrac on the shoulder. Sedrac steps back and bows, Buris bows and Alisha curtsies. Buris kisses her hand and then draws her into his arms. You do that every time you change partners. Ooh," she squealed. "There's Robo, Ambassador from Chaleen. O-oh awesome tunic. Nice."

"Luciana, I can't do this," Sylvia wailed. "This is much too complicated. I'd suffocate being in a room with that many people. Forget Sedrac's plan."

"The Lady of the Forest is afraid of a little dance?" Neither girl had heard Bart open the door behind them.

"Captain," Luciana greeted him with a curtsy and a radiant smile. "I didn't know you knew about this place. How pleasant."

"I always thought this place was my secret. It's delightful to share secrets with good company," Bart answered as he kissed

194

Luciana's hand. He raised his eyebrows when Sylvia followed suit. "Nice." He took her hand and kissed it, then broke out laughing. "Sylvia, you're supposed to smile when a man kisses your hand. Not stick your tongue out at him. Luciana, didn't you tell this lovely barbarian that a kiss on the hand is merely a formal greeting?"

"Over and over, Captain. She seems to be a slow learner." Luciana looked dejectedly at the dancers below her.

Sylvia tossed her head. "Hand kissing is repulsive. So is all that bowing and kneeling and small talk."

"Ah, the filly is showing her true colors," Bart said. "Maybe we should apply the whip."

"I'm not a horse," Sylvia snapped.

"Then start acting like a sensible human being," Bart growled.

"Let's try it again, Captain," Sylvia said. "Pretend you just came into the room." She curtsied gracefully and thrust her hand in his direction.

Bart bowed and kissed it.

She smiled prettily and said, "it's good to see you, Captain."

"Little stiff with the hand, need more emotion in your greeting. I thought you liked me."

Luciana giggled.

"Not while you're kissing my hand! Would you please explain why it is necessary for me to learn all this?"

"Danians are very formal people, Sylvia. We mostly keep to ourselves. We spend hours conversing about the weather. But when we step on the dance floor, we relax and allow ourselves a certain degree of intimacy. We often broach subjects that ordinarily we wouldn't dream of sharing. If you can modify your behavior to the Danian way of life, your appearance on the floor will shock everyone into conversation. We might be able to discover the truth about the black death. Err I mean the powder."

"All right. I'll keep working at it." Sylvia drew a sharp breath. "There is nothing I'd like more than to see Prince Conder decorate a wall." She glanced at Luciana whose eyes were widening by the moment.

195

"Your distaste for the King's brother is understandable, but I doubt that he's guilty of any misdoing," Bart said. "Sylvia, I see how strange this is for you. You lived very well on the mountain without any of our customs. I wouldn't even ask you to do this except I'm desperate. I smell treason, but Betren's not the villain. To save him we need to unearth the real culprit. It could be anyone on that dance floor."

"But Lance is speaking on the Knife; I was at the Hall of Justice in Delmarath. I know he saw Conder steal the book of weapons. Isn't it logical that Conder is your traitor?"

"Lance only saw Conder borrow the book of weapons, nothing more. Who's to say that someone else didn't steal the book from Conder?"

"You mean Lance lacks the knowledge to convict anyone of anything? Then why is my brother here?"

"To save my brother's city. To prove that the powder's a threat. Who'd believe that a few bad smelling grains of grit would quickly turn a wall to ash?"

Luciana put her hands on her hips, glaring at Bart. "You're talking to her like she is a man. Why?"

"Because this is the kind of conversation, Sylvia understands. She grew up with three— no five brothers if you include Bet and me. She was never treated like a Danian girl. She never knew another girl until she came here."

"Captain?" Luciana had tears in her eyes. "Are you saying that you have known these barbarians all your life? You consider them friends?"

"Yes," Bart answered his face expressionless. "You might as well learn it now from me, rather than discover the truth when Lance speaks on the Knife." He took Luciana's hand. "The sons of Bromwell have sworn an oath of friendship with the sons and daughter of Robert."

Luciana gasped as she jerked away from him. "How could you? I— I thought the gossip was just malicious. Now, I find it's true. You really approve of your brother's behavior."

196

"Betren's my brother," Bart said tonelessly. "He did what was necessary. Only Lance can prove that this danger exists." He stared intently into Luciana's horrified face. "I see that none of these reasons matter to you."

"Matter! It makes all the difference in the world. It means that what is being said is true. Your house is doomed and I've been trying to protect you!"

The Danian girl brushed by Betren as he stepped through the door. "Seems that I missed something. I'd say, my private observation post is a little crowded."

"Luciana just found out about our friendship with the House of Robert," Bart said. "She'll never speak to me again."

Sylvia touched his arm. "Big Brother, you really like her, don't you?"

Bart nodded. "Not that it matters. I could never marry her under any circumstance. She comes from too high ranking a family for a border lord, but I enjoyed dancing with her. It's not the court's reaction that upsets me so much. That's to be expected. It's the reactions of people I consider friends that hurt." He glanced at his brother. "Sorry Bet, I know you did what had to be done."

"I understand," Betren said. "I feel like I'm in an empty room filled with shadows. No one speaks to me, but they certainly do converse with each other."

"I fear that Lance and I toppled your world into scrap," Sylvia said slowly.

Bart touched her arm. "Little Sister, it's not your fault. You can't help being from some other part of the world. You didn't give the prairie-men the ability to destroy our cities. It's just the way it is, that's all. Danians never associate with non-danians."

"What? Are you saying all Danians are shallow, self-centered and bigoted?" Sylvia pursed her lips into a pout.

Bart turned away from her and watched the dancers below him. "How do I explain this to you? Your family sold horses to both Danians and prairie-men. Your family considered the individual; it didn't matter to your folks where they came from. Danians— well Danians have no tolerance for anyone undanian."

"Oh, I remember Bet telling Lance something like that. I thought my brother was being stupid that day."

"Now you're experiencing it head on," Betren said.

Bart let his hand fall from the drape and faced them. "I'm glad you're here. Betren, something that was said earlier has been bothering me and I decided to wait until the three of us were alone to inquire about it. Reig brought some evidence to Metrox. It's what I'm holding off showing you until the others are present. What I'm wondering is how? The market is closed, so are the Western Gates. Will be until the night of the Gathering of the Greens. At least that's the way it use to be five years ago."

"It still is," Betren said. "Reig the Storyteller? What's this about?"

Bart fiddled with his signet ring. "How could Reig contact anyone? Is he one of our agents? Would he know about the secret door?"

"No."

"He — he just popped in out of nowhere," Sylvia explained. "He held a magic ball, said that he found it in a cave under Trac's lodge. It brought him to the Hall of Justice."

"Oh, Sylvia, living in the palace must be going to your head!" Bart grabbed her arm. "People don't pop in."

"I'm telling the truth." Sylvia stamped her foot and headed toward the balcony door. "Reig also used the ball for talking with a wizard in Megara," she shot over her shoulder.

"Hold it Bart." Betren held up his hand. "Sylvia, stop, this is important. Besides, you'll never find your way back to the girls room. Just when did Reig 'pop in'?"

Sylvia faced him. "Why, about six days after you left for Megara. That's when he spoke to the wizard. It was fascinating."

"And on the sixth day the King rode out of Megara and rescued Lance and me," Betren said slowly as he studied Bart. "That's why Talman rode with the King? In case his report was false, he'd have to walk back to Megara?"

198

"I suppose." Bart shrugged. "He came to the King with some mumble jumble and persuaded him to ride. Claimed he saw something in his crystal ball."

Betren frowned and nodded. "I owe Reig for that. Tell me, Sylvia, is Reig a prisoner in Delmarath?"

"Oh no. I'm pretty sure he saved Maris from death on the wall. He left that night and Maris was no longer around. I think there was an adoption." She noticed the expression on Betren's face. "Oh my, was that something I wasn't supposed to tell you?"

"Metrox might think so. Never mind Sylvia, you said nothing that will hurt anyone."

"Well, that answers one or two of my questions," Bart said. "Now I have about six more, but they'll wait. Sylvia, what were you and Luciana planning this evening?"

"She was going to teach me to dance. There should be a fiddler by the time we get back to her room."

"I'll be a better teacher than either of the girls on this one," Bart said quietly. "None of them have ever led a lady around the dance floor. Come here, Sylvia. Give me your hand. I'm going to slip my arm around your waist just like they're doing it down on the dance floor."

Sylvia took his hand as Bart gently pulled her toward him and let his arm rest around her waist.

"Any questions?"

"How come you call this place a secret?"

"It is, Little Sister," Bart assured her. "Most people don't come here."

Betren tapped Bart on the shoulder. "Now, I'll show you how to change partners, Sylvia. Bart and I bow." Betren bowed then glanced at his brother. "Bart, you're not doing this right."

"I wasn't finished." Bart stepped back and bowed.

Sylvia sighed. It was going to be a long evening.

Chapter 25

"This is yours." Reig gently laid a large bundle on the table in the cabin where Sylvia and Lance had lived in the Citherian Mountains. He tossed his long gray braids over his shoulders. "I must check the traps we set on that rabbit trail. Hopefully, we'll eat fresh meat tomorrow. I also mean to investigate the area where the Danian ceremony of the Gathering of the Greens will be held." The storyteller slipped into his sheepskin jacket. "I'll be gone most of the day. You'll remain here to work on your first assignment as my apprentice."

"My first assignment?" Maris gulped.

"You must create a song about your life in Delmarath and how you became my son, Mar. Put your feelings into this piece. Leave nothing out."

Maris stared at Reig's pale weathered face. He opened his mouth, but no words came out.

Reig nodded as he touched Maris on the shoulder with his wrinkled hand. "I know, this is going to be hard, but it is your first step in becoming Mar, a master storyteller. I refuse to continue your education until you accomplish this."

Storm, who looked more wolf than any self-respecting Danian dog should, rose from his bed in front of the fireplace and trotted to the door wagging his tail.

"No, Storm. Not this time." Reig hefted his knapsack over his shoulders and gave Maris one of his penetrating looks. "Oh, yes, Mar, I understand perfectly. Any Delmarthian pig would recognize your defiant expression. Regardless of your feelings, I expect a song when I return." He closed the door firmly behind him.

Maris watched Reig's retreating figure from the window. "Sing a song about my disgrace and waste this day of freedom dwelling on my real father," he muttered. "Besides, I need an instrument, never create a song without music. I'll tell Reig I can't work without an instrument. Since he depends on others to play music, I'm safe for the rest of the winter. Wonder what great surprise he has for me on the table?"

The teenager reached for the package and pulled on the end of a rope. The knot tightened. *Wished I'd paid more attention to that class on knots during my first year in the guard. Wait, I got it; if I tug on this loop... Yes.* The rope came free. He undid the outer wrapping.

Inside were several objects, various sizes and shapes, each one enclosed in cloth. His attention focused on the weapon that rested on top of these bundles.

"My knife," he cried, drawing it out of its sheath. "The one father gave me on my seventh birthday."

The exquisite blade forged from iron in a far off border town in Northern Dana, then shipped to and etched in Chaleen with the image of a swooping eagle— the very essence of Delmarath. It balanced well as a weapon. The craftsmanship of the bone handle felt as if it had been lovingly shaped to fit comfortably in his hands alone.

Every Danian boy received a knife when his father deemed him capable of learning to use it without slicing off a finger, a treasure that most kept until the day they died. A symbol stating that babyhood was over; the child had reached the age where he was capable of owning his first tool. But his blade was a notch above most everyone's because his father earned the honor of holding the rank of Captain of the Guard. Rank came with privileges.

He fingered the cutting edge. *Somebody recently sharpened it. It's ready for any kind of work, cutting meat, whittling wood, defending my life, or* — he froze at the thought — *ending my life.*

The knife clattered on the table. *Father's behind this. Father's giving me one last opportunity to die as a Danian. I can slash my wrists. It can't hurt anymore than the brand Reig cut into my arm. I'll finish it.*

As Maris retrieved his knife, his hand brushed against the other objects on the table. *What else has Father? No; he's not my father, not anymore. What did my dear beloved Captain of the Delmarthian Guard send me? Those bundles can't hold some kind of fast working poison. They're too big.*

Maris reached for a long narrow package, took his knife and cut the rope that held the cloth in place. "My flute?" He stared at it, open mouthed. "Storm, I'm holding my flute."

The dog's tail struck the floor at the sound of his name.

The teenager tore open the other bundles. His lute, the guitar, his horn, they were all there. He could hardly believe his eyes. He picked up the lute and plucked the strings as he tuned his instrument, then laid it back on the table. *My 'real father' sent me all my tools to survive if I decide to live. I thought them burned along with everything else I owned. Guess those weren't mine. Father must have substituted cheaper ones.* Maris sighed. *Father grants me yet another chance to die with honor. Reig wishes me to become his son. I'm trapped. Those two old geezers are forcing me to choose. They've set this up so I must decide today.*

So far, living with Reig is better than expected. At first I felt like a servant because what's required for living is girl's work, but no matter what the chore, Reig toils along with me. At the end of the day he rubs ointment on my wounds. Applies warmed towels on my bruises. It would be easy to love Reig as an uncle if he were Danian.

Maris sauntered to the window and stared across the cleared land encircling the cabin into the forest beyond. "Reig's not

Danian," he muttered. "Neither am I." He rolled up the sleeve on his arm and contemplated at the "S" mark carved into his skin. "To die as a Danian, or live as a prairie-man, that is the question."

"Would you miss me, Storm?" Mar knelt beside the dog and hid his face in the animal's silver fur. "I deserted my post," he said, hugging Storm. "I was only gone a moment. I didn't figure anyone would notice, but my brother did. So did Father. Up to the end, I trusted Father would rescue me on some loophole, but he didn't. He conducted the proceedings as if I was only a mere guardsman, not his son."

Maris considered his last hours in Delmarath. It was dark when he walked from the small room off the Hall of Justice to stand before his father and the guard. He held his head high as he stood at attention while Metrox read a long list of infractions. Maris' head was an anvil, each crime a hammer that smashed his skull, his mind, his being. Only his pledge to honor his father stilled his tongue. He kept his eyes on Metrox's grim face.

The Captain of the Guard laid the parchment on the table and rose to his feet. "Maris, Son of the House of Melron, how do you plead to these charges?"

"Guilty, Captain," Maris managed to keep his voice steady. Every misdemeanor was recorded in Captain Evander's records.

"Then I pronounce the Sentence of Banishment. Tonight we strip you of your citizenship, your dignity. When you leave this room, you are nothing — a bit of garbage to be driven out of the city to die in the wilderness. I needn't spell out the procedure. You know it as well as I."

"Yes, sir." Maris took several steps away from the table, and turned toward the assembled guard. Everyone in the room waited for his father's order.

"Guardsmen, he's yours. Take him."

The guard surrounded Maris, threw him on the floor. Evander, as was his right, having Maris under his command, struck the first blow. He cut off Maris' belt and yanked open the fastenings on his clothing. Leaping to his feet, Evander waved the belt in the air, signaling the guard to complete the job, which they did with enthusiasm. When they finished, they hauled Maris upright, naked, disheveled, and bruised. He shivered as the clammy air of the hall engulfed him. Evander caught his arm and forced him to stand a few feet away from the fire.

More guardsmen entered the hall, carrying baskets of his processions which were dumped on one side of the fireplace. The men taunted Maris, daring him to reach out for his cherished belongings as they tossed them into the fire. The guard would have been delighted if he protested. One word or movement entitled them the right to dangle him over the fire. As long as he remained at attention, they couldn't touch him.

After the flames consumed the head of Maris' favorite toy horse, the one his mother gave him before she died, his last possession, Evander led Maris to the other end of the room. The guard formed two lines, their swords drawn ready to beat him.

The Captain of the Guard always delivered the first blow to the condemned. His father shoved Maris beyond first four guardsmen into a shower of punishing weapons. Blows rained down on his back and legs. Someone tripped him, forcing him to crawl on the stinging frigid stone floor.

When Maris managed to regain his footing at the end of the line, Evander struck a final blow which sent him reeling though the secret door which closed with an ominous thud. Echoes of cheers of the guard bounced off the twisting dark tunnels. Maris knew he was finished, the letter of the law satisfied.

Maris stroked Storm's head. "I didn't cry out or protest their cruelty. I handled the whole trial with honor. The guard will have to admit that I behaved as a member of the House of Melron should. No one except my family knows I'm still alive. My father can keep his head high in Delmarath."

Maris returned to the table and lifted the knife. It represented everything he knew, everything he had lost. Could he put together a tune about his punishment? The tellers of tales sang lots of songs about men who faced death bravely. What about the horror that awaited him that night in the underground room? He reached for his lute and plucked several cords.

The result was discord.

"I can't do this." He slammed the lute on the table and fingered the knife. His clammy hands turned the weapon over . "I can't slash my wrists just yet, either. I haven't made a choice, just understood my real father's reasoning. I must try to obey Reig's orders."

Storm whined and nuzzled his water dish across the floor. When Maris failed to respond, the dog nudged the boy's hand with his head, each time with more force.

"Oh, all right, Storm." Maris dipped water out of a bucket into Storm's dish, petted his head. "Leave me alone so I can work."

"Perhaps a song about my knife." Maris picked up his lute. "If I start there, I can work into the other. Either this will be my last song or my first." The tune that emerged was a happy one.

Maris remembered himself as a boy in Delmarath; yes, life had been wonderful. As he played, he pictured his father, straight, tall armed with his sword flashing in the Delmarthian sunlight. He frowned and laid the lute down. *How to work my father into the music?*

He picked up the knife, fondled it in his hand. *Father always knew a quality weapon when he saw one. Will Reig keep it after I'm gone?*

Holding his knife brought back a memory of the time when Maris was eight years old and had lost his knife. Oh, it was found all right, next to the spot where the cook had placed a cake to cool. It was a very special cake, the one that was baked to celebrate Lord Bromwell's birthday. And it was gone, his knife screaming that Maris was the thief.

Maris had furiously denied his father's accusations until his father quietly laid a firm hand on his shoulder and silenced him with the words, "fine, just fine. We'll see."

Those were dreaded words. The innocent party had nothing to fear, providing he was truly innocent, however the guilty one could look forward to double the punishment as he not only committed the misdeed, but also lied to protect himself. When their father decided to investigate a crime his sons had committed, he vigilantly pursued the matter until he obtained proof of what really occurred. And he had the manpower to do it.

205

In this case the real thieves were not far away. Father caught Menes and Bart feasting with friends on the stolen cake in the marketplace.

The older boys were marched to the place of punishment on one side of the marketplace, had their pants pulled down and forced to lean across two wooden horses where they were publicly and soundly spanked. They really didn't want to sit down for a day or so — Father's punishment. Then Bart and Menes were hauled up to the Hall of Justice where Lord Bromwell sentenced them to serve Maris for the rest of the summer.

At first Maris forced Menes and Bart to obey his every wish, until Betren, with that amused look he reserved for the younger boys when they were making absolute idiots of themselves, took him aside.

"Just how are you going to handle things when Bart's and Menes' punishment is over?" Betren asked. "That guard who is always with them these days will move onto other duties. You really think Menes and Bart will forget every insult and not plan some suitable revenge?"

Maris swallowed. He hadn't thought of that. "No," he said slowly. "I suppose not."

"Then I'd start supposing if I were you." Betren started to walk away, then turned back. "By the way, my father wants to see you in the Hall of Justice."

Betren disappeared into the stable leaving Maris very much alone. Betren's father was the Lord of Delmarath. He was often in Maris' house, and the boy was often in Bromwell's quarters.

This was a very different matter. To be summoned to the Hall of Justice meant that whatever was to be discussed was serious. Maris slunk slowly into the courtyard and climbed the six flights of winding stairs to where Lord Bromwell waited. Those stairs were the most intimidating structures in the whole world. Every step took you closer and closer to unknown, but certain disaster. Many who climbed those stairs did not live to see another day. By the time he reached the first landing his legs felt heavy. By the time he reached the bottom of the last flight, he felt like the biggest stone in the wall was tied around his neck.

One of the guards motioned him to stop. "Wait here, Younger Son of Metrox. Lord Bromwell is occupied."

Maris became aware of voices raised in anger. The door was closed so he couldn't hear what was actually being said but he recognized them. One was his father's, the other Lord Bromwell's. A shaft of fear shot through him. *What horrible thing have I done, that my father would argue with the Lord of Delmarath?*

Father opened the door with a frustrated frown on his face. "Upstairs," he ordered.

Maris climbed the last six stairs with dread in his heart.

However, when he reached the top, Lord Bromwell looked at him and smiled. "Maris, come here. Sit down." He indicated the bench in front of the table.

Maris scooted up on the bench. He was much too small for it to feel comfortable. His legs were too short to touch the floor. His eyes barely saw over the top of the table where his lute accused him of stolen moments of unfinished chores. Oh, to grab the instrument and run. He glanced at his father, no help from that direction. Father's face remained expressionless.

"Well, Maris," Lord Bromwell said. "Are you enjoying the last two days? How have you been spending them?"

Maris looked at the edge of the table. He tried to figure out how much Bromwell and his father knew about his recent activities and decided to be honest. "I was making life miserable for Bart and Menes," he said in a small voice. "But Betren talked some sense into me and it isn't fun anymore."

Bromwell studied him gravely. "It is not an honorable action to kick a person when he is down. Perhaps you should apologize?"

Maris gulped. He was old enough to know that anything said over this table was not a suggestion. It was a command. "Yes, my Lord."

"Good. So what are you going to do with the next two months? You have no chores, so that opens up a lot of free time."

Maris gazed longingly at his instrument. "I want to play my lute." He glanced up at his father and knew he was saying the wrong thing. He didn't care. "I want to learn more tunes and invent some of my own."

Lord Bromwell leaned back in his chair. "Do you now? Will you play me something?"

Maris timidly reached for the lute. Once he touched the first note, he forgot everything except his music.

When he finished his song, Lord Bromwell watched him intently. His father wore a rueful smile on his face.

"My Lord," Maris stammered. "Did I do something wrong?"

"No, lad, You have done everything right." Bromwell nodded toward the door of the small room off the Hall of Justice and called. "Franklin." A man with black curly hair appeared.

"Well?" Bromwell said. "You heard him play. Will you teach him?"

"My Lord." The man dropped to one knee. "I thought this a punishment for starting a quarrel in the marketplace with that red headed barbarian storyteller. Instead, I will gain great pleasure in teaching the lad. He plays well."

Maris was actually going to have a teacher. He stared at Bromwell and stammered, "thank you, my Lord." He looked up at his father. "Father?"

His father threw up his hands. "Fine, just fine, my Lord. I surrender. Let it be on record that I protest that too much music is bad for anyone, but I said I would agree if the teacher was pleased. My Lord, I hope we don't live to regret this decision."

"Maris, you'll begin tomorrow," Bromwell said. "That gives you today to settle some unfinished business with Bart and Menes. You may go."

Maris suddenly darted around the table and knelt to Bromwell and pressed Bromwell's hand against his forehead. "Thank you, my Lord. Thank you." Then he jumped up and sprinted out of the Hall of Justice.

The thought of even speaking to Menes and Bart slowed him to the speed of the slowest snail. *They'll laugh at me.* He found the

208

older boys on the steps of the Hall of Justice. One of his jobs had been to help sweep out the Great Hall once a week. "Menes, Bart," he called as he approached them. Maris dropped to one knee. "I'm sorry about making life miserable for you the last couple of days."

"Why are you kneeling to us?" Menes demanded. "We should be kneeling to you." He yanked Maris up on his feet.

"He's right," said the younger son of Bromwell. "We're the ones who tried to get you in trouble and stole the cake. Talk about acting stupid."

Menes stroked his right hand with his left. "We were reminded that the normal punishment for stealing is to lose a hand. We deserved what we got."

"And to accuse someone falsely is usually punished by death on the wall," Bart said. "We got off easy."

Maris didn't expect this. Bart and Menes never apologized to him. Usually they ignored him. They even had their own private language when they didn't want him to know what they were talking about. After all they were eleven, almost twelve years old and he was only eight. He felt speechless. The silence was becoming unbearable. He stared at their boots and the older boys stared at him. At last he mumbled, "can we call it even?"

"Yes," Bart said quickly. He knelt before Maris.

"Little Brother, you are more than generous," Menes said and also knelt.

Each boy took one of Maris' hands and pressed it against his forehead.

"All right, you two scamps," the guard opened the door and beckoned to Bart and Menes. "Inside. Get to work."

Maris started to run. He didn't look back. He couldn't believe how grand this day had turned out. He raced past Betren and Evander leading their horses out of the stable to join the patrol that was forming just inside the city gate. He rushed into the marketplace. Lance called to him, but he did not answer. He wanted to sing, dance, yell and laugh at once. He dashed by merchant's stalls and a short way up the mountain. He was going to have a teacher. His father was letting him learn everything there was to know about music.

Even after Franklin had moved back to Chaleen, Lord Bromwell insisted that Maris had afternoons free to work on his music.

Maris set the knife on the table, picked up the lute and fingered the strings. Miraculously, he projected his feelings of that wonderful day into his song. Yes, he could create the pitter-patter pounding of the heart of a frightened small boy climbing the stairs to the judgment hall and he certainly could make it sing of his joy of being given a teacher. To be honest, life hadn't been all that bad until he joined the guard.

Unconsciously, he strummed the chords of a Danian marching song. Startled, he dropped the lute on the table. *Despise that music. Hate the songs sung by the guard. Loathed serving my time. It was prison. Degrading. I was full of songs that needed to be sung, but instead I had to stand on watch for hours. No one with my talent should have to serve.*

He had no choice in the matter. All Delmarthian boys entered the guard when they were fourteen. They served four long miserable years until the day of freedom arrived. Then boys decided their future— stay in the guard or move on to some other career.

Metrox assigned him to Evander's command. His cousin took the time to know every boy that served under him. *Evander.* Maris thought of him fondly. *Always inspired us to do better. Everyone, that is except me.*

Shortly before Lance returned, Evander called Maris into the Hall of Justice to show him his progress report. Not only was Maris incompetent with weapons, a fact that kept him the laughing stock of the guard, he rarely showed up where he was suppose to be at any given time.

"One more incident and I'll be forced to report you to the Captain of the Guard." Evander warned. "That's not a threat, Maris, your father wants to review my records."

A few days later, Maris took the matter out of Evander's hands. And his father did exactly as Evander predicted. Forcing his

210

youngest, dearest son through an adoption ceremony with a barbarian added a terrible indignity above the letter of the law.

Noise from the shed attached to the cabin penetrated Maris' brain. The restless ponies nickered, their hooves clattered on the floor. One of them pounded the door with his hoof.

"How could I forget to feed them?" Maris groaned. "It's something I've done every morning since we arrived. Not their fault I'm trying to compose a song."

Maris scooped up an armful hay stored in the old library and opened the inner shed door. He threw the hay under snatching chomping heads, grabbed a bucket and hurried outside to the pump. The water rushed into the bucket and slopped over his legs as he jogged to the shed and splashed the leftover contents of the bucket into a wooden trough.

He flew into the main room, fed the fire another log and plopped down in the chair in front of the fireplace. *I can live with the punishment dealt to me in the Hall of Justice, but can I live with the horror that awaited me in that underground hall? What hold does Reig exercise over my father that he and his house deviated from the law; no, actually they broke it. No Danian defies the law to accommodate a barbarian. I refuse to dwell on this.*

Storm brought him his bone and pleaded with his brown eyes for Maris to throw it. "Not now, Storm. I'm busy. Reig said to include everything; leave nothing out. That storyteller can read my mind. If I don't do this, he'll know somehow."

Maris stared into the fire. The flames dancing on the wood reminded him of the Delmarthian black and red uniforms. The crackling sparks floated up the stone dark chimney in a single file as if they followed orders from a superior officer. He poked at a charred log laced with red embers. It split in two. Sparks sprouted in a chaotic shower upwards as if he had broken a law by severing a log.

Menes, his legalistic brother broke the law when he provided Maris a cloak and slippers to fend off the frigid temperature of the tunnels and guided him to the underground room.

211

When they almost reached the entrance, Menes unfastened the cloak from Maris' shoulders and confiscated the slippers. "Now, go meet your new father as naked as the day you were born." He shoved his brother into the room where Reig waited.

Maris stumbled forward. All the torches were lit. Their flickering light created an eerie atmosphere. Damp air invaded his body.

A dark monster approached him clutching a torch.

Maris reeled back, legs and feet itching to bolt so he could hide forever in the tunnels. The teenager froze as the light blinded him, then it was lowered as it illuminated his body.

"Easy, boy, I'm not going to touch you." The light circled him as Reig stepped behind him. "Just want to see how badly they damaged you up there." Reig's voice sounded sympathetic.

Father had warned him about an adoption ceremony. Maris had ripped it out of his mind as an atrocity his father would never sanction. Numbness seized his mind and limbs. He failed to realize that his family waited in the room until his father caught his arm and escorted him to a tub filled with water forcing him to stand in it.

Menes and Evander held him firmly as his father washed him from head to toe.

"I cleanse you of everything Danian," Metrox said while he scrubbed. "Not one inch of your skin has any part of me, you are not my son, you have no call on the House of Melron, and you have no brother or cousin. You are nothing." When he finished, he nodded to Menes and Evander who led Maris in front of Reig.

"On your knees," his father ordered. "Both of them."

Reig's voice boomed, echoing in the stone chamber. "Tonight this wretched Danian known as Maris, son of Metrox, Captain of the Delmarthian Guard, died at the hands of his father's men, executed for crimes committed against his city. Tonight, new life graces this pathetic carcass of neglect and treachery." Reig poured warm liquid over Maris' head. As it spilled into his face and down his back, the storyteller said, "a new clean bold spirit replaces the old brittle spoiled one. Washing away much. Promising greatness.

Embrace a redeemed heart." Reig set the jug on the floor and slid his hand under Maris's chin forcing the teenager to look up into his bearded face. "I, Reig, Master Storyteller of the great prairie, name you Mar, and claim you as my son."

Overwhelmed by shame, Maris' muscles refused to operate. In truth his father had sentenced him to a fate worse than death.

"Let's finish this." His father's voice lacked emotion.

"Lay him on the table," Reig ordered.

His father scooped him off the floor, carried him to the table and laid him on his back. Evander forced his cousin's shoulders flat against the rough wood, restraining him. Menes sat on his legs. His father leaned on Maris' chest pinning his left arm with his body and clamped his right arm out toward that horrible filthy barbarian.

"Hold him steady," Reig said. "This will take a few minutes."

Maris couldn't see Reig approach, but he felt his arm being rubbed with a cold liquid. Soon it felt numb. His eyes snapped shut as a warm blade traced a pattern into his skin. He clamped his teeth as the knife penetrated into his arm and then screamed as Reig cut a curved line through his flesh following the original mark. "You bear the mark of an apprentice storyteller. You are born anew." As Reig withdrew the knife, he slashed his hairy forearm.

Maris arched his neck and managed to peek at his elbow. Reig's bloody arm flattened on top of his.

"You no longer are pure Danian," Reig announced. "You were born again when the sacred oil sealed your skin from Danian pollution. And now my blood has mixed with yours. This blood sacrifice authenticates our relationship as father and son." He wiped the blood off his knife as Maris' family left the room without another word.

Storm plopped two large paws on his lap and licked his face.

"Cut it out," Maris cried, pushing the dog on the floor. The sleeve of his shirt slid back revealing the hated 'S' mark. Even when it completely healed it would be visible. "How can Reig ever fathom that I could write a song, much less sing about this horror? I'll end it now."

213

He shuffled over to the table, picked up his knife and lowered it over his wrist. As the knife scratched his skin, a sudden thought riveted him motionless. *Is this what is meant by facing oneself on the Knife of Truth? Thank all the gods in the universe that I'm alone in a cabin in the mountains, as opposed to standing before the King and court in Megara. I should be dead. Danian law decrees it. If anyone discovers that I'm alive because Father allowed me to escape proscribed punishment, dooms him to die on the wall. He's put his life in jeopardy.* Maris' knife fell onto the table. *Why? For me? For my music?*

Sobs racked his body as he sank on the bench and buried his head in his arms. An ancient saying that all Danian boys memorized from the scrolls of great wisdom as part of their schooling came to mind with awful meaning. *'Greater love has no man, then this, that he lay down his life for another.'* He stood and paced the floor. *I don't deserve that kind of love. I did nothing but cause father grief all my life.*

He lifted his knife. *Cut my veins? That's what most people do in my situation. No big deal. I'll simply finish what I tried to do in Delmarath when Evander apprehended me.* As he thought of his cousin, Evander's words crossed his mind like a well-laid whip. *'Suicide is a coward's way out. You are no coward. You'll learn to live on the prairies. You'll become the greatest musician that ever walked the grasslands.'*

The word "live" stuck in his mind. His father had given him the greatest gift any man could give another — life. Maris laid the knife back on the table. His survival was the only thanks he could offer his father.

He studied the mark Reig had carved into his skin. It branded him as a prairie-man; in Dana any mark of that sort spelled death.

Maris reached for his lute. His fingers found the notes he searched for; his mind formed the words and he put it into story and song.

Chapter 26

That evening Reig returned to the cabin. After they had eaten, Reig stretched out in his favorite chair, warming his feet by the fire and said, "play a song, Mar. Any song."

Maris chose a ballad that was actually a dialogue between a father who insisted that his son follow in his footsteps as a blacksmith, but the son desired nothing more than to farm.

Reig listened, his eyes half closed.

Maris noticed a little smile playing around the storyteller's lips. The teenager realized that he was putting more feeling into the song than he had ever achieved before.

When he was finished, Maris peered at Reig hesitantly. "I have another song," he said slowly. "Should I play it for you?"

Reig smiled. "The song I told you to work on today?"

Maris nodded.

"If you want. Some songs are not for others but for ourselves, to be stashed away in the corner of the brain, to be let out little by little as you did in the ballad you just sang. Use your special song to enhance the tale you are telling, to have a character make a point, to give something feeling that only you can give it because you have experienced it in your life. Do you understand what I'm saying, boy?"

Maris looked into the flames. "I think so. That ballad I sang for you is one that I've heard and sung many times, but tonight I knew what the father felt, I knew what the boy thought. I made it real." He looked up at Reig. "Are you saying I could not have done that without..."

"Without living it? More than that— without facing it and understanding it." Reig laid his hand on Maris' shoulder. "A lot of what we do is acting and I can teach you that, but the best is what we feel in our heart. Mar, that song you worked on today— if you wish to share it with me, I would be more than honored. If not— I understand."

Before Maris could answer, a knock resounded on the door. Storm leaped to his feet barking. Reig drew his knife and positioned himself so he'd be behind the door when it opened.

"Hello the house," a deep voice bellowed. "Will you shelter a weary traveler?"

"Drom, my friend. I thought I'd missed you this year." Reig stepped into the doorway and raised his hand in greeting. He spoke in Danian.

The newcomer was almost as short as Maris, but a barbarian in dress and speech. His ruddy face sprouted a grin as he raised his right hand. "Reig, glad I found you." Rough hands scratched Storm behind the ears. "Is there a reason for using the Danian tongue?"

"Good practice for performing in the upcoming festival. After all, our audience will be Danian. We'll be right out to help you stable your horse."

Reig snatched a candle from the table and shielded the flame with his hand as he strode outside followed by Storm. Maris grabbed his cloak and hurried after them.

Drom had two horses, but Maris paid no attention to the gray, laden with a heavy saddle from the prairies designed not only to

216

carry a man, but equipped with hooks and rings which supported gear.

The teenager caught his breath as he recognized the bay that sported an unadorned Danian bridle and light saddle with a swooping eagle carved into the leather, a guardsman's horse. Only one gelding in Delmarath had such a wide blaze on his face that the white hair broadened at the muzzle. The horse arched his head toward Maris and whinnied in recognition.

"Wipperwill," he greeted the horse softly. "What are you doing here? Did you pick up a stone? You're favoring your front leg." The teenager ran his fingers over the horse's neck and down his legs, stopping at the knee as his hand touched something gooey. "Reig, shine the candle over here." He studied his hand. "Blood."

"Yeah," Drom said. "He's been down. Found him this evening as I came along the Danian side of the mountain. Took some time to drag his dead rider off the trail and cover his body with stones."

"Danian side?" The curled lip on Reig's face illuminated by the flickering candle gave him a fearsome appearance.

Drom threw his saddlebags on the ground. "There's an advantage being short. No one looks too close when all men traveling through the Chaleen mining tunnels wear cloaks and scarves, so long as we're the same height and our telltale beards are stuffed smugly out of sight."

"Drom," Reig exploded. "How many times must I warn you that one of these days you'll be noticed and killed?"

"Reig, you worry too much," Drom protested. "Only you tall characters have a problem. I was running late and didn't want to miss the Delmarthian festival so I used the shortest route to Delmarath.

"We'll talk later," Reig said. "Let's take care of your horses. Mar, fetch some of that water that I put on the fire. We need to clean that Danian horse's legs."

"Good old Reig," Drom grumbled as they led the horses into the barn. Always concerned about an animal's comfort before feeding a starving friend."

Maris swallowed. *Only one person is assigned to ride Wipperwill. That's Laris. Why would my father — no, he's not my father anymore — why would that miserable Captain of the Delmarthian Guard order a son of Lang to use that dangerous trail during the fall rains? One of my best friends is dead.*

"Mar, get up in that loft and throw down some hay," Reig ordered.

The two men and the youth, all experienced horsemen worked quickly, and soon the horses were bedded down for the night. They hurried back to the cabin were warmth from the fireplace welcomed them.

Drom untied his scarf and removed his cloak, revealing a head of long curly red hair that hung below his shoulders and a red beard to match it. He joined Maris and Storm by the fire and held his hands over the flames. "What did Reig call you? Mar? Have you known Reig long?"

"Not long." Maris used the prairie-man's language. He had been working very hard at learning it.

Drom stepped away from the fire and studied him. "Danian, aren't you? Only a Danian speaks our language with that accent." He ran his hand through his red hair. "And that Danian horse recognized you." He spun toward Reig. "So that's why we've been speaking Danian. The boy doesn't know our language."

Reig stepped briskly to the fire. He stirred the stew with a long metal spoon then tasted it.

"Oh, good. A mystery." Drom grinned. "One that the great storyteller Reig would rather I didn't solve."

Reig dished up a bowl of stew and handed it to Drom. "I suppose there's no stopping you."

Drom laughed. "A little food never kept me from talking. Not while I'm enjoying your discomfort." He turned to Maris. "Now, I ask you, boy, what kind of a name is Mar for a Danian? Mart? Maybe. But I doubt it. A short time ago, you answered to the name of Maris, didn't you?"

Maris stared at him. *How can this barbarian know anything about me?*

218

"Answer me, boy. You use to be Maris."

"Yes." Maris studied the wood plank floor.

Drom caught Maris' arm and pushed back the sleeve of his tunic. He eyed the 'S' shaped mark, his face lined with displeasure.

Storm cocked his head slightly, glaring menacingly at Drom.

"Drom, let go of my son," Reig said. "Now!"

Drom shoved Maris away from him and faced Reig. "Son? You actually put that boy through one of our adoption ceremonies?"

"I did."

"So there's truth in the rumor flying through the land that the son of the Danian Fox was banished. Now, how did Maris, the son of that Danian fox, Metrox, Delmarath's captain of the guard, come to be adopted by Reig, the master storyteller from the prairies?"

"That's a good question, Drom." Reig scowled. "But the answer lies in the realm of nothing you need to know."

"And you've taken him into our order?" Drom spat. "A Danian. By the great god above all others, Reig, if anyone told me that you'd have anything to do with this little rat, I'd have called him a liar and slit his throat. You have colossal nerve making this little rodent excuse of a son, one of us."

Reig grinned. "Eat up, Drom. Mar, play something."

Drom scraped a bench across the floor to the table, picked up his spoon, skimmed it along the edge of the bowl, and sampled the contents. "Hmm, rabbit, not bad. Where did you get onions?"

"From a well-stocked pantry. Enough food to carry us through the winter."

Maris took his flute and chose one of his own songs, one that Lord Betren had especially liked. It was a song of the mountains, the soft breezes, the flowing water of the streams, the wind rustling through the leaves, the dark forests and bright meadows with flowers dancing in the sunlight. When the song was over, he felt dismayed to see Drom, his spoon in the bowl, the food untouched, staring at him. "Is there something wrong with the stew?"

Drom looked at his dish and then at Maris. "No, there's nothing wrong with the food. It's your music. I saw the mountain in summer." He rubbed his forehead. "He has talent. No doubt about that, but can he muster what it takes to live on our side of the mountain?"

Reig shrugged. "I'll teach him what he needs to know. The rest is up to him. Are you going to eat, or should I put that food back in the pot?"

"Half a minute," Drom grunted and started swallowing stew in earnest.

Maris focused on the bowl as Drom chewed on well cooked carrots speckled with slivers of rabbit. *The toughest part of living with prairie-men is refraining from conversation while eating.*

Drom glowered at him. He leaped to his feet and leaned over the table. "What's wrong, little rat? Haven't ever seen anyone eat before?"

"I'm sorry," Maris said. "I wondered when you'd finish. So many questions about that Danian horse puzzles me. Why would anyone ride that wilderness trail to Chaleen when he could choose a real road?"

Drom continued eating until he polished the bottom of the bowl clean. "Good stew. I don't suppose I could have another?"

"Later," Reig said. "I'm just as curious as Mar about that horse. It's time to pay for your supper."

Storm pleaded with his brown eyes, thumping his tail, hoping to lick out the bowl.

Drom scowled, shoving the bowl to the center of table as he rose to his feet and wiped the stew from his beard on his sleeve.

Storm's tail fell between his back legs and he trotted to the doorway and scratched on the door.

Pivoting after the wolflike dog, Drom said, "be that way. I plan to use that bowl again. But I'll let you out. Go on. Catch your own supper." Drom scuttled to his belongings and freed his backpack from under his cloak. "Suppose to feed a dog well enough that he shouldn't be begging from a guest." Strong stocky fingers wrestled out a packet of parchment and thrust it in front of Maris. "Perhaps these hold the answer. I assume you read Danian."

"I can read, but I need better light." Maris shifted a candle to one side of the table and examined the first page of several pieces of parchment cut into identical sizes. "This isn't a letter. Letters are written on scrolls so the whole letter can be read without turning a page. This is an official report. Captains use scraps of parchment like this for sending messages."

"Interesting." Reig peered over Maris' shoulder. "There are several pieces. How do you know which one to read first?"

Maris pointed to a number 1 at the top of the page. "This was written first." He leafed through the pages. "Each page has a different number meaning that the writing was done over several days."

"And this was written by one of your captains? Evander for instance?" Drom asked.

"Not Evander. This isn't his handwriting."

"What do you mean handwriting?"

Reig raised his hand. "Enough. Read the document, Mar."

"It's entitled *Conditions in Delmarath*. There are several items listed." Maris glanced over his shoulder up at Reig. "Why would anyone in another city request current news of Delmarath written in an official report?"

Drom plopped on the bench opposite Maris. "Oh, I can dream up a few reasons." He leaned forward placing his elbows on the table, resting his chin on folded hands. "Well?"

Noble Prince of Chaleen,

Maris read. He gasped. "This is addressed to Conder."

"Remarkable," Drom said. "A letter to the Lord of Chaleen frightens this little rat."

"Yes," Maris said. "It does." He cleared his throat. *They don't know how dangerous Conder is.*

"Any information you find unnerving keenly intrigues me," Reig said, "and I'm sure the Danian Fox would be interested."

"What difference does it make?" Maris stared at Reig. "You'll ensure Metrox will never see this; no matter what is written here."

"Read it," Reig sat close to his adopted son. The storyteller eyed the parchment as if he could decipher the words.

Maris swallowed and started:

> *My prince, this report covers*
> *events which occurred during the*
> *last few weeks. I delayed sending*
> *this until I acquired a suitable*
> *messenger to entrust this vital*
> *information. The first matter*
> *concerns the absence of Lord*
> *Betren. He has not walked*
> *among us for over two weeks.*
> *Obviously, he remains in the city,*
> *or is no longer among the living*
> *as all his horses are stabled.*

Drom sneered as he sat up straight. "'Obviously remains in the city?' So? The Lord of Delmarath doesn't know how to walk?"

"No Danian Lord ever leaves his city on foot. It's a disgrace. He always rides a horse unless—" Maris caught his breath.

"Unless what, Mar?"

"Unless he has been banished by his people or forced out of a city other than the one he rules." Maris muttered. "Let me finish reading this part."

> *The white Citherian stallion*
> *resides in our Lord's barns.'*

"Warrior? Living in a Delmarthian barn?" Drom's belly shook as he laughed. "We don't have to worry about destroying Delmarath. That devil horse will do it for us. Wonder how many Danians he's killed. Unless—" Drom rubbed his forehead, his

222

fingers pushing his hair off his face. "Lance is dead. That stallion never left Lance's side while the Citherian lived with us. In that case Lord Betren might keep the demon beast as a stud to breed more warhorses."

"Lance isn't in Delmarath," Maris said and continued reading:

Perhaps that renegade Lance, consumed with vengeance, murdered our noble Lord Betren. Obviously, that despicable barbarian knew a secret way into the Hall of Justice. I submit that the House of Bartran sanctioned this knowledge. Their infatuation with these barbarians who lived on the mountain was known by all.

My lord, the people will cheer your legal right to execute Bromwell and his sons and that miserable Captain Metrox.

The teenager's lips tightened. *Normal end for the leaders of any town that falls to the right of rank.* "This next part is ridiculous." Maris stared at Reig as he picked up the second piece of parchment. "It must have been written a day or two later."

"Let's hear it," Reig and Drom chorused.

> *Another rumor of interest;*
> *Metrox, Captain of the Guard*
> *turned on his master and*
> *murdered him. A possibility as he*
> *is now in charge of Delmarath*
> *after Lord Betren's*
> *disappearance. No proof here.*
> *The city bursts with wild*
> *speculations.'*

Drom whistled. "Delmarath is ripe for conquest. Now is the time."

"Impossible," Reig said. "Snow buries the road to Kans; the Danian gods protect Delmarath until spring."

Maris dropped the second parchment on the floor as if it burned him. "I can't read this. You'll use it against Delmarath."

Drom grinned. "Who are we going to tell, Danian boy? With the snow on the mountain, we'll winter right here."

Reig leaned over and scooped the parchment off the floor. "We were just stating a fact, Mar. A city divided like Delmarath is weak, hence easy to conquer. Read the rest of it." He handed the piece of parchment to Maris who laid it on top of the first one.

Maris picked up the third parchment. "This one must have been written the next day. It has to do with my father." He read it silently and groaned.

"Is the Danian Fox dead?" Reig stretched his arm across Maris' shoulder.

The teenager wondered if he would ever get use to Reig's pale hand. He shook his head and resumed reading aloud:

Metrox finalized his summons to Megara by calling a meeting of the captains. Naturally, he placed his nephew, the apathetic Evander in charge of the city.

Maris blinked back tears. "My real father's doing exactly what Evander said he'd do. He won't allow Lord Betren to face the Knife alone; not when he carries half the blame."

"Blame? What blame?" Drom looked from Maris to Reig. "Oh, don't tell me, nothing I need to know."

"It's private," Reig said. "Go on, Mar."

Maris took a moment to locate his place in the report. "Listen to this!" He forgot to keep his voice impartial as was proper when reading a report. He spoke quickly, raising his voice in outrage.

When I deliver the city to you, my great and noble prince, I anticipate your favor for my House by appointing me Defender of Delmarath. I pledge my life to continue in your service.

Maris gasped. *Inconceivable!* He glanced from Drom to Reig. "You're right, a conquest is planned, but you're innocent."

"Explain."

Maris detected sympathy in Reig's face. He gulped. "Conder hates us. Five years ago, Lord Bromwell forced Conder out of Delmarath; mounted riders escorted the Prince and all those with him to walk home to Chaleen. Evander, Metrox, Menes— all who support the House of Melron will pay the ultimate price."

225

Drom hooted. "I assume this traitorous rodent plays the part of a loyal citizen in Delmarath."

Maris felt nauseous. "Several captains who serve in command positions in the guard have relatives in Chaleen."

"Mar, I can't wait to hear the rest of this." Reig clutched the parchment holding it in front of Maris' face.

"That's all that's written on this page; we have to move onto the forth one." Maris held the parchment close to the candle.

That fiend Metrox snuck off to Megara without announcing the day of his departure. Deprived the city of a farewell ceremony. The white stallion and the mare that Evander's woman often rides are missing. So is her sidesaddle. This perplexes me as I saw Lavine with her maid at the well, yesterday. Checked the lists of arrivals and departures at the city gate. None of our lovely ladies left Delmarath, so, what woman would Metrox be escorting to Megara? Is he involved in an illicit affair?

Drom frowned. "I wasn't aware anyone could ride Warrior except Lance."

"My father can." Maris studied the fifth piece of parchment. "We can skip this part. It's only about me."

"Don't even think you can omit that," Reig said as he twisted Maris toward him by seizing his shoulders. "Leave nothing out."

Maris sighed as Reig released him.

The rumor that Metrox banished his worthless son is correct. His precious offspring should have graced the wall long ago.

Maris felt his face grow hot. If he needed proof of the results of how his actions during the last three and half years shamed his father, it was in front of him, a written accusation.

"Mar," Reig spoke, his voice compassionate. "Finish reading."

Maris nodded and read, his lips quivering:

I was off duty so I missed the pleasure of watching Metrox's boy handle his disgrace. My eldest son reports he will die with honor. May it take him days to freeze to death.

Drom eyed Reig. "Why do I have the feeling you didn't stumble on this Danian rat dying on the mountain? What did you barter for his well-being? Perhaps this new son of yours is a Danian undercover agent. Or do you and the Delmarthian Fox have some sort of agreement?"

"I'm not a spy," Maris protested. "All I wish to do is learn how to live on the prairies and entertain people with my music."

"Don't let your imagination run away with you, my friend," Reig snapped. "I'm not beyond dragging someone who falsely accuses me before our order's council at Arondo. Go on Mar."

"Take it easy, Reig." Drom pushed back his bench and stepped away from the table. "It's just that I'm unsettled about what I'm hearing. Go ahead, little rat, read on."

> *Discrediting Evander's ability to rule the city is an easy task. Many desire a proper Lord to rule. Enough fools will support our cause; it will be child's play to convince the guard to serve their Prince instead of a Delmarthian captain. You'll be pleased with them. It's a well-trained unit. I guarantee the gates of the city open for you, my Prince, by spring.*

"That should be a blood bath," Reig commented.

"No, you don't understand!" Maris cried. "Conder is the Crown Prince of Dana. To oppose him would be the same as declaring war on King Cadamire. If Evander lacks the loyalty of the guard and the city gates are opened for the prince, Conder can ride in and declare Right of Rank."

"Right of Rank?" Reig questioned as he stood. "Explain."

"Right of Rank is a law which permits any lord to takeover a city while no noble is in charge. The only lords in Delmarath are of the House of Bartran. Currently, they're all in Megara. Conder plots to rule both Delmarath and Chaleen."

228

"Thereby opening the door for our overly ambitious headsman, Cole of Kans to destroy Delmarath and lead our tribes to their death in the Sistra Gap," Reig stated, his face grim. "Our women will starve without their men. Our people will be annihilated."

Drom drummed his fingers against the stonework of the fireplace, the same as Evander did when he was troubled. First disbelief, then horror crossed Drom's face. He resumed his seat at the table and gawked at Maris.

Maris held his gaze, suddenly conscious of the crackling fire, the whistling wind. He felt cold inside.

"Little rat, do you mean to say the people of Delmarath would forsake Evander whom they know and follow this Conder without a battle just because he's a Lord?" Drom asked after awhile. "What's wrong with them? Are they sheep?"

"It's the law," Maris explained glancing at Reig. "Danians live by the law, or die. No one decides if it's good or not." Maris examined the parchment. "There's one more page."

He read:

> *A personal note. You requested me to inquire if a teller of tales named Greylen had come to Delmarath. He is here on Lord Bromwell's recommendation. If all goes as designed, you will have the pleasure of watching this loudmouth tale spinner die on the wall this spring along with the current command.*

"That teller of tales might prove useful," Drom said. "Anything else?"

"Just the name of who wrote this." Maris caught his breath.

This by the hand of Lang of the House of Langfield.

The teenager held the report closer to his eyes. "It's hard to believe. The House of Langfield, traitors."

"Friends of yours?" Reig asked.

"Laris, the one you found on trail, was." Maris added the last sheet to the pile. "I'm certain that he was the messenger. I guess it's good that he's dead. As soon as Evander receives this packet, the House of Langfield will be punished."

"And I suppose you plan to warn this Delmarthian captain?" Drom started to laugh. "What have you taken under your wing, Reig? A Danian crybaby who will rush back to Delmarath every time someone threatens his city? You're a prairie-man now, boy. You had better change your loyalties— fast."

Chapter 27

Reig stared thoughtfully into the fire. "I assume that the Captain of Delmarath delays informing his people of their upcoming doom?"

"We hoped to wait until Lord Betren and Lance cleared Delmarthian territory," Maris said, "in an attempt to prevent one of our own people obeying the law by killing Lord Betren. You know it's death for a barbarian to enter Dana." The yellow and orange flame curled around two crossing logs.

"Well?" Reig prodded.

"Evander will postpone briefing them until the Winter Festival finishes. It would be his gift to the city." *And how I wish, I were there.*

"A gift that might prove disastrous for your cousin." Drom glared at Reig. "Suppose you fill me in on what's going on."

"You haven't been to Kans lately, have you?" Reig snatched a stick from the wood pile and sat next to the fire.

"No, been up north, entertained the five villages with my stories. Enjoyed myself; let the months fly by until I realized I must make haste to Delmarath. I cut across the plain and stopped at the Chaleen Market to restock supplies. Met a few friends, had a few drinks and before I knew it, I needed to join you here at the cabin and only had four days to complete my journey, so I slipped through the miner's tunnel, hurried along the edge of the great swamp, then ended up here."

"Heard no rumors about black powder or maybe black magic?" Reig drew a square building in the center of a city.

"Black powder? Magic? No, can't say that I did." Drom stared at Reig as he rubbed the red beard on his chin. "Wait a minute. Yeah, it was mentioned in Chaleen."

Maris gaped at Drom. *Chaleen? How could anyone in Chaleen know about the powder? Is that proof that Prince Conder is involved? What's Reig drawing now?* He bit his tongue, not wanting to interrupt.

Reig destroyed his drawing and started another. This time he outlined a stag, the symbol of Chaleen. "Knowledge of this evil spreads."

Drom shoved his bench back and paced around the room. "Condor's guardsmen fastened two bodies to the wall— barbarians. The strange thing was their hair. Thought Lance wore his hair short when he came to Kans. It crawled down the back of his neck, but these men wore their hair clipped above their ears. Never saw anyone on the prairie wear hair that short."

Drom's jaw stiffened. His eyes narrowed; the floor creaked under his feet. "Conder ordered three of his own men executed. Had them stripped, forced them to kiss the feet of the dead barbarians. 'You lost the battle,' he roared."

"Of course that's normal procedure for an extremely painful Danian execution." Drom said as if he read Maris mind.

"Easy on the boy, Drom," Reig said. "Our own methods of execution are not exactly painless."

"True," Drom admitted, but the noble prince's behavior went beyond a normal Danian execution. Conder encouraged the executioners to be brutal without causing death. He ordered his men to pull fingernails off their first victim. Commanded them to cut off

232

the fingers of the second. Bleeding to death would shorten the poor devil's life, so he ordered the wounds cauterized so the flow of blood stopped. Had scalding water thrown into the face of the third. When the men were finally hung on the wall, he ordered his guard to take red-hot torches and apply them to naked flesh." Drom glowered at Maris. "Your prince is a demon. The grin on his face sickened me. The man enjoyed himself."

"Conder's Danian slime!" Maris looked at his favorite tapestry, the one depicting Warrior as a colt. "My father never brutalized condemned men. He drugs them to ease their pain. Sometimes they die before their flesh ever touches the wall."

Drom sighed. "The first poor devil on the wall cursed Conder as he watched the torture of the other two. 'Curse you Conder and your filthy black powder' he moaned. Conder ordered his bowmen to silence the poor rat. I didn't understand the significance of the black powder, but I packed my gear and left."

Reig frowned. "Only two barbarians on the wall? Are you certain?"

"That's right. Why?"

"Because there were four or five that brought that powder to Kans." Reig stroked his beard. "Your report tells me Trac could still be alive. I commissioned him to investigate these strangers. And yes, that powder is a weapon— so powerful it turns stone walls into rubble."

"Powder that destroys city walls?" Drom joined them by the fire and gaped at Reig, disbelief in his grayish green eyes.

"Sit down, Drom. I planned to inform you in the morning, but we might as well discuss it now." Reig tossed his stick into the fire and rose to his feet. "Tell me, Drom, if you can. What would a map of Dana drawn on parchment be doing in the Sacred Cave at Kans? A map meant for our people, with pictures instead of words of names and places."

"Oh." Drom grimaced. "I've seen that map. There's more than one. It's being shown to people in all the villages in the north."

Maris caught his breath. *Copies? Only a lord who employed a scribe would make copies of anything.*

"I questioned the use of parchment," Drom continued. "Besides it's all wrong. The gap of Sistra is omitted and it must lie somewhere between Delmarath and Megara."

"Ah, you believe the old stories rather than the map?" Reig smiled at his friend with approval. "Take note, Mar. Always rely on the old stories when seeking the truth."

"Yes, Reig." *Use stories to impart information?*

Drom nodded. "Someone is inciting our people to war. Ven was killed warning the village of Brie about the gap. And Fin and his son were chased out of Lou for the same reason. All members of our order."

"Hmm." Reig picked up a stick and sketched a sod hut in the ashes. "Trac was right about our people losing their wits. He saved my life in Kans and I really didn't appreciate it." He gazed at Drom. "Sorry about Ven. He was a good friend. Sooner or later, Brie will pay for his death."

Drom fingered his knife hilt. "We can set it up this summer."

Maris shuddered. *Reig's changing even as I sit here. He reminds me of Lord Betren. What happened to my good natured easy going foster father?*

"So far we have a deadly black powder, maps written on parchment showing the way to Megara, a city no man has ever seen," Drom said. "I've had it, Reig. I'm tired of feeling like I'm in the middle of a story."

Reig sighed. "If you insist. Mar, get your lute, I'd like an accompaniment."

"Which story?" Maris asked as he hurried to the place under a beautiful carved wall cabinet where he had stored his instruments before the evening meal. "I need to know the tale first; then I can match it with music."

"You'll find this story familiar," Reig said. "Improvise."

Maris' mind squirmed. "Don't quite understand what you want me to do!"

"Make up the music as I tell the tale." Reig rose to his feet and loomed above Drom. "Listen, my friends, and listen well." The fire flared as if Reig could cue it to do so, on a whim, illuminating his white braided hair and pale bearded face in an eerie orange glow. "I tell a story of friendship between two boys. One, the son of a Danian lord; the other, the son of a barbarian who dwelled in this very house here in the mountains of Citheria."

Maris blinked. *Now Reig's a storyteller again.* He struck a happy tune as Reig spoke of the strange relationship between a Danian Lord and a barbarian horse breeder.

Maris allowed the tune to slow as Reig told about the books made of paper, and showed Drom, Sylvia's tattered storybook. His music became low and threatening as Reig mentioned the <u>Book of Weapons</u> with its information about unbelievable ancient tools of destruction.

He chose the highest notes on his lute as Reig described the black powder called black magic by the men of Kans which reduced walls to rubble.

Reig paused for a dramatic moment. "The boys grew into men as all boys do."

Maris let his fingers flow into a favorite tune common in Delmarath. This was a part of the story he was unfamiliar with and he wanted to hear every detail.

"The family that lived in Citheria ran afoul of Danian law, an easy thing to do, as the Danians have so many of them." Reig allowed his voice to become sorrowful. "The males were branded, hung on the wall. The brash youngest son, Lance escaped the cells and rode through the mountains to the prairies where Trac the trader adopted him. And Lance betrayed the man who nursed him to life, the man who pledged his word to the council that the Citherian would grow into a productive citizen of Kans. Lance repaid him by stealing a sacred bag of powder from the cave and smuggling it to Delmarath."

Three distinct cords followed this statement.

"Drom, this is really serious." Reig gave a short bow, handed Drom the storybook. He unbraided his hair as he spoke. "The men of Kans own two great barrels of the deadly stuff. In spring, men from all over the prairies will gather to destroy Delmarath." He crawled into his bed on the floor and pulled his blankets up to his chin.

Maris laid down his instrument and gazed into the fire. *No one in Delmarath considers Lance a traitor.*

"That's it?" Drom asked.

"That's enough," Reig grunted.

"But what's the ending?"

"There is no ending. We're living this story. I suppose it'll end with the destruction of Delmarath, or it could end with the destruction of Kans and the other prairie towns, including yours for that matter." He pulled the blanket over his head. "Good night."

Chapter 28

Maris couldn't sleep. *Drom says I have to readjust my loyalties. How can I? Lang is committing treason against Delmarath. Evander admires the House of Langfield. The last thing that would cross his mind is Lang's betrayal. The only one who can stop Lang is Evander, and he requires solid evidence in order to execute the house of Langfield. If I fail to deliver this report to Evander, my cousin, my brother, my father — everyone dies a brutal death like Drom described.*

Drom lay still on the floor under a blanket, his breathing even. Reig snored lightly. *Where's the wolf-dog?* Storm hadn't returned from his nightly hunt. *Tonight's my only opportunity. Drom thinks I'm a Danian spy and this will prove him right. Can't avoid that.* Maris tiptoed to the table, snatched the Danian documents and tucked them under his shirt.

Reig grunted and flopped over in his sleep.

Maris flinched. His heart pounded loudly, earsplitting, but not enough to wake sleeping men. Reig housing the ponies at the end of the hallway, beyond the bedrooms, behind the door leading into the woodshed, seemed like a well thought-out solution for caring for the animals, until now. Maris' feet creaked on the hallway floor as he inched toward the closed inner shed door. *Can't go this way; I'm creating enough racket to wake the dead, let alone Reig and Drom.*

Maris held his breath as he backtracked into the main room without rousing the sleeping men.

Neither moved.

Maris slid into his cloak and slipped outside. The cold air robbed his breath as a gust of wind slapped him in his face. He pulled his hood over his head. *Fortunately, there's almost a full moon. I'll have light to find the trail. Good. No sign of Storm.*

He crept to the back of the cabin, unhooked the latch and stepped inside the woodshed.

A pony snorted and drummed his hoofs on the wooden floor. The other whinnied.

Maris retreated, closing the squeaking door. *Never mind, I'll use Drom's horse.* He trudged through the ankle-deep snow into the nearest barn and stumbled over a water bucket. One of the horses whinnied in alarm. "Easy boys." Maris lifted Drom's bridle off its hook and stepped inside the stall.

Drom's gray gelding snorted and reared, his hooves striking the wall.

"Going somewhere? On my horse?"

Maris didn't answer. The knife Drom held at his throat made speaking next to impossible. The bridle slipped through his fingers as Drom yanked him out of the stall and slammed the door behind them.

"Listen, you little Danian rat, you might have left the land of too many laws, but we also have rules on the prairie."

"I didn't do anything."

"The penalty for horse stealing is death, a death as painful as the owner of the animal can imagine and I have a great imagination. Consider yourself fortunate that Reig is your father and has the right to deal with you. Step out of this barn. Don't try anything. I'm an expert with a knife and enjoy putting a horse thief out of his misery."

Maris swallowed and struggled to obey. *Where's Storm when I need him?* He stumbled over a fallen branch.

Drom restrained him with one arm; his other hand positioned the knife against Maris' back. When they reached the door, Drom stopped him. "When we get inside, you'll hang up your cloak, and then return that report to the table. Understand?"

"Yes." Maris unfastened the clasp on his cloak and pulled the stolen parchment from under his shirt.

Drom slammed the front door behind them, halted beside the table permitting Maris to obey him; then shoved the teenager onto the floor in front of the fire. "Caught him stealing my horse. He's all yours, Reig."

Reig propped himself up on his elbow and studied his adopted son. He glanced at Drom. "Are you certain you wish to relinquish the right of punishment? It is your horse."

"He's 'your' son. You carry high rank in our order as you reminded me earlier, I'm only a three-line storyteller." Drom kicked the table leg. "I hate Danians."

Maris hoped he betrayed no emotion. *Why should there be such a fuss over a horse?*

The wind whistled around the cabin, slipping through cracks between the logs forcing the heavy tapestries to billow into the room.

"Well?" Reig said at last. "Explain."

"I wasn't stealing the horse," Maris said slowly. "I was just borrowing it."

"Why?"

"So I could deliver those reports to Evander. I wasn't running away. You're my father."

Reig sat up and folded his arms. "First law of the prairie," he said sternly. "Do not steal another man's horse or borrow it without permission. A man's horse can mean the difference between life and death. It's a prairie-man's most valued possession."

Maris gulped. *Drom would enjoy tearing me apart limb by limb. Dislike the expression on Reig's face. I'm in real trouble.*

239

"Talk to me, Mar." Reig's voice invaded the teenager's thoughts. "Why do you think it's all right to take someone's horse?"

"You're not angry about me touching the reports?"

"We'll get to the reports. The bigger crime is stealing a horse. Surely they feel the same about horses in Delmarath?"

"Oh no, they'd be more upset about stealing the reports. In Dana the horses belong to the city. No one except lords own horses. The guardsmen are allocated mounts while they serve on active duty, but when they retire, the horse is assigned to someone else. I was the son of Metrox, captain of the guard. No one would question me taking any horse from the stable. Oh." Maris stared at the mark on his arm. "I'm no one's son here."

"That's not true," Drom grunted. "You're missing the point, boy."

Reig emitted a low heavy sigh. "Our laws, although different on the prairies than in Dana, apply to everyone when it comes to horse thievery. Who you are, who your father is, makes no difference. I do believe the law is similar in Delmarath."

A piece of wood snapped, sparks landed on the floor beside Maris. The red embers glowed brightly for a moment and then died leaving behind a diminutive pile of ashes. "I didn't know horses were so important," he mumbled.

Drom spoke sharply in the language of the prairies.

Reig answered him.

Drom replied.

Maris looked from one man to another as their endless conversation continued. Reig's face was turned toward Drom, his long hair hung down his back. He emphasized his statements with deliberate hand motions. Drom glowered in the shadows, his angular face half-hidden in the darkness.

Maris stifled a groan. *My fate is being decided, I'm sure of it and I can't understand one word.*

"Mar," Reig said in Danian, "if you are going to live long enough to become a master storyteller, you are going to have to learn to use your head. In order to live in a place, you have to know

240

its laws, understand how people think." Reig shook his head as he said, "Mar, you're a living disaster. You want to help Evander, so you plow ahead into failure. Your friend died of a broken neck because the trails at this time of year are too muddy and too slippery for speed. You really believe Drom's horse could handle a gallop down the mountain any better than that Danian horse? Drom, his actions shout that he's a child. When he grows a beard, we'll try him as an adult. For now, we treat him as a child born on our side of the mountain.

Drom grunted.

Reig glared at Maris. "Morning is almost upon us. Just how do you expect to get into the Hall of Justice in broad daylight?"

Maris couldn't look at Reig. "I guess I'm stupid."

"I begin to understand your captain's dismay at your performance. You must have driven Evander mad."

"I did the best I could," Maris said sullenly.

"Did you?" Reig asked. "As a Danian, you owed your city four years of your life. You seemed to fancy yourself better than any other young man in Delmarath, that you could ignore the rules. That behavior is why you sit before me, a prairie-man, instead of sleeping in the house of your fathers', safe behind the walls of Delmarath. Are you going to repeat the last few years here?"

Maris knew Reig was right. He pushed himself up on one knee and took Reig's hand in his.

"Here, what are you doing?" Reig jerked his hand away and rammed Maris back on the floor. "Prairie-men don't kneel like that."

"But when I want to say something I really mean, I kneel to the man I'm speaking to." Maris remained sprawled in front of Reig, the fire hot on his back.

"Don't kneel to me, ever."

Maris felt death's cold fingers crawling up his spine. "You've decided how you'll handle this. I must pay the price for stealing a horse." He sighed. "I faced plenty of punishment in Delmarath, but this is different. I want to do the right thing, and I've blundered into disaster."

241

"Mar, come sit beside me." Reig patted the floor next to him. Maris obeyed slowly.

"The only time prairie-men kneel is when they participate in a ceremony. Now, what did you want to tell me?"

Maris stared at the fire. *It would be easy for me to say, if I could speak while kneeling.* "No one does this in Delmarath."

"Duh, where do you think you are?" Drom growled.

Reig waited, patiently.

Drom took an ax and hacked a log into a multitude of kindling. He built up the fire, then snatched some candles from a shelf and lit them.

"Danian law demanded my death. I should have been executed," Maris said haltingly.

"I know that, Mar. What of it?"

"My father— my real father cheated the law so I could live. He risked his life for me."

"So, who's to know that the Danian Fox did anything illegal?" Drom backed from the fire, an interested spectator.

"My father knows what he did," Maris said. "And if ever he takes the Knife and is questioned about his family, he must tell the truth. The punishment for letting me live is death."

"The Knife?" Reig scratched his head. "Are you talking about the Knife of Truth?"

Maris nodded.

Drom whistled. "We have a couple of stories about that weapon. I didn't think it existed."

"The point is I've been a fool," Maris said. "I spent the last few years believing that if I couldn't devote all my time playing instruments and making up songs, it didn't matter what I did. I never considered how my actions affected anyone else."

"You are saying this to the wrong father," Reig said softly.

"I know, but I'll never see him again." Maris looked up at Reig, unable to stop the tears that welled in his eyes. "The only way I can thank him is to live this life he made possible for me, stay alive and learn everything."

242

Reig drew Maris close to him. "Cry, lad. Let yourself grieve as a prairie-man. It's your first lesson."

"You mean it's all right to cry?" Maris gasped between sobs.

"Of course it's all right," Drom said. "We cry, we scream, we roar, we throw things, we have ceremonies which encourage us to do this." He groaned and ran his hands through his red hair. "Oh, don't tell me. I know. Danians don't cry. It's death on the wall to weep. Right?"

"It's enough for this boy to know there is no shame in tears," Reig said quietly.

Drom threw another log on the fire and then wandered over to the wall cabinet where Maris had left his instruments. He picked up the guitar and strummed it softly, humming quietly to himself.

Slowly Maris' sobs subsided. For awhile he just sat with his head in his fists, Reig's hand on his shoulder. *No Danian ever cried in public.* Finally, he mumbled, "I'm sorry."

Reig's hand tightened on his collarbone. "For what, Mar?"

"For attempting to steal a horse; for being such a cry baby."

"I'm not going to punish you for the horse, not this time. You didn't know, but if you ever do it again, you'll pay the price like any other prairie-man. Understand?"

"Thank you," Maris whispered.

"As for crying, it is not the way of the prairie-men to hide sorrow. You have a right to mourn. You suffered a great loss. Not only your father, but your family, your city, your way of life — everything that you once knew is gone.

"It was my fault."

"Yes. It was." Reig grabbed Maris' chin forcing Maris to meet his eyes. "You made a mistake, that's all. I must say it was a rather large one, but all men make mistakes. And once made, must live with the consequences. For you that means learning a new language, a new way of life, living with people, you have been taught to hate since birth and who have been taught to hate your people. It won't be easy, but you're my son, an apprentice storyteller and will be treated as such. I agree with you on one point. Your feeble

243

attempt to relay those reports to Delmarath bordered on stupidity, nevertheless, Evander should be alerted."

Chapter 29

"Reig!" Drom's green eyes turned as hard as stone. He said something that sounded threatening in another language as he stomped toward Reig.

"Repeat what you said in Danian." Reig stood and nodded in Maris' direction.

"I said:" Drom stared up at Reig's stern expression. "Whose side are you on in this conflict? Are you a traitor to our people?"

Reig met Drom's gaze. "No, although our leaders will probably say that. I've no intention of riding with Cole to conquer Delmarath."

Maris sat on a bench and held his stomach. *Why should I tell Drom and Reig anything? Aren't they the enemy? But I'm no longer Danian. Does that make me an enemy? How can I help destroy the place where I've spent my life, murder my friends, people who loved me?* He glanced at Reig and saw understanding in the storyteller's face.

"I plan to be in the caves of Arondo by spring." Reig side-stepped behind Maris and patted his shoulder. "Mar has so much to learn and I want only the best of our order to teach him. Besides, he needn't be caught up in a battle against his own people."

Maris sighed in relief.

"Nothing wrong with that," Drom said quietly, "but—"

"Nor, have I any intention of warning the Danians when the attack begins," Reig said as he strode in front of Drom, leveling his finger at him. "If they lack the intelligence to put outlooks on the mountain, that's their business."

Evander would have no problem with that one, Maris thought. *Conder wouldn't bother.*

"I don't understand. Where in the name of loyalty does delivering these reports to Delmarath fall?" Drom fingered his knife.

Maris gaped at Reig. When his ex-father had suggested the pact between the storyteller and the Lords of Delmarath concerning Danian involvement, Reig held his tongue. In Dana that was the same as a refusal, and so the matter had been dropped. But silence must have a different meaning on the prairie.

Reig gave Drom a long hard look. "I haven't told you everything. This Danian report convinces me, the Prince of Chaleen is enticing our people with a dastardly scheme to rip apart the walls of Delmarath. Walls which protect us from Delmarthian guardsmen and their ridiculous laws down through the ages."

Drom nodded; his eyes narrowed. "Then lure us into ambush in the valley of Sistra. Danians also sing a version of that old tale."

"What do you think Mar? Would Conder gain great honor achieving this victory?" Reig asked.

Maris grinned. "Questionable honor, Reig. He's obviously just after the throne."

Drom grunted backing away from Reig. "My dear, friend, and teacher, you know too much about Conder. Where do you dig up your wealth of insider-facts concerning Danian politics?"

"Remember the year of the great snow?"

Drom nodded.

"Trac and I rescued the Prince and his crippled son from certain death." Reig sat on the bench next to Maris and stroked his beard thoughtfully. "That might have been a mistake."

"Definitely," Drom agreed. "And?"

"We found our way to this cabin and spent the winter. I had the questionable pleasure to live in the same house with Conder. The Lords of Delmarath were also trapped here."

"Must have been one big happy family. It's a wonder that anyone survived. That's where you first heard about this powder of death?"

"Yes, that's why I distrust Conder. No proof, of course, just a nagging hunch."

"My ex-father thought so too."

"So destroy the powder." Drom pounded his fist on the table and threw up his hands. "That shouldn't be so hard."

"Except no one knows how to do that." Reig started to doodle with a long stick that reached into the ashes. "Besides, do you really imagine that would slow that fat old Danian rat? He'd just obtain more powder and try again, or bide his time and try something worse."

"So, let's give him an untimely death."

"Drom, my friend, I taught you better! You're forgetting the tale of Megu."

Drom screwed up his face, tapping his index finger as he considered the tale. "Well, let's see," he said in Danian with only a slight prairie-men's accent.

Maris watched in fascination as Drom paced about the cabin counting off the parts of the story on his fingers as he spoke.

"There's the horse race, the disappearance of the prairie-men and the death of the Danian. There's a bit about Megu, the builder of sod houses, great chief of our people and creator of our laws. So?" Drom ran his hand through his hair. "What's your point?"

"Keep going," Reig said.

"The violent reaction to the disappearance of the racers, the death of Megu. Withdrawal of the Danians into the mountains... Oh. This is the part you mean."

Reig grinned. "Let's see you tell our version of the tale in Danian."

Drom thought a second, stood in front of Maris and Reig, spread out his hands and translated from his language into Danian: "A great anger arose among our people. The drums sounded day and night summoning warriors from other villages. Songs of retaliation and battle were sung. Each man boasted of his valor, described his conquest and danced showing his valiant intent. Danians murdered Megu. Everyone savored the sweet honor of revenge."

"Bravo, bravo, magnificent," Reig exclaimed. Maris applauded enthusiastically.

Drom bowed. "All right, Reig, I got it. If we kill Conder it would be considered an act of war. Give the Danians an excuse to attack. Our villages lack walls to protect us."

Reig clapped his hands. "That parchment, my son Mar tried to deliver has nothing to do with our people, but everything to do with our people's welfare. You buy and sell at the Delmarthian Marketplace. The Lords of Delmarath keep order. You trade in the Chaleen Market. In Chaleen your life depends on the whims of the insanely sadistic Prince Conder and his henchmen. These parchments may fuel the Delmarthians toward preserving our livelihood. Only Delmarthians can solve this sticky situation."

Drom howled. "Reig, you're playing with fire. Who'd ever guess a few smart barbarians could control the entire fate of Danian oppressors. I don't suppose you'd care to elaborate a bit on how Mar ended up here."

"Some other time, perhaps." Reig yawned as he laid down in front of the fire. "Enough for one night." He pulled his blankets over his head. "Tomorrow, we have much to do. Must get ready for our part in the Delmarthian Gathering of the Greens."

"Yeah," Drom agreed, "maybe even create a new song. What was the name of that teller of tales?"

"Greylen," Maris rolled up in his blankets and closed his eyes. In a few hours he and his new father would figure out how to rescue his ex-cousin Evander.

Chapter 30

Greylen found Delmarath exhilarating. The locals welcomed his songs, especially the ditties which told of the activities of the lords of the land. He considered replacing his well worn patched cloak with the new one Evander's wife fashioned for him, except that his many colored cloak still attracted an audience.

The beginning of the Winter Festival unsettled him. He had a difficult time fathoming why the storytellers from the prairies somewhere over the mountains participated in any Danian celebration. Not only were these barbarians, an important part of the Gathering of the Greens, the Delmarthians expected him to sing with them and tell a story as his contribution to the event. All the teller of tales in Delmarath were expected to participate. This year he held the dubious honor of being the only one. Greylen's part in all this wouldn't begin until sunset, but he wanted to get a feel for the stage and work out his act.

And so Greylen stood on the mountainside observing groups of people as they searched for small pine trees to erect in their homes to decorate with ribbons, pinecones, beads, and popcorn. Young and old, hacked conifer branches for their shelves, windows and counter-tops. Wagons hitched to teams of farm horses stood ready to be loaded to transport the evergreens to the city.

Following Captain Evander's instructions, the teller of tales located the area where the evening's activities would begin, an arena built by the gods, flat on the bottom, with gentle slopping hillsides providing room for people to stand and listen. He tried a small ditty. He didn't appreciate the quality of the acoustics of the place, until Evander called to him and clapped his hands.

"Greylen. One moment." Evander half slid, half climbed down the side of the natural amphitheater. "That was great," he said as he reached Greylen's side. "However, why aren't you wearing the cloak Lavine sewed for you? Don't you like it?"

"It's a wonderful cloak, my Lord. Give your woman my highest regards."

"Lavine is beside herself in disappointment. She is sure her sacrifice was completely wasted on an ingrate who masquerades as a teller of tales."

"I've been told you would not attend the festivities on the mountain this evening." Greylen hoped to change the subject. "The lord or acting defender must be in the Hall of Justice. Your part is to welcome the people back into the city and declare that the Winter Festival has begun."

"I've shared Levine's grievances with you. Her maid put much time into stitching your new cloak which could have been spent on preparations for the Winter Festival. Start wearing that cloak."

"Captain," a small boy cried. "Come look at the greens I've collected for my mother."

Evander smiled as he scanned the pile of spruce boughs surrounding the youngster.

"I'm trapped. Can you help me?"

Evander lifted the youngster into the air, swung him over his branches and placed him on the ground. "Better?"

"Yes, Captain. Now, all I have to do is figure out how to get them down to the city." The boy raised a pair of pleading eyes. "Any suggestions?"

"I was recently reminded that by the time you reach the city, I'm supposed to be waiting for you." Evander grinned. "I'll watch for you from the Hall of Justice. I'm sure you'll make out just fine." He turned, raising his hand in farewell and headed for his horse.

Thoughtfully, Greylen climbed up the mountain away from the people already piling greens into the wagons. *If only I could dream up a brand-new story appropriate to this festive occasion. Wish I could deviate from the old traditional tales, I feel so much more comfortable with my repertoire of current affairs.*

He found a small hollow out of the wind and was about to build a fire, when he was surprised by a stocky man, about his height, but dressed in the fur lined leather garb of the prairie-men. Surprised wasn't exactly the right word — befuddled, perhaps. The barbarian's knife at his throat was very persuasive in him relocating away from his original spot to one further up the mountain, where an older man waited for them by a small fire.

"Ah, good, you found him," the older man said. "I hope we are not causing you any distress. Did Drom hurt you? Sometimes his methods are a little rough."

"But effective," Drom protested. "I doubt any argument I could sprout would produce the same results so handsomely."

Greylen gawked at their pale faces and rosy cheeks. Reig's long gray braided hair, Drom's shoulder length red curls, and both men's full beards unsettled his already queasy stomach. "Who are you? What do you want of me?"

"I am Reig, master storyteller, of Kans and the surrounding lands," the gray hair man said. "Drom here," he pointed to Greylen's captor, "is also a storyteller and my friend. You must be the teller of tales from Megara. It is said you wear a coat of many patches."

Greylen nodded. *If I wore my new coat, these two would never have recognized me.*

Reig sat on a log next to the fire. "Sit. Let's talk."

251

Drom turned the rabbit roasting on the spittle above the flickering flames.

Talk? Greylen wondered if he heard right. *What could I possibly say to these barbarians?* He waited.

"You are new to Delmarath?" Reig asked.

"I've been here before." Greylen stared at Reig. His pale skin and his piercing hazel eyes stirred his memory. "I remember you. You told those dazzling stories in the marketplace years ago. My father demanded that I follow his footsteps as a silversmith. I felt quite uncertain on how to select a career but I sensed it was other than that of a craftsman. Then I witnessed your performance and knew I found my calling. I joined a group of visiting tellers of tales and they kept me on as an apprentice. But this is too much about me — and to complete barbarians. Storyteller, what business do you desire with Greylen the Great?"

"I inspired a Danian to take up storytelling? What a compliment." Reig gave him a long hard look. "Where is Lord Betren? Where is Metrox, the Captain of the Delmarthian Guard? Why aren't they on the mountain this day?"

Greylen shrugged. "No one has seen Lord Betren for sometime. Some say he's dead." He stopped. *How much do I divulge to these strange looking men?*

"But you don't think so?" The older man smiled.

Greylen stared at the fire.

"Well? Answer me. Or would you rather Drom beat it out of you."

Drom stood up and unfastened his sheepskin cloak letting it fall to the ground exposing muscles developed from other duties than telling stories. He clenched his fists. "I always enjoy pounding Danian flesh."

Greylen's lip quavered. "I don't know."

Reig looked skeptical.

Drom advanced toward him; his hand lashed out and knocked Greylen into the snow.

Greylen considered a quick roll out of range of the barbarian, then realized he had no room to maneuver. A large half-rotten log blocked that idea.

Reig motioned Drom to stop. "Are you so loyal to Delmarath that you prefer death, to sharing a little innocent information?"

Greylen sighed. He pushed himself up and leaned against the log. *Why couldn't I have just said 'thank you my Lord,' when Bromwell handed me my recommendation?' Life would have been so much easier.* "Delmarath is Bromwell's city. I swore an oath to the noble Lord Bromwell that I would not harm him or his house in anyway."

"Danian oaths," exclaimed Reig. "It's beyond all belief of reasonable men to understand how mere words can bind one man to another, even in the face of death." He motioned Drom back. "Forget it, friend. You could beat him to pulp and we'd be no further ahead. We'll try my method." He stood.

Greylen remained still.

Drom put his leather cloak back on and stepped behind the teller of tales, his long sharp knife in his hand.

Reig's features relaxed as he smiled. "Pay attention, Greylen. I'm about to tell you a story that will explain much."

A story? Will I die at the end?

Reig raised his arms assuming the opening stance of his story-telling position. "Once there were two boys, one the son of the Defender of Delmarath, the other the son of a barbarian who lived in the mountains of Citheria."

Greylen forgot about Drom standing behind him as he listened. *Friendship between Danian and barbarian? Why would Bromwell permit it? And I considered the House of Bartran too dull to make an interesting tale. Now, because of my oath to Bromwell, I can't use it.*

The fact that the family that lived in Citheria ran afoul of Danian law did not surprise him. Death by hanging on the wall was a normal punishment. However, the fact that one escaped from the cells in the Hall of Justice suggested that one of the House of Bartran had broken the law.

Stories written in books on something called paper? Horrible idea. If everyone could read about the songs I sing, I'd be out of a job. He heaved

253

a heavy sigh. *The men of Kans have an ancient weapon that they plan to employ against Delmarath?* He shuddered.

When Reig finished, Greylen said, "Bromwell is a Lord whose reputation is beyond reproach." He sifted through the facts of the story. *Actually such a friendship is not unlawful. It just isn't done, that's all. But a weapon that could turn walls to rubble? Where did these barbarians gain this knowledge?* Somehow he was quite sure he didn't want to know. He looked from Reig to Drom. "The destruction of Delmarath should please you. Why should you care?"

"We don't." Drom said flatly. "But we have uncovered information that may point to a Danian prince at the back of all our trouble. It bothers us that such a one could manipulate our people into an ambush for his own purposes."

"A Danian prince? The only man that holds that title in Dana is the King's brother, Conder of Chaleen!" Greylen gaped at them. "The King's brother a traitor? Do you have proof?"

"No. Unfortunately, not enough to prove it one way or the other," Reig said. "What we do know is that the Prince of Chaleen is trying to stir up trouble in Delmarath in order to ride into the city and proclaim the Right to Rule."

Greylen stared into Reig's hazel eyes. *Conder in Delmarath is an unwelcomed prospect. I'll join any that oppose his takeover of the city. This attempt to oust Evander from position of defender must be a well-kept secret.* "Where did you acquire those facts?"

Even as he asked the question, Greylen considered comments and conversations in the last week or so — yes, now that he thought about it, *people had been complaining that Delmarath should be ruled by a lord. Evander is merely a captain. The only reason he received the appointment of acting defender was because he is related to Metrox who rode off with a woman to Megara.*

Reig looked at him shrewdly. "I don't need to reveal my sources. You've already compiled information to collaborate our claim. So now I will ask a question that you should be able to answer without betraying your pledge to Bromwell. Do your people know about this threat from the other side of the mountains? Have they heard about the black powder?"

Greylen shook his head. "Evander will keep that foul tidbit to himself until after the Winter Festival. He's unusual for one in his position. He actually cares about people. It would be just like him to let everyone celebrate the holidays without the thought of death hanging over their heads."

"That may be a mistake for Evander," Drom said. "The comments I overheard while I hunted for you, shout that wondering where Lord Betren is undermines this season's usual holiday cheer. They actually feel threatened unless a lord sits in the Hall of Justice."

"They are." Greylen shrugged. "It's an intrinsic part of Danian society. You wouldn't understand." He stared into the fire. He wondered if the two barbarians had any better luck searching for answers in the flickering flames. A piece of wet wood sizzled and snapped. The wind blew the smoke in circles. Sometimes it was hard to breathe, much less concentrate. An unpleasant thought invaded his mind. *Anyone coming across two barbarians and a Danian sharing a fire would only have one word for it. Treason.* He jumped to his feet. "Why are you doing this? What's the point?"

Reig smiled. "Or more to the point, what do we want you to do?"

Greylen tapped his foot. "Is it usual for storytellers of the prairie and Danian teller of tales to plan this event together? I was told that you did your thing. I led some songs and sang a story or two and that was it."

"That's how it works most years," Reig said. "Sometimes we acquaint ourselves with the Danians who are participating. Ensure we aren't using the same material. It's a professional thing." He took the rabbit off the fire. "We don't usually kidnap them, but if we are seen conversing, no one will think it improper. We're outside the walls of the city, remember. This is neutral ground."

Greylen gulped. *Neutral territory. There's no law here.* "Same material? How can that be?"

Drom shook his head. "We don't know, Danian, but songs about this time of the year, our ancient stories about this holiday almost always have a Danian counterpart. Delmarthians love our versions of Sanclaw and the mysterious child born in a stable.

"Oh, you mean, 'Silent Night, Holy Night'?" Greylen asked. "I never imagined that song meant one particular child. I fancied it as a tribute to all new born children."

"Sometimes, I think as you." Reig sliced a chunk of the rabbit and offered it to Greylen. "But at other times it seems that a specific child is meant. There is one village on the edge of the great plains, miles from here where that child is thought to be the son of the Great God above all others." He shook his head. "Teller of Tales, I see that we could spend hours learning from each other."

"Reig, my friend," Drom interrupted. "The shadows are lengthening. We don't have hours." He smiled at Greylen. "Teller of Tales, we want you to sing a story, your type of story about what's happening here and now."

"Starting with 'Once there were two boys, one the son of a Lord and the other the son of a barbarian.' I don't think so, Prairie-men. That story has too much supposition in it, information that I have no way of substantiating."

"Figured that might be the case," Reig said.

"I can see only one point where we agree. None of us wants to see Prince Conder become Defender of Delmarath." Greylen swallowed the rabbit as he returned to his seat on the log. "My reason is personal. Yours?"

"We know enough about how Conder runs the market outside of the Chaleen mines to know that we prefer the House of Bartran in that position," Reig answered.

Again, Greylen felt that Reig omitted important details that he secretly knew and acted on. "Why should I believe you? How do I know that you aren't trying to set me up to appear to be a complete idiot?"

Reig looked at Drom and nodded.

Drom removed a packet of Danian parchment from his pack. "Read this. You'll be especially interested in the last entry."

Greylen chewed his lip as he slowly read the documents. It had been a long time since he was a child and attended school. He hadn't had reason to read anything except Bromwell's letter of recommendation which he read on his way to Delmarath. He had totally missed a sentence or two there. It took him awhile to decipher the cursive writing. When he reached the last entry, he felt like he had been struck with a six foot staff. It was Conder who was involved with the beautiful Elana. Conder had a wife. Adultery was punishable by death.

For a hundredth time, Greylen wondered how he could have been so stupid as not to check the facts before singing that song in the palace. Before reading this, Conder was one of several possibilities. Now, Greylen knew that his greatest fears were true. If Conder ruled Delmarath, Greylen's days were numbered. "Evander should see this," he muttered.

"Already taken care of," Reig said. "This is a copy. Are you convinced of our sincerity?"

Greylen shook his head. "The only detail I really understand is Conder's ambition to rule Delmarath. You're right. The people need to realize the danger threatening them." He knew a way to initiate that process. It was harmless enough. He looked at Drom's guitar. "May I?"

Drom nodded and handed it to him.

Greylen strummed a few cords. "Nice sound." He picked out a little tune and started to sing:

"Good people of Delmarath.
Gather round and listen well.
I have questions I would ask
Can you their answers tell?
Where is the Lord Betren?
Is he dead or alive?
Come now, tell me the answer?
Perhaps Evander can try.

Did Metrox kill our Betren?
Has he gone to tell the king?
Who is the woman with him?
A long lost lover's fling?
Power flooded his head?
Rooting a doleful dive?"
Come now, tell me the answer?
Perhaps Evander can try."

"That's good," Drom said. "Never thought of that form of song before. I like it."

"Excellent!" Reig agreed. "Can you make up more verses?"

"No problem," Greylen said. "I can create enough verses to sing our way down the mountain to the city gates, but that's not how I work. I'll start by singing softly to myself ensuring that I'm within the earshot of any group of people. When their conversation turns from the fun of the season to the problems of the city, I will slip away to another group and repeat my performance. If I'm successful, the songs of the season will be replaced by my song. At the end of your performance, I'll rise and sing my song claiming that I listened to people singing about this all afternoon and so I will express the feelings of the people on this day of celebration."

Drom nodded at him with approval. "I like your methods, Teller of Tales." He handed Greylen some rabbit. "Come on let's eat before we work. Then I'll walk you back down the mountain to the place where we left your instrument."

Greylen followed Drom down the mountain with a dry taste in his mouth. He could have used a goblet of wine with that rabbit. *I'm trapped between the barbarians and Conder. Wished I understood the storyteller's game, I might feel better about what I'm about to do. My song will rouse the people. Conder must not rule Delmarath. Only one weak point in my plan, there's no one below Evander who can hold the people together until the House of Bartran returns. What will Evander do when confronted with an infuriated mob?*

258

Chapter 31

"Reig's right, I would've never made Delmarath in the dark," Maris muttered as he jerked the pony's rein. "Trail's traitorous." Slippery snow plastered leaves on the ground. The sun slid behind the mountains.

Maris' idea had been to approach the city while the storytellers entertained most of the people on the mountain and reunite with Reig and Drom before the crowd paraded back to the Hall of Justice. Reig suggested that he travel in daylight and lay low until show time. Maris had waited until noon to leave the cabin. Perhaps he should have started earlier. Night covered the land with blackness. The entertainment provided by the storytellers might have already begun.

Maris sighed. *Loved the Winter Festival but I won't ever partake in the Gathering of the Greens again. Not unless I return as a storyteller and I'm sure Reig will prohibit that for a long time to come, certainly not until I learn to act, think and speak like a prairie-man.* It was only because he still looked Danian and the fact that the sons of Bromwell had left clothes at the cabin, that he could pull this off.

Maris reached the clearing where Lance once tied Warrior when he visited the marketplace. Having fastened the pony to a tree, Maris hurried down the mountain. Voices stopped him. He tried to slow his heavy breathing as he waited in the darkness until a party of people passed him, then joined the group in the rear. The stable master's voice caused his heart to jump and settle in the pit of his stomach. This man taught him how to care for his first pony. Maris tied his hood tight around his face, his heart pounding. Still, no one noticed the addition of one more person coming off the mountain.

As they reached the marketplace, the group dissolved, some to warm themselves by the fires, some to gather wood. Others cheered on a hockey game that was in progress. Maris followed the few who sauntered toward the city gates. A shaft of confidence lightened his steps until a snowball hit him in the back of the neck. He resisted the urge to bend down and pack together his own as another one struck his back. *I recognize these voices — the brothers and sisters of one of my friends. I spent many marvelous hours in that house.* He forced himself to ignore them and maintain the same pace until he reached the city gates.

He ducked to one side of the gate number three, and crouched in the darkness, as some first year guardsmen darted into the marketplace. Obviously off duty, they laughed, shouted, and wrestled each other into the snow.

Maris slipped up a dark vacant side street which led to the Hall of Justice in the middle of town. His timing was as excellent as he had hoped. Everyone either attended the program on the mountain or participated in the activities in the marketplace.

At last, the Hall of Justice loomed in front of him. *Good, it's unguarded. No one manning the stairs. Use to sneak up these stairways at night when I was a boy. Must be careful. Stop. Listen for anyone lurking around as I approach these torch-lit areas.* He paused to catch his breath and rest his sore legs. *How much farther is it?* His lungs felt like collapsing; his legs as heavy as stone when he swung open the door to the Hall of Justice, allowing it to close with a bang and struggled up the last six stairs.

Evander sprang to his feet, his hand on his knife. The blue glowing magic ball lit the area around the table and then dimmed.

"Captain," Maris panted.

Evander froze. "Maris! Are you out of your mind? What in the name of all the gods are you doing here? You're dead!"

"Maris? I'm not Maris. I'm Mar, apprentice to Reig, a Master Storyteller, one of the greatest storytellers, who lives on the prairie. I have a package for you. It's important."

"You, barbarian! I should kill you now." Evander held his knife against Maris' gut. "It better be important to risk all our lives with your presence in Delmarath." Evander returned his knife to its sheath and shook Maris by the shoulders.

Maris or rather Mar, drew the packet out from under his cloak and shoved it in front of him. "This was found on Laris of the House of Langfield on the trail that runs along the mountain to Chaleen."

Evander snatched the stack of parchment and flipped through the contents. He looked up and studied Mar. "You're sure of your facts?"

"Drom, one of our storytellers delivered it to Reig. I saw Laris' horse. He had been down; there was damage to his knees."

"You're sure Drom didn't kill Laris and steal his horse?"

"As sure as I can be without seeing the body to verify cause of death. None of this matters. What is written on this parchment does. You can't accuse Drom of writing it. He's prairie-man."

Evander nodded. "You're right, but you've got to leave. If anyone sees you, we both will be executed. Our House, wiped off the map Dana. Besides, no barbarian is permitted on this side of the wall."

"What do you mean no barbarians? Reig, Sylvia, Lance; they're barbarians."

"They're not welcomed here. Not under my command." Evander glanced out of the window. "Wait. Everyone is coming off the

261

mountain. Don't go yet. Anyone traveling in the opposite direction will be noticed."

Mar gulped. *What have Reig and Drom been up to while I traveled to Delmarath? I'm sure it has something to do with the torches advancing on the city.*

"Can I use the secret passage?"

"No, last night's storm sealed it for the winter. It's frozen shut. Hide behind the tapestry. Now!"

A blue light flooded the room.

"There's something in magic ball," Mar exclaimed. He leaned over the table. "Look, there's a room exactly like the cabin in Citheria."

"Forget the ball! Hide!"

Mar dashed toward the spot where the wall hangings concealed the man-sized opening behind the table. Unintentionally, he stumbled into Evander.

"Watch out!" Evander shoved Mar away from him.

Mar flew backwards; his right hand brushed the back of the ball.

Evander vanished in a flash of blue light. The Hall of Justice faded away.

Chapter 32

Trac gazed through the window in the main room at Trail's End in the land of Merkan, a country unknown to all men on the prairie. The snow glistened in the moonlight; the open land between the cabin and the forest buried under wind sculptured drifts obliterated the trail that led through the forest to freedom. The snow-covered trees that crowded the edge of the clearing projected a feeling of imprisonment to the prairie-man familiar with open grasslands. *Long for home, but I'd be a fool to pretend that I can out-ski men who have used this excellent means of transportation all their lives. I must find some other way to escape.*

"The good Lord showers us with his gifts of beauty even in the cold, cruel winter," Karl remarked quietly. "I believe you share my feelings." The head of the 12 Districts of Merkan joined Trac.

"I stand in awe of winter's beauty. I know the season's cruelty only too well. Frigid weather slaughters the unprepared." Trac sighed. "I keep hoping that I'll see Peter and Marcia skiing toward the cabin. They've been missing for three days and told no one their plans."

"I'm sure we've seen the last of them." Karl crossed his arms gathering the blue and green plaid blanket that he had draped over his wool shirt and dark trousers snugly around his body. "I surmise they've sneaked off to celebrate the Thanksfest with relatives. It's tomorrow, you know."

"Odd that your Thanksfest occurs about the same time as our Winter Festival. My people will be lighting fires soon, they'll be gathering to celebrate the holidays." Trac stuck up his lower lip at Karl. "I long to be home, but this early winter holds me captive with its unusually deep snow and severe blizzards." *Not that these leaders of Merkan would permit me to leave. They consider me dangerous. I've intruded into a land where people believe they are the only race who inhabits this earth. I am proof that their point of view is wrong. Some here wish me dead. It's only a matter of time.*

"Counselor John, you are staying here for the holidays." Sybil, head of the Thunderhills District strode into the main room from the kitchen, her back rigid, determination written in her face. Her sharp voice filled the room. "We will celebrate Thanksfest in this cabin." Sybil always used formal Merkan titles when exasperated.

Karl winced.

"I have a district of my own to run." John lumbered after her, a hunk of bread in his hand. "Besides, I have an escort eager to be home with their families." He shoved a piece of the bread into his large mouth and chewed nosily. "Councilor Sybil. You are not head of the 12 Districts. How dare you order me about?"

"Our rangers will survive." Sybil whirled to face him. "We need you here."

"I intend on spending our Lord's birthday at my homestead in Hio," John bellowed. He turned away from her and sank down on a bench near the kitchen door. "I have some important issues to address."

"There's too much at stake here for you to abandon us." Sybil glanced at Karl and smiled. "Councilor Karl, I know I'm right, but I will submit to your auth—"

Brilliant white light flashed into the cabin turning the night outside to day, accompanied by a horrendous noise. The floor greeted Trac as Karl's wiry body slammed into him, shielding the prairie-man's face with his blanket as window glass shattered. The floor shook. The blanket scrunched under both men. Dishes rattled in the cupboard. Screams erupted from the kitchen where the women slaved on the feast to be held the next day. Outside, trees snapped; a branch struck the building.

"Lie still. This is what a lot of gunpowder does when someone ignites it properly," Karl hissed. "Wait until everything settles." Blackness flooded the room, most of the oil lamps extinguished by the blast.

"My ears," Trac groaned. "I can't stop them from ringing." He stared unbelievingly at the shattered window above his head as a blast of frigid air entered the room.

"Result of that horrible noise. We're all affected. Easy, it will pass," Karl assured him.

"Thought it was lightning, or a giant landside," Trac gasped. "Makes the worst thunderstorm I've seen on the prairie insignificant." An acid aroma assaulted his nose drying his throat.

Blue light flashed across the room accompanied by a yelp of pain. A slender figure sprawled on the rug in front of the fireplace. "What happened? This room was in one piece a moment ago."

Trac froze. No one spoke Danian in Merkan.

"Who's that?" Karl grabbed the only lamp that remained lit and rose to his knees holding it so it illuminated a brown face beardless youth wearing a red cloak flowing over leather boots, tan tight fitting pants, and bright red tunic. "Where did this — this mutant come from? What gibberish is he babbling?"

Trac focused in the direction of Karl's hand and recognized Maris, the talented son of Metrox, Captain of the Guard of Delmarath. He motioned the teenager to be silent as he lurched to his feet.

"Good Lord in heaven, is this a storm of biblical proportions?" Sybil asked as she staggered to her feet, her blue slacks, tunic, and long gray braids pinned tightly around her dust-covered head. "Dear Lord, what happened?" She picked up a lamp, lit it and surveyed the room, her face white. "Anyone hurt? What a mess! Oh

265

my!" She gasped, pressing her hand over her heart when she saw the young Danian. "Where did you come from?"

"What was that?" John moaned, stumbling to his feet. His large fleshly arms attempted to close the door to the kitchen. He gave up the effort as the door now hung on the remaining hinge. When no one answered, he sank onto an upright bench which creaked under his weight.

Sybil lit two more lamps. "Oh, nobody's hurt. The Lord be praised. Bow your heads, everyone. We must give thanks to our Lord." She bowed her head even though no one else responded. "Thank you, most merciful Father that we are all alive. Amen."

"Everyone all right here?" Chad poked his ash-covered head through the doorway from the kitchen. He pushed his sandy hair out of his eyes and hung his lamp on the wall. "Sounded like an explosion. Karl, your hand is bleeding. Oh, what have we here?"

Everyone stared at Mar.

Chad lifted Mar to his feet. "Well, well, look what the magic ball dragged in."

Karl struggled out of the blanket which had captured his legs. "Of course. The magic ball brought this stranger to us. I knew it could transport people from place to place, but this is the first time I've experienced it actually happening." He stared at his hand and frowned. "You're right, I'm hurt."

"Here, let me see it." Sybil snatched a handkerchief from a pocket in her slacks. She took Karl's hand and pressed it on his wound.

Chad picked his way through the debris to the counter and inched the ball around. "There, I got a stronger signal. Anybody know that mutant? Strangest hair cut I've ever seen. His skin's not the right color. And his outfit; it's black. Black hair, black shirt and a red cape. I'm looking at a real live devil."

Sybil hobbled behind Chad, spied over his shoulder and gasped. "Oh, my, my, my!"

Trac's legs felt weak, but he managed to stumble to Chad's side and peek into the ball. He bit his lip to prevent laughing. "He's a Delmarthian captain. Let me talk."

266

"Come with me, Karl, Come into the kitchen," Sybil said quickly as she hurried toward Karl's side. "We need to wash this. Check if there is any glass lodged in your hand." She maneuvered Karl around a bench and dodged the door hanging on one hinge.

"Go ahead, Prairie-man, talk." Chad stepped aside, keeping his hand on the controls located in the back of the ball to allow Trac full view of Evander.

Trac spoke in Danian. "Evander. I'm Trac, the trader from Kans. You bought those prime silver fox furs from me at the Delmarthian Marketplace last summer. Can you see me?"

"Yes. Where are you?" Evander rubbed his hand over his eyes. "I can't believe the condition of your location. Were you set on by a mob? The place looks like the results of one big fight." He caught his breath. "Is Maris with you?"

Mar pushed in front of Trac. "No, no one here by that name. You don't listen, Evander. I told you I am Mar, the adopted son of Reig."

"I thank you, Mar." Evander raised the parchment so it was visible. "My awareness of this information will save Delmarath and the Houses of Bartran and Melron. I take it you are safe?"

"I'm all right. So far. Will you do something for me?"

"Granted."

"Tell Reig where I am— what happened to me. I left my pony where Lance tied Warrior when he visited the marketplace. Tell Reig I want to come home."

"All right. That's enough foreign chatter for now." Chad said. "How do we know you aren't relaying instructions for an invasion?" He shoved Mar aside.

"Chad, keep that line open." Sybil commanded as she entered the room. "Order that mutant to stick around. We may want to communicate further. Oh, Karl's wound is not serious."

"How can I, Councilor? I don't speak his language."

"I do. Please try to remember I am an ambassador. As Councilor Sybil would say, 'This is my jurisdiction.'" Trac stepped close to the ball. "Captain Evander, please leave the ball where it is, and remain in the Hall of Justice. These people want to talk more. It's about the black magic."

"Black magic?"

"He means the black death," Mar yelled.

Evander frowned. "Impossible. Duties demand my immediate attention. Tell that barbarian that I won't touch the ball. I'll return shortly with many questions."

"As will they." Trac stepped away from the ball and translated his conversation with Evander to the Merkans. Karl joined them, his right hand wrapped in a white bloody bandage.

"I won't close it down," Chad said. "I may not find that signal again. Anyone touch that ball and we'll have you for dinner." He rubbed his hands together and smacked his lips. "Remember, I know the cook. Right now, I need to check the damage in the barns."

"Check on our rangers while you're at it," Karl said. "They should have reported in by now."

Trac stared at Chad putting on his plaid jacket.

"Relax, ambassador," Karl said. "Chad doesn't mean what he said about the cook. It just his way of communicating orders to his boys."

Trac grunted as he grabbed Mar's arm and hissed in Danian. "Who did you say you are?" He pushed Mar's sleeve up until he came to the 'S' mark. He gawked at the teenager. "You? A Danian rat? Reig chose you to join the Order of Storytellers?" He dropped Mar's arm and studied the course texture of the planks on the floor. "My son, Trav, was to hold that honor, but Trav is dead. I knew Reig would pick someone in my son's place, but a Danian? Doesn't seem right somehow." He glared at the youth. "Newly adopted I see."

"Yes," Mar said.

"Prairie-man," Sybil demanded. "Who is that demon in the ball? And who is this boy?"

Trac faced her and spoke in Merkan. "The man is a captain of Delmarath, Evander of the House of Melron. The boy is a son of Reig, one of the greatest storytellers of them all."

268

Sybil smiled and reached out her hand. "Glad to meet you, Son of Reig. I'm Councilor Sybil. Welcome to Merkan."

Mar stared at her dedicate white hand.

"But he's brown like that captain," John objected.

"Trac, why does this boy resemble the captain, yet you claim he is a prairie-man?" Karl asked.

Trac took out the medallion Reig had given him and pointed at Mar's bare arm. "The boy wears the beginning mark of the great storytellers which is the same sign that I carry as an ambassador from the prairies. Storytellers are always searching for apprentices. Keeps the old tales alive. You need a good memory in order to qualify. Race or village doesn't matter— much." He took Mar's hand and connected it to Sibyl's and shook it. "Easy boy," he said in Danian. "The medallion I wear on my neck qualifies me as a friend. Pull your sleeve down. Sit over there and relax." He pointed to a toppled chair near the fire.

"Are we prisoners?" Mar asked. "What are they going to do to me?"

"At the moment, nothing," Trac assured him. "But, for all intents and purposes, yes, we are prisoners."

"Hmm..." Karl looked at Mar, then at Trac. "His language is a problem. He doesn't understand anything we say, does he?"

"He only speaks Danian. He hasn't lived on the prairies long enough to master my tongue."

Karl's eyes widened as his mouth dropped open. "And you speak Danian, as well as Merkan. How many other languages do you know?"

"Several. I'm a trader, err, vendor. I need to know how to communicate to people."

"Then communicate to this boy," Sybil ordered. "Find out what he knows about the gunpowder."

Probably a lot, Trac thought. Aloud he said, "I doubt he knows much. Such information would be known only to the Defender and his closest advisors." He walked over to the fireplace and laid his hand on Mar's shoulder. "Mar, what do you know about the black magic?" He nodded in the direction of the council. "They want to know."

"Why should I tell you, Prairie-man?" Mar jerked away from him. "It's your people that are going to try to destroy the walls surrounding my childhood home."

"Only that it can destroy city walls," Trac translated, then spoke in Danian. "Reig is my friend," he said to Mar. "Is he alive?"

"Yes, he found one of these stupid balls and appeared magically in the Hall of Justice. I refuse to talk about it, even though you wear the great seal of the Storytellers. Not to you or anyone."

Trac nodded. "I've one more question and it's a biggy. I know Lance brought the powder to Delmarath. Did the Lord Betren believe him?"

Mar nodded. "Lord Betren and Lance took the powder to the King in Megara. Whether they arrived there or not, I don't know. And that's all I know. Tell them that."

Trac spoke to the Merkans. "The Danians know about the powder. They are informing the High King."

"Good," John said. "So now the King can take care of it."

"How?" Trac asked.

"For Heaven's sake, John," Sybil said. "These people know nothing about gunpowder except the damage it can do. Use your head."

"Councilor," Trac said, surveying the upturned table, broken glass and benches around him, "they have no idea of what havoc this weapon causes."

"What are we supposed to do about it?" John snapped. "Just a few days ago, we Merkans discovered intelligent life in the forbidden lands beyond the forest. It's beyond our jurisdiction."

"Unbelievable!" Chad plopped two empty buckets next to the door. "You stand here ankle deep in glass, snow flying in through the window, furniture every which way and all you can do is chitchat."

"Normal reaction." Allen followed Chad inside and grinned. He handed Sybil a broom, Trac a shovel and leaned the rest of his tools against a wall. He laughed as he surveyed the councilors.

"Hope, I came through this better than you folks." He absently dusted off his brown pants creating a fine cloud of ash.

"I wouldn't talk if I were you," Sybil said. "You look like you've aged twenty years. Never thought brown hair could turn grey in such a short time."

Allen brushed the hair on his chin and started coughing.

"That was some explosion, folks and it was close." Chad stamped some snow off his leather boots. "I bet we'll find our missing hoodlums somewhere in the vicinity, if they're still alive. I need someone to go with my boys to see if we can locate them first thing in the morning. Any volunteers?"

"I'll go," Allen said. "Better send some of your boys to board up that window." He picked up a bench. "John, you oversize lump of lard, are you going sit there and watch the rest of us work?"

John rose to his feet. "I don't have to take insults from you," he muttered. "You don't expect a councilor from Hio to do manual labor." He pushed aside the broom Sybil handed him. "Besides, I feel a little dizzy. Got to lie down. Hope my room is still standing." He paused in the doorway and announced, "this finalizes my decision. I'm leaving for Hio. Why didn't you lock those scoundrels up like I advised? If you listened to me, Marcia and Peter would still be here. They've been gone for three days. If Allen doesn't find them soon, you can be sure they're dead. I'm leaving, Councilor Sybil. I'm leaving tomorrow right after the feast." The floor quaked under John's weight as he yanked the door off its one remaining hinge and allowed it to crash to the floor.

Chapter 33

Sylvia gazed at her image in Alisha's mirror, a lump in her throat, her stomach queasy. Tonight, she must participate in Megara's Winter Festival Eve Dance. She sighed, wishing she was home. Since Reig sheltered in her house, he would have let her come with the storytellers and sit beside him dressed in a scarlet Delmarthian cloak and a pointed red cap while he recited stories of Sanclaw and the strange baby. Instead, she must attend this miserable dance that Megarans maintained was the only way to start the holidays.

Touching her ornament, a small wooden horse attached to a black velvet ribbon around her neck, she pivoted, admiring the way her dark blue skirt flowed around her ankles. She patted her hair hoping that the blond mass of curls attached on her head with silver and red pins would remain in place until her ordeal ended.

"Excuse me, my Barbarian Princess, I need to use the mirror." Alisha nudged Sylvia with her elbow.

Sylvia stepped away. *Don't see why she needs the mirror. She's the picture of perfection.* "I hope I remember all your Danian manners tonight."

Alisha twisted her head side to side as she inspected her black curls flowing down her back. She reached for a small silver box filled with charcoal power and carefully painted her dark eyelashes making them even a darker shade of black.

"I've been in the palace for three days and they were some of the busiest days in my life," Sylvia continued. "I can't be sure if I'll survive this crash course in Danian etiquette until this stupid dance is over." She pushed the seat back slightly as she plopped herself on the cushioned chair next to the fire.

Alisha stared into the mirror and brushed some pink powder on her cheek. She checked the clasp of her silver necklace and repositioned the matching circlet on her hair, showing it off to an exquisite advantage.

"Of all the stupid ways to start the Winter Festival, this has to be one of the strangest. If I were home, I'd be decorating my cabin with pine."

Alisha patted her green and red panel skirts, slid her puffy sleeves closer to her shoulders and fastened a silver belt around her waist. She spun slowly in front of the mirror, and nodded. "There, I'm ready."

She could wear rags and still be ravishingly gorgeous. She belongs to this place. I certainly don't.

"I'm going down now. You must wait for Bart." Alisha stepped back and studied Sylvia. "You're beautiful. Only—"

"Only, I'm too tall, too blond and too foreign for this to work. You and Luciana ignore me unless you're teaching me one more thing about Danian protocol."

"What do we have in common with a barbarian?" Alisha shrugged. "On the other hand, what I do know to be certain is that we only have one opportunity to draw traitorous information from high-ranking nobles. Some return to their homes tomorrow morning. Conder's already in Chaleen. Every year he attends the early part of Chaleen's festivities, then returns to the palace to

273

celebrate the Great Banquet with his brother." She smiled. "Well, I'll forgo fretting about anything tonight. I mean to indulge in a wonderful evening. Good luck, Sylvia." She drifted down the corridor.

Left alone, Sylvia relaxed in front of the fire. It was the first time she had to reflect on matters in three solid days. Some of that time, she visited Lance. Her brother's recovery from his ordeal proceeded slowly. Betren kept to his father's quarters. She had seen nothing of Bart since that night he had taught her to dance. When she asked, Alisha told her tartly that Bart had duties.

A bedroom door opened and Luciana dressed in a simple emerald green dress styled much like Sylvia's ambled over to the fire. A wreath of golden berries crowned her straight black hair.

For the last three days the younger daughter of Lord Andros had meandered throughout the palace as if she might burst out in a shower of tears at a moment's notice, but tonight, a look of resolution replaced her sorrowful expression.

Sylvia sensed that Luciana had come to some sort of decision about Bart.

Luciana gave a tight little smile. "Ready for tonight?"

"No. Positively not. Two minutes on that dance floor without you by my side and I'll feel like a fish out of water." Sylvia stood and gazed at the mirror. "It's ridiculous. I've never been around so many people, never felt so alone. The last thing I want to do is to attend this dance."

Bart overheard the last statement as he entered the parlor from the hallway. He wore his scarlet tunic and black pants, the dress uniform of the guard, his sword hung loosely at his side. "Don't tell me the daughter of the forest fears a few harmless Danians."

"There's not a few and they are not harmless," Sylvia snapped. "I'd give anything to be in the mountains tonight. This is the night of the Gathering of the Greens. The storytellers will be there."

"I empathize. However, there are many ways of celebrating the first day of the Winter Festival. In Megara we hold a dance. Come on." Bart offered her his arm.

"Might as well get this over with," Sylvia said through clenched teeth.

"Captain," Luciana said. "May I have your other arm? I do not wish to enter the hall unescorted."

Bart dropped Sylvia's arm and whirled facing Luciana. "Younger Daughter of Andros, is this wise? The House of Bartran is under the King's sword. Haven't you noticed? People of proper breeding stopped speaking to me. You'll put yourself in disgrace. Besides, the wrath of your House will fall on my head."

Luciana smiled. "Leave Lord Andros to me, Captain. I can handle my father. Besides, who is going to hold this little indiscretion against me when there is so much to be gained by ignoring it? Property gives men short memories."

"Short or not, Luciana, I refuse to damage your reputation. I fail to understand.... When you left me the other night, I felt sure you discarded me like everyone else in the palace."

Luciana nodded. "Surely it seemed like that." She looked away from Bart. "The very idea of a long time friendship with barbarians unnerved me. Actually, the results of this friendship scare me to death. The House of Bartran in disgrace— A weapon so powerful it crumbles city walls —" She glanced at Sylvia and then peered out the parlor window. "I also thought about you, Captain, standing alone against the whole court. And I arrived at a decision. I have no intention of deserting you during this time of trouble. Would you deny my support?"

"Of course, not, Luciana, but you needn't support me in public." Bart's face was troubled. "I want to protect you."

"What? Snide remarks? Cold shoulders? People not speaking to me? Not a problem. They don't anyway. Captain, you are forever confusing me with my sister." She laid her hand on his arm. "Don't you see if I stand with the House of Bartran, everyone will ignore me as one beneath their notice. It grants me freedom to converse to you openly in public without comment. If I pretend to go along with the court procedure, and am caught discussing anything with you, it becomes scandal. And you and I will be

275

scrutinized, no matter what we do. We should shun that notoriety as we strive to solve the problem of the black death."

"Luciana, Luciana." Bart looked at her in dismay. "Sylvia is a bad influence. You are much too logical. This is your first appearance at the opening dance of Megara's Winter Festival. The world is yours. Why give up all that for the House of Bartran?"

"Surely the man who preferred a public whipping to the death of a child would not ask. Or do you surmise only men act on the knowledge of right and wrong?"

"But the risk?"

"Captain, the risk is minimal. Let's speak no more of this." Luciana motioned to the hallway door. "Our battlefield awaits."

"Just one minute." Sylvia glanced from Bart to Luciana. "Are you saying being whipped is the reward for saving a life? How could that be possible?"

"Only if you're in the guard, Sylvia," Bart said. "It's a Danian thing. I haven't time to explain."

Sylvia put her hands on her hips and mimicked Bart sarcastically. "It's a Danian thing and I haven't time to explain. How convenient."

Bart glanced ruefully first at Luciana, then at Sylvia. "Right now it's time to march into battle as Luciana so nicely put it. Heads up, ladies, nice smiles, walk as if you own the world." He escorted them through the winding halls and down the stairs to the grand stairway.

As they descended to the ballroom floor, the thick red carpet squished softly under their feet. Honoring the season, red and gold cords entwined the wrought iron railing. Wreaths of red, gold, silver and green ribbon decorated the walls. Musicians played softly unnoticed by most of the population who engaged in greetings and well wishes of the upcoming holidays.

As Bart's party neared the halfway mark on the stairs, someone noticed them and pointed. All motion stopped, followed by a buzz of conversation. It didn't feel friendly.

"Sylvia, loosen your grip on my arm," Bart murmured. "You've nothing to fear."

Lord Sedrac extracted himself from the crowd.

Sylvia glanced at Bart, his eyes riveted straight ahead. She swallowed. *Calm down. A familiar face — Sedrac. Certainly looks better when he's not in uniform. That outfit of green hose and white tunic with red trim makes him almost handsome.*

Sedrac approached the stairway.

He plans to dance with Luciana. Good, I like dancing with Bart.

The crowd stretched their necks, watched and waited.

When Bart, Luciana, and Sylvia reached the bottom of the stairs, Sedrac saluted Bart, than bowed to Luciana who curtsied.

"Do you need rescuing, my Lady," he murmured.

The younger daughter of Andros laid her hand on Bart's arm.

Sedrac faced Sylvia and kissed her hand. Sylvia managed a smile and a curtsey.

"You will dance with me, my Lady," Sedrac said.

Sylvia whispered, "I'm not very good. I tried it earlier."

"Nonsense, just follow my lead." Sedrac started to escort her to the dance floor but he halted at the sound of a trumpet.

Buris and Rieman stepped out of the crowd and met in the center of the floor. Rieman cradled his horn.

"What's this? A salute?" Sedrac glanced around him. He and Sylvia were the only couple on the floor. He whistled under his breath as he gaped at Sylvia.

People nudged each other and chattered excitedly. A crescendo of voices filled the room.

"No woman has ever had this honor, but as we are the center of attention, and since I have done nothing to warrant a salute, I surmise this is for you." Sedrac's lips tightened. "By all the gods, Buris is out of his mind. As second in command I should have known about this."

Sylvia felt herself blush. *I'm causing more problems.*

"Alisha," Sedrac muttered. "I'll have her head. Who else would inform Buris of my plans for this evening? And me out of uniform. Step back on the stairs, Princess. We need to give the guard room."

Buris nodded to Rieman who silenced the people with his horn.

"Hear me, my lords, ladies and townspeople." Buris pivoted as he spoke, his strong voice penetrated the corners of the hall. "We, the King's Personal Guard, select this moment to honor the people who risked their lives so that we, the sons of the lords of the land could participate in the glorious celebration of this Megara's Winter Festival Eve Dance. I need not mention how our guard trains to be super heroes in service of King Cadamire, may he live forever. We braved the wilderness infested with horrhounds that harassed us from Delmarath to Megara.

"First, we acknowledge the exceptional regard we hold for the Delmarthian archers who held the monstrous dogs at bay. These brave men will not be joining us tonight as they are on duty in the holding center along with Metrox, Captain of the Delmarthian Guard." He nodded at Rieman who raised his horn to his lips and summoned the King's Guard to the floor.

From all parts of the hall, the King's Guard, dressed in red tunics and black hose formed two lines, reaching from the stairs to the center of the room where Buris and Rieman stood at attention.

"We, the King's Guard welcome the Barbarian Princess, Sylvia of Citheria to our opening dance of our Winter Festival. Treat her with gentle courtesy, my friends, for without her, our safe return would have been most unlikely."

Sylvia wanted to disappear through the floor. She grasped Sedrac's arm.

"True," Buris continued, "We often salute valiant men, but never have we honored a woman in this manner. Sylvia of Citheria. We salute you." Buris raised his sword above his head. "This barbarian princess will be remembered by our teller of tales for future generations. We recall her amazing horsemanship, her steed under complete control as horrhounds harried us. We stand before you tonight."

"Don't move, princess," Sedrac murmured. "I'll walk you through this."

"What next?" Sylvia whispered.

"Steady." Sedrac forced a smile. "You're being presented to the court in such a way that no one will dare make fun of you. Lighten your grip on my arm. I'll tell you what to do and when to do it."

"Lastly," Buris said, "tonight we, the members of the King's Guard, honor our youngest captain, Bart, son of Bromwell of the House of Bartran from Delmarath as captains of the King's Personal Guard are rarely honored. Your wisdom, to place the barbarian princess in the lead, for surrounding our camps with fire-- keeping those demons at bay throughout the night, for foresight to spare our horses until the end. Not one man was sacrificed to the hounds."

From somewhere in the crowd, a lone person began to clap, from other parts of the hall, others followed. Someone cheered and soon the hall rocked with cries of approval.

"Guardsmen, draw your swords," Buris ordered.

As one the men drew their swords and formed an arch of glittering metal. Together Buris and Rieman marched through the arch to the stairs.

Buris knelt in front of Sylvia. "My Lady, accept this token of our gratitude. Tonight, every man will have an opportunity to dance with you."

"Thank you," Sylvia ventured.

Buris reached for her hand and kissed it and then rose to his feet.

Sedrac's twisted his wrist from under Sylvia's grasp in one quick move. His fingers tightened on Sylvia's arm, forcing her to stand motionless.

Sylvia glanced at Sedrac about to question it, but Sedrac's expression made her think it better to remain quiet. *Life in Megara is so confusing. I thought I was supposed to curtsey when a man bowed or kissed my hand. Oh well.*

Sedrac loosened his grip on Sylvia's arm. "Don't say anything," he murmured. "Don't let on that I'm speaking to you. Smile your acknowledgment of this honor and accompany me." As he escorted her through the archway, he said, "when we pass the last swords- man, I will turn you to face them. Then I will take one step back and you will make the lowest curtsey you can without falling on your face."

It seemed to take forever to pass through the arch created by the swords. Sylvia didn't dare look into the men's faces. Her impression of that walk would always be a blur of red on black with silver overhead. At the end, Sedrac turned her gracefully in a small circle and stepped back.

Sylvia gazed at the stairway where Bart and Luciana waited.

Bart held his head high.

Luciana looked up at him and smiled.

Sylvia got the feeling that Bart was the only one that mattered to the younger daughter of Andros. *How nice they looked together. Can't disappoint them.* She sank into a low curtsey; it had to be the best she ever made. As she stood up, Sedrac took her by the arm and led her to the side of the dance floor.

Buris saluted Bart and dropped to one knee. "Captain, you have proved your worth in the eyes of your men. No one will ever question the King's decision of selecting the youngest member of the King's Personal Guard as our captain. Accept this expression of our regard." Buris rose to his feet and smiled. "Escort the lovely lady on your arm though the arch."

Rieman played a dignified march on his horn.

Sedrac and Sylvia watched Bart emerged from the arch. Luciana stepped back as Bart pivoted on his heel and drew his sword in a salute. "Thank you gentlemen," he said to his men. "The honor is yours as well as mine. It took all of us working together to survive the horrhounds." He returned his sword to its scabbard. Buris barked a command, and the guard sheathed their swords. He nodded to the musicians.

Sylvia held her breath. *Heaven help me if they play music for a dance I haven't practiced for.*

"You're performing admirably," Sedrac said as he wrapped his arm around Sylvia's waist and stepped back onto the dance floor. He spun her gently toward him. "Place this hand on my shoulder, and this one around my waist. Fine. Follow my footsteps and don't step on my feet."

Sylvia recognized the dance as one she had worked on with Bart and Betren, slow-moving music that encouraged couples to glide around the room. Sedrac was a good dancer and easy to follow.

"You've learned your lessons well, my Lady," Sedrac whispered in her ear. "Just keep going. Before this dance is over, you'll have a turn with every member of the guard."

A moment later, Buris approached Sedrac, touched his shoulder. The men bowed to each other. Then Buris bowed to Sylvia who remembered to curtsy. Sedrac drew Alisha onto the dance floor. As each member of the guard finished their turn with Sylvia, they too went to the sidelines and chose another girl as a partner. Soon the floor was filled. Sylvia started to relax. This was rather fun.

The music stopped. The dance ended. Bart strode to her side. "The next dance is a reel. We rehearsed this the other night. Alisha and Robo are the lead couple. When we're not dancing together, keep your eye on Alisha."

Sylvia nodded. "Where's Bet? I haven't seen him."

Bart grinned. "My brother abhors dances. It's not a major event in Delmarath." He nodded to the balcony where Sylvia had her first look at a dance.

She followed his gaze and glimpsed Betren standing in the shadows. The music started again, this time much faster. Sylvia remembered to skip as they promenaded in a circle. When they returned to their original spot, Bart swung her around several times, then she followed Alisha as the girls danced in a single file surrounding the men who clapped their hands in time to the music. Then the men changed places with the girls who clapped as the men danced around them. Bart's advice was good. Keeping an eye on Alisha kept Sylvia from making a complete fool of herself.

As the dance ended, Bart said, "I see Lord Robo working his way toward us. He's going to insist on a dance with you. Robo is a second or third cousin of Conder and ambassador from Chaleen. Be careful. Remember, you are a woman and know nothing about gunpowder, or law, or maps. Understand? Oh yes, under no

281

circumstance do you repeat your performance with him as you did with Sedrac when you first met, no matter how much he insults you. If you find him disgusting, remember our goal is to see the one guilty of the destruction of Delmarath hang on the city wall."

"Captain, may I have the pleasure of you partner." Robo tapped Bart on the shoulder.

"My Lord, may she bring as much delight to you as she has to me." Bart released Sylvia who curtsied.

Robo took her hand and kissed it.

Sylvia felt like her hand had been kissed by a snake. Her first reaction was to shrink back, find her way to the balcony and beg Betren to protect her, but she managed a smile.

Robo took her in his arms and guided her into the middle of the dance floor. "So, my Lady, can you tell me what's going on across the mountains."

"I don't know my Lord. I don't live there," Sylvia said. *Wonder if Bart would think that is vague enough.*

"Oh, my pardon, my lady. I assumed you were from the prairies." Robo smiled. "Of course you know why Lord Betren brought that barbarian to the King. I understand you are his sister."

"Indeed I am, but good heavens! Do you really expect a woman, especially a barbarian to know anything? It's all beyond me." She smiled sweetly.

"Of course," Robo smiled back. "Forgive me for prying. One doesn't expect a barbarian to adapt to our ways so successfully. It's being said all over the palace that Captain Bart calls you Little Sister."

"It's something from when I was a child. My family raised horses. The Lords of Delmarath visited our house to buy mounts for their guard. I was much younger than my brothers. Everyone called me Little Sister then."

Robo whirled her around in a small circle so that her skirts flowed out around her ankles. "Any other Danians buy horses from you? My master, the Prince of Chaleen for instance?"

Sylvia nodded. "Yes, he came once, or twice." The look on Robo's face reminded her of a cat who had just caught a mouse.

"Ah, I now know the secret of Conder's prize horses," he purred. "Thank you, my Lady."

As the dance finished Buris rescued her from Robo. "Would you like something to drink?" he asked as he led her to a chair.

Sylvia nodded.

"Sit here until I return. I'll bring you something."

Sylvia sank back in the chair with a little sigh of relief. She became aware of the chatter of girls standing near her.

"Look at that stupid Luciana dancing with doomed Captain Bart of Delmarath. She should have her head examined." The girl who spoke had her back toward Sylvia.

"His brother is under the King's sword. Certainly, Bart's head will fall too, and Luciana right along with him," another girl said.

"Look at Alisha, she pretends she's unaware of what her sister is doing," the first girl observed.

"Does she ever notice? All she thinks about is men."

"What is Lord Andros going to do about this?" A third voice lower then the others spoke. She was taller than the other two. Sylvia noticed her long nose.

"Well, Luciana belongs in the dungeon. It would bring her to her senses!" the first girl said. "Look, there's Lord Andros."

Sylvia couldn't see Luciana's father.

"Look at Lord Andros! He's ignoring the whole matter," a girl whispered.

"Just proves that what's said is true. That barbarian girl, did she really deserve that salute?"

There was a shaking of heads, then silence as Buris strode past them with a cup of mulled wine in his hand. The girls wilted before his scornful look and wandered off in several directions.

Bart and Luciana stopped dancing and walked over to where Sylvia was sitting.

"Good job, Little Sister," Bart said. "That was some stunt you pulled, Buris. Why wasn't I informed?"

"Lack of time, Captain." Buris smiled. "I thought it went rather well." He raised his voice. "Wilfred and I depart for Chaleen tomorrow. I hate to leave. I'll miss Alisha. Such beauty deserves appreciation." He put his hand over his heart and sighed. "I doubt if I can live without seeing her beautiful face."

Sylvia frowned. "You could write—"

"Write?" Buris stared at her.

Bart grinned. "You know, put your feelings for her down on parchment. Send her a letter."

Buris nodded and boomed, "I have men and horses under my control. I hope I have enough."

"Enough?" Bart raised his eyebrows.

"Yes, such a beauty as my Alisha deserves a letter every day."

Bart laughed. "So take a crate of the messenger pigeons with you."

"Good idea." Buris slapped Bart on the shoulder. "You will write me the requisition?"

"See me tomorrow before you leave." Bart regarded him disdainfully.

Alisha and her newest partner danced by them.

"Excuse me, Captain, I must profess my devout affection to Alisha." Buris saluted, whirled on his heels, strolled onto the dance floor, graciously replaced her partner and danced her to the other side of the hall.

Bart stared after the couple. "Buris must have had too much to drink."

"How much longer must I stay? I feel exhausted." Sylvia spoke in her own language.

"The dance has just started, my Lady. You must stay awhile longer," Bart answered.

"I'm sitting this one out," Luciana said. "You gentlemen go find other partners before you are ostracized by every lady here."

"That might not be so easy," Bart said.

Luciana looked at him. "Oh, I forgot." She wrinkled up her nose. "Well, then you may keep me company."

"Perhaps our guest would relish an opportunity to visit her brother." Cadamire bowed to the company, his face sober.

Bart stiffened into a salute. Sylvia rose to her feet and followed Luciana's example of a curtsy.

284

"Yes, oh yes," Sylvia breathed as she gaped at the King. Cadamire's tunic was made of scarlet and golden threads woven together. He wore a silver crown with golden stars on his head. A gold medallion with three red stones set into it hung around his neck. He looked just like the picture of the prince in her old Cinderella book.

"Bart, a celebration awaits you in the holding center." Cadamire said quietly.

"My King, you wish me to leave the dance?"

"I wish you to celebrate with Lance and his sister. I've learned that even the barbarians partake in a Winter Festival this night. I find that information extraordinary, but your father insists it is so. Something to do with pine trees — so I ordered pine bows to be cut and delivered. I surmise that any man, alone, captive in a strange country, hearing the music of the dance and knowing what day this is, needs friends to distract him." He looked at Bart keenly. "We can heal his body, but his mind? His spirit? Only acceptance by those he considers friends can accomplish that. Your brother is already there. Lady Luciana, you will attend Sylvia."

Luciana curtsied. "Yes, my King."

Cadamire smiled at Lance's sister. "I'm unsure what the play is, but you have acted your part well, my Lady. You'll be the topic of conversation all evening."

Chapter 34

While Sylvia conquered the Danian dance floor in Megara — a feat Evander would learn of via carrier pigeons in a few days and while Mar struggled to cope with a new set of barbarians in Merkan — a nasty family secret, Evander labored within the tapestry lined walls of the Delmarthian Hall of Justice studying the documents that Mar left him.

The signature on the treasonable report was signed by Lang but what if another forged his name? Evander hoped a loathsome disreputable felon who lived outside his noble city seeded this treachery as he selected a box filled with written requisitions from the shelves hidden behind the wall hangings. Lang had joined the Delmarthian guard the same day as Evander. They served together. The minute before Captain Metrox named Evander Defender of Delmarath, both men had held equal rank. *In many ways Lang's the better guardsman. I recommended him as Acting Defender.*

Spreading the reports and requisitions across his desk, he compared the signatures with the one on the report and groaned.

The incriminating signature matched perfectly with every form and letter on file. "Thank you, Lord Betren, thank you very much — you too, Uncle Metrox, for leaving me this heart wrenching predicament," he grumbled as he gathered up the parchment and returned the files to the shelves behind him.

He cracked open the window anticipating the songs of the season. *Strange, they're not singing one of the holiday favorites. That song projects turbulent anger.* "What has Greylen been up to?"

Torches bobbed up the narrow building lined streets.

"Confounded infernal festering! Barbarian storytellers preform long-winded productions on this first festive evening. Our citizens delight in egging them on. Much too early for the people to be coming off the mountain." He slammed the window shut. The ball on his desk flashed blue briefly, and transformed into its normal clear crystal form. "Maris, I mean Mar, can thank his maddening perpetual klutziness for his timely escape. Praise all the gods, the magic ball is still intact."

Evander inhaled a deep calming breath, and then buckled on his sword as he hurried down the stairs. "With me!" he shouted to the few guardsmen who were on duty in a room below. He led the way into the Great Hall where he positioned his men and himself on the dais.

The Delmarthians swarmed into the building waving their pine boughs like weapons. Men, women and children pressed into the great room.

"Easy," Evander warned his men who laid their hands on their swords. "Spilling blood is no way to celebrate the Gathering of the Greens."

Cahart, a Delmarthian sub-captain and his men pushed through the crowd and joined Evander on the dais.

"Steady," Evander murmured to counteract any sudden reaction by his guard to the unnerving dull undercurrent of voices.

When the hall was full, Evander raised his hands for silence. "Good people, what is this? What happened to our traditional anthem, 'Deck the Great Hall with boughs of pine, tra-la-la-la la, la, la'? I've been anticipating singing with you all evening. The hall wants decorating. When do we start?"

"Soon, Captain, after you address a few discrepancies." A man in a captain's uniform stood on the lowest step— Lang.

"Which are?" Evander questioned.

"Oh, little details." Lang's dark eyes glinted angrily from his swarthy face. His deep voice boomed to the farthest corners of the room. "For instance, where is Lord Betren? For that matter where is Metrox? What are you concealing, Captain Evander?"

"Why are the eastern gates closed?" shouted one of the boys standing on the floor below Evander's feet. "My big brother is needed at home at this season."

"Why is the outpost manned?" croaked an old man. "Our grandson is stuck there for the entire winter festival."

"Enough." Evander raised his hands and paused until the crowd decked in scarves of red, green and white quieted. "My people, proceed with the festivities. We'll discuss all of your concerns after the holidays."

No one budged.

Evander surveyed the crowd. *I know what they want to hear, but I'm not to tell them, not now. How many of them will be alive after the snow melts off the mountain? How many will suffer the prairie-men's wrath as the walls collapse around them?* "Enjoy the holiday," he shouted.

The crowd remained hushed, waiting, watching.

For what?

His guard, men he trusted, men like Lang who had served under Bromwell, Betren and Metrox, drew their swords and advanced toward him.

He held his position.

The guardsmen formed a semi-circle behind him, their swords held directly at his back.

"You risk much."

"You risk more," Cahart, who had served many years in the guard, answered. "I only risk my life; you put everyone's life in peril."

"Explain."

Cahart knelt holding his curled head high, his dark eyes glued on Evander. "Captain, there's been too much wild speculation throughout the city. We, the people you swore to protect, demand to be informed. We understand you are honor bound to the House of Bartran to keep their secrets, but we give you a choice. Tell us or die."

The drawn swords behind Evander touched his clothing.

Evander understood. His guard opened the way for him to reveal classified information, at swords point so he could maintain honor. He could refuse. He had supporters in the crowd. But it would create a bloodbath. Every man, every male over the age of seven carried a knife and knew how to use it. Women and small children would be injured.

Evander sank to one knee. "I submit to the will of my guard and my people."

The guard returned their swords to their scabbards.

Evander stood up. "What worries you?"

"Captain," Cahart spoke. "We always knew of Lord Bromwell's friendship with the barbarians on the mountain. It's common gossip that Lord Betren and Captain Metrox aided Lance's escape from the cells. We suspect Lance returned. Several of us witnessed that white stallion in Lord Betren's stable, and now the horse is missing. Captain, is it true that Metrox murdered our Lord?"

"Speech," several people yelled. "Speech!" Soon everyone joined the leaders. The chant spread through the hall.

Eventually, I'll answer for my decisions to the Lords of Delmarath. Divulge too much and I betray them. Evander raised his hands in the air signaling for silence. When the people responded to his actions and order was restored, he said, "my people, our situation is dire."

"The Lord Betren is dead?" The speaker wearing a long white sheepskin coat was one of the herdsmen from ring three.

"No, he is in Megara. So is Metrox."

"Why?" people wailed. "Our Lord and his captain always spend the first part of the holidays with us."

"Yes, yes," Lang bellowed. "Custom decrees our Lord and Captain attend."

"My people, we face grave danger. The prairie-men wield a new weapon." Evander paused looking into up-lifted faces. *Perhaps, there is no good way of informing the people of impending disaster.*

"Weapon?" two or three voices chorused. "What kind of weapon?"

"A weapon that will reduce our walls to rubble. Barbarians plan to overrun us in the spring."

A silence followed, a silence different from the one when everyone waited for explanations. This stillness was one of fear, of despair. It started in the front lines and then crept back into the darkest corners of the hall.

"Go on," Cahart said, still on his knee. He chewed on his heavy lip.

"Lance visited Lord Betren with this news. Lord Betren escorted the weapon and Lance to the King."

This time a weaver from the first ring waved his red and yellow plaid scarf to catch Evander's attention. "But that's against the law. It's death to bring a barbarian into Dana."

"Yes, it is," Evander agreed. "But the King won't believe Lord Betren unless Lance speaks on the Knife of Truth."

"But Lord Betren will be stripped of his rank; the King may even hang him on the wall. We need our Defender!" This time it was Rolan, a Danian merchant.

"Can't expect the King to save Delmarath," Lang yelled. "Lord Betren's duty is to remain here and prepare our defenses."

"Exactly. Our Lord is saving his own skin. He'll be in Megara when the attack begins."

Evander recognized the last speaker as Lang's brother. *Know those squinty eyes anywhere.*

"How dare you speak of our defender like that?" Theo, the blacksmith threatened the speaker with his fist, a sizable weapon.

"Order! Order!" Evander glanced around the hall. His archers positioned above the crowd had their bows strung, arrows ready to shoot if necessary. *That is if they still support me.* He glanced at Cahart.

"They're loyal to you, Captain," Cahart said quietly. "Most of the guard is."

"Anymore violence and you will learn what bloodshed entails." Evander gestured to the armed contingent of archers.

"Onto Megara. We must convince the King to return our Lord!" shouted one of the guardsmen.

"Onto Megara. One and all." The shouts of agreement were deafening.

Evander raised his hands for silence. "My people, we can't all go. Who would defend the city? Is it your desire that any lord with treachery in his heart waltz on in here? Besides, what would the King think if the whole population of Delmarath stood before the gates of Megara? Might it not be received as a declaration of war?"

"The King knows of our loyalty," Lang shouted. "Let's leave tomorrow."

"Cahart. On your feet," Evander ordered. "Arrest that man."

Two of Cahart's men leaped down the stairs, seized Lang and dragged him in front of Evander.

"On what grounds?" Lang sputtered as he knelt.

"Treason," Evander said evenly. "Interesting documents smeared with your signature have fallen into my hands, documents proving that you plan to give Delmarath to Prince Conder come spring. A request to execute the entire House of Melron."

Lang paled. "Curse you, Evander. I should have been appointed Temporary Defender. I'm far more capable than on you." He caught his breath. "What happened to the messenger?"

"Found dead on the trail along the mountain to Chaleen. Cahart!"

"Orders, Captain?" Cahart saluted Evander.

"Arrest Lang of Langfield and his entire house. Put them in irons."

"Yes, sir." Cahart motioned to his men and stepped off the dais.

Evander addressed the crowd. "No one moves under the pain of death. My archers are ready to shoot anyone instigating a disturbance."

He watched his guards pick out members of the House of Lang and drag the doomed men and their families through the door leading to the dungeon. *I'm losing several good officers tonight. Men who have served Delmarath well most of their lives. The law requires death of everyone related to the guilty in a case concerning treason.*

"Captain." Cahart saluted. "All members of the House of Lang who attended the Gathering of the Greens are accounted for."

"Good. You and your guard, take care of any remaining in their home."

"Yes, sir."

"The law demands their death." Evander raised his voice as he addressed the citizens of Delmarath. "Know that I have proof of this treason, a handwritten report by Lang addressed to Conder to transfer the rule of this city to the Prince of Chaleen, advising death on the wall to all who are loyal to the House of Bartran."

"Captain," Theo, the blacksmith boomed. "We do want to go to Megara. Obviously not under Lang's leadership. Regardless of what took place tonight, Lord Betren is in trouble on our behalf."

"But not everyone," Evander said firmly. "Listen, my friends. Each ring of the city will hold a lottery. Anyone who wishes to travel to Megara at this time of year will submit their names in a box and they will be drawn in two days. The winners will display our banner as a symbol that this is an official visit. And I'll provide a detachment of guardsmen ensuring your safety."

A murmur of agreement rang through the crowd. Several voices called out, "long live Lord Betren." More joined in the chant: "Long live Captain Evander."

"Thank you." Evander permitted himself to relax just a little as he saluted the crowd. "In spite of the treason discovered tonight, this is the eve of our Winter Festival. We are Danians, obedient to the law. Everyone involved in this treason knew the penalty of his actions. We have no cause to mourn traitors. We are Danians and tonight we shall celebrate despite our knowledge of future

292

calamities. We will deal with them in due time. Not to observe our joyous festival would give our enemy a victory before they ever appeared in front of our walls. Hang greens in the Council Hall. Trim the tree, then return to your homes. Let the aroma of fresh pine seep through your rooms in honor of our celebrations. Enjoy the feast tomorrow. Prepare for the joyous days ahead. Spread winter merriment throughout our city. Let the Gathering of the Greens continue!"

Greylen hopped on the dais, his patched cloak flying behind him. The crowd hesitated, then cheered as the teller of tales bowed to Evander. He strummed familiar cords on his guitar and the people broke out singing, "deck the Great Hall with boughs of pine. Fa, la, la, la..."

Before Evander left, he steadied the huge pine wreath decorated with nuts and pinecones as men secured it on the wall behind the dais. Women passed garlands of pine trimmed with ribbon to men on ladders who strung the greens across the room. Several other women took covered pans and prepared popcorn. Boxes of ornaments crowded tabletops so children could adorn the tree. First and second year guardsmen assisted them.

Evander took the time to walk among the people admiring their efforts and wishing them a good feast on the morrow. When the hall resounded with songs and laughter, shouts of "hold that ladder steady," and women passed out bowls of popcorn to be strung, Evander retired to the Hall of Justice and the magic ball.

Chapter 35

Trac savored the aroma of roast venison and a type of fowl which penetrated the whole cabin at Trail's End being prepared in the kitchen for the Thanksfest. Beeswax candles and oil lamps flickered in the dim room as no light filtered through the boarded windows damaged by the explosion the day before.

A ranger, one of the men who first accompanied the councilors, made his morning inquiry on the status of their stay with Councilor Karl. As usual, Sybil and John's voices rose in anger from the small room adjacent to the larger one. Trac had given up trying to follow their disagreements, but a nasty feeling plagued him. Today they argued about his future.

The Merkans, especially John, maintained that he and Mar were exotic creatures. The councilor from Hio suggested too many times that the two mutants be hauled into the interior of the country and displayed to the Merkans, probably the same way Danian entertainers showed off a tame bear, or trained dogs.

The prairie-man and the Danian teenager occupied a corner, their conversation muffled by Chad's rowdy boys who dragged tables across the floor, and arranged chairs around them.

Trac leaned toward Mar. "Listen to me. Whatever you do, don't let them know you sing. Don't touch any musical instruments that might be around. Understand?" *Thank the great god above all others that no one here speaks Danian.*

Mar frowned, and then nodded. "I'll follow your orders. I don't even comprehend their language. Hope we eat soon. I'm hungry." He pointed toward the smaller room. "Are they ever going to stop shouting at each other? And that other man— the old skinny one, he's watching us."

Trac grunted. "Guarantee that racket will continue until the meal is served. Get use to it." He shrugged then sighed. "Imagine. We're going to celebrate the first day of the Winter Festival with a Thanksfest. These people fill their stomachs in honor of their god."

Mar grimaced. "What can you expect from barbarians? My people would be awake by now. Pine fills the houses with a wonderful aroma. The children decorate their trees, and the women cook a meal of stewed mutton representing the sacrifice made by the gods for man. Pumpkin pies for dessert." He rubbed his eyes. "Every house in Delmarath is decorated for the holidays."

"Delmarath is not among your options." *Am I seeing tears? I thought Danians were born without emotions. Could it be that they have them like us, but are trained to hide their feelings?*

Mar stared at him. "Who told you about me?"

"No one. You wear the mark of a storyteller, an honor in my land, a death warrant in your city. I don't need to know the details that brought you to this strange land to understand that any mark burned or cut into the flesh is a death sentence for a Danian." Trac tentatively touched Mar's shoulder. "Doesn't matter where you live this year, you can't escape the pain of losing your Danian family."

The boy jerked away, he stared at Trac his features expressionless. "No barbarian—" He dropped his eyes and shook his head. "I'm sorry; you're trying to be friendly and I…"

"You're acting like a Danian." Trac smiled. "Easy boy, you are Danian. Never be ashamed of that. In time you will learn the way of my people and be able to combine the best of both races."

Mar buried his head in his arms. "Sometimes, I wish I could forget that my father was Metrox, Captain of the Delmarthian Guard, forget my former cousin Evander or even my brother Menes. I never thought memories could hurt so." He sighed. "I almost miss Reig as much; he's been good to me."

"If Reig was able to cross the mountain to Kans and you accompanied him, you'd see how my people celebrate the season. You'd find it as strange as what we're watching." Trac sighed. "Look, the longest table stretches the length of this room; the smaller one is close to the fireplace. Bet the important people get to sit there."

"Oh, today must be special, even here; women spread cloth covers on the tables. Gold and brown — earth colors." Mar brushed a tear off his face. "Lavine used a red and green plaid one. She wove it herself and only used it for the Winter Festival." He turned away from Trac. "Funny looking plates," he observed. "They're not pewter."

"Some kind of pottery." Trac nodded at the grayish-blue plates. "Be very careful not to drop one. They break. At least they use normal spoons and knives. Oh, no, they have those miserable forks just like the House of Robert. Ever seen a fork before?"

"You mean those tiny gray utensils that look like miniature pitchforks? They remind me of the long iron prongs our cooks use to fish potatoes out of red-hot coals. Are we supposed to use them to eat?"

"That's right."

"They look dangerous. You could stab the insides of your mouth with silverware like that. Do they season their food with human blood?"

"It's not that bad, you'll see." Trac smiled at the boy. "Cheer up. It's the first day of the Winter Festival and we'll enjoy a good meal. Try thinking of something pleasant."

Mar stared at his hands then glanced at Trac. "How do you celebrate on the prairies?"

Trac sighed. "In Kans we spend the night singing praises for the blessings we've received during the past year and dance to the music of seasonal carols, acting out our gratefulness to the great god above all other gods around bonfires. Sometimes storytellers come and spin tales. Otherwise, we take turns telling the old stories that have been handed down to us from ancient times, tales about Sanclaw and the baby. Our celebration continues until dawn. Right now everyone would be sleeping."

Mar poked Trac. "That old man is still staring at us."

"I know. Ignore Councilor Karl."

Having finished decorating the tables for their feast, the women retreated into the kitchen. The men grabbed their hats, gloves and put on their wool plaid jackets to accompany Allen to investigate the source of last night's explosion. They trooped outside, fastened their skis to their feet, their masculine voices faded leaving the cabin in comparative silence.

"Why does that old man gawk at us so?" Mar whispered pointing to Karl. "Every time we talk, he does that."

Trac shrugged. "Merkans can't understand what we say when we speak Danian. That bothers them." He motioned the boy to be quiet. *What obnoxious plan is the Councilor of the 12 Districts forming in his devious brain concerning us?*

"This wouldn't be a bad place if those two would stop talking so loud," Mar muttered.

"What did he say?" Karl asked.

Trac glanced at Mar. "He said he's tired of all the noise in the next room."

"So am I," Karl agreed. "Come, warm yourselves by the fire while we wait for the great feast. Sometimes I can block loud voices from my ears by gazing into the flames and dreaming of better company."

They spent the rest of the morning soaking up the heat from the fire, and inhaling the delicious mouth-watering scents from the kitchen which stimulated their stomach's cry for food.

297

Trac sat in a position where he could watch the progress of rolls and condiments en route to the table. He frowned as one of the girls placed a bowl of cranberries near him but inconveniently out of reach. He stroked his beard wondering how they tasted.

The door to the smaller room opened and Sybil appeared. "John, we'll continue this conversation later," she said over her shoulder. She disappeared into the kitchen, then came back to announce, "it's time to eat, Karl. Trac, inform our newest guest he's to join us at our table next to the fire. This is a very special day. I'll show you where to sit."

"You're not going to wait for Allen Stacy and those that went off this morning?" Karl asked. "Has anyone told our staff we're about to eat?"

"They should be here already." Sybil placed her hands on her hips. "The food's ready now. Our hosts worked too hard on this feast to let the food spoil just because a few people are missing. They'll keep their meals hot in the kitchen."

"Sybil," Karl protested, "it's the Thanksfest. It's only proper that we wait—"

"Karl, for the first time today, I agree with Sybil. Let's eat." John slid out a chair and lowered his heavy frame into it.

The door burst open and Allen stepped into the room. "Stop lagging behind, Peter. I want to close the door."

"I was waiting for Marcia," Peter said sullenly. He started to remove his outer clothing.

"She's coming. Oh, before I forget, I have some bad news for Councilor John." Allen smirked. "The explosion did you in. No one will be leaving Trail's End today or any time soon. Three large trees are down across the tracks."

John groaned. "But I must be back today."

"Sorry, Councilor." Allen hung his jacket on a peg. "No one's going to chop wood today. It's the Thanksfest and sacred to our Lord."

Marcia charged into the room. "Trac, we did it!" she cried, her cheeks cherry red from the cold.

"I'm glad you're both safe." Trac leaped up and met the children halfway toward the outside door.

"We destroyed the powder! No one will ever use it again. Isn't that wonderful?"

John sprang to his feet like an overfed puffed up rooster, ready for battle. His chair crashed to the floor. "No, it's not wonderful! How dare you destroy government property?"

"It doesn't belong to the government," Marcia declared spinning to face him. "We manufactured it and we had the right to destroy it."

"I agree." Sybil strode to the center of the room and glared at them all. "These children, heaven help them, developed this all by themselves. It was theirs and their right to do with it as they wished, without breaking our laws of course."

Trac pressed his lips together. *Give them time. Surely they'll find some law to punish my young friends.* Peter stepped to Trac's side.

"You don't know what you're saying," John sputtered as he paced in front of the small table. "I spent time and effort locating the right information so Tom could create that powder. Even planted that technical manual on ancient weapons where that enterprising young man could stumble upon it..." His voice faded as Karl's face constricted in horror. Sybil's face wrinkled up in disgust. Marcia's and Peter's eyes grew wide in surprise.

Trac placed his hand on Peter's shoulder. *Should have known that someone in power is behind this black magic.*

"You're involved in this? You, a trusted councilor of Hio?" Karl stood up slowly from his spot near the fire. "Are you saying we, the Merkan Council, are responsible for a war? It's one matter for these children to be tried for this crime, but you have jeopardized the credibility of the entire council. The children may not be aware of the law, but you certainly are. Councilor John, what were you thinking?"

"Oh, hogwash, Karl. You and your supporters want us to descend to the Dark Ages. Have no better life than our mutant here." John waved his arm at Trac. "It's bad enough that we've lost so

299

much. When we do achieve a little progress, someone like this idiot girl sets us back a hundred years."

"And just what improvement in our lives would the production of gunpowder make?" Sybil smiled at Marcia. "Take off your scarf, dear and sit down. We're just starting the Thanksfest. You too, Peter. Trac, Allen, I reserved places for you at our table. Chad, tell your boys when they get inside and their families to sit over there with our staff." She pointed to the long table and then faced John. "Will gunpowder give us electric lights, or miracle cures, or gasoline engines? Oh yes, I've read those books too. The ancients lived in a world of luxury. They had marvelous possessions at their fingertips and threw it all away." She paused, her eyes narrow, her lips pursed. "Councilor John did you tell these children to sell gunpowder to mutants?"

"Of course not." John's face reddened. "They did that on their own. And they'll hang for it." He hoisted his chair and slammed it on the floor in front of his place causing the plate, cup and silverware to dance on the table. "I'll call for a Ringing of the Bells, summoning the people to the Caves of New Hope. We'll hold a public trial."

"No matter what I do, I never get it right," Peter whispered to Trac. "I can't win."

"When these two delinquents are declared guilty, I'll enjoy watching them dangle from a rope. No one's going to incriminate me of warmongering with mutants that might not even be truly human."

"We can hold a public trial right here," Sybil snapped. "Must I remind you that you are in my district? I could have you strung up on a tree. After all you just admitted that you are accountable for this criminal remaking of gunpowder."

"Trac? Tell me what they're saying," Mar said.

Trac raised his finger to his lip. "Not now, they're talking fast, so I have to concentrate on their words in order to understand."

"Don't worry Trac," Marcia whispered from across the table. "No one's likely to hang. Council members talk much and do little."

The mouths of the councilors snapped shut when Chad's boys, as he called his loud enthusiastic followers, stomped the snow from their boots while they entered the lodge.

One of them reported to Chad. "We found those two." He indicated Marcia and Peter, "on their way to Trail's End. Back-tracked to the crime scene to survey the damage. The saltpeter cavern is completely destroyed. We won't use our underground hall to celebrate this New Year, or ever again."

"No chance of digging it out?" Chad looked grim.

"None. The whole front chamber collapsed under a ton of rock."

"Great." Chad glared at Sybil. "Councilor, if anyone should be punished, it should be these two kids. Sentence them to dig out the cave opening. It'd keep them busy for the rest of their lives."

All the men glared at Marcia and Peter.

"Great idea," John muttered.

Trac struggled to recognize an entourage of nine men, as they trooped inside, leaving their wooden staffs in a tepee formed pile, and adding their brown coats to the pegs on the wall.

"Councilor Sybil," a ranger asked as two more men joined Chad's boys. "Are we really supposed to eat at the common table?"

"We're still heavily involved in negotiations, Frank." Sybil 's voice rose. "Everyone's here now. Be seated. The food is ready. Karl will you bless this meal?"

Chad, his workers, their families and the rangers, gathered around the large table and sat. All reached out and held each other's hands.

"Hold it, both of you." Karl spoke quietly, yet firmly. "As members of the council it is our duty to set a high example to our people who elected us. For this reason, John, I'd really hold off on a public trial. If you did that, it'd be my business to expose your part in this."

Everyone at the long table looked blankly at each other. Several of the men released a heavy sigh, as they dropped their neighbor's hands and glared at the table closest to the fire.

"When are we going to eat?" one of the men muttered.

"Now's not the time for debate," a few others groaned.

"You don't have anything on me," John protested. "It's legal to mine the caves." He paused and studied Karl. "Why? What are you up to?"

Sybil frowned at Karl."It's prohibited by law to conceal re-discoveries. And gunpowder is on our list of restricted items. Tell me, my ears are deceiving me. Surely, I didn't hear you say you wanted to protect John of Hio from justice?"

"Be seated, Sybil," Karl said as he took his place at the table. "We can discuss this as we eat."

The people at the second table nodded in agreement when hearing, 'discuss this as we eat'.

"Not only will the cooks' work be ruined if we stand around debating, but nobody can eat until we start. Let's hold hands around our tables signifying peace while we say our blessing." Karl smiled as Sybil sat and reached for Peter's and Karl's hands.

Trac grabbed Peter's and John''s hand and said in Danian, "take Marcia's hand and the hand of the fat man next to you. It's the custom here."

Mar glanced at the others seated around the table and copied them.

"Karl, now will you say the blessing?" Sybil asked.

All the Merkans bowed their heads.

"May the Lord keep us and bless us. May the Lord's face shine upon us and give us world peace. Thank you for our food. A-men."

"A-men," the Merkans chimed.

"Finally," John said. "Now we can eat. Chad," he shouted, "Bring on the feast."

Chapter 36

"Don't start eating until everyone has food on their plate," Trac warned Mar. "It's the custom here."

"Barbarians." Mar snorted.

Marcia wrinkled her nose at Mar. "If you said what I think you said; that wasn't very nice. I'm not a barbarian. Are you a mutant?"

Sybil kicked Allen under the table, who then pinched Marcia. Sybil frowned at Mar. "No antagonizing, please. Trac, tell him to behave. This is the Thanksfest after all."

Trac stroked his beard and twisted it while he stared at the rafters. *Why don't these 'chosen people' and the Danian understand you're supposed to be cordial to each other on the first day of the Winter Festival?* "Mar, the Merkan girl understands more than you suspect. Keep your comments to yourself," Trac said in Danian.

For the first time that day, Sybil and John became quiet as they concentrated on handing platters laden with meat and bowls of vegetables around the table allowing the participants to load their plates. A contented buzz of conversation filled the room. Words like have some, please and thank you came from around the councilor's table.

Words like New Years, the destruction of the Great Cave, the loss of the still and a winter's supply of whiskey penetrated Trac's hearing as he stuffed his plate. Warnings to be quiet accompanied with furtive glances at his table interested him. What was wrong with drinking whisky? What did his young friends destroy? The place where they had made the black magic seemed to be important to the people at the long table. Something to do with another celebration.

"Who's the wild looking man seated with the councilors?" a woman from the large table asked.

"Has to be the wild one who lives in the middle of the forest," was the answer. "He's always accompanied by his pet elf that he captured in one of the caves."

As this information was passed around the table and accepted by everyone except the rangers, the conversation returned to the really important issue: What to do about the New Year's celebration?

Conversation at the smaller table ran a somewhat different course. "I'm satisfied by the noise level in here, that no one cares about us councilors," Karl said. "There's a problem none of us have addressed. Are our people ready to accept the fact that others besides our own ancestors escaped the horror? We think of ourselves as the chosen people, like John here, acknowledging that if any others survived, they'd be monsters. It's part of our religion. It makes our people proud to be Merkan, proud to be the only descendant of the old ones. Please pass the potatoes."

Sybil frowned as she spooned potatoes on her plate and handed serving bowl to Karl. "When Allen called us here, I expected that he had some wild animal to show off, a horrible creature that might threaten our safety."

"They might indeed still be animals and they do threaten us." John took a large piece of venison off a platter. "They threaten the very fabric of our civilization. The best idea would be to dispose of them. Hide the fact that there are others in this world besides us."

Trac lost his appetite. *Can't expect mercy.* Peter and Marcia gloomily helped themselves to the food and ate without comment. Mar chased a bean across his plate with a fork. *Fortunately, Mar doesn't understand what's being discussed.*

Mar looked up from his plate and said softly, "are you sure we should be sitting next to this fat man? He's so loud, he makes me nervous. It looks safer over there." He nodded at the long table where Chad and his men sat with their families and the councilor's staff.

Trac forced a smile and reached for the potatoes. "Try some of this. They actually take the potatoes out of their skins and pound them into pulp."

Allen surveyed the councilors and shook his head as he passed a steaming bowl of squash across the table to Peter. "Sometimes I wonder at the stupidity of our leaders," he said softly. "We've already made contact with Danians. When Trac speaks to them, we don't understand a word he says. For all we know he might have given that Evander fellow direction on how to get here."

"Exactly," Karl said. "Thanks to that magic ball, we've been discovered." He chewed on a large bird leg thoughtfully and glanced at Trac. "Prairie-man, eat up. It's the Thanksfest. This day we are grateful to our Lord for our harvest. Not to eat is to dishonor our God."

Trac picked up a piece of meat. "What is this?"

"Turkey. They run wild in the woods. It's a traditional dish from the ancient days. We always eat turkey on Thanksfest."

Trac bit into his meat. *Grainier than chicken, but moist and tasty.*

Karl sighed. "I can't get the picture of that Danian's face out of my mind. I'm talking about the captain that was on the magic ball."

"It was a poker face," John said. "No emotion whatsoever. I doubt that he cares about anything. Pass the corn, please."

"On the contrary." Karl laid his turkey bone on his plate. "I gazed into his eyes and saw his concern for our guests. I saw his fear, not for himself, but for his people who would die when the walls crumble. A happening, I may add, for which we are responsible. I had the feeling that with even knowing where the powder came from, he wasn't sure the guilty would be punished, that he didn't have enough evidence. All he has is hearsay and I doubt that's good enough. It wouldn't be here."

"Karl, you're crazy. You're reading your own thoughts into the face of that Danian," John said. "Besides, you're assuming they live by some sort of law. Don't you think that's stretching it?"

Trac couldn't help it, he choked back a laugh.

"Hold it." Sybil placed her fork on her plate. "Let's find out. Trac, ask the boy about this. These Danians, are they civilized enough to live by law?"

Trac smirked. He struggled not to choke on his food. *This is why men from Kans never talk until after everyone finishes their meal. It's impossible to swallow and laugh at the same time.* He coughed and the food flew back on his plate.

The councilors gaped at him. Peter and Marcia pretended not to notice.

When Mar put his mug of wine down, Trac spoke in Danian. "They want to know if a man can be convicted by another's word when the accuser is repeating something he heard."

"Hearsay?" Of course not." Mar's horrified expression told Trac that the Danian boy considered him an idiot. "It's death to falsely accuse someone. You can die for trying to get a man in trouble without solid proof."

Trac nodded. "Danians do not convict anyone on hearsay," he said in Merkan. "They must have proof."

Karl slid back his chair and stood. "Trac should take us to the High King in Megara: Peter, Marcia and myself. This gunpowder tragedy must stop. We are witnesses to the truth and directly responsible for what our history books call an international disaster. I've spent the last week observing our guests. You, Trac, and the young man across from you seem very human. Neither I nor any in my assembly will be stained with the identical mass destruction that damned our ancestors. Trac, can you do it? Could you get us to the High King to testify?"

306

Trac whistled. "The King lives in a big stone castle surrounded by leech infested waters in Megara. Fortified— Well guarded— Danians tend to kill strangers first, ask questions later. We'll probably all end up dead, before we ever testify, but if we did succeed, death would be a certainty for Peter and Marcia." He switched to Danian. "Mar, are there any crimes not punishable by death in Dana?"

"Very few."

John snorted. "It doesn't make any difference in their case. They're dead no matter what happens."

"And they'll take you down with them," Sybil snapped. "I'll see to that myself."

Peter and Marcia stared at John with big wide eyes.

"But you set us up," Peter gasped. "Councilor Sybil? What are you going to do to us? This isn't our fault!"

"Hush up, Peter." Marcia gave him a kick from beneath the table. "We should go to Megara. We're not exactly innocent by-standers in this affair."

"I'm not going anywhere," Peter declared. "And you can't make me."

"Of course not, Peter," Karl said. "It would help if you decided to come with us, but I'm sure Marcia will be able to handle a trial in a foreign land without you."

Peter shoved back his chair, bolted toward the outside door, and grabbed his jacket off a hook.

"Peter! Where are you going?" Marcia wailed. "I need you."

"I'm not going to stick around and be dragged to some strange land to die," Peter yelled. He slammed the door behind him.

"Oh, good," one of the men at the long table shouted. "They're going to execute that delinquent for destroying our cave."

Everyone at the long table picked up their spoons and pounded them on the table in time to shouts of, "death to Peter. Death to the cave destroyer."

"Quiet down!" Chad shouted. "Agreed, hanging's too good for the boy, but it won't happen today. Remember, we don't have executions on Thanksfest. It's the day of God, the same reason we're not chopping up trees."

"Aw…" The noise at the long table subsided to a low hum.

"Trac?" Mar had a big question in his eyes.

"They want me to lead Karl and the Merkan youngsters to Megara," Trac said in Danian.

"Don't do it." Mar's dark eyes widened with concern. "You don't know the way, and you'll be killed." He stood, squeezed around John and then laid his hand on Trac's arm, frowning. "Why did Peter leave? Oh! That's a silly question. He doesn't want to die. Trac, I don't want you to die either."

"Hang on. This may be our way out of here. Return to your seat and eat all the food on your plate. To leave some is probably an insult to their god." Trac switched languages as Mar obeyed. "Dana is not my homeland. In your land I'm a mutant, in theirs, a barbarian. But Mar explained to me that our Order of the Storytellers agreed to aid in Dana's search for justice on subject of gunpowder on the prairies."

"As an ambassador, it would be appropriate to gain the cooperation of the foreign country," Sybil said. "We will trust you to secure political immunity from Evander."

"Translated," Karl said, "she means 'convince Evander'."

"Only if you send Mar home." Trac stood up and folded his arms. He eyed Karl.

"Let's both be seated, Trac." Karl nodded toward the other table. "Need to cool down a little as we're attracting way too much attention."

Trac scanned the curious faces at the other table and sat.

"Sybil, you never passed the applesauce to Trac's end of the table." Karl said, raising his voice. "No wonder our friend is upset."

"Sorry." Sybil passed the applesauce to Trac who took some for himself, reached over the table and spooned some on Mar's plate.

Mar tasted it. "This is good. It's sweet."

Allen tapped his cup with his spoon. "May I have a word?"

"Of course," Karl said. "You are our Deputy of the Forest Border. You are welcomed to take part in our discussion."

"When you send Mar home, I'll accompany him," Allen said.

"What?" Sybil exclaimed. "This is madness. Allen Stacy, what will your mother say?"

"Easy, Aunt, I'm sure you can handle my mother." Allen smiled. "You forgot to inform her of my promotion to the position of Deputy of the Forest Border. New duties always come with higher position. Two reasons: One, if something goes wrong and we don't end up at the boy's home— it's been known to happen; two heads are better than one. Two, our vendors are already venturing out on the forbidden lands. We need to know whom we're dealing with. I volunteer to gather information. We don't need anymore disasters like this powder thing."

"But you don't even know their language," Sybil protested.

"Mar doesn't know mine either. We'll learn from each other. Can't think of any better way of mastering a new language."

"And if you wind up in Reig's company, the boy's father, you'll learn plenty." Trac stroked his beard. "But what's in it for you?" He tasted the applesauce and wondered what sweetened it.

"The world is changing," Karl said slowly as he grimly stared at Allen. "It seems to be growing. We need the information to transform our people's perceptions." He glanced around the room. "We'll proceed slowly of course."

"But, I already own a cabin built on the other edge of the forest," Allen said. "I hope to set up a market like they have in Chaleen, a self-sufficient fortress to deter strangers from crossing our border. But I need to know something about the people I'm trading with; I've already tried sign language. You don't know how fortunate you are to see me." He pushed his plate away from him, indicating he had enough to eat.

"I agree. Good research always takes substantial time." Sybil pursed her lips. "From now on all vendors must go through Thunderhills. A covert fortress on the other side of the forest is a good suggestion." She laid her fork and spoon on her empty plate. "Can you imagine the three of us standing before a Joint Council

Meeting of the 12 Districts stating that we have proof that one of our most cherished sacred beliefs is wrong? We'd be stoned for heresy."

"Parading the mutants throughout the country would shock our people into reality." John's knuckles turned red as he stood leaning against the table.

"Our people require time to adjust their world-point-of-view," Karl said. "And so, John, the deal is this. You say absolutely nothing about what has happened here to anyone. The last thing we need is the 12 Assemblies up in arms about something we know so little about. And you will cease your activities in the caves."

"And just to keep you honest," Sybil added, "I'm taking your son under my care. I know he is in the Great Cave doing his writing assignment. John, your son will live as long as you stay honest."

Karl nodded. "I back you in this decision, Councilor Sybil. We will discuss the technicalities of building and maintaining a secret defensive fortress at another time."

"What about the other men here," John sputtered. "How do you plan on silencing them? A little mass murder, Councilor Sybil?"

"Unnecessary," Chad said, approaching the councilor's table. "Who'd believe them? Your rangers don't. My boys spend their whole life on the edge of the forest. Men have been known to loose their sanity here. They even believe wild stories that the mutants might be friendly."

Trac smiled. "You may want to expand on that legend, and let it spread throughout your land."

"As pure fantasy of course." Karl said.

Chad grinned. "Good idea. Do you want dessert served now or wait until later. Our cooks want to know your pleasure."

Karl glanced around his table. Everyone's plate was empty except John who munched on a turkey leg. "Let's save desert until we make contact with... What's that captain's name?"

"Evander," Trac said. "The current Defender of Delmarath is named Evander."

310

Chapter 37

With expressions of fear and disgust, Chad's boys retreated toward the fireplace and the small table as Chad activated the ball. The rangers and train-crew watched with interest as Trac and Mar stood in front of the ball in the mist of Allen, Marcia and the councilors.

"All right Trac, talk to this— this Evander. Then we will send these two, the elf and our noble Allen, who just made Deputy of the Forest Border on their way." Chad pushed a switch on the magic ball.

"Trac, no." Mar protested when Karl's plan was explained to him. "Already, two men have risked their lives for me. That's quite enough."

"It's all right, Mar." Trac laid his hand on the boy's shoulder and lifted the storyteller's medallion from his neck. "I do this for Reig, not you. He is my friend and it is my privilege to return his son. It is the way of the prairie-men."

"All right." Chad pressed a button on the back of the ball. "Let's hope someone is in that Hall of Justice." They could see the huge fireplace, the tapestry lined walls, the table and the benches. "Looks empty."

At that moment Evander stepped out of a little room, rubbing his eyes and ambled toward the magic ball in the Hall of Justice. The blue glow of the ball lit his brown face as he peered into it.

Chad motioned to Trac. "Go ahead," he growled. "I'd feel better if I could understand your language."

Trac approached Chad's ball. "Evander."

"Trac, I see you."

"Good. They are sending Mar back to the cabin. He'll have a Merkan with him, a vendor called Allen."

"Vendor?"

"Trader— oh—" Trac floundered for the right Danian word. "Merchant."

"'Allen.' Strange name. Why should he wish to come here?"

"He desires to learn about our side of the world."

Evander shrugged. "All right. Not that I can prohibit his presence there. I hold no power outside Delmarthian territory."

"Just that they'll be spending the winter at Sylvia's cabin. Thought you should know."

"And the black death?"

"We have eyewitnesses of Conder's involvement with the black powder." Trac glanced at Chad. He could see the man growing agitated. *Better keep it short.* He pulled Marcia close to the ball. "This girl's involved."

"A girl?" Evander shook his head. "That's difficult to believe."

"Better believe me," Trac answered, "because you'll have more difficulty believing this. A Merkan leader asked me to bring him and this lass to Megara so they can testify to the King."

Evander gaped. "You must be out of your mind! The risks are horrendous. Once you arrive in Dana, every hand will be raised against you. I've been informed that Lance is healing from his ordeal of a similar attempt." He eyed Trac and then walked over to the fireplace and poked the wood with an iron poker.

312

"Hah!" Chad exploded. "That mutant lost his tongue. He walked away from the whole issue! Move over so I can shut my ball down."

"Wait!" Trac held his ground. "You do not understand the enormity of Counselor Karl's request. Give the good captain a moment."

"Chad, a little patience, please," Karl said. "I agree, it's spooky listening to strange languages. We either trust our ambassador, or perhaps, it would be wise to commit mass suicide here and now. The death of everyone here will keep our secret of other Great Disaster survivors hidden for a few more years. The truth will come out. It always does."

John's face paled. "That truth is worse than mass murder! I'm surrounded by lunatics."

Sybil scoffed. "Mass homicide is what may happen if we ignore this problem that's been dumped on us. Karl, don't be so drear. Chad, give Ambassador Trac some leeway."

"I'm only emphasizing how dire this situation is," Karl explained. "It's suicide not to acknowledge possible hostile forces beyond our border, and suicide to give the first people we meet cause to despise us."

Slowly Evander returned to his desk and sat. He sighed. "If you do insist on committing suicide, Trac, how long will it take you to reach our land?"

"I don't know. It's winter. Travel will be slow." Trac forced himself to think out loud in his best Danian. "I would guess a good two or three weeks to the Citherian pass; at least a week to cross the mountain in the snow, plus however long it takes to go from Delmarath to Megara."

"That long." Evander drummed his fingers on the table. "You'll never reach Megara before Lance is required to speak on the Knife of Truth. The King's decision will depend on the little Lance knows, and Reig's map. I could send a carrier pigeon, but anyone could intercept the message, and it might not ever reach the King."

Chad glared at the Councilors and poked Trac in the ribs. "Enough," he growled. "Time for a little translating. What in the Lord's name is all your chatter about?"

"Hold on, Evander. I need to interpret our conversation to these barbarians." Trac switched languages as he faced the Merkans. "I told Evander that we have proof of who's responsible for the powder, that Karl wants to take Marcia to Megara. Evander worries that we lack the hours to arrive at the palace in time to testify at the trial. The Danian commander considers Karl's plan suicidal."

Chad groaned. "Suicide or suicide. Are those our only options?"

"It took a long time to say that little," John grumbled.

"And he didn't have to tell us it would be too dangerous to attempt," Sybil said. "A strange country and all that. I don't see a problem. Just ignore anyone you happen to meet."

Trac winced.

"I could get you to that Hall of Justice, lickety-split," Chad said. "Better yet, if I knew what the King's city looked like, I could send you right there."

"Tricky." Trac stroked his beard. "We know what the walls of Delmarath look like, but we can't go there. Even Evander would lose his life if he tried to pass a party of four barbarians though his city. That's an act of treason for any Danian." He turned to Mar and spoke in Danian. "Any idea what Megara looks like?"

Mar shrugged. "My family's not of the nobility. I've never been there."

"Half a second." Allen pushed his way past Marcia, Peter and the councilors toward the ball. "How many can we send through the ball at one time? How strong is our signal?" What happens if the ball can't handle four people? Do they disintegrate into molecules?"

Chad looked perplexed. "Do they what?"

"Never mind. Is it safe to send four people anywhere at one time?"

"I know it works with two people."

"Trac." Evander spoke from the ball.

"I'm here."

"If I understood how to use this ball-contraption, I could attempt contacting the wizard. Inform him that we have gained more evidence to present to King Cadamire concerning the black powder, delay Lance's session with the Knife as long as necessary."

"Give me a moment." Trac turned to Chad and spoke in Merkan. "Can you teach Evander how to use the ball? If he can communicate with the castle, he might be able to arrange safe passage."

"Did I hear you correctly?" Chad blustered. "Teach that mutant to use this ball? No, way. I'm not sharing technical expertise with a mutant."

"Do it," Sybil commanded. "Not one word, John, or I'll have Chad lock you up, in his not too comfortable jail," she added as the heavy man opened his mouth.

John clamped his jaw shut and glared at her.

"Aunt..." Allen interrupted. "We should know —"

"Quiet, Allen." Sybil snapped. "We'll discuss your concern later."

"Sybil's right, that Danian captain might be able to help." Karl faced Sybil and John. "I, Director of the 12 Districts take full responsibility for this action of training this mutant how to use our ball. Chad, now it's official."

"I'll do it, but remember I'm not responsible for any of this." Chad sighed. "Trac, tell Evander that the first step is to clear every landmark, every town, every place he knows out of his mind. He must not want to be anywhere except in the Hall of Justice."

"Evander," Trac translated. "Don't let your mind wander. Just thinking about another place will send you there."

"Understood."

"Can he do that?" Chad asked.

Trac snorted. "Believe me, Evander's qualified."

Chad glared at him. "There are a couple of details he must understand before he touches that ball. Tell him that it picks up wavelengths that travel through the air. In order to stay in contact with us, he must keep the ball stationary."

Trac ran his fingers through his beard. "Wavelengths? I don't see anything coming toward us. Ball-stationary? What's that?"

"This is impossible!" Chad pushed through the councilors to pace around the room. "Oh, tell him if he moves that ball, he'll lose contact with us," he said finally.

"Evander," Trac translated. "Leave the ball exactly where it is. If you move it, we won't be able to talk."

"Understood," Evander pushed his chair away from the table.

"Why is he backing away?" Chad shoved the councilors aside as he returned to the ball. "It won't bite. My ball is a command model. I can override the ball Evander has so we can carry on a conversation. But his ball won't do that. If he wants to talk to someone other than us, he has to use the switches on the back."

"Command Model? Override? Switches?"

"Blast it!" Chad growled. "Might have known a mutant would have no idea of common words."

Trac frowned, his face wrinkled in thought. "You mean in order to use Evander's ball you have to touch it?"

"Yes!" Chad exploded.

"Evander," Trac translated. "You have to touch the ball if you're going to use it. There are a couple of lumps on one side. Use your eyes and touch nothing but those uh— switches. Switches, yes, that's the right word for them. Be careful."

Evander stretched his hand toward the Delmarthian ball. The Merkan view of the Hall of Justice inside Chad's ball dissolved into it's normal crystal orb state.

Chad threw his arms up in the air and resumed pacing. "Lousy mutant devil, did it. Just what I told him not to do. Maybe he thought of someplace he wants to go. This isn't going to work."

A flash of blue light flooded Trails End. Evander's features reappeared. "Fascinating," he said in Danian. "If I slide it here..."

The Trails End clear ball sparkled in the candlelight momentarily. With another flash of blue light Evander's face once again filled the ball.

"Will you tell that mutant to leave it in one place!" Chad pounded the table.

"Evander, be a good Danian," Trac translated. "Stop playing. That thing's not a toy."

Evander grimaced. "Well, all right. Next step?"

And so it went for most of the evening. The effort left Chad kicking whatever happened to be near him.

Women carried in a stack of desert plates and set them on the table, studied the current situation, collected the plates and retreated to the kitchen.

"Let us know when we can serve dessert," one of the women shouted.

Clanking silverware and the clinking sound of dishes followed as if it were the background orchestra for muffled ladies' voices of righteous indignation.

"We'll be washing dishes after midnight," one woman complained.

"If it wasn't the Thanksfest we could skip dessert," another responded. "The good Lord will be angry if we don't complete his feast."

Chad's boys huddled around the fireplace, chuckling and swapping stories. The rangers and train-crew played cards at the long table. Allen, John, Sybil, and Karl retreated into the smaller room; their voices rose in another heated discussion. Marcia led Mar out of Chad's way into a corner of the room near the door leading outside to possible escape.

"Thunderation!" Chad roared as the ball became a shining crystal. "He's back to moving the ball again."

Evander's face reappeared.

Chad snorted. "Brain damaged mutant doesn't listen to anything I say."

Trac didn't think he should translate that one.

"I got it. I got it," Evander said. "This device has to be in a certain location to work. And something's wrong. Last time I lost you, I slid the ball to the spot where Reig used it to talk to Talman. The ball turned black."

Chad groaned and sank into the nearest chair when Trac informed him of Evander's latest experiment. "The ball in Megara is covered with something. We cover ours with cloth. Black shows it's making contact, but the ball is in storage. When you use the ball and there is nothing for it to contact, it looks like clear glass. After all this aggravation, those brain damaged mutants in the castle have stashed our only source of communication where it's useless."

When Trac translated that to Evander, Evander said, "I'll keep trying. Talman uncovers the ball when he predicts the future. Maybe he practices sometimes."

Trac was fairly sure Talman's use of the ball was not anything Chad needed to know. "He'll place the ball where it can let him talk to Talman. He'll try contacting us later."

Chad threw up his hands in disgust. "Now, I suppose you want me to send Allen and the boy back to wherever the boy-elf came from and then you four to— well— where?"

"Let's take a break from all this," Karl said as he poked his head into the main room. "We must remember that this is the day of giving thanks to the Lord. We must partake of the last course of our dinner. I smell delicious pumpkin pie aromas. Something hot to drink would be good too."

"There's a pot of chicory near the fire. Last summer the women dried enough mint to serve tea all winter," Chad answered.

"Mint," Trac said. Mint brought a painful memory of a delightful time spent with his woman and son collecting mint and other herbs from edges of the great swamp after a successful week at the Delmarthian Marketplace. "I'll try the chicory."

"Before we eat dessert, let's offer a prayer that Peter will find it in his heart to return to help Karl when he leads these people to Megara," Sybil said.

"We'd better expect a miracle if I'm doing the leading," Karl grumbled. "I submit that Trac needs the Lord's help, not me."

The door swung open revealing Peter. "Thank you, Lord," Sybil murmured. "My prayers have never been answered so quickly."

"Well?" Karl's face reddened with anger. "So you decided on crawling back here hoping to share our pie."

Peter's defiant face cringed as he banged the door shut. "Don't need your pie. I have friends who'd feed me."

"Then why?"

"I can't let Marcia face that king alone. It's not fair. Accept me as a member of the team headed for Megara."

Karl winced as he pressed his lips together. "It's Trac's decision."

Trac nodded. "He's with us."

"Now that we've settled that—" Allen approached Chad. "I still want absolute assurance that ball is powerful enough to transport four, or now it's five people over the mountains."

"Could your magic ball transport my pony too?" Trac asked. "Me and Fleetfoot go back a long way."

Karl glanced at the kitchen. "Allen, we need to finish the Thanksfest. I suggest we return to our seats and dessert."

"Oh, wait a minute!" Chad exclaimed. "Try out this solution. We don't need to test the ball's ability for transporting five people and a pony. A tunnel cuts through the mountain, something created during the Great Destruction. Suppose our Lord provided an earthquake, perhaps for this very moment. Old tunnels would have smooth walls and these are all jagged. Hooks up to what might have been a road once. Followed it with my girls quite a distance to where the ground was still damp. That's where we found all the mint. The trail itself sank under-water, but we could see where it continued on the other side. That wouldn't be a problem this time of year. Not with skis."

"This road— it goes to Megara?" Karl asked.

Chad shrugged. "I better guide you to the other side of the mountains. A couple of minor passages veer off the main tunnel. Other than that— who knows? It heads north. Is Megara north?"

"Let's do it," Trac said. *The other side of the mountains will free me from Merkan. After that? Only the Great god above all other gods knows.* "First things first. Send Mar home."

319

"Sit down," Karl ordered." "We will not insult our Lord by leaving the dinner prepared in his honor unfinished."

"Everyone," Sybil commanded, "back to the tables. Ladies, bring those dessert dishes in and let's eat pie."

Murmurs and confusion followed immediately as everyone headed back to their places while dodging the women carrying in trays of pies from the kitchen.

When the last crumb of pie had been devoured, women and children hurried to the kitchen with the dirty dishes, the rangers and train-crew dealt out playing cards. Chad's boys filtered in front of the fireplace as everyone who had sat at the first table approached the ball and stared at it.

"All I have to do is imagine the cabin, right?" Allen asked. "I've no idea what that cabin looks like."

"You're going to have to trust our little elf-friend here," Chad said. "How does it feel to have your life dependant on a mutant?"

"Scary," Allen said. "But, we're going to have to trust our neighbors sometime."

Chad fiddled with the controls on the ball. "I'm ready. Remember, Allen, keep your mind blank. Trac, tell Mar to picture nothing except that cabin and what surrounds it. Tell him to hang onto Allen's hand and rub his other one here, on the back of the ball."

That magic ball was truly a wonder. Trac saw the cabin, its roof piled with snow as Mar and Allen sprawled in a big drift before it. Gray smoke snaked up toward the white blanketed tree branches that touched the earth.

As they struggled to their feet brushing off their clothes, Reig peaked out the door. A gray and white wolf-dog with a wagging tail bounded past him greeting Mar, knocking him backwards into the snow.

Reig opened the door wide, his ruddy weathered face wreathed in a smile. He held up his right hand which was the only way a prairie-man would welcome a guest.

www.ingramcontent.com/pod-product-compliance
Lightning Source LLC
Chambersburg PA
CBHW071102250626
47159CB00002B/568